CW01481138

INIQUITIES TI

Book 3

Runaways

ALSO BY CAROLYN MCCRAE

Iniquities Trilogy 1: The Last Dance
Winner 2007 David St John Thomas Prize for Fiction

Iniquities Trilogy 2: Walking Alone

Both published by Troubador

INIQUITIES TRILOGY

Book 3

Runaways

Carolyn McCrae

Copyright © 2008 Carolyn McCrae

The moral right of the author has been asserted.

Apart from any fair dealing for the purposes of research or private study,
or criticism or review, as permitted under the Copyright, Designs and Patents
Act 1988, this publication may only be reproduced, stored or transmitted, in
any form or by any means, with the prior permission in writing of the
publishers, or in the case of reprographic reproduction in accordance with
the terms of licences issued by the Copyright Licensing Agency. Enquiries concerning reproduction
outside those terms should be sent to the publishers.

Matador
9 De Montfort Mews
Leicester LE1 7FW, UK
Tel: (+44) 116 255 9311 / 9312
Email: books@troubador.co.uk
Web: www.troubador.co.uk/matador

ISBN
Paperback: 978-1906510-732
Hardback: 978-1906510-848

Mixed Sources
Product group from well-managed
forests and other controlled sources
www.fsc.org Cert no. TT-COC-2082
© 1996 Forest Stewardship Council

Typeset in 11pt Stempel Garamond by Troubador Publishing Ltd, Leicester, UK
Printed in the UK by The Cromwell Press Ltd, Trowbridge, Wilts, UK

Matador is an imprint of Troubador Publishing Ltd

For my husband and best friend, Colin
For his help and for all he has put up with
Perhaps now Iniquities has reached its conclusion there
will be more time…

Also for our very special friends
Pachelbel 1988–1999
Solomon 1988–2007
and
Beaver 2000–2007

Iniquity

The word has two meanings according to the *Shorter Oxford Dictionary*:

1. Immoral, unrighteous or harmful action or conduct; gross injustice, wickedness, sin.

2. Inequality, inequity, unfairness. (obsolete).

Something by Way of Explanation

I told Susannah Donaldson on July 24th 1976 that I had been writing a book about her family.

I'm not sure why I did, I think perhaps I needed to change the subject as we had been talking of serious things, of misunderstandings, of lies deliberate and accidental, of love permissible and forbidden and of the damage caused by lies and deceit. 'I always wanted to be a part of your family,' I had explained, 'I've loved you all, one way or another, and I wanted to write everything down so it wouldn't be forgotten. One day you will read it and it will help you understand'.

"Aren't you going to let me read it now?" she had asked, expecting to be able to get me to do what she wanted. As she always had done.

I had known Susannah since she was born. I had been 26 years old when I had driven her mother, Alicia, to the nursing home on a Bank Holiday Sunday when the man who should have taken her was more engaged with his cricket match than his wife's impending confinement. As Susannah had grown up through a very disturbed childhood I had worried about her more than her parents had ever done. I had wanted to stop her marriage in April 1964 even though she was pregnant; 17 was far too young to get married whatever the reason. I watched, helping her where I could, as she had child after child in that most unhappy of marriages. I was able to give more practical assistance when her husband drowned and she had a breakdown. I was looking after Alicia at the time so it seemed sensible to have them both live with me. I had hoped to get them to know each other before it was too late. After Alicia's death Susannah had resumed her education, reclaimed something of her life and it was four years before we met again.

Susannah had always managed to twist me around her little finger. But not this time.

"No. Not yet."

"When?"

"It'll be some years yet."

She tried another approach. "You couldn't explain all about the family, it's all too much of a mess, not even you could make any sense of it."

"We all have secrets," I admitted, "even I have kept things to myself that should have been shared. I'm not innocent in all this, my secrets have been just as damaging to your family as your mother's." I'm not sure she believed me.

"And what about Max?" She asked disingenuously. I knew she had spent much of the previous four years learning more about Max than I would ever know. "Max has been behind so much of what has happened in our family."

"I've written more about the family. Max is involved, of course he is, but he …."

She interrupted me as she frequently did.

"Tell me now! I don't want to have to wait to read it all."

"You will have to wait, along with everyone else in the family, until Max is dead." I didn't relent when she argued that that could be years. "Your family's secrets are so tied up with his and we must respect him. We all owe him that much."

"But you said everything was his fault."

"Did I? I don't think I used the word fault if I did it would be the wrong one. The complications of your family and all your lives cannot be one single person's fault but Max was undoubtedly behind much of it."

"And David?"

There were some things I hoped never to have to explain in detail to Susannah and one was my long standing relationship with her grandfather.

"Yes, David."

An atmosphere descended as it was obvious I was not telling her the whole truth.

We had both looked out through the window of my flat across the golf course towards the sandbanks, Max's house Sandhey, the river estuary and the islands. It was a view Susannah had known since she was a baby as she had lived in this house before it was broken into flats. I didn't think there was anything sinister in the fact that I had bought the one that occupied the nursery floor but I'm sure there were people who would read something unsavoury into it.

Although I would be the last to tell her, Susannah was right.

Maximilian Fischer had been involved in the lives of every generation of the extended Donaldson family over a period of more than seventy years yet so little had been known about him until Susannah had begun her investigations. She had probably already discovered that Max and her grandfather, David McKennah, had known each other before they had 'met' at her mother's funeral.

"Is there much in your book about me?" She made the pleading face she had used when, as a child, she had asked her Uncle Ted for favour or for flattery. It was a tone of voice that usually made me smile and it didn't fail this time.

"Absolutely, and most of it not particularly complimentary. But you still can't read it until Max has gone."

And now, 22 years later, he was finally going.

Although I am nearing 80 and should have retired years before I still spend most mornings in a room above a shop that I call 'my office'. When asked why I drive into town every day I say it allows me to believe I am still the young man I feel myself to be. 'Few people look behind the speckled skin, the thin grey hair and the wrinkled hands. If they think of me at all it is as an old man, but as long as I work I am still the person I was 40 years ago'.

There is, of course, another reason. I love my wife dearly but there are things I need to do without her fussing around me.

This morning I had a phone call from the past.

"He told me to telephone you when the end approached." Max's housekeeper spoke without introduction, her accent accentuated by her distress.

"Thank you Monika. Everything will be as he has requested." There was no need for a longer conversation, any words of comfort or reassurance would have been insincere. We had not left on good terms.

At last Max was dying. 92 was a good age, especially for one who had led such a life as his.

I spent most of the morning locating all the documents I had known would one day be required. Many I had not looked at since January 1984 when Max had sold the business I had run for him and I had moved from Merseyside to Kent. The last of the phone calls I made was to Susannah. Without preamble I told her Max was dying.

"Oh." It seemed somehow an inadequate response.

"I've just spoken with Charles."

"Charles?" she seemed surprised. She had no idea that I knew how to get in touch with her half-brother. Although they lived fewer than fifteen miles apart they had not spoken for over ten years, not since they had argued so vehemently when she had told him who it was she intended to spend the rest of her life with.

I tried to be patient. "Before you ask, yes, you will soon be able to read my book. But it is incomplete. I was pretty clear on what happened until your mother died, but then I lost touch. There were so many things I could not know. I have asked Charles to write about the time when you and he were growing up and… Well he's going to write about all that." I finished rather lamely.

I had always regretted losing contact with her family after Alicia had died. Somehow 'I was too busy with work' seemed a feeble excuse.

"Why?" It seemed that Susannah couldn't believe that Charles meeting and marrying Holly, a pretty blonde American, would be of any interest to anybody.

"You don't think he was free to do as he liked do you? Holly's father was not who his family believed him to be, both he and his wife died in mysterious circumstances, your cousin Graham was involved, as was Max. He was involved in everything your brother did at that time. And…" I continued quickly ignoring her attempts at interruption, "you know more than any of us how Max came to be in such a position of influence over the family."

Susannah had learned a great deal about Max's life over the years. Although it was an endeavour in which I sometimes assisted we had avoided talking about the details.

We all have to have secrets.

"Will you?"

"Will I what?"

"Oh come on Susannah!" I didn't often call her Susannah, when I did it was to let her know I was being serious. "Will you write down the truth about Max? Tell the whole story? You are the only one who can possibly do it. You are the one who had those long conversations with your grandfather, access to Max's papers, the only one who has read Maureen's diaries. You are the only one who can possibly help us understand everything."

She answered unenthusiastically "I suppose so."

"I know so. And," I continued quickly trying to be firm, "I think it would be fair to tell your ungrateful family how much they owe you. I think they should be told. It's only fair."

"Nobody ever said life should be fair."

It was a mantra in the Donaldson family. Alicia had repeated it as if trying to convince herself that nothing that went wrong in her life was her responsibility. I thought it depressingly negative.

"No but we can make it as fair as possible. When the family is gathered for Max's funeral and for the reading of his will I want them all to get copies of three books; mine, Charles's and yours."

"But…"

I knew I was asking a great deal of her. In the telling of what she knew of Max and David she would have to give away much about herself. During the years she spent learning about Max there had been times when she had not behaved well, when she had been self-centred, thoughtless and gullible. In telling the story she would have to acknowledge much she didn't like about herself.

"Be honest, my dear, in writing it all down you might remember why you did the things you did, and perhaps even forgive yourself."

"Face up to my ghosts?"

"As you say, 'face up to your ghosts'."

"All of them?"

"All of them, even the ones you have never shared with me." I wasn't entirely successful in hiding the hurt in my voice.

"What are the rules?" She seemed to have accepted the task.

"There is only one. Tell the truth, the whole truth and nothing …."

"I have always tried not to tell lies so telling the truth as I saw it won't be too hard, it'll be the 'whole truth' bit that's the problem." I could imagine her grimacing ruefully.

"It always is, my dear, it always is."

Ted Mottram
Brasted, Kent
August 1998

Chapter One

We were members of the same extended family but we who slept at Max Fischer's home the night after my mother's funeral were all strangers.

I had recently, reluctantly, moved to Sandhey to live with Max Fischer, my half-brother Charles and their housekeeper Monika. Max had thought it unsuitable for me to remain in Ted's flat, where I had been living, helping him look after my mother in her illness, even though I was a 25 year widow and Ted, a perfectly respectable solicitor and an old family friend, was in his 50s.

Charles and I had never been close, we had lived in the same house when we were very young but that was all. When he was 16 and I was 11 he and Monika, who had been our nanny, went to live with Max. I didn't see them for years even though we lived only a couple of miles apart. Charles had always done what he wanted to do regardless of how it hurt others and, rightly or wrongly, I blamed him for so much that had gone wrong in my life.

The night before the funeral, in the dark days of January 1972, we had been unexpectedly joined by a motley collection of people who turned out to be my grandparents David and Edith McKennah, a cousin Graham Tyler and Maureen Shelton my step-mother's sister, none of whom I had knowingly met before.

I was not looking forward to having to talk to any of them as I walked down the stairs to breakfast.

"Ah, Susannah, my dear, come and look at this most beautiful drawing." My grandfather did not even say 'good morning'. Wondering why he wanted to talk about art before breakfast I did as he suggested and stood next to him looking at a picture I must have passed hundreds of times over the years. The drawing was of a young man in shirtsleeves with a blue tie sitting in a chair.

"I've never noticed it." I was trying to be polite but, not being really interested, I must have sounded irritable and churlish.

David was not put off by my lack of enthusiasm. "You should have

1

done, it is a very interesting and very valuable drawing. You should look at it and appreciate its unique beauty."

Reluctantly I did as he asked. "I like the colours."

"What else do you notice?"

"His right hand is facing away from him, his left hand towards him?" I ventured, hoping I didn't sound too stupid. My grandfather nodded before continuing. "That was always considered very odd. It is a portrait of an actor called Albert Kiehtreiber."

"Who painted it?"

"A little known artist called Egon Schiele. He painted this in 1918. His wife had died of influenza and with her his unborn child. Within three days he had joined them. Very sad."

"Ted's father had that." I remembered Ted admitting how he had felt cheated by the fact that his father hadn't fallen heroically in the Great War, but had simply died of the flu that had swept Europe immediately afterwards.

"He and over 20 million people in Europe." David seemed lost in thought for a few seconds and I realised he must have been a young adult in those years and perhaps had seen it first hand.

I brought his thoughts back to the pictures. "What was the artist's name again?"

"Egon Schiele. He was Austrian. He lived in Vienna in the early 20th century and was …"

As was my no doubt annoying but incurable habit I interrupted him. "Like Max?"

But David was patient. "They would have been in the city at the same time but Max would, of course, have been far too young to have known him. When was Max born? 1906?"

"Probably, I don't know." I had never thought about Max's age, in all the years I had known him he had seemed an old man.

"Well he would have been there but a lot younger than the artist set."

I looked at the picture, "I like it." and went to turn away towards breakfast but David gently caught my arm. "Stay, just look at it." and we stood together for a minute or two in silence. I felt a bit uncomfortable and broke the silence with the first comment that came into my head. "It must have been thought very peculiar back then."

David didn't seem to mind my lack of artistic appreciation. "Some of his work was considered very modern indeed, in fact he was arrested and imprisoned for pornography. Some of his later works …" As he talked I realised I was concentrating on the rise and fall of his voice as much as on the words. He spoke quietly but with authority. I listened carefully to everything he said and remembered it all, not just because the subject was actually interesting but because he made it sound vital. And he made me feel important, answering my questions slowly and carefully, as if they had merit.

"Do you think Max has any more of his work?" I asked, conscious that I had lived and visited this house many times over the years and David had been here only one day.

"He has another, look over there. Very interesting…" We were just walking over to a darker corner of the hall when a loud voice interrupted us.

"Hey, I need some coffee. Where's breakfast?"

"Good morning Graham, in the dining room I expect." David and I had no choice but to follow my cousin and our conversation was ended. But perhaps David had realised what he had set out to achieve.

"Where's your brother?" Graham asked me pointedly as he sat down in Max's seat at the head of the table. "And Max isn't here either. Bloody rude if you ask me." There was an unpleasant leer in his voice. He had made it obvious the afternoon before that he knew of the rumours about Max's relationship with Charles. There had always been uninformed gossips in the town implying there was something unnatural about Charles living with an older man, they assumed there must be 'something to it'. I just thought Charles saw living with Max as a way of not having to earn his own living.

"He had to go out." I said, giving as little of my emotions away as I could. I had heard Charles' car drive away about an hour earlier. Despite all our history I felt I had to defend him against Graham's insinuations, I suppose it was that I disliked the cousin I had only met two days before more than I disliked my half-brother. "He won't be back before you've gone." I tried to make my voice ooze sophisticated disdain but it didn't work with Graham.

"Shame, I'd have enjoyed winding up the queer little toe rag."

Before I could think of a suitable reply Maureen had joined us and slipped me a scrap of paper "Susannah, my dear. You will come to stay with me won't you? One day you will need somewhere that is not filled with old men," she looked at David and smiled, "and I may be useful to you. Here is my phone number. When you're ready you will call me won't you?"

Maureen had been the only person who had helped me through the afternoon of the funeral when Charles had disappeared leaving me to deal with the many people who had come back to Max's house to eat his food and drink his wine and take the rare opportunity to observe our family at close hand. I slipped the paper into my pocket with little intention of taking her up on her offer.

Four months later the situation was very different.

Charles didn't return to Sandhey that day, or the next, and a week later there was a postcard from Cornwall saying he was staying away to have a look at his life. Monika seemed hurt and Max disappointed though the formal, inflexible routines of the household were undisturbed.

Through those early months of 1972 Max never implied I should leave Sandhey and get on with my life. I spent most of my time in my room overlooking the Dee Estuary and Hilbre Islands, with the hills of Wales in the distance, reading romantic novels, meeting Max and Monika only at mealtimes. There was nothing about the books of Georgette Heyer I did not know. Dark, mysteriously rich and powerful men always fell for invariably beautiful yet unsuitable young women; they would charge about Regency England having improbable adventures before finally overcoming all misunderstandings, marrying and living happily ever after. I saw myself in every poor unfortunate, but ultimately successful, heroine and every romantic hero was Carl.

I loved Carl more than anyone and always had. We had been inseparable through our childhood but I hadn't seen him in the nine years since the day we had been told that we were half brother and sister. All my life since then had been spent waiting for Carl to realise that that didn't matter, that caring for each other was the most important thing, that sharing a father didn't mean we couldn't share our lives. But Carl wasn't going to come to my rescue and the formality of Max's household quickly became oppressive. At Easter, more out of curiosity than expectation, I phoned the number Maureen had given me.

"Well, my dear, I live in a small village where not much goes on, but we have a good library and I have plenty of time to spend with you."

"I would like that." I hadn't thought I meant it, the words were spoken more from an ingrained politeness than real expectation.

"Just give me a day's warning to get your room ready."

"I'll let you know."

Perhaps I was being rude, ringing her and then not making a firm arrangement. Whatever the reason I rang Maureen again a week later.

"Is it still OK?"

"Of course it is dear, but only come when you're good and ready. How are you getting on with Max and Monika? It must be very difficult."

During our third telephone conversation in as many weeks Maureen asked me whether I had done anything about going back to university. She knew about my ignominious academic career, how I had scraped a third because of my ridiculous marriage to Joe and the birth of my four children within five years. "It will be too late if you don't apply soon. You don't want to lose another year do you sweetie?" I liked Maureen, she asked me about myself, never mentioning my children who I had had nothing to do with since their father's death and my breakdown.

I admitted I had done nothing, throwing up problems. "It was so easy at school. They just presented you with all the forms. I've got no idea what to do now. And how am I going to pay for it? I won't get another grant."

"Don't you worry about that, dear, I'm sure something will turn up." She sounded cheerful and confident. I began to look forward to our phone calls and fell into the routine of calling her every Sunday evening.

Towards the end of May Max announced that Charles was at last coming home, he had tired of Cornwall. Monika was delighted. "Oh that is wonderful I have missed my Charles so much. When will he be home? I had worried he would miss his birthday dinner. It would have been so wrong for him not to be here, for Mister Ted not to be here for dinner for his birthday. It is an important one. Thirty years. Oh that is wonderful that he will be home."

I sat listening to Monika's gushing about my brother feeling the familiar jealousy and anger. Monika had always cared for Charles more than she did for me, even when we had been small children and she was supposed to be looking after both of us. The feelings of resentment welled up as they always had and I knew I could not be in the house when the prodigal son returned. "Would you mind if I wasn't here?" I asked.

Max appeared to understand. "You seem so much better than you were but living in the same house as your brother may be one step too far. Perhaps you are ready to go back to your children?"

"I am much better Max, thank you but I can't cope with the children."

"You must not let them forget you. It is unnatural for a mother." Monika's disapproval hurt as she, more than anyone, knew the difficulties of my marriage.

"I can't. Not until I've done something for myself, done what I should have done before I had them." I ignored the look on Monika's face and found myself repeating words that Maureen had said when she had been trying to explain my behaviour to me. "I need to get a good degree, do myself justice, and then I will be able to face the years of not being me."

"You sound so like your mother." Max's voice was uncharacteristically gentle. "Alicia always said that she had never had a chance to be what she should have been."

"Well you understand then. Three, maybe four years, that's all I need and then I'll get to know them and I won't resent them, I'll be a far better mother when they really need one. They're too young to miss me."

"Josie is seven now, Jack will be starting school soon. You will not be there for them? The poor children have no father and no mother. You are a very selfish young woman." Monika's accent was more pronounced when she was angry.

"No. I'm not ready for them." I could be firm when I wanted "I've got to do this for me first."

"You're absolutely adamant about this Susannah?" Max had known my mother, perhaps he understood me better because of that.

"I am. Absolutely."

"Then I will give you every help I can."

Monika stood up and ostentatiously began to clear away the dishes, even though we had not finished, her disapproval made painfully clear.

Max kept silent until she was out of the room and what he said amazed me, reeling off instructions as if reading from a list. "You will go to Maureen, she will be a friend to you as she was to your mother. I will make sure the children are looked after. I will pay your fees and an allowance. You may take the Humber as I have no need of it. In return you will work hard at your studies and when you get your First I will hold a party for you in the garden."

"You don't have to do all that."

"I know I don't have to, but I shall." He smiled and I could see that years before he would have been an attractive man. "I shall because of your mother. It is what she would have wanted you to do. It's what she would have done. Do not let us down. And one more thing Susannah."

I was surely going to agree with anything Max asked of me.

"In the time it takes you to achieve what you have to achieve you will not come back here, you will not contact us in any way until you have done what you have to do and until you are ready to meet your children and take up your responsibilities."

That was going to be easy, it would have been exactly what I wanted anyway.

"Agreed. And thank you Max. No wonder my mother loved you."

Monika returned with the coffee and sat frowning at the end of the table. I wondered what to say as we surely couldn't talk about our arrangement in front of Monika.

"You know that drawing in the hall?" I ventured.

"Which one is that?" Max was relaxed in his answer "There are several."

"The Schiele." He seemed surprised I knew the artist's name. I had surprised myself by remembering.

"You know Schiele's work?"

"David was telling me about it, in January, after the funeral. How sad the artist's life was."

I was unprepared for the change in him.

He stood up without speaking, wiped his mouth deliberately on his napkin and, having folded and rolled it, placed it carefully in the silver ring and left the room without another word.

"What have I done? What have I said?" I asked Monika.

"You always were a thoughtless little girl." She said in her clipped, accented voice. "Can you not see that it disturbs him. The mention of that man."

'No' I thought but did not say 'How can I know if no one ever tells me anything?' Perhaps there was some history between Max and David that neither had acknowledged in January. I hadn't been entirely convinced that they had never met before.

So in May 1972 I ran away to Maureen for the first time.

Chapter Two

I drove south to Surrey the next day, carefully keeping off the motorways as, although I had passed my test a few years before, I had rarely driven any distance and I was unfamiliar with Max's old Humber. After trying, unsuccessfully, to get the radio to work I had time to think as I drove along the unfamiliar roads.

I wondered what it would be like being in the village where my mother's life had been after her divorce and I looked forward to seeing the places she had seen and learning more about her life. I had lived under the same roof as my mother for only three years of my life, my first two and her last one. She had left us soon after my second birthday party and I didn't live with her again until we had both been given refuge by Ted, she dying of cancer and I recovering from a nervous breakdown.

That last year we had not known how to act with each other, and I had begun by hating her. But Ted made us talk and, as we spent more time together, she had explained her reasons for leaving Charles and me to others to bring up. She had married the wrong man to escape her parents. She had had children too young. She had resented those children. She had not had enough time in her life to do the things she wanted to do. She was someone's daughter, then she had become someone's wife and too soon after someone's mother. Towards the end she had asked me 'when could I have been myself if I hadn't run away?'. I could not answer as I realised that we had so much in common.

Did my daughter Josie, feel as much anger towards me as I felt towards Alicia?

My mother's excuses were mine also.

Maureen called her house 'the cottage' but it was really more substantial than that, having probably once been the rectory or vicarage of the small Surrey village. She showed me straight up to a surprisingly large bedroom saying this was my home for as long and as often as I needed it.

I couldn't possibly have known how many nights I would spend there over the next few years, in such varying circumstances, and how important that house was to my future.

Maureen made me feel immediately at home and anything more different from the rigidity and formality of Sandhey would have been difficult to imagine as we sat in the garden that evening drinking wine and getting to know each other.

"There'll be five of us for supper tomorrow night. I hope you don't mind. It has been long planned but is extremely fortuitous." I'm not sure whether she expected me to believe her.

"Five?" I repeated, "I'm not very good at dinner parties."

"Oh it's not a dinner party, nothing formal like that. We'll just sit in the garden, as we are now, with a few bottles of wine and talk. I don't eat much and if you knew what an awful cook I was then you'd thank God I'm not producing any food! We will provide the wine and our guests will bring salads. There's far more time to enjoy the company that way." I noticed the 'our guests' and relaxed even more, remembering with horror Monika's plans for Charles's formal birthday dinner. "Who are the guests?"

"That's the wonderful coincidence, and you must believe that this was not a set up, two are David and Edie, your grandparents."

"Great!" And I meant it. I was intrigued by the idea of meeting David again, there were things I wanted to ask him. "And who else?"

"A friend of mine who lives in the village, her name is Joy and she just happens to be in the History Department at Sussex University."

"Are you sure you hadn't just planned this when you heard I was coming?"

"And you think such people would be able to make plans at one day's notice?"

It was only later as I lay in bed unable to sleep, too excited by the difference a day can make, that I realised she hadn't actually answered my question.

I liked the look of Joy. Although she was far too old and plump for the tight denims and t-shirt that she wore she obviously had enough confidence in herself not to worry about what others thought. Her first action was to give me a hug.

"Susannah. I am so pleased to meet Alicia's daughter."

"You knew my mother?"

"Of course, this is a small village so I saw quite a lot of her before she got so ill. I didn't get to the funeral, Maureen said…"

I never knew what she was going to say about Maureen and the funeral as we were disturbed by the arrival of my grandparents.

"Susannah, my dear girl, it's so good to see you again."

9

"You look so much better than you did in January. Then you were so strained, now you look wonderful. Doesn't she David?"

"You're absolutely right Edie, she looks good as new. I gather we're to sort…"

"Now now… time enough for all that later." Maureen interrupted. "We must sit down and work out what we're all going to call each other."

"I refuse to be called 'grandmother'." Edie smiled broadly at me, reaching over to take my hand in hers and give it an encouraging squeeze.

"And proud as I am to be your grandfather I refuse to be called Grandpa or any such like so you must call me David."

"I've always thought of you as David." I ventured.

"I've always hated 'Edie' but you may call me Edith."

"Edie is a perfectly respectable name." David grinned at his wife.

"But so ugly." She grimaced. "I've always hated it. Alicia changed her name. Imagine if she had had to go through her life as Alberta." Looking at me she added in explanation. "That was her given name you know."

I hadn't known. It was a perfect illustration of our family circumstances that I hadn't known my mother's real Christian name.

"What would you rather have been?" Her husband asked with a smile.

"Ann, something that couldn't be made ugly by abbreviation, I would like to have been Ann. I would have a completely different life if I had been called Ann."

"I'm rather happy that you are Edith." David's smile swept passed his wife and focussed on me.

"Are you always 'Susannah' or do you ever shorten it? Susie perhaps?"

"No." I knew I had spoken too sharply. I realised I had been rude. "Sorry, it's just that 'Susie' brings back all sorts of memories."

"I know. Carl called you that." Maureen looked at me smiling mischievously. "You'll have to face up to the fact that I knew that young man. He spent quite a bit of time here and he talked about you quite a lot."

"Carl, wasn't he that beautiful young man…" Joy began only to be cut short by Maureen.

"If we can't use the 'Sus.' bit of your name how about the '..anna' bit? Susannah's such a mouthful. No, not Anna, that's too formal, but how about Annie?"

"I like the name Annie, a new name for my new life." I wasn't just

10

saying that, I really did like the idea of changing my name.

I had won three or four years of freedom before having to face up to the children and I had every intention of enjoying them. A change of name would make it seem so much more a complete break. Annie Donaldson would not have to be Susannah Parry. Perhaps I need never be Susannah Parry again.

The time passed quickly, we drank the wine and the wide ranging conversation flowed easily. It was one of the most interesting but enjoyable evenings I had ever spent.

Maureen spent most of the next morning on the phone. I heard snippets of the conversation; 'Oh dear she will be disappointed.' 'What a good idea.' 'Are you sure?' 'I'm sure she would find that very interesting. I'm sure she will.' 'I'll talk to her and get her to call you back.' 'Leave it to me.' I was obviously the subject of the conversation.

"Well well Annie." She put the emphasis on my new name. "You made quite an impression yesterday."

"What do you mean?"

"That was Joy on the phone." I felt certain there had been other calls but if Maureen only wanted me to know about her call to Joy that was fine. I'm sure she had her reasons. "She hadn't wanted to say anything last night, in fact I had wondered why she was quieter than normal, but she was very impressed with you."

"I didn't realise I was on trial." It showed how much better I was now that I could make a joke of it.

"Not 'on trial' more 'being interviewed'."

"But I'm not looking for a job."

"What Joy said on the phone was that you've left it a little late for your plan to start a university course this year."

"Oh." I couldn't help showing my disappointment.

"We knew you would be frustrated but she was very helpful. She said she didn't think there would be a problem for next year, in fact she practically said there would be no problem at all."

"That's nice of her."

Maureen chose to misunderstand. "She wasn't being nice, sweetie, she was simply saying what would be the case."

"Max has given me the money and the car, but he'll be expecting bills for fees, expecting me to be doing something positive. What can I tell him if I'm not doing anything for a year?"

"Don't worry. Joy had a request."

"A *request?*"

"She's working on a project at the moment, she's not sure whether it's going to be a book or not but it's something she's been progressing when she's had time from her teaching. She needs a researcher, someone to do the leg work for her. She can't travel as much as she'd like to and so it would mean time away from home. Would you be interested?"

"What's it about?"

"That's where I thought you would be interested. In central Europe in the 1930s there were a lot of very wealthy people, not all Jews but many were. By 1945 much of their wealth had disappeared. Joy is studying where it went. There are apocryphal tales of much of it ending up in America. Apparently it was not only the Nazis who stole."

"What does she mean by 'wealth'?" I was beginning to understand what Maureen was getting at.

"Certainly not just money."

"Paintings?"

"Certainly. A lot of very valuable and important art was lost."

"Has this anything to do with David?"

She looked at me sharply and I wondered if I had gone too far. "I mean he knows a lot about art. He was telling me all about Max's Schieles and stuff like that." I finished weakly.

She relaxed and answered in her normal, gentle voice. "David knows a lot about a lot of things."

"What would I have to do?"

"As I said. You must do whatever Joy asks you to do with common sense and intelligence. I've never thought they were the same thing."

"Where would I live? Would I get paid?"

"So many questions! You need to speak with Joy, I said you'd call her back after I'd had a chance to talk to you, but you know you will always have your room here."

I gave her a hug. "You know when I first met you I thought you were going to be like Kathleen but you're nothing like her."

"Should I take that as a compliment?" she seemed amused. "I always thought my sister was very clever and quite beautiful."

It was the measure of how well we had got to know each other so quickly that I didn't feel awkward about replying truthfully "I always thought my step-mother was a selfish, bossy, ungrateful, miserable cow."

"Perhaps she was all those things at different times."

"Perhaps you should have been my step-mother instead."

"There's one problem with that scenario."

"What's that?"

"I always disliked Arnold."

Perhaps now was the time to clear the air in case there was any awkwardness between Maureen and myself. "It was a real shock for Mother when she found out you were Kathleen's sister. You were her friend and you had never told her though you must have known your sister was her husband's mistress all those years."

"Kathleen and Arnold had been close for many years."

"Before he married my mother?"

"Well before."

"Why did he marry her then?"

Maureen thought for a few moments before answering "He needed a wife and Kathleen couldn't be that."

"Why not? They got married later, when he'd divorced my mother."

"She would have been totally unsuitable as the political wife Arnold thought he would need. She was far too strong for him."

"But they had Carl together. Dad arranged for her to marry someone else so his son wouldn't be a bastard. He probably kept seeing her all the time. You must have known and you never told her."

"Yes I knew. No I didn't tell her. I knew if she learned I was Kathleen's sister she would never want to see me again and then I couldn't be any good for her could I? She needed a friend to help her through her loneliness and her illness. I had to be that person so I couldn't tell her."

I had to admit it made sense. "I'm learning more about her all the time."

"And all the time you stay with me I'll try to tell you more. You need to know your mother before you can understand yourself. You know you are very alike."

I was beginning to realise that many people thought that.

"When did she find out?" Maureen asked almost tentatively.

"It was my fault. I was reading out the death notice from the paper. She had laughed saying she hadn't realised how much older Kathleen was and then the notice mentioned 'Maureen'. It could only have been you. She died a few hours later."

We sat in silence for only a few moments before she spoke again, brightly, as if our conversation had not happened. "You'd better call Joy. What are you going to tell her?"

"Of course I'll definitely say yes."

Chapter Three

"David?"

He didn't answer immediately. I waited for my grandfather to break the silence which, though not uncomfortable seemed to be too long for comfort. We were sitting together in Maureen's garden taking advantage of the late summer sun, it would soon be September and I would be leaving for the unknowns of working for Joy in Brighton.

I did what I could to help Maureen and be a trouble-free houseguest but she had insisted that I spent my time preparing for the demands Joy would make of me in the coming year. 'She will expect a great deal from you, you will not let her down.' Maureen had said as I had read the long list of tasks Joy had set for my summer. I had seen David and Edith two or three times and I had enjoyed telling them how I was progressing and practising my German on David, who spoke the language quite fluently.

The month before Edith had appeared tired and she had lost a great deal of weight. Now I was spending the afternoon with David while Maureen took his wife to a hospital appointment in London. It was my job to take David's mind off what his wife might be going through.

"Yes my dear?" David finally answered me, still staring at his fingers which were intertwined on his lap.

"Tell me about your childhood."

He looked up as if he had been a long way away.

"Ah Annie, it should be so easy."

"What's not easy?" I knew I should probably back away, go into the kitchen, leave an old man with his thoughts but I couldn't. I thought at first he was going to say 'everything' or 'nothing' but his answer made me think that perhaps I had a lot to learn about what made and hurt people.

"Because in telling you about myself I won't have anywhere to hide. You will know me. I don't like people knowing me."

"Even grandmother?"

"There are many, many things about me she does not know."

"But you've been married for how long? 25 years?"

"Since March 1st 1948. It will be our Silver Wedding anniversary next year. I didn't think we would have so long together." Again he fell

14

quiet, perhaps wondering whether Edith would still be with him in six months time.

"I'll make sure we have a wonderful celebration." I'm not sure it was the right thing to say but it seemed to help as when he began speaking his voice had its usual lilt.

"For many years we conducted what could be described as an affair of the heart. We met maybe twenty times in as many years before her husband died. Then we married. We have had many good years together but there are many things about my life she does not know. She has never asked me to tell her anything I didn't volunteer. She loves me as she finds me."

"I would want to know everything there was to know about any man I married."

David raised his eyebrow. "I think you will find that you will know only what he wants you to know."

"How depressing."

"But human nature I think."

"Well *are* you?" I didn't want to think of marrying again, my first experience of marriage had not been a happy one but I did want to hear about my grandfather's life. My interest in history was not only academic.

"Am I what?"

"Going to tell me about where you came from, your childhood, your work, how you met my grandmother, why you didn't marry for so many years?"

"Are you really interested or do you just want me to think of other things?"

It seemed only fair to be honest. "Both."

He made a show of thinking for a few moments, as if coming to a decision. "I will tell you about how I came to get my first job."

I wondered later why, of all the things about his early life, he chose that.

He cleared his throat as if about to make a speech. "One Saturday evening I watched my mother, her name was Alice…"

"Alice? That's very like…"

"Yes it is like the name Alicia. I like to think your grandmother had heard me mention my mother when she decided she wanted a secret name for our daughter."

"It doesn't seem like a coincidence."

"As I was saying, I was sitting in our kitchen watching my mother drying the dishes and putting them away carefully on the rack above the sink, everything in its place…"

15

"Where did you live?"

"South London, Crystal Palace, in a house like many others, in a street like many others, though they had recently planted trees along the pavement outside our house and it almost seemed like we were in the country. You must stop interrupting me Annie or we'll never get through even the beginning of the story."

"I'll try." I meant it but I was worried that he would leave something out and I so much wanted to know everything.

"Alice was wondering why my father had had to go to work that particular Saturday. He normally worked on Saturdays but she had asked him to take a holiday on the 29th January, it was her 40th birthday and she wanted him to be at home."

"What year was it?" I interrupted, biting my tongue as I did but needing to know the answer.

"Nineteen hundred and ten."

"How old were you?"

"18. I was born on April 2nd 1891. The same day as Max Ernst."

"Who's Max Ernst?"

"Another artist you should have heard of. Now, Annie, no more questions."

All the time he spoke he looked down at his hands, turning them over as if he had never seen them before, stretching his fingers out, turning his hands palm up and then curling his fingers over almost as if he was a nervous interviewee for a job he wasn't qualified for. But throughout his voice was strong and clear.

Chapter Four

From Monday to Saturday every week Arthur Redhead left his house at precisely ten past nine in the morning to make the fifteen minute walk to the railway station. He always exchanged a few words with the newspaper seller where he bought his copy of the Daily Mail. During the journey into London Bridge Station he read the articles about the main stories of the day and then would turn to the Editor's page to read what he should believe about the events he could not hope to fully understand. As he approached London Bridge he would carefully re-fold the paper and place it with the sandwiches that Alice had made that morning in the small attaché case that was part of the uniform for someone of his grade. All the other clerks in Arthur's department carried identical brown cases which would also contain sandwiches their wives or mothers had made for them along with their copies of the Daily Mail.

Arthur had worked in the same office for fifteen years, since his son David had been a small boy. There were some days when he had found what he did interesting, but there hadn't been many. He sat every day at his desk alongside four others, spending every working day writing words and numbers on pieces of paper in an identical script. They never knew the entirety of the documents, seeing only a page here and a page there of complex reports which must have meant something to someone. 'Perhaps the editor of the Daily Mail understands' Arthur had thought.

He talked about the generality of his work with his son, who, he hoped, would follow him into the service. There was talk, that armies of women would take over their jobs using machines called type writers, that they would lose their jobs to these 'type writer girls'. It had taken years for Arthur and his colleagues to perfect the Vere Foster script that they, and all civil servants, had to use. Women would be able to copy the documents operating type writing machines just as easily as they could use a sewing machine. Arthur could not afford to lose his job, and he reassured himself that there would always be a need for the experience and skill of proper clerks to ensure the vast libraries of documents required by government were created correctly.

When the government changed in 1906 Arthur found his life transformed.

He still left at the same time in the morning, but it was often well past 7 o'clock in the evening before he left the building off Whitehall to walk over Westminster Bridge and under the dark network of arches and bridges to catch his train to the suburbs. For the first time in his working life he was finding the documents he was copying interesting. For fifteen years he had written many thousands of pages of dry words about taxation followed by more thousands of pages of numbers in neat columns. He had copied them all taking no notice of the content 'from the eye to the hand without passing through the brain' he had said. But in 1906 he had been moved to the new Foreign Office. No longer was he copying dry and meaningless figures, now there were memoranda about places and people he recognised from his reading of the Daily Mail. So interesting were they that, not only did Arthur extend his working days, he also began to spend his Saturday afternoons in the library pouring over an atlas of the world to see where these places were that he was writing about.

Arthur was never told why he had been chosen to move from the Finance Ministry to the Foreign Office, he had made no formal application and had not even known there were positions available but it was promotion and a timely one for him personally. David had left school and was working for his Civil Service exams so Arthur and Alice had not expected to have another child, but the unexpected baby Elizabeth had brought laughter to the household despite the increasing gloom of international events.

Everyone knew a war was coming. Whatever Kaiser Bill said about his friendship with England the Daily Mail knew that the German people would force a war.

It would be over quickly, Arthur told his son, there was so much preparation going on. Although bound to secrecy Arthur told David of the young men in the best public schools being trained to be officers, young and fit men being trained as a Special Reserve, the build up of arms of a quantity more than sufficient to overcome any foe and the lessons of recent wars all learned. "There won't be a chance for you to cover yourself with glory," Arthur had said, "Once it starts we'll have sorted it all out in a few weeks."

In common with many men of his class, Arthur would never discuss anything of world affairs with his wife. He would never have expected her to understand what he was talking about let alone have an opinion that might have value. The papers, and what they reported, were men's business and Arthur felt it best not to worry his wife with such details. He did not for one instant think that his attitude was patronising and he was totally unaware that she read every page of the newspaper he gave her at the end of each day. He assumed that she put them to good use for wrapping up the waste or rolling into tight fire lighters, which of course she did for she was a thrifty housekeeper, but not before she had read every word. Frequently she bit her lip when he said she wouldn't understand or shouldn't be interested in what occurred in the widening world around them. She kept quiet with Arthur, but spent many happy hours discussing 'events' with David.

Arthur was older and more experienced than the other clerks in his department and perhaps that was why he was singled out to do special work. If a particularly sensitive or difficult document was to be copied it would be Arthur who was instructed but he had still been surprised when was called to the front of the room and asked to stay behind after the bell that marked the end of the working day sounded.

"I have a favour to ask you, Mr Redhead."

"Sir?" It was extremely unusual for his Manager to address him in this way and Arthur couldn't hide his curiosity.

Mr Fowler nodded down at a parcel on his desk wrapped in brown paper, tied with string and sealed with red wax. "This must be delivered to The Metropole Hotel in Brighton tomorrow. I would take it myself but I am unable, for reasons I need not bother you with, to make the journey. I would be indebted to you." Mr Fowler had a way of asking his staff to do something that made them feel they had a choice when they knew they hadn't, so Arthur had nodded, put the parcel in his attaché case along with the envelope containing the rail tickets and wondered how he was going to tell his wife that he would not be with her until the evening on her birthday.

Alice had tentatively ventured 'you said you would take a holiday' when Arthur had told her he would not be at home until the evening. She didn't mention her birthday. 'I know' Arthur had answered unhelpfully 'I have not forgotten it is your birthday. I'm not going into town, I just have an errand to do for Mr Fowler.' He had smiled as he kissed her cheek and something in his eyes reminded her of the man she had fallen in love with 20 years before. 'I promise I'll be home for tea.'

But he wasn't.

David had been out most of the day as well. He sang in the local church choir, not because he was any more religious than the next man but because he liked to sing. The choir always met on a Saturday afternoon to practise the hymns and psalms for the services the following day. Afterwards David would go to an ale house for a glass or two but on his mother's birthday he made sure he was home in time for tea.

He watched his mother and four year old Elizabeth lay out the thin slices of ham and carefully spread just enough butter on the freshly baked bread. The parlour was warm and homely, the kettle filled and ready to put on the range as soon as Arthur returned.

He had said he would be back in time for tea. And he always did as he said.

Alice wasn't worried until she began to light the lamps. As the clock on the mantle struck 5 o'clock she decided they would have to start without him. It was an unheard of situation but Elizabeth was getting tired and fractious, so the three sat down around the table and tried to ignore the empty chair.

David tried to distract his mother as they ate but without success. He even helped her to tidy away, explaining his uncharacteristic behaviour by saying that it was her birthday rather than admit the reality that he was very worried. His father had told him what his errand was and David realised how unusual the request had been.

"Perhaps he had to go into town after all." Alice said, as if thinking aloud as they heard the mantle clock strike seven.

"Perhaps he ..." But David couldn't think of any reason for his father not to have been able to make the journey to Brighton and back in ten hours. Elizabeth had gone to bed at 6 in a sulk so David was sitting alone with his mother by the fire in a heavy silence when there was a knock on the door.

They looked sharply at each other, both recognising that there was no reason Arthur would need to knock.

"Mrs Redhead?" The well dressed man at the door spoke too well to be a policeman.

"My mother is in the parlour." David answered formally. When the man moved into the light of the hallway and removed his hat David saw the look on his face.

"My name is Fowler."

"Of course Mr Fowler, I was forgetting my manners, do come in. Do you mind the back room? That's where the fire is." David took the visitor's hat and coat and hung them up, pausing barely perceptibly as he noticed the empty hook where a more familiar coat should have been.

David led Mr Fowler through to the back room. Alice was standing, her back to the fire, her hands firmly in the pockets of her apron. If either of the men had looked they would have realised her fists were clenched under the thin checked material.

"Do sit down, I'm afraid Arthur, I mean Mr Redhead, I'm afraid my husband isn't back yet. He said he would be back for tea, you see it's my birthday, but he isn't. It'd be him you're wanting to see." She saw her son frowning at her. She knew she should stop talking but she thought that as long as she talked the visitor couldn't say what she knew he was going to say. "Come in Mr Fowler, David, this is my son David, say 'how do you do' to Mr Fowler." But she didn't give him time to say anything as she fussed about the visitor. "Are you quite comfortable, can I get you a cup of tea? The kettle won't take a moment. It won't take a moment to ..."

"Mrs Redhead. Please. Sit down." Mr Fowler shifted his glance between the two involving both in his words.

"Mrs Redhead, David, you will realise I am not here with good news." As the words were spoken David walked round to stand behind his mother and put his hands on her shoulders, pressing firmly on them to give her something else to think about as Mr Fowler continued. "In fact it is the worst." He paused, knowing the effect his words would have. As he had entered the house he had recognised that the Redheads lived quite well for their class, probably due to the boy's wage as well as the father's. The room was clean and well appointed, there were interesting pictures on the walls and there were good rugs on the floor. They probably had a girl to help in the house, a man to help in the garden. This prosperous home was to be broken with the news he had to give them.

"Arthur, may I call him Arthur?" he looked across at Alice who nodded her head very slightly in assent. "Arthur kindly stepped in to undertake an important task for me. It was imperative that a package was taken to Brighton."

"Brighton?" Alice asked, uncomprehending.

"The Hotel Metropole in Brighton. Arthur agreed to take the package for me and if everything had gone smoothly he would have been back by the middle of the afternoon."

"If everything had gone smoothly?" David asked, knowing that something must have gone wrong.

"Unfortunately, and it with great sadness that I have to tell you, there was an accident, a very bad accident. A train was derailed, it crashed into a station and your husband, your father, he was amongst the casualties." He seemed to realise he had said the wrong thing, David knew his father was dead, but by using the word 'casualty' Mr Fowler had given Alice hope. David looked at him sharply and Mr Fowler spoke quickly to overcome his regret at any misunderstanding. "Arthur was, most unfortunately, amongst the fatalities. He was one of the seven people killed at Stoat's Nest railway station when the Brighton train was derailed."

He paused, waiting for some reaction from Alice; a cry, a sob, something to show that she had realised how suddenly her circumstances had changed. It was some time before the silence was broken.

21

"Will my mother have any form of pension?"

"That's very practical of you young man." Mr Fowler was relieved that he was not to be faced with hysteria, practicalities were far easier to deal with. "Pensions are very much in the news are they not." The question had not been directly answered, but in the evasion David understood the negative as much as if the word 'No' had been spoken.

"So I will have to become breadwinner."

"You are a remarkably sensible young man."

"I have a mother and a young sister to support. I will have to be."

"Indeed you will."

Mr Fowler had been expecting the boy to speak with the broad south London accent Arthur had always tried to hide. Through this exchange he had an opportunity to assess the young man who spoke courteously, with no hint of the servility Alice couldn't help displaying when dealing with someone she would consider 'above her'. David spoke as he did to visiting choir-masters at the church, with respect but as to an equal.

"What will you do to help us? After all is said and done if you felt no responsibility you would have left it to others to come to break the news to us."

Mr Fowler bowed his head slightly in acknowledgement of the truth in David's statement, his interest in the young man growing.

"When the police arrived at my house some two hours ago they had believed it was to tell Mrs Fowler that her husband was dead. The body had been..." he hesitated endeavouring to find the right word and David, whose hands were still on his mother's shoulders, felt her wince in anticipation "...damaged and identification was ... difficult. They had found an envelope addressed to 'Mr Harold Fowler' at my address and so they had made the assumption that the dead man was the said Harold Fowler. Having discovered their mistake they were relieved when I said I would take it upon myself to visit the family. The police had six other calls to make. You are quite right, your father would not have been on that train had I not requested him to go to Brighton this morning."

"And we would not now be facing penury."

"And you would not be facing a change in your circumstances. I suggest that you would always be able to maintain your family above penury."

David understood that this man was testing him, perhaps to see if he might be useful to him. Wise to the probability that Mr Fowler would be more likely to assist them if he felt he had won the bout he changed the tone of his voice. "I will support my mother and my sister for as long as they need me."

"I am absolutely certain you will for you are the head of the household now."

Alice seemed to be taking little account of the conversation that occurred above her head. She heard the rise and fall of the voices as if in a dream and the words made no sense to her. Her Arthur was dead.

There had been no passion between them for years, Elizabeth had been a mistake, she had thought she was too old to conceive when they had been husband and wife that one last time. They were companions, good friends, partners, albeit unequal ones, in the business of bringing up their family. She would mourn him and she would miss him but she would get on with the business of raising their daughter and keeping her home together.

She thought of how he would have felt in his last moments. Would he have known? Would he have thought of her? As her son's voice rose and fell above her head, she banished such thoughts and never again let herself think about her husband's last moments.

"Where is he? We must make the necessary arrangements."

Some years later she told her son that she wished she had been listening more carefully that evening because he must have given a truly wonderful performance. The following week a letter from Mr Fowler called David to his office. David was taken under his direct tutelage and, far sooner than he should have been, David was working in the Ministry of War. He began the accelerated charge through the grades of the Civil Service that was possible for a clever and ambitious young man in that Ministry as spy fever swept the country.

Chapter Five

David's story answered so many questions, but raised even more.

"You speak of your father as 'Mr Redhead'?"

"Indeed. That was our name."

"But you are David McKennah."

"Indeed I am."

"Why?" I had to ask the question directly because he was not going to volunteer the information.

He thought for a while before answering.

"For many years I was both David Redhead and David McKennah. They had separate work, separate lives and in the end I preferred to be David McKennah. David Redhead was not a particularly nice man."

"Will you tell me?"

"Not now. I am not David Redhead. David Redhead was the product of a time now, thank God, a part of history." He drank the cold cup of tea that had been sitting untouched on the table and continued. "It was not unusual for people to change their identities. There were very few demands to prove that you were who you said you were. Many men in the great strikes of the 1920s and the depression of the 30s moved from area to area using different names whenever it suited them. Many people during and after the war disappeared and re-appeared with a completely new name. They did it for many different reasons."

"Was Max one?"

"Of course. Max's real name was not Fischer. He chose that name, just as many, many people did in those years."

Again David was not going to volunteer any information, again I was going to have to ask the question directly. "What was it?"

He teased me for a while pretending not to remember.

"I was wondering how long it would take you to realise there was no such man as 'Maximilian Fischer' before the 1930s."

"Would you have let me waste my time?"

"Probably not."

"Well... what was it? You're not going to make me guess are you?"

"I'm sure you could get close."

"I don't know any Austrian surnames."

"You know one."

"Monika? Heller?"

"When Max brought Monika to this country after the war he gave her a new name. She didn't remember her old one after the awful experiences she had had. Her couldn't give her his name so he just adapted it. His name was Hellermann."

"You seem to know a lot about Max. I thought you hadn't met till the funeral."

"Why would you think that?"

"Well you said so."

"Did I say that?"

"And you hardly talked to him."

"Do you know what we all did those two days? Do you know I didn't spend many hours in Max's study that night talking until we both heard your brother drive away?"

I tried to remember that morning and I wondered if I had imagined the door to Max's study closing as I came down the stairs just before being greeted by David.

"Do you know we didn't talk? No. Of course you don't. You have assumed things Annie. You must not *assume*. You must *know* and until you know you must not think you do. What do you think you know of Max?" David slowly changed his focus from the sky to my face.

He really wanted to know my answer.

"The bare bones I suppose. He was a refugee from Austria in the early days of the war but he wasn't interned. He should have lost everything but seems to have limitless funds because he not only bought into the firm of solicitors Ted and my father worked for but also purchased Millcourt, a substantial house on 'Millionaires Mile'. He was married and had a daughter, but they died."

"Are you fond of him?"

"I wouldn't say that. I suppose I'm a bit afraid of him. He always seems to have so much control and so much power. But he's never been anything but kind and generous to me. Look at what he's doing for me now."

"You're going to spend a year working with Joy and then go on to study for your degree. You will no doubt spend much of that time finding out more about Max."

"Will I?"

"You are an inquisitive lady, you have an inquiring mind."

25

"You've known each other for years?" I asked tentatively.

He nodded. "Yes we have known each other."

"But you don't like each other?" It seemed obvious now.

"Liking each other doesn't come into it my dear Annie. We have known each other for five decades, but, until your mother's funeral, we had not met for more than half that time."

"You worked together?"

"Yes, we worked together."

"But you worked for the government."

"Indeed I did."

"Does that mean Max did too?"

"In a manner of speaking."

"Will you tell me something about him?"

David at first seemed reluctant to talk, taking a few moments before he composed himself.

"In the beginning Max and I were very alike. We both had the disadvantage of fighting class prejudice, we both had to work to rise above the station in life our birth should have dictated. As I have just told you I had the assistance of an older man who felt obliged to sponsor me. It was the same for Maximilian."

"I always thought Max was an aristocrat.."

"You *assumed* he was. I have told you not to make assumptions and not to think you know until you do. You must ask particular questions about him, and me, and you must find the answers to those. Have you any in mind?"

"I suppose it's where he came from, why he came, how he got his money, why he's so ashamed of his money, why he's so mysterious about himself, why he gave a home to Charles, why…"

"That should keep you busy." David was smiling.

"If you know all the answers why don't you tell me now?"

"I do not know all the answers. You must find out for yourself and then ask me specific questions. It is the only way."

"What do you want me to find that you don't know?"

"Well done, my dear Annie. You have seen through me." He laughed but didn't answer my question. "You know Annie, you will find out so much about this man but you will find out about other people too."

"You?"

"And people you do not know."

"Is there much you wouldn't want me to know? David Redhead?"

26

He nodded, "I'm afraid so."

"But you want me to get involved don't you? When you started talking to me about that lovely picture. You were trying to get me interested."

"Annie. I wish that things were that simple. I want someone to know what we did, it should not be forgotten. Also, I am hoping that you might find another man who worked with us."

"Then you must tell me everything you know."

"That isn't possible."

"Why not?"

"There is such a thing as honour and, incidentally, the Official Secrets Act. I consider myself bound by that. I will tell you what I can, Annie dear, when you ask me, but you must find out what I know but cannot tell you."

"It sounds like what you were all doing wasn't particularly legal."

"It was …" He paused as if he wasn't quite sure how to answer. "… They were different times, they cannot be judged by the standards of today."

We had been in the garden for a long time and I noticed David glancing at his watch, I wondered how long it would be before Edith and Maureen arrived back.

David also seemed to be calculating whether he had time to tell me another part of his story.

"Shall I tell you how I met my wife?"

Chapter Six

Since early in the war, when the first codebook had been captured detailing the enemy's operating ciphers, David had spent his working days interpreting the messages which enabled the Navy to locate enemy ships and submarines. Many of his colleagues were Naval officers and wore uniform but, as a civilian David was exposed, whenever he walked the streets of London, to the unjustified attacks of women with their malicious words and white feathers.

He felt they should have known better.

He was not normally required to go into work on a Saturday but January 1917 was a particularly busy time. A message had been intercepted which was believed to be of critical importance to the progress of the war. David had heard enough to know that, if their interpretation was correct, America would have to enter the war against Germany. Such was the pressure that Saturday that David had worked even longer than he had meant to.

It was nearing the anniversary of his father's death and he knew his mother and Elizabeth would both worry if he was not back on time so he was running to catch his bus when he bumped into Edith Tyler on the pavement outside Charing Cross station. In the collision the contents of her shopping basket were spilled on the pavement. He remembered two brown parcels, a small bag and a newspaper. He was surprised to see a woman with a serious newspaper, he did not think women were interested in such things.

As David helped her retrieve the contents of her basket from the pavement he noticed her wedding ring, but so many women with rings were widows that he had no qualms about asking her to join him for a pot of tea, 'it's the least I can do after crashing into you like that.'

His concern for his mother's feelings were forgotten. It was important to him to get to know this young woman. As they talked he had found that she was interested in current events, and obviously not only carried a newspaper but read, and understood, the contents.

He wondered whether she was one of those modern women who considered themselves equal with men. He had thought that the recent Act of Parliament giving a vote to women was simply a reward for their work in the war, it implied, he felt, nothing more than that. Women had risen to the occasion of the war and had taken on many of the jobs

28

that had been men's but when the war ended, they would return to the kitchen as those men who could returned from war. Would they then give up the vote? He found himself asking this young woman what she thought and their discussion lasted as they drank two pots of tea in the Lyons Corner House. They did not talk about themselves, they said nothing about their personal circumstances, but they did arrange to meet the following week.

It was at that second meeting that Edie told David she wasn't a widow, her husband was serving in France and she had two young sons. But she also told David of her unhappiness, of how unsuited to each other she and Bert were, how he had changed since his business had failed and how resentful he had become at being recruited in the ranks.

Her marital status made no difference to David. He wasn't in a position to support a wife with his mother and sister to support, but he wasn't averse to developing a friendship.

Perhaps he should have been.

They met every Saturday afternoon. They would walk through the parks or, when the weather was inclement, they would visit museums and art galleries. David's afternoons with Edith were the highpoint of his week.

In early September they were walking in Kensington Gardens. The trees were turning to orange and gold and they talked about where they would be when new leaves appeared and the walks were once again green. They stood, hand in hand, looking at the grey and lacklustre memorial to Prince Albert wondering if it would ever be returned to the shining gilt that had been removed 'in case Fritz used it as a navigation aid for their aircraft'.

'Perhaps it was that reminder of our mortality and of the bombs which were falling more persistently over the capital,' David thought years later, 'or perhaps it was just meant to be'.

They had held hands on their third meeting and then, some months later, he had kissed her on the cheek as they parted. It was Edie who had first kissed him on the lips as though she meant it. After that they had always tried to find a quiet corner where they could kiss and cuddle. Many people were shocked to see young couples sitting close together on park benches but it was not an unusual sight in the city so much changed by the war.

As the months had passed and their need for each other had grown David had been careful not to get into a situation where what they both wanted to happen would be possible.

As they walked away from the Albert Memorial, and that September afternoon turned to dusk, Edie made no move to end their afternoon. She didn't mention missing her train, or her children waiting for her at her parents. She just, rather defiantly, walked with David.

"The park will be closing soon, the gates will be closed." David had ventured.

"Let them lock us in."

They both knew what she meant.

Their Saturday afternoons changed after that day.

David took the lease on a small flat near Kings Cross Station where they could spend their afternoons privately together. News from France was improving and they were both conscious that when the war ended Bert would return. They had so little time left to be together. Neither felt that there was anything wrong in what they were doing. They loved each other and they were simply doing what people in love did.

They had been philosophical when Edie told David in July 1918 that she was expecting.

"Bert will know it can't be his but he'll take it on. He'd know he'd have to. He can't do without me." It was hard for David to take. He couldn't ask Edie to leave Bert and the boys to live with him, divorce was out of the question and he had his mother and sister to consider.

"Will I ever see it?" He had asked trying not to let Edie know how sad he felt.

But no one ever saw the baby that died almost as soon as it was born in January 1919. Bert was back from France and he knew it wasn't his, his experience was not unique, others of his pals had returned from war to a larger family. He wasn't particularly interested in who the father had been as he re-established his rights over his wife, very soon showing her she wouldn't get a chance to stray again.

There were so many other things changing now the war was over. The freedoms that women had achieved were removed as soon as the men returned. Edie's job in the office of the West End store was given to a man who had no experience but since he had lost a leg on the Somme her employer felt he was owed the work. She returned to dependence on her husband, as so many other women had to.

David's work necessarily changed.

He began to concentrate on the next, inevitable, war.

Everyone in his section knew there would be another, sooner rather than later 'I'll give it 20 years' he had told his mother 'It's the small weak states that have been created by breaking up the Habsburg empire, that's where the trouble will brew.'

So David had set about becoming an expert on Austria.

Opportunities for Edith and David to be together were rare but when she knew she could get away from Bert she wrote a postcard detailing a time and they would return to the flat in Kings Cross. She would never know whether he could make the assignation or not but, when he did, their feelings for each other were only stronger. It was the first time they felt there was anything deceitful about their relationship.

In April 1920 Edie knew she was expecting again.

David had known he may never see Edie again when he visited the flat and found a letter, several months old, saying simply

My dear
You have a daughter. She is healthy and will survive.
Goodbye, God Bless, I will love her as I have loved you.
Perhaps one day...
E

Chapter Seven

"They'll be back soon." I tried to fill the silence that had followed David's monologue. I had been fascinated and moved by the story but it had obviously been difficult for David as he faced up to losing the woman I now understood so much better. "I'll put the kettle on."

David sounded very old and tired as he replied "No, Annie, don't leave me alone. Let me talk. If I talk I cannot think."

I wondered what we should talk about, perhaps something less personal, perhaps I could learn more about his work.

"You said you knew the Second World War was inevitable?"

David half shook his head as if bringing himself back to the present and eventually answering with his voice, once again, strong and confident.

"Before the First War we knew there was conflict coming and the powers in the land prepared for it even though we had no idea what the horrors were to be. Ten years later why didn't we acknowledge the same signals? Some of us did."

"Why didn't you stop it?"

"It is so easy for your generation, with the benefit of hindsight, to ask that."

"You saw it coming why didn't you do anything about it?"

"We did." David corrected himself. "Some of us did."

"Wasn't it in your minds every minute of the day, every day?"

"Some of us *did* see it coming, some of us *were* worn down with fear and dread, some of us *did* have it on our minds every minute of every day. But only a few of us did anything about it." He sounded very bitter. "You and your generation don't have to imagine the destruction of that war, you've seen the endless television programmes and films," David looked across at me, and smiled sadly "but at that time we had no idea what it would be like. No idea at all. We knew there would be a war but we imagined a war like the previous one, with men fighting away from home, few dying on home soil, the dead being listed in tight columns in the newspapers, carefully arranged by rank and surname, but life for the vast majority of the population passing more or less normally. We couldn't have imagined how different this war was going to be."

"We shouldn't judge people in history," I suggested tentatively, continuing when I realised I had David's attention "because we know what happens?"

"Thank you Annie, thank you for recognising that. We had a saying in our department *'Do not judge us too harshly for things we could not know.'*

"I've heard that." I recognised the phrase. I had a vague recollection of Ted using it and also my father and, since they were both lawyers, I had assumed it was some kind of legal phrase probably translated from Latin.

"Bear that in mind, Annie. Too many people don't."

"Did the fear of war hanging over you affect everything in your lives?"

"Certainly for some of my generation the answer would have to be 'yes'."

"Did you fear it?"

"Yes indeed I did. From the very end of the Great War there were some of us who recognised what was going to happen. We knew the German people would never accept the terms of the Treaty of Versailles. They had been dictated by short-sighted politicians seeking re-election and it seemed obvious they would lead directly to another war. The people seemed unaware, believing that those politicians would not lead us into another conflagration. It was our job to prepare as well as we could."

"Our job?" I interrupted.

"The government, the services."

"But you weren't in the government or the forces."

"No, strictly speaking I wasn't, but I was in a position to watch and influence. Any information that could have led to fear was suppressed. It was important that young men worked to achieve their ambitions despite the fact that we knew their careers would be truncated. We had to make sure they didn't know that their world had such a very short time left."

"So you let people live in a fools' paradise?"

"There was no alternative. What would have happened if woman had known there was to be a war in 20 years time?" David continued without giving me time to answer. "They would not have had children, they would not have had the next generation of cannon fodder. There were few enough men around to be fathers anyway and there were serious concerns in government that the birth rate would drop so low that there wouldn't be enough young men to allow us to fight the war when it came."

"That is awful." I couldn't believe a government could be so cynical.

"I'm afraid that was what we were required to do. They wouldn't re-arm, they wouldn't invest in developing modern techniques of war. In our department we did what we could, quietly and without fuss, but also without any support."

I was intrigued. I had never thought of the world my mother and grandparents had grown up in.

"What did you do?"

David was about to answer when we both heard voices and David leant forward, put his hand on my knee and spoke quickly. "Annie, you will learn many things in the next years. Some of the knowledge will not be comfortable, you must approach your work with no pre-conceptions. Just because we are your family does not make what we did right. What you learn, and what you do with that knowledge, I leave in your hands."

What David said just made me want to learn more but I had no chance to ask anything further.

Maureen had arrived home and, judging from the look in her eyes, she did not bring good news.

Chapter Eight

I had no chance to keep in touch with either Maureen or my grandparents during that first year working with Joy. I travelled to Austria and Germany several times and the work was very time consuming. When the year was up and I became a student again my life hardly changed.

I was determined to use the years that Max had given me well and so spent my time working for my degree and still undertaking specific tasks for Joy. David and Max could give me some help but I knew I had to know more about Europe in the 1930s to both ask the right questions and understand their answers.

I had little social life, soon finding that I had little in common with those students, only a few years younger than me, who were happy to waste their student years partying and drinking.

There was always so much to do that I never got around to visiting Maureen or my grandparents. I sent them postcards and wrote short letters but I hadn't visited them since beginning at Sussex. The phone call from Maureen just after the end of my first year examinations was short and to the point.

"You must come back. Your grandmother has taken a turn for the worse. Get here quickly."

I drove up the next day feeling guilty that I hadn't made the short journey many more times in the two years I had been away. I arrived at Maureen's cottage to be told I was too late.

"She knew it was coming, she was very brave."

"Long illness bravely borne." I quoted dryly.

I was more upset than I could explain. I hadn't known Edith very well at all but I had liked her, and having learned what I had through the previous years there had been very specific questions I knew she could have answered.

"Somehow you think people are a fixture don't you?" I asked Maureen as we sat in her unchanged kitchen drinking tea. "You think they'll always be able to tell you what you want to know, answer your questions and just *be* there. There was so much I could have asked her and I didn't, I always thought there'd be more time."

"David is bereft. I really don't know how he'll cope being on his own. They've loved each other for so long. We must keep an eye on him, you must visit him. We both will." Maureen was urgent in her concern for him.

"You knew them well." I had never really questioned Maureen about how she came to be a friend of my mother's parents and I hoped she'd tell me. I didn't believe that she had just met them by chance on the train on the way to their daughter's funeral. They had seemed to know each other a great deal better than that.

"I knew David better than Edie." Maureen rarely answered a question directly.

"Had you known him a long time?"

"I was surprised to see them on the train to Liverpool on the way to the funeral. I recognised him but I wasn't sure he knew me at first. It had been a long time, over 25 years."

I did a quick calculation. "So you must have known him during the war? Tell me about him."

It was some years before I realised what an opportunity I had lost by asking Maureen about David and not about herself.

She nodded briefly. "David is a wonderful man," she said firmly "but he had to do many difficult things in his work. So much he couldn't tell anyone, so many secrets…"

"Was he a spy?" I interrupted. David had talked of politics and intrigue.

"Such a silly word 'spy'." Maureen sounded weary "There are many different kinds of jobs that we hear so little of. For every James Bond there are ten, twenty, thirty people whose work involves nothing more exciting than commuting to sit at desks in gloomy rooms in narrow streets off Whitehall or in ornate rooms in grand houses tucked away in the country."

"You sound like you know a lot about it."

"It's where I worked too."

"I thought you did something academic."

"No you didn't, Annie, you thought I did nothing. That's if you ever thought of it at all. Those days around Alicia's funeral must have been incredibly difficult for them both. David and Max worked together for years but had never liked each other, and then of course Max had married David's sister …"

"What?" That really was a surprise and diverted me from the fact that, again, Maureen had not taken the opportunity to be honest with me. Perhaps I hadn't asked the right questions.

"It's not common knowledge of course. Elizabeth had been left a widow quite early in the war. Max married her. I'm not sure whether it was a marriage of convenience or a love match. There was a daughter."

"Veronica?"

"I think that was her name."

"She died of whooping cough."

I remembered, very vaguely, discussions about the whooping cough epidemic and of Veronica. We had all been infected at a party, I was far too young to remember but all of us had been ill, Carl and Charles and me.

"So we were cousins?"

"Well it's a bit convoluted, her mother was your grandfather's sister."

"So she was my mother's cousin? Did she know? But she was so much younger."

"Generations aren't always clear cut you know. David was still quite young when your mother was born and Elizabeth quite old when she had Veronica. And no, Alicia never knew of the relationship. She certainly never knew David, or that her mother's husband wasn't her natural father, though she always believed she had nothing whatsoever in common with her brothers."

"Unless Max told her, during their affair." I knew Max Fischer and my mother had had a relationship that had lasted several years. "I can't understand them being together, he was old enough to be her father."

"Not quite. There was probably no more than ten or fifteen years between them. I don't think either of them would have talked about anything that really mattered. I don't think they had that kind of relationship. But maybe they did." She seemed to have forgotten I was there as she added wistfully. "Perhaps it is impossible to truly know what goes on between two people."

That afternoon I made the first of many visits to David.

"I am so pleased you are here, Annie, darling. I have so much to tell you, to ask you to do for me. I don't need to keep secrets any longer, now Edith's gone." He spoke the words as if he had to in order to remind himself that he was alone. He seemed twenty years older than the last time I had seen him.

"You must stay and talk to me. There are so many things I haven't done, so many things I should have done but didn't because I couldn't upset Edie." He stopped talking, a tear running down his cheek. I couldn't bear his pain and could say nothing while he collected himself. "How are you getting on with your studies?"

He listened while I told him something of what I had been doing. "I must thank you David. Really. If it hadn't been for you I wouldn't have got involved in such a fascinating period. I would probably have done Napoleon or Edward III. But you put me on to a period where there are still people alive who can tell me things that aren't just to be found in books."

"It worked then."

I made two mugs of tea but I had hardly sat down before he spoke urgently, as if he had been wondering whether to say anything but, having decided to, had to blurt it out.

"There are things that must be done. There are things that must not die with me. You will do these things won't you?"

"I won't know until you tell me what 'these things' are will I?" I tried to sound cheerful.

"I've told you something of what my life has been, I'm sure Maureen has told you more, if she hasn't she will. You must write it all down and to tell everyone when it is time."

"When will I know it's time?"

I was surprised by his answer.

"Ted will tell you."

"How do you know Ted?"

Nothing at my mother's funeral had been as it seemed. I had assumed they were all strangers but David and Max had known each other, David had known Ted, and Maureen had known them all. Perhaps I hadn't looked closely enough.

"I have known Ted for many years and we met again at your mother's funeral. We have kept in touch. He is the single most responsible member of your extended family."

"But he's not family."

"Not in the strict sense of blood and parentage but has he ever let you down? Has he ever not been around when the right thing had to be done? Isn't that what 'family' means? I've always thought too much was made of blood ties. It is love that matters and Ted loves you dearly."

"Sometimes he's seemed the only friend I've had." As I spoke the words I realised the truth in them.

Ted had been there throughout my childhood, he had been there when I had desperately needed a friend in the final days of my marriage and in the days immediately following Joe's death. He had been there for my mother in her final months and had let me live with them and learn about her before it was too late.

"Ted is a lonely man. He was mesmerised by your mother many years ago and has spent his adult life looking after you and your brother in deference to that feeling. He is very fond of you all."

"I haven't been in touch with him for years."

"Don't worry. You will when you need to be."

On my visit the following day his sadness had become a belligerent defiance against convention.

"I won't go to Edie's funeral. I hate funerals. I've said goodbye and neither of us believed there was anything after life has left the body. What's the point? She lived, she made me happy, I hope I made her happy and now she's dead. Singing songs won't do any good."

"You went to my mother's." I pointed out perhaps with less tact than appropriate because he looked at me with something approaching irritation.

"I didn't go to Alicia's funeral to say goodbye to Alicia. I went to be with Edie. She wanted to go. She had to go. I was with Edie. That and ...." I wondered if what he had left unsaid was 'that and to see Max'.

"Talk to me David. Tell me more of those times. Tell me about Max." I would try anything to take his mind away from Edie. "Tell me more about your work, in the 1930s. You began to tell me two years ago but there were so many gaps."

"You know so much already."

"Never enough." I sat with him, holding his hand, trying to ease some of the pain of his loneliness.

"I told you my job through those years was to develop contacts." He began hesitantly. He hadn't but I didn't argue with him.

"Was Max one of them?" I remembered him saying he would answer direct questions if I asked them. Now seemed the time.

"Yes, he was. I knew of him, indeed I knew a lot about him but I didn't have to meet him until 1935."

"What were these contacts for?"

"They were people who would be able to go into unfriendly countries."

"This was before the war though?"

"I've told you we all knew the war was coming."

"Who were they?"

He began to relax a bit and his answers flowed more freely. "Anyone who we could trust we recruited to report what they saw as they travelled around Europe. Actors, businessmen, anyone who could legitimately be in Germany, Austria or Hungary at that time. We had a wonderful network of information but everything we did was secret."

"How did you know of Max?"

"He was a young lawyer, learning his business. He was ambitious but it wasn't long before he realised that a great many of his contemporaries were more successful without having to do the work."

"They came from the right families."

"Indeed. Max's family was lower middle class, his parents were shop keepers. He had none of the advantages of his contemporaries and he felt it keenly. Max needed to be accepted as a person as well as someone good at his job."

"Just like you."

"Not quite, but you're right neither of us would have been expected to do well. I think we always understood that about each other though we were practically different generations. When I was born Queen Victoria had nearly ten more years to reign. I was 44 and he was not yet 30 when I met Max."

"And in meeting Max everything changed?"

"For him, certainly, meeting me opened doors to an entirely new life. He had a chip on his shoulder, he was sure he was a better, possibly more intelligent, certainly more devious, lawyer than the people he wished were his friends. He spent drunken evenings in bars thinking that if he acted as they did he would be accepted, but at the time he didn't realise quite how much they despised him."

"Did they know he was Jewish?" I had always suspected this and it seemed a question worth asking.

"Max was not Jewish. His mother was probably of that faith, his grandparents certainly were. But it was not his religion that set him back in life, it was his class. And, Annie, before you argue with me, they are not necessarily the same."

"Some religions have always been…"

"Underdogs? Scapegoats?"

"I wasn't going to say that, I was going to say economically disadvantaged."

"What a peculiar way of putting it. If Max was 'disadvantaged' it was because his family were shopkeepers, not because his mother's parents were Jewish."

"But why was he a shopkeeper?"

"Because he was not a farmer." David's tone was final. He was not going to pursue that conversation. "Max acted as though he were the aristocrat he wanted to be but since he couldn't achieve a position of power and authority by right of birth, he had to do it through hard work and luck. Max's life and mine have been inextricably linked on many levels. In the beginning I was the one who dictated to him and at other times the roles were reversed and he was able to dictate to me, but for over 40 years we have not been free of each other."

"That's an odd way of putting it. Weren't you friends? Didn't you like each other?"

"No, I can honestly say neither of us has ever liked the other."

"Even though you were brothers-in-law?"

"What do you know about that?" He spoke sharply.

"Elizabeth... your sister... " I didn't answer properly, I had been shocked by the pain in his voice. Please tell me about her. I'd love to know more about her."

He thought for a while before answering.

"Elizabeth's story isn't just about her, it is about the influence she had on others. She had no life of her own. She was simply a pawn in a bigger game."

"A game?"

"A game between me and Max."

Chapter Nine

It was 1948, more than 27 years after he and Edie had last met that David unlocked his mail box in the dark lobby of the block of flats in Connaught Square where he had lived since his mother had been killed in an air-raid in the early days of the war he had worked for more than 20 years to help prevent.

Every evening he walked from his office to St James's where he would spend an hour having two drinks in the peaceful smoking room at his club. He was 57 years old and would be retiring soon, it was not a welcome prospect. He knew he would be leaving loose ends and he felt disappointed with himself. He remembered how, when he had been young and new to the service, he had resented and despised the time servers, now he had become one of them. Whatever purpose he had was now over, those skills he had were no longer needed. Unusually he had not been offered a knighthood in recognition of the grade he had achieved in the ministry. He recognised that would only be because too much was known of his failures, his mistakes and his questionable activities. His work was particularly difficult as the new post-war generation took over and he had had great difficulty pursuing his own objectives. He was involved, much against his better judgement, in helping one of his fishermen to bring a young woman in from France under the refugee evacuation programme. And he had lost contact with his second, final, surviving fisherman. Loose ends which would only cause problems.

After his hour at the club he would thread his way through the streets and squares of Mayfair to the company flat that he would have to leave when he retired. It was another reason for his depressed mood. He didn't like change. He had always resisted it and worried about it as it became increasingly imminent.

He put his hand into the dark wooden cubby hole and drew out a clutch of envelopes. He knew immediately who the letter in the blue envelope was from. Edie rarely wrote to him but when she did she always used the same Basildon Bond notepaper.

Climbing the stairs to his first floor flat he wondered what his life would have been if he had not had to go to work on that Saturday morning 30 years earlier. Would he have met someone, perhaps had children that he could openly care for? Would he have had a happier more fulfilled life? Would his work have been any different? But he knew he could never have felt for any woman as he felt for Edith and that he could never have been happy with anyone else.

He placed the envelopes on the small round table and carefully arranged them so that all overlapped by the exact amount and all angles were perfectly right. He placed the tumbler and the bottle of malt next to the envelopes, carefully edging them this way and that to form a perfect pattern. He then turned away to his small kitchen and opened the oven to see what Millie had left in the oven for his sustenance this evening.

Millie came in for an hour every day during the week to clean the flat and to leave him 'something hot' on a plate in the oven. It was never very appetising, but it was food and he was grateful for that. He knew men who ate every night at the club, but it was enough for David to endure the club's turgid cooking at the weekends. He lifted off the covering plate to display a meal evenly divided into three colours; one third brown stew, one third yellow potato and one third green cabbage. He put the plate on the small Formica topped table and ate his dinner with no pleasure. Placing the knife, fork and plate in the small sink he returned to the sitting room, altogether, he thought, a more civilised room.

Sitting down in his leather wing armchair, he carefully poured the malt into the tumbler, as he always did, thinking to ration himself to half a glass for the evening ahead.

He looked at the envelopes on the table. He was going to leave the blue one to the last.

It was some years since he had last had a letter from Edie. She had written early in the war to tell him that Alicia had been involved in a bad accident *'Her back is broken … she is desperately depressed but Bert will not let me visit her … the accident was his fault … I will never forgive him.'* A letter a year later told him of Alicia's marriage to Arnold and another, shortly after, to inform him that he was a grandfather. *'I don't like the name Charles,'* she had written *'it is a very pompous name and it will undoubtedly be shortened to Charley which is very ugly'*. There had been a long gap to the letter he had received the previous year announcing the birth of their second grandchild, Susannah. *'I'm pleased it's a girl then there will be no comparisons with her older sibling, she will have a chance to have a life of her own'* David had tried not to read her own pain in the words.

He had only received letters when there was something important to record. 'I dislike giving important news on the telephone,' she had said to him early in their friendship, 'there's no record to look back on, no piece of paper to take from a drawer and re-read to experience afresh the joy of hearing good news. Even bad news should be

43

recorded in this way, otherwise it is almost as if it didn't happen or it wasn't of any importance.'

David, my dear

Bert is dead.

He has not been well for some years. I don't think he ever recovered fully from the accident. We all rather overlooked what it must have done to him to damage the life of our daughter so. I think perhaps he was rather fond of her in his own way.

It was the cold weather that finally brought his suffering to an end. His mind has been wandering and he has been living so much in the past. Our neighbour found him sitting on the ground that had been his allotment. He was frozen to the marrow, he thought he was back in the trenches. I put him to bed but he never woke up.

Perhaps that's the way to go, David dear, in one's sleep.

We have been good friends, you and I, for many years, but you must not think that the news contained in this letter puts you under any obligation.

If you want to contact me I am here.

If you don't wish to I will understand.

David re-read the letter, trying to identify Edie's true feelings from the words she had written. Was she sad? Was she relieved? What did she want him to do?

He drank the whisky and, breaking his self-imposed rule, poured himself another.

He knew there was only one thing he could do.

He would go to her.

"Edith my dear," David sat in the comfortable kitchen of the house that was now their home, "come here will you, stop that washing up, I'll help you later."

Edie wiped her hands on the dish cloth and sat down opposite her husband of two weeks. For two people well into their middle-age and who didn't really know each other very well they had settled into married life together remarkably easily.

"What is it David? You look worried."

"No, not worried, nervous."

"Why?"

"I think perhaps I've married you under false pretences. You haven't asked any questions about my life. You haven't asked why I use a different name, what I have done for a living, what I *do* for a living. You have asked me nothing."

44

"I trust you."

"Aren't you curious?"

"You'll tell me what you want to, when you want to." Edie was calm and secure.

"I might be all sorts of things, a criminal even."

"I know you're not."

"Didn't you think it odd that you are Mrs McKennah not Mrs Redhead?"

"I knew there would be a good reason."

Edie sat patiently waiting for David to tell her what he had to.

"After the Great War my job changed. I still worked for the government but what they wanted me to do was wrong, they were planning for peace when they should have been planning for another war. I worked for a branch of the government, always remember that, what I was doing was not for myself, it was official, perhaps not something the governments of the time would want publicised but certainly necessary."

"It sounds very mysterious. Were you a spy?"

"Spy is such a silly word."

"Sorry." Edie was quick to sense she had done something wrong.

"No I didn't mean you were silly to use it, I mean the way people think of spying as somehow glamorous or clever, something that involves secretive meetings in dark alleys, a smoky black and white world where no one trusts anyone and killing is an every day activity. Spying isn't like that for the most part. Secret operations, covert operations, dirty tricks, doing things that need to be done but which are, perhaps, a little difficult to justify. If that is 'spying' then yes, I was a spy."

"Have you ever killed anyone David? Have you ever taken a gun or a knife and killed someone?"

"No, Edie, I have never done that. My work was far less adventurous."

"Have you ever told anyone to kill someone?"

"No, though that isn't to say that none of my team ever killed anyone, I'm sure they did, but we have just gone through a long and dirty period of war. We have been at war since 1914, never think that the 20s and 30s were 'peace'."

"You sound very bitter, do you want to tell me about it?"

"No, Edie, I don't want to tell you but I must. Things are happening that I cannot control and which may rebound on me, us, personally. I shouldn't have married you, I shouldn't have involved you."

"Please don't say that. I am your wife and have thought of myself

45

as that for many years." When David said nothing for several minutes Edie prompted him "I'm listening."

"In 1920 I was given a task. I had to liaise with a man in Vienna. Münz had employed a number of young people who he hoped would be useful, in time. He had great hopes of three of his recruits but it soon became obvious to him that it would be one of them, a man called Max, who would be the most useful. He was a chameleon, he could be an aristocrat amongst aristocrats, a labourer amongst labourers or an intellectual amongst intellectuals. He had proved himself to be brave, if not foolhardy. Münz thought he would be perfect for my team of fishermen."

"Fishermen?"

"The job they were to be groomed for was exciting and dangerous. We had a good network of informants but we needed more than information. The fishermen were to travel around middle Europe locating valuable artefacts and securing them from the inevitable ravages of a Nazi invasion. They were required to steal and appropriate beautiful and valuable objects so these could be returned to their rightful owners after the war. And if, after that war, they weren't able to return the goods to their rightful owners, they would be valuable additions to the inventories of museums and appropriate accessories to Ministerial offices. They had to employ improvisation and imagination only where it was required for that job. If they survived they survived, if you didn't there were plenty of others to take your place. Max drove around Europe in a car with several compartments that even the most stringent of searches could not find. The border guards and customs officers knew him and believed his cover; that he was a journalist. He was always polite and patient with them, his command of language and dialect allowed him to joke in a relaxed fashion when they, with copious apologies about how unnecessary it was, searched his car. Towards the end of 1938 I began to suspect Max was not being entirely accurate in the inventories of contraband. I had carefully logged the results of each of Max' trips and both the volume and the value were markedly reduced. But since he was one of a dwindling band and we had little alternative it was allowed. Max continued his trips backwards and forwards across the channel until the end of April 1940 when his final trip was only completed by travelling south to Spain and into Portugal. In the secret compartments of his Daimler were several rolled up canvasses, the deeds to many properties and several large bags of jewellery. He became a 'liaison officer', an all encompassing term that allowed him flexibility to wear different uniforms, be different nationalities, live different lives, as it suited us.

"Is this Max still alive?"

"He is."

David saw Edie looking round at the pictures on the wall.

"They aren't prints are they?"

"No."

"They're originals?"

"Yes."

"They must be worth *thousands*."

"They are."

"But they're not yours?"

"In a way. In a way there is no one with a better claim."

They sat quietly while Edie wondered what her husband really meant.

"By the end of the war there were only two of my fishermen surviving. Only Max and Vijay were left. I have told you more than I meant to of Max, the other Vijay, is a ..." He paused, trying to find the right word, "an enigma."

"You don't sound particularly fond of them."

"Fondness doesn't come into it. They were recruited to do a job. It was mine to keep them under control. It was inevitable that, doing what they did, they would keep some of the merchandise for their own use. It wasn't my job to stop them, that would have been impossible, but it was my responsibility to ensure that any personal gain they made was put to good use. I have to keep contact with them, their lives have moved on, the war is over, but I have to keep them true to the unwritten agreement. They can only do good with the illicit gains. They had done well, they had saved much that would have been destroyed, they have made post-war reconstruction possible for so many people. They were paid next to nothing for the risks they took, it was only fair that they had something. If it hadn't been agreed formally they would probably have taken even more than they did. I don't particularly like them but I must keep in contact with them, I must still control their actions as I have for 20 years or more."

"So a peaceful retirement is not on the agenda?"

They smiled at each other, each understanding what they were asking of the other.

"The fishermen met on the third Friday of every month at Rules Restaurant in Covent Garden. It was not a social event, the meetings were intended to operate checks and controls on the individuals, to keep them under some control."

"You talk in the past tense."

"Max for complicated reasons married my sister, you remember Elizabeth? She couldn't cope when she was left widowed whilst pregnant and I'm afraid I suggested a marriage of convenience. They moved to Liverpool."

David noticed the change in Edie immediately. She had as little belief in coincidence as David did.

"Liverpool?" she asked with heavy understanding in her voice.

He looked at her. It was a critical moment. If he lied or prevaricated she would know and their marriage would be damaged. He was not going to risk that.

"Yes. The firm that Arnold Donaldson worked for became available. I arranged for Max to buy it, he was well qualified to run such an organisation and there was a good man there, Edward Mottram, who would assist him."

"And you."

"Indeed, and me. I do not like Arnold Donaldson. I did not like his father, George, who I knew better. George was a Victorian man out of his time, he kept mistresses and had children he never recognised and who didn't recognise him. Arnold has inherited that trait from his father. I knew he would not make our daughter a good husband. He would only make her unhappy. I wanted someone over whom I had some control to be near to keep an eye out for her and report to me any problems she may have that I could assist with. From a distance you understand. I would never make myself known to her."

Edie began to realise the extent of the concern David had had for her over the years. He had never forgotten her. "Thank you." she said "Thank you for doing those things and thank you for telling me."

"We must have no secrets, my dear, there are too many secrets in the world."

"Secrets are only born out of unhappiness and fear. We have no need for them."

"George was a profiteer who made a great deal of money out of the war which he proceeded to give away in the hope that he would receive an honour in recognition. I made sure he didn't but if Max is faithful to his promise he shall have one."

"Is that in your gift?"

"I am in a position to block unsuitable appointments."

"Max is settling into his new life in Liverpool, becoming a pillar of the community and, apart from time he insists on spending in France working with the displaced persons camps, he is manageable. I cannot fault the way he has looked after Elizabeth."

"How lucky she is to have him."

"Max knows which side his bread is buttered. If he cooperates he has a comfortable life with a knighthood for 'services to the community'..."

"If he doesn't?"

"Unfortunately, my dear, there are ways and means of evening things out in the end."

"I don't understand."

"It is a harsh world, if he breaks his side of the bargain then we break ours, he would no longer be protected, events in his past would come into the open, he would be faced with exposure and prosecution. There would be powerful organisations who would be very glad to know where some of the merchandise they thought was theirs had found a home."

"That is a lot to hold over someone's head." Edie was trying to grasp the enormity of what David was saying. "You could have him eliminated?"

"You've been reading too many novels, my dear, we don't 'eliminate' we 'deal with'."

"But the result is the same?"

"Not always, but Max will know the likely consequences of breaking the bargain. He knows he is safe, at least while he is looking after Elizabeth."

They were quiet for a time. David wondered if he had broken too many of Edie's illusions and that perhaps he shouldn't have told her so much. But she had to know enough and it was best to tell her all at once. There was nothing worse, he thought, than a slow drip of information. There were too many opportunities for confusion. Tell Edie everything, then he could relax.

"You said you had two surviving fishermen. What of the other one?"

"Vijay? He had no scruples, nothing to hold him in check. He had a chip on his shoulder against the world..."

"And against you?"

"Undoubtedly. You see I made sure he left the country with far less than he imagined. He left at the time of partition in his country, he was originally from India, and when he left he thought he had trunks of silver and jewels, paintings and dollars. He didn't. I think perhaps, one day, he will turn up again and try to take what he will probably believe should be his. It is likely he will try to wreak some kind of revenge for being tricked."

"Are you in any danger?"

"So long as I have control of Max and Vijay is nowhere to be seen then you and I and our daughter and our daughter's children are all safe. But you see I have to keep looking for him. It is very important to me to find him, make sure he cannot harm anyone that is dear to me. It is the only thing I can do. I have tried to keep Alicia safe."

"Surely Vijay wouldn't hurt Alicia?"

"He would use her to hurt me."

"And me, now we're married?"

"Of course. I'm so sorry."

"Why are you sorry? I always knew loving you would not be the easiest way through life." She stood up from her chair and walked over to plant a kiss in the middle of her husband's forehead.

He put out his hand to hold hers, he squeezed it and looked into her loving face. "I am so incredibly lucky."

Edie walked over to the cabinet and poured some malt whisky into her husband's tumbler, and a thimbleful for her in a similar glass.

"Tell me more about Vijay?"

"I didn't recruit him, I wouldn't have recruited him because I did not trust him at the outset and I have never trusted him. It was the nature of the role that traditionally trustworthy people would have been unsuitable..."

"Hence Max."

"Exactly. But I knew where I stood with Max. I understood him. But I neither knew nor understood Vijay. I never believed the account Vijay had given of his life. I never understood how he managed to travel across Europe for his appearance was distinctive. With his dark skin and deep brown eyes, and black hair he could never melt into the background as a north European. He should always have been caught, he should never have been able to cross borders as he did. But he had always managed it. Sometimes he was Portuguese, sometimes Brazilian, sometimes Persian, He held various passports that would allow him to be anything other than the South African Indian lawyer he claimed to be."

"He was a lawyer too?"

"He was, that was the one thing I could believe about him. But his life, the account he gave was, to my mind, literally incredible. He claimed to have been born in Bombay of a comfortable merchant family. In 1896 his family had paid a not inconsiderable sum to send him, first class, to South Africa equipped with a complete western wardrobe and a considerable amount of gold. In Johannesburg he had always worn western suits, with a pristine white shirt with starched collar and dark tie. He was, to all appearances, a successful barrister. He claimed to have enjoyed his life in South Africa in the early 1900s despite increasing complaints about the petty restrictions he experienced because of his colour. With his money, good looks and impeccable English manners and speaking voice, no door should have been shut to him. He felt he should have mixed freely with all races and, although he married the daughter of a fellow Indian, he undoubtedly kept black mistresses. It was what was done by well-to-do middle class people at the time. He cultivated an ability to speak, act and write exactly as the ruling classes wanted. After the Great War the limitations on being an Indian in South Africa became more frustrating to him. After years of being the equal of whites increasingly incidents occurred that made him conscious, and almost ashamed, of his race. He was ejected from a first class carriage in a train despite being respectably dressed and in possession of the correct ticket, the cases he was given were increasingly insignificant. By 1929 he knew he had to leave South Africa and he sailed to London."

"It must have been very difficult for him."

"Difficult certainly, but I'm sure he never ran away from confrontation."

"What brought him into your group of fishermen?"

"He began by writing letters to the newspapers. They were clever and articulate. They came to the notice of my superiors."

"What was his name?"

"Vijay Thakersey. He was well educated, he lived comfortably and had an exceptional knowledge of, and interest in, western culture. He was a rare being and it was felt there had to be a use for such a person so he was recruited."

"You don't sound as if he would have been your choice."

"No. As a fisherman Vijay was undoubtedly a success, but he was a loose cannon."

Edie was interested in the different ways that David talked Vijay and Max. "You respected Max didn't you?"

"I suppose I did."

"But you were afraid of Vijay."

"Afraid? No I don't think 'afraid' is the right word. I mistrusted him, and that was everything to do with his character and nothing to do with his race. He was a nasty piece of work."

"In the middle of the summer last year, just as India was granted independence and the subcontinent was partitioned Vijay disappeared. He did not attend the meeting on 15th August. We searched his house, it was empty; his bank accounts were closed. We tracked him down when his ship docked at Aden. The contents of his trunks in the hold were replaced with worthless linen, his cabin was searched and anything of value removed. He would have had sufficient to give him a good life but it would have been nothing like the riches he was expecting. He was followed whilst on the boat and in Bombay, but then he disappeared. It was the time of Indian partition, the country was in complete chaos. We do not know what has become of him."

"And he knew everything."

"And everybody."

"Have you heard from his since?"

"No. I am, we are, vulnerable to Mr Thakersey. I have no idea where he is or what he has done. He is a loose end and I don't like loose ends. We haven't heard from him for months now, perhaps he just wanted a life of his own in India, perhaps he had returned during partition and had lost his life, along with the millions of others."

"Perhaps he's just biding his time."

They sat together in silence for some while. Eventually Edie broke interrupted her husband's thoughts. "I am very pleased I am Mrs David McKennah."

"I hope so. There is nothing to stop us being together now."

"Not even your fishermen."

"What do you know about my fishermen?" She knew he was testing her.

"Absolutely nothing, my dear, absolutely nothing. So tell me about Elizabeth and Max, your sister and her husband."

Chapter Ten

The bar of the White Hart was packed on the Sunday evening in the late summer of 1940. There were people drinking because they were happy to be alive and others trying to forget someone who wasn't.

Elizabeth sat quietly, unnoticed and alone at a corner table. She was staring into the half pint of beer that she had had in her hands for half an hour. She glanced at her watch and realised it wasn't yet 9 o'clock. He wasn't very late. She wanted so much to see him but she knew he wasn't coming. She knew he was dead.

She knew it as much as she knew she was pregnant with his child.

The large clock on the wall moved slowly. The next time she looked the minute hand had moved barely five times.

He would have been on time if he could. But he couldn't. She just knew it.

Any tiny hope she may have harboured was wiped out when she saw her brother standing in the door with a look on his face that told her everything. David walked over and sat opposite her without saying a word.

"It's Jim."

"I know."

"He's bought it."

"I know."

"How could you?"

"I knew the minute he was a minute late."

"There's worse."

"What could be worse?"

"Mum."

"What about Mum?"

"There was an air raid. Yesterday. Last night. Crystal Palace was hit. Mum. She's gone. It was a direct hit. She wouldn't have known anything."

"Other than the fear of the raid, the sound of the bomb." Elizabeth was too familiar with having lived through the sirens and the shrill sound of bombs falling to believe that her mother had felt no fear. She would have wished the bomb away from her before realising that meant she was wishing it on to someone else.

"She wouldn't have known anything." He repeated, trying to convince himself as well as his sister.

"Oh bugger." Elizabeth's words seemed inadequate. She had lost her mother and the father of her child in one minute. "Bugger bugger bugger." It didn't make her feel any better.

"I'll get you a drink. A large one."

She watched her brother, so much older than she was, with whom she had so little in common, as he waited to be served. She watched as he exchanged words with the bar-maid, and as he took the drinks from her. Somehow focussing on him stopped her thinking.

"Here. Drink."

Elizabeth drank the scotch in one.

"Another?"

"Yes. Please."

She looked at pilot's names chalked on the blackout screen by her table and wondered how many of them were already dead.

"David. What am I going to do?"

"You'll forget. In time. You will. Everyone does."

"You don't understand."

"I do. I try."

"You can't. You can't because I'm pregnant."

It was only a week since he had given her away to Jim in the quiet wedding in the small village church a few hundred yards from the base. He was not shocked, this was wartime and most of the couples he knew had anticipated their wedding night but he was not sure how best to help her.

"Are you pleased about that?"

"I would have been. If Jim... If Jim had been here, everything would have been wonderful."

"But he isn't. But that doesn't mean you're on your own."

They sat at the table in the window and talked about Jim. About the times they had all enjoyed. 'Remember the fun, don't think about anything else."

"How did it happen? I need to know how he died."

"His crate had been shot up but it was still flying, he was making it home, he was nearly home, he should have made it."

She wanted him to say that he crashed avoiding a school or houses, that he saved lives by losing his but she knew it would be more mundane than that.

"He just ran out of luck. He'd got over the cliffs, he'd nearly reached base but he'd lost too much fuel and too much height. He tried to land but he would have known it was hopeless, he went in hard. It would have been quick."

"Like Mum was quick."

"No." David knew he couldn't lie and he knew it would be kinder to tell the truth. "No. He would have known he wasn't going to make it."

"He would just have looked out of the cockpit at the world."

"He loved flying, he loved being in the air. He would just have looked at the ground, his last sights of the world..."

"Maybe he would have thought about me."

"He would have known they were his last moments. He would have seen the fields coming towards him."

"But when it happened it would have been quick."

"Instantaneous."

"There'll be a funeral won't there? His parents, his family. They won't know me. Should I go? I don't know what to do."

"Of course they'll want you there, they'll want all Jim's friends to be there. No one likes the church to be empty at a funeral. Even when..."

"...the coffin will be." Elizabeth finished the sentence for him.

"There will be one. It's easier with a box, even when there's nothing in it."

"Does that happen often?"

"More often than anyone would know."

"So Jim is part of a field in Kent. His atoms will be part of next year's crops. Someone will eat him."

"Is that so bad? To know that there is life after death."

"In a way."

"It's the only way."

"My turn to buy I think." And Elizabeth stood up and walked to the bar with their two empty glasses.

"Same again love?" the bar-maid said. "On the house."

Elizabeth took the glasses from her and nodded an acknowledgement before walking back to their table in the corner.

"Are you going to be in touch with his parents? Can you tell them I need to be there? Oh!"

Elizabeth had cried out, as if in surprise or pain.

"What is it?" David was full of concern."

"It's my camera, I still have the photographs from ... last week ... the wedding ... they're still in my camera."

There were pictures someone had taken at the church and pictures taken when they had gone back up to the base and told everyone that they had got married. There would be several of the small group of uniformed men laughing at the camera, throwing their caps in the air. There was David and his colleague Kipper, a strange, tall man who looked shy of the camera and surprised to be included with the group. And there was Jimbo who would always be young, who would always be remembered looking just as he did in that photograph.

"One week. We had one week."

And she burst into tears.

The next day David talked of things he had hoped he would never have to share as he drove Elizabeth up to London.

He admitted that when he had given her away at her wedding, he had been relieved that she was no longer his responsibility, responsibilities were not what he needed as he headed into the next phase of his war.

He had liked Jimbo and was pleased that his sister had finally found someone she could love. She was a lot older than most of the unmarried women around the base and the airmen had pretty much their pick. Elizabeth wasn't conventionally attractive, she didn't think anyone would want her so she didn't try. He was older than many of his fellow pilots, had had experience in the war in Spain and had seen first hand what it could do to people so he didn't join in with the gung-ho enthusiasm of his comrades. They were drawn to each other's quietness. He had invited her to one of the base dances and in a matter of a few weeks they both knew they had found the person they wanted to spend the rest of their lives with. However long or short a time that might be. She had never made love with anyone before and she hoped she would get pregnant, before it was too late for her. She knew for certain the week before Jimbo had proposed and she had answered 'we'd both like to marry you'. He had understood immediately.

It was on his unborn child that Elizabeth hoped Jimmy Morton's last thoughts were focussed and she imagined him wishing the child the best possible life with all of his heart as it burst the instant his plane hit the ground.

"Elizabeth," David spoke as the car climbed the steep hill away from the base, "There's some things we've got to sort out before we get to town. Do you feel up to it?"

Elizabeth didn't answer directly, she was staring, unseeing, out of the window. After a few moments she nodded her head and David turned the car off the road onto a rough track in the woods. Carefully turning the car to face the road and switching off the engine he stared ahead as he said "I want you to marry Max."

She jerked her head sideways, a look of disbelief on her face.

"You must listen to me. Kipper, Max I mean, would never make any... demands ... on you. He wouldn't be a husband in anything other than name. But as Elizabeth Fischer you would have security, a home for your child, someone to look after you if anything happened to me. He would never expect you to love him, I don't think he would want that, nor would you expect him to love you, but I'm sure a mutual friendship and regard would develop that would mean that life would not be too uncomfortable for you."

He was aware he sounded pompous.

"You wouldn't even have to live with him if you didn't want to. Not immediately, though the wedding should be as soon as it can be arranged. You can live at my flat. I won't be there very much in the next few months. When the baby is born, then you could take over Max's household."

She shrugged her shoulders in a gesture of unenthusiastic acceptance, saying nothing as her brother mapped out her life.

It made no difference to her, she no longer had a life with Jimmy so any life would be as good, or as bad, as any other.

"There's one more thing you should know."

David had agonised about how much he should tell his sister about his work. He knew that 'Careless talk costs lives' and he should 'Be like Dad, keep Mum' but he had decided she had a right to know as it was just the two of them left.

"What do you think I do?"

She didn't answer, so he repeated the question. Eventually she spoke.

"I suppose you do something at some ministry or other. You must be quite high up though, you've got the flat in London and the house in the country."

"Yes, you could say I am 'quite high up' but don't forget neither the flat nor the house belong to me. David Redhead has done very well for himself, his father would be proud of him."

"You say that as if 'David Redhead' were someone else."

"In a way he is. He is your brother who has had a staid and respectable life in the ministry, looking after his mother and sister as well as he could, as he should have done. But there is another David who has had a far more interesting life."

Elizabeth began to listen, she turned away from the window and looked at the distinguished looking man sitting next to her. She hadn't spent much time with him since he had left home at the end of the previous war. He sent them money regularly, they received cards on their birthdays, he had always spent Christmas with them, but he told them very little about his life. She had assumed there was very little to tell.

"There is another David, David McKennah is his name, whom you do not know. He performs tasks for the ministry that David Redhead could not undertake. He has a far more exciting life."

"Which David does your Max know?"

"He knows them both."

"Who is he?"

"He is someone who has served this country well over the past few years. You need not know the details, but he is an intelligent and resourceful man. He will look after you and your child well."

"He knows about the baby? You've agreed this all with him already?"

"Libby," David used the pet form of his sister's name that he hadn't used for many years. "These are not easy times. Many of us have to do things we could never have imagined only a few years ago."

"What will he gain from the arrangement?"

"It is not easy for him in England. He needs a family, he needs respectability, marriage to you would undoubtedly provide that. Certainly we discussed all the details but he was adamant he would not go ahead if you were against the idea."

"Do I really have any choice?"

"Of course you do."

"I get security, as you said, for me and my child." The words still did not come easily. "He gets a loveless marriage of convenience looking after someone else's child?"

"He gets a life story." David spoke plainly. "When you move to wherever it is you are going to move to, he won't be a mysterious alien presence. He will have a respectable English wife and a child. People will not suspect that he is anything other than what he says he is, a respectable lawyer who just happens to be a refugee from middle Europe."

"Are you going to tell me what you do? What he does?"

"Of course not."

"That answers my question."

"Elizabeth, there is one more think I must tell you. It is too important for you not to know. We have lost our mother in a raid, you have just lost your Jimmy. The only thing in life these days is uncertainty. I must tell you something, in case anything ever happens to me."

He turned in his seat and took hold of his sister's hands in his, his long tapered fingers wrapping round hers. "I have a daughter." It was his turn to turn his head, unable to meet his sister's gaze.

"She will be 20 next month. She lives with her mother and her mother's husband. Her name is Alicia, at least that's what we call her. I'm not part of her life but I will always be there if she or her mother should ever need me. I keep an eye on them from a distance but it's unlikely I'll ever meet her."

Elizabeth sat motionless. Her brother had kept this information to himself for over 20 years. Had he told their mother or had she died not knowing she had a grand-daughter? Of all the things she had learned about her brother in the previous half an hour that was the one that shocked her the most. That he led a double life, had two names, was probably a spy, knew other spies, was going to marry his sister to one to provide him with a cover story; that all paled into insignificance in the face of the revelation that he was a father.

"Which David is this?"

"At the moment Redhead, if ever I have a chance to be with her I shall start again as McKennah. You must believe me when I tell you, quite simply, Edith is the love of my life. We have never been able to be together for reasons I won't go into, but I can never love anyone else. If it was meant to be that we were never to be together so be it. But we produced, between us, this wonderful, beautiful, talented young woman. That makes it all worthwhile."

He turned back towards his sister and saw she was crying silently, tears rolled down her cheeks. She took her hands out of her brothers and put them on her stomach. "Thank you for telling me. Somehow it makes me feel less alone. Yes, I'll marry your Max. I can't have the life I wanted either, I know I'll never love anyone as I love Jimmy, but I'll do anything to make the best possible life for this little one."

David patted her stomach, an intimacy he would never had presumed two days ago. 'That's my girl.' He put the car into gear to drive back onto the road and towards London.

Elizabeth let her brother take control. He formally identified the body of their mother, and arranged the funeral in the quiet churchyard in which she had fed the birds for so many years as she sat by her husband's grave. Neither he nor Elizabeth believed they were 'reunited in death', though that was what they agreed to add to the headstone. There were few people at her funeral and most of those who were there had been at the one immediately preceding and stayed for the one following. There had been a long series of bad raids.

Jimmy's funeral was arranged by his parents, but they were gracious in allowing Elizabeth to be chief mourner at the service held in the parish church in the Shropshire market town. They had not met Elizabeth before and they never met their son's wife again. She didn't think it was sensible to tell them she was expecting their grandchild so she left very little mark on their lives.

Elizabeth's wedding to Jimbo had been a joyful ceremony. Two weeks before the girls in her outfit had found a white wedding dress that nearly fitted and there had been a lot of laughter and a blind optimism for the future. For her wedding to Max both she and the groom were in uniform and there were no flowers, no laughter and no photographs to record the event. She hadn't even met her bridesmaid before that morning, David having asked his secretary to perform any necessary tasks. Elizabeth was contained and dignified throughout the short ceremony, barely looking at her new husband though she very nearly broke down when she saw herself described as 'widow' on the Marriage Certificate.

The four participants in the subdued ceremony were silent as they were driven away from the Register Office down the Marylebone Road heading for Claridge's where David had arranged a small lunch. The traffic was always difficult the morning after a raid but their journey was even slower than they had anticipated.

"There must have been an accident." David said as he heard the bell of an ambulance close by.

"I'll see if we will be moving soon." They sat in awkward silence while their driver went to see what their prospects were.

"Is anybody badly hurt?" Elizabeth asked when he returned.

"I'm afraid so, a young woman appears to be quite badly injured."

"Is there anything we can do to help?" David's secretary asked.

"I shouldn't think so, there are people helping and it all seems under control." The driver wanted to be on his way.

"Best not to get involved." David spoke firmly and the awkward silence resumed while they waited for the road to clear. One woman's accident didn't amount to a great deal when hundreds were being killed in raids every night.

It was a week later that David got a phone call in his office and he began to regret his lack of concern the week before.

"Mr Redhead? David Redhead?"

"Yes."

"You don't know me, I am a friend of Edith Tyler. She has asked me to phone you."

"Edith? Has she been hurt?" Some time before David had given Edie the telephone number where she could reach him in an emergency. This was the first time it had been used.

"Edie is well." The nervous voice on the other end of the line reassured him. "She asked me to call you to say that Alicia has had the most awful accident. Can we meet?"

David followed Alicia's progress as she was transferred from one hospital to another. He was very discreet and no one was aware of his particular interest in the progress of a young actress who was struggling to walk again. It was weeks before he heard that she was improving but her recovery was being hampered by her not receiving any visitors. She had been transferred to a hospital in Buckinghamshire and none of her friends or family could visit. Again he called on his secretary to help.

"The daughter of a friend of mine is in hospital and is not getting any visitors. Your sister works out that way doesn't she? If she can't do anything perhaps she has a friend who could spend some time at the hospital?"

"I'm sure she can organise something." Maureen knew her sister Kathleen would visit once or twice to satisfy her curiosity about being asked but she could be relied upon to find somebody to take over once she had lost interest.

A week later Maureen was able to report some degree of success.

"Funnily enough one of Kathleen's colleagues knew your friend's daughter, she taught her. So she's happy to visit." How much Maureen guessed of his interest David could not know, even if she guessed the true level of his concern he knew he could rely on her discretion.

Just before Christmas 1940 Maureen reported that Alicia was being visited by a gentleman. "There's a Captain Arnold Donaldson who appears to be in regular attendance."

She did not tell David that she knew Arnold Donaldson and that he had been her sister's lover for several years but he discovered that soon enough for himself. He found out a great deal more about Arnold and his family background and he did not like what he discovered. Arnold Donaldson's father, a businessman who was doing very well out of the war, kept several mistresses himself, one of whom was Kathleen's mother and David had every reason to believe that Kathleen and Arnold were more closely related than either of them seemed to think. David was unhappy that Alicia was getting involved with this man. He could do nothing as reports came in of the time they spent together and, as 1941 progressed, their engagement was announced.

David felt that both of Alicia's fathers had brought her disaster. Bert had made no amends for causing her accident but, feeling responsible for introducing Alicia to this most unsuitable husband, David made plans to protect his daughter.

Elizabeth had not been well through the winter and had spent most of the last weeks of her pregnancy in bed. Both David and Max were away frequently and she was left alone apart from regular visits from Maureen. At first she had been happy to go out to shop, and would talk quietly to the other women in the queues. Those who she met learned that she was a widow, that her baby was due in March or April and that she was looked after by her brother. She never mentioned that she had a new husband. To her Jimmy was her husband and always would be. She still wore Jimmy's ring, having removed the one Max had put on her finger within hours of the wedding.

As the weeks had progressed she had convinced herself her baby would be a son. She would call him James and he would grow up in a peaceful world. She would tell him from the earliest time possible that his real father was a brave and wonderful man who had died in the war to make his world better. She would tell him that his father had known that he existed and had loved him. James would always know that Max was not his father and would be suitably grateful to him, his legal guardian, but would never love him as he would love the memory of his true father.

Elizabeth knew what to expect when the time came. She had read the booklets and she knew that she would spend several hours with short sharp pains lasting only a few seconds with perhaps 20 or 30 minutes in between. Then the pains would be stronger, last longer and become more frequent until they were almost continuous. But that was a good sign as it meant the pain would soon be over and Jimmy's son would be born.

To have Jimmy's son would be worth the hours of pain.

Max was concerned that she seemed tired when he paid her his regular Sunday afternoon visit.

"I didn't sleep too well last night. It is very uncomfortable you know." She had tried not to sound annoyed at his concern. He had been very kind and had made no demands on her whatsoever. He was happy that she lived in David's service flat and that he could only visit her on her invitation.

"I will telephone you tomorrow to ensure all is well."

"Of course all is well." She had snapped at him, instantly regretting the tone in her voice but unable to do anything to change it. "What could possibly be wrong? I'm seven months pregnant, I haven't been able to go out for weeks because of the weather, I depend on Mrs Whatever-her-name-is to do my shopping, I have no independence, no life of my own. Everything is completely perfect."

"I will still call." He had said, making allowances for her sarcasm.

She was not sure whether the discomfort was indigestion or a touch of cramp, but then discomfort became pain. By dusk a day later she realised that the cramps were quite regular and she began to be afraid. It couldn't possibly be the baby.

She walked around the flat finding a notepad and pencil and began noting down the times when the pains occurred. They were still regular when it began to get light. For the second night in a row she hadn't slept and she was very tired.

She saw no point in calling the midwife. The pains weren't getting any closer together and they weren't too bad, she had plenty of time to recover in between them and she began to know when to expect them.

She thought she had better call the midwife when, by lunchtime, nothing had changed. She was exhausted. Apart from sips of water she had had nothing to eat or drink since Max had left two days before.

It was Maureen who insisted on calling the doctor as soon as she saw the state Elizabeth was in when she called that evening.

The doctor left after only a cursory examination. "False alarm my dear, often happens with the first. It is your first isn't it?" The pains will die away, you have a few more weeks to go."

"Will you stay with me? Elizabeth asked Maureen. "I don't want to be alone. He's wrong you know. This isn't a false alarm. I'm not an imbecile."

Maureen stayed with her through the afternoon which they spent watching the clock, filling up the notepad with times and symptoms as they watched the snow falling. The pains didn't get any worse, but neither did they go away.

"My baby's going to die isn't he?" Elizabeth had said with resignation. Maureen helped her get into bed and tried to reassure her. "I'm going to call the midwife. Perhaps she will be more sympathetic."

The midwife tried to sound more reassuring than she felt. "No deary, of course your baby won't die. It's just taking a little longer than normal. Only to be expected what with your age and it being your first."

"And only." Elizabeth said wearily.

Maureen let herself out, she had to tell David the danger his sister was in.

As it began to get dark Elizabeth dozed fitfully between the pains. "This isn't right is it? Nothing's happening.".

"I'm going to call Doctor." She said, and Elizabeth could hear from her tone of voice as she spoke into the phone that she realised she should have called him some time before, before the snow and the raid made his journey difficult.

Elizabeth was only vaguely aware of the doctor's presence and what was happening to her body as the night progressed. She was aware of some of the words about her 'husband' 'brother' and she wondered why they should be involved. But the doctor had given her injections and kept asking her to lie in different positions. She just did as he said.

Early on the Wednesday morning she was aware that the pains were more frequent and she began to feel changes in her body. The doctor and the midwife were telling her to push but she had no energy left. She barely remembered being led down the stairs into the ambulance, even less did she remember the journey in the ambulance and the hospital.

She just remembered the pain of waking up to be told that she had a daughter.

"It was alive and, though weak, would survive. So will I ." She told Max when he visited her the next day. "Have they let you see her?"

"Yes, they said I have a beautiful daughter."

"I will learn to love her won't I? I was so sure it was going to be a boy."

"You will, when you see her, you will love her." Max was surprisingly tender as he held the baby they called Veronica.

A little under six months later Max had answered the telephone warily, it usually meant he was to fly somewhere that night. But it wasn't the perfectly modulated voice of David's secretary naming a time and location, it was Elizabeth.

"I think you need to come over."

He tried to analyse the tone in her voice, he couldn't be sure whether it was tiredness or impatience. He didn't know his wife well enough.

"Is anything the matter? Veronica?"

"No. She's fine. Just come over now please."

His flat and David's, where Elizabeth was still living, were a little more than two streets apart so he had little time to wonder about the reason for the summons.

"David?" Max was surprised when it wasn't Elizabeth who answered the door.

"Come in Max. I think we need to talk."

"Elizabeth?"

"This very much concerns Elizabeth."

They sat down to drink tea in the gloom of a rainy day in late July. Veronica was asleep in her cot as Elizabeth poured the tea and sat down with her brother and her husband.

"We have the perfect move for you." David explained that a legal practice had been located which was run by two old gentlemen who found the world changing too quickly for them and who wanted to retire. The firm was being bought for Max as was a comfortable family home. David did not tell Max that a bright young clerk in the office, Ted Mottram, had been instructed to report regularly on the Fischer family.

"Liverpool?"

David explained the perfect situation of a legal firm in Liverpool, the nearby transit camp meaning Air Force comings and goings were common place, the safe environment on the Wirral, well away from the docks and the risk of bombs.

He waited until Elizabeth had left the room before explaining to Max his additional responsibilities.

"You will look after my sister and my niece as if you loved them both. You will do everything you can to make their lives comfortable and happy."

Max nodded his assent, it was, after all, what had been agreed.

"You will also look to the well-being of another lady. She is shortly to move to the area and you will report to me what happens in her life and you will do your best to protect her from harm."

"Is someone out to harm her?"

"They will be."

"Her name?"

"Alicia, soon to be Alicia Donaldson."

"And her relationship to you?"

"Of no concern of yours."

"That is no answer."

"It will have to do."

Veronica was eight months old when, in October 1941, the Fischer family moved into Millcourt, a large grey stone house overlooking a golf course a few miles outside Liverpool.

Elizabeth grew to love Veronica with a possessiveness she hadn't thought possible. As her child grew she saw James in her eyes and the colour of her hair, every milestone in her daughter's life she longed to share with Jimmy, but they had to be faced alone. She spent many hours playing with Veronica on the beach in the shelter of the rocks, she felt calmer there, less depressed and less anxious. The sudden noise of gulls didn't startle her as much as any sudden noise in the house did. She never could get used to the nanny, the maids and the other staff that Max thought were important to make their lives more comfortable. They seemed to spring out on her and so when she was in the house she was always jumpy, waiting to be startled. When she was on the beach telling her uncomprehending daughter stories about her father, she felt safer.

Early in 1945 they moved to Sandhey, where her bedroom looked out over the sea to the islands in the estuary and beyond to the hills of Wales. Elizabeth was interested in nothing but her daughter, rarely leaving the house, never seen in the town. She spent any time when she wasn't tending to Veronica's needs doing tapestry work. Max was rarely at home. He was abroad for many weeks at a time and even when in the country he would spend 18 hours a day at his office.

She never asked about his work, what he did or where he went when he was away. She knew enough from what David had told her not to ask questions. She was grateful to him for the life he had given her and Veronica. And for keeping his promise to leave her alone.

When Elizabeth talked about her daughter he would listen conscientiously and ask what he considered to be 'the right questions' but he never interfered, so she was surprised when, in September 1948, he asked if Veronica had been invited to Susannah Donaldson's birthday party.

"Funnily enough, yes she has. I wondered why she was invited. I know Arnold Donaldson works for you but I couldn't see why they had invited Veronica to the birthday party of a two-year-old."

"There is a son, Charles, who is only a little younger than Veronica and there will be other children of that age. I suppose Arnold wouldn't want me to feel slighted."

"But we have nothing to do with them socially. Why would we feel slighted?"

"He is a snob. He wants to have all the children of the better families to his child's birthday party. He believes it will further his business and political ambitions."

"You are cynical."

"I am correct."

"Do you want me to accept?"

Much would have been different if Max's answer to that question had been 'No'.

But Max said 'Yes' and Veronica went to Susannah Donaldson's birthday party where she caught the whooping cough that killed her.

After Veronica died Elizabeth spent weeks lost in depression staring out of the window watching the tide coming in and going out.

For five years she rarely left her bedroom.

The decision to move her to a nursing home early in 1954 was not taken lightly as she was only 48 years old.

It was four years later, three days after Charles Donaldson and Monika Heller had gone to live with Max at Sandhey, that she finally succeeded in killing herself.

"Max?"

David was not surprised to hear Max's voice on the intercom of his flat. He had been expecting him since he had received the letter from Maureen Sheldon saying that not only was Elizabeth dead but the Donaldson household had split and sixteen year old Charles had left home with his nanny Monika to live under Max's protection. Ever since he had had that letter he had been wondering how the balance of power between them would change.

"Come up."

As they settled in the leather wing back chairs Edith discreetly closed the door behind her leaving them alone. She had been aware of the change in her husband's mood over the previous few days but since he had said nothing to her she did not ask what the problem was. In the ten years they had been married she knew he would tell her if he felt she needed to know.

"She's dead. I'm sorry."

David was quiet for a few moments. He was not going to let Max know that Maureen had already told him the news.

"It had only been a matter of time."

"Ever since Veronica it has only been a matter of time."

"We would have lost her years before if it hadn't been for Veronica."

"She died the day Jimmy crashed."

"Would it have been better if she had?"

They left that question hanging in the air between them.

Max changed the atmosphere by speaking energetically, "It's on another matter I'm calling. There have been other developments. Charles."

"What about Charles?"

"Charles has left his home and run to me. And he brought Monika with him."

"You've given them both a home?"

"There is no alternative. I have no choice."

"You have never had a choice." David agreed. His tone changed to polite enquiry when he asked "How much? How much did you filter away?"

"Enough" Max answered in the same conversational tone.

"What precisely?"

Max didn't answer the question directly. "How much do you think keeping Elizabeth and Veronica cost? The firm isn't very profitable. How do you think I have been able to keep your sister and her child in the correct manner without ..."

"... your ill-gotten gains."

"All right. I kept some things for myself. Didn't you?"

"No."

"But I did. I have known what it is like to have nothing. I wasn't going to go back to that for anybody."

"I asked you 'how much' but I don't need an answer. I know something of it. I know some of the bank accounts and the names you have used, I know some of the dealers who have given you valuations on the more obscure of the paintings and jewellery you have kept. I know something of their value, something of the extent of your theft."

Max said nothing. He didn't know how much David really knew and how much he was guessing.

"We'll make a deal."

Max indicated his willingness to listen by a slight inclination of his head.

"I will not make this formal if you use your wealth well. You will give to charity, you will assist the weaker members of society, you will only spend that money to the benefit of others."

"Does 'others' include Alicia Donaldson?"

David nodded.

"And her children?"

David nodded slowly a second time.

"Why David? Why is it necessary to help them? What are they to you?"

"That, as I told you at the outset, is none of your business."

"That is still no answer."

"It will still have to do."

Max's voice changed, his accent subtly more noticeable. "Alicia has a lovely singing voice."

David hoped he did not know where Max was leading.

"She has told me she is a stranger in her family, she says her father and brothers are 'imbeciles'. You are her father."

David took out a cheque book from the drawer of his desk and quickly wrote the words and numbers.

"Take this, it is for Charles and Susannah."

"Your grandchildren."

David said nothing, he saw no point in lying.

"It's a lot of money."

"Invest it well for them."

"How do you manage to have so much money? There's only one way you could have that sort of money on your salary. You accuse me of keeping back what should have been handed over but you must have been taking your cut too." David made no move to answer but his anger was almost tangible as Max pressed home his point. "Is that all or have you kept even more back for yourself?"

"If you think for one moment I would steal any of the goods you brought back you misjudge me. This, and he pointed to the cheque, is legitimate. My family's house, my mother's savings, my savings. You know nothing of me if you think I would steal as you did."

"So you're blackmailing me because you know of my wartime sideline and I'm blackmailing you because I've guessed your dark family secret. It is not a basis for friendship is it?"

"We were never friends."

"There is no need to be."

"You must always do what you have to do to protect them, Max, all of them. I will be at the end of the telephone if they need help you cannot give. But we will not meet again."

And they didn't for 23 years.

Chapter Eleven

In June 1976 I graduated, my university career finally, successfully, completed.

I had a final drink with Joy before setting off to Cheshire for the long promised, and long dreaded, reunion with Max. Although I owed him so much I returned armed with so much knowledge above and beyond the formal learning of my degree.

On a whim I decided to call in on Maureen. It wasn't far out of the way and it was nearly a year since I had seen her. I needed to ask her why she had never told me she was David's secretary.

She opened the door to me with the familiar hug but as we sat in her garden drinking coffee I was aware that something was wrong.

"It's David he's in hospital."

"How long?"

"Do you mean how long has he been in hospital or how long has he got?" Maureen was characteristically forthright.

"Well both really."

"He was taken in yesterday. They don't think anything is imminent, there is so much they can do nowadays, so much more than when your mother was ill."

"Is it cancer then?"

"I'm afraid so. But, as I say, they can do so much these days. They won't operate but they will stabilise him. What he'll hate most is his loss of independence. He has a lovely room and the hospital is more like a hotel in some ways, there are lovely grounds and when he's a bit better he will enjoy that."

"But he's not going to get better is he?"

"No my dear."

"Can I ..."

"Of course you can stay here tonight. Go and visit him. Carry on up north tomorrow. I'll phone Ted and explain."

Now wasn't the time to tackle Maureen about the past.

David was propped up in bed and looked remarkably uncomfortable but pleased to see me.

I had never visited anyone in a private hospital before and was amazed at the room. Maureen was right, it could have been a good hotel. David had his own bathroom, television and telephone, there were several nice pictures on the wall. I looked around the room thinking it wasn't a bad place to die. There was a lovely view out of the window over the grounds of the hospital towards a lake with swans serenely causing slight ripples across the surface. I noticed the window was sufficiently low for the occupant of the bed to be able to see the view as well.

"Ah Annie, I hear you did well." He sounded tired but alert.

"Not badly."

"I'll have none of that. You did us all proud. Maureen told me. But did you learn the things you wanted to?"

"I'm getting there, David, I'm getting there. There are mysteries but the bits of the jigsaw are beginning to fit together."

"Not too clearly I hope. Not until I'm dead and that, I trust, will be some years in the future. And my girl, I forgive you for abandoning us these past two years."

I was saved from having to respond by the telephone ringing. He reached over and lifted the receiver.

It was a very strange phone call, David said little but the gaps between his answers were short.

"Yes."

"If it is necessary."

It didn't seem like a social call but David must surely have retired years ago.

"Very well."

"Leave it with me." Without a 'goodbye' he put his finger on the bridge of the phone cutting off the caller but obviously intending to make another call.

"Annie, can you leave me for a few moments, some tea? I believe there is a machine in the corridor."

By the time I had walked ten yards and poured two cups from the machine and returned he had finished that second call. It must have been as short and to the point as the first one.

We sat looking out of the window sipping at the boiling tea in silence for a few minutes before David broke the silence that had not been entirely comfortable.

"You were wondering about those phone calls? They tell me he has woken up. The Indian has woken up."

"The Indian?" I had no idea what he was talking about.

71

"You know I told you how Edith and I met?"

"Yes, that day she and Maureen went to the hospital."

"Well let me tell you the rest. Much of it you undoubtedly know already and there will be some gaps which you may have to fill but I think perhaps now you need to know."

"It is not possible to retire you know Annie. There are always things to be done, loose ends to be tied."

"The Indian is a loose end?"

David didn't answer so I asked him if he wanted a drink of water. Still there was no answer.

When he did speak again it was with deep sadness. "Oh Annie, my dear young Annie, he is a loose end. I have been waiting for this to happen. The Indian will be wanting revenge for what he thinks we stole from him. He will want to harm us, you, any of my family. He will feel we have cheated him, ruined him. Mistakes were made but we do not know, we cannot know…"

I sat with him a few more minutes all the time wondering how anyone could know of the connection between David and our family and, if they did know, whether David's fear that we were in danger was a realistic one.

"I believe Vijay has woken up, he has decided the time has come."

"Vijay?"

"He is undoubtedly behind the trouble your cousin Graham has caused in the family."

"What trouble?"

"Things have been happening while you have been away. You will have a lot to learn when you return. Ted Mottram will tell you what you need to know but in everything he tells you read the hands of Vijay. He will find people who have grudges against your family and he will use them."

We were interrupted by a knock on the door and the arrival of a nurse so I had to leave and try to remember all that David had told me.

On my visit the following day David seemed much weaker and he wanted to talk of other things

"Annie. I love seeing you every day but I am not going to die yet. My life hasn't been saved, lives can never be saved as we all will die, but my death is being postponed. Death is only ever postponed."

He gave me no chance to interrupt or disagree.

"You must go back up north to Max and to your friends. But remember what I have told you. There are people who wish our family harm. Promise that you will keep alert, watch out for events that go ill for your family and find out who is behind it. It will be Vijay.

"I promise I will be vigilant."

"And I promise I will not die till we meet again."

It was a promise he kept.

I did not keep mine.

Chapter Twelve

Charles said Carl and I taking my children and living together in Cambridge was a bad idea and his final words as we left Sandhey were hardly encouraging.

"When it doesn't work out you know the children will always have a welcome here."

"That sounds like you have such confidence in me." I couldn't stop the sarcasm that frequently came into my voice when I talked with my half brother.

"It shows that I have absolutely no confidence in you." His reply was just as I had expected.

Carl and I had waited years to be together. So many misunderstandings had kept us apart but Ted had cleared them all up and now, as the wonderful summer of 1976 came to an end, we were going to be together. All my plans of getting a job and finding out what happened to David's missing fisherman were forgotten. David's warnings that harm would come to his family seemed a million miles away from the realities of love in the sun-drenched summer.

The only important thing in my life was that Carl had asked me to live with him. He didn't seem to mind that he was taking on a complete family though 'family' was probably the wrong word. I hadn't lived with my children for years and it was Max who insisted that we take Josie, Al, Jack and Bill. I didn't realise that Carl had thought it all through no more than I had. We had not considered that I and four children aged between 12 and 7 might be far more than he either wanted, or was able, to cope with.

We had spent a little over a month getting to know each other after 13 years apart. I hadn't seen my children since Jack's fourth birthday in 1970. None of us knew each other. It was, as Charles anticipated, a disaster waiting to happen.

"We'll be fine." I answered Charles. There was no way I was going to suggest that I had any doubt whatsoever.

The car was unnaturally quiet as we drove to Cambridge. The children seemed to be on their best behaviour, there was no shouting and argument but neither was there any laughter or teasing. I sat next to Carl still excited by our closeness, determined to be confident. But I still played my superstition game. *If the third vehicle in the opposite direction is a lorry everything will be work out. If there's a red car before I count to 20 everything will be all right.* Whenever one of my tests failed I'd try again until it succeeded. I so wanted everything to work out. After all, we were risking everything on the feelings we had had for each other years before that had been rekindled in the few short weeks of the summer.

Had we loved each other all the years we had been apart? Of course we had. Did we love each other enough to make this work? Of course we did. Were we thinking of anyone else but ourselves? Of course we weren't.

There was no honeymoon period as the moment we arrived at Carl's house we were facing up to unpleasant realities. Carl had said his house was large, but what had seemed large for a man on his own was not so generously proportioned when shared with a woman and her four children.

The argument that began the moment we got into the house over who would have which bedroom was only ended, after what seemed hours of shouting and bickering, when Carl agreed to move all his books out of the box-room. That first day did not auger well.

I did my best to pack all the things we had brought with us away unobtrusively but when the van arrived the following week with all the children's clothes and toys, bicycles and books, along with all the other things that had been essential in their lives, I despaired of our fitting into the house, let alone keeping it tidy.

"Whose are those bloody things?" Carl yelled on the first evening when he tripped over the pile of boots and shoes I had been trying to tidy away in the cupboard under the stairs.

It seemed that every day Carl would find fault with something as I tried to sort out the house. There *were* boxes and piles of books and toys on the floor and it probably *was* difficult for him to find things but I didn't think he tried very hard to understand.

It was soon obvious that he didn't want to change anything about his life. He was busy with his work at the university and he was planning a series of television programmes about The Duke of Wellington to be made in Spain. He seemed happy that he had someone to come home to, someone to talk over the events of his day with and to make love to but he was not happy about practically everything else. The music the children played was too loud; their games too raucous, their choices of television programmes were not his.

I had dreamed for years of being with Carl, being able to see him every day. I had imagined intimate conversations, eating in dimly lit restaurants while we discussed our work, for I had always hoped to work with him on his radio and television projects. Instead of interesting things to talk about at the end of the day my conversations were largely made up of complaints about my life being an unending cycle of housework and incessant arguments with the children about homework or tidiness or noise. As the weeks passed I found it difficult even to suggest to him that I had ambitions of my own which could be as important to me as his career was to him.

Perhaps I had expected too much.

In the early days Carl and I talked about the problems. We discussed getting a larger house, one that was 'ours' rather than 'his', where he could have his books out on shelves instead of having been hastily piled on the floor in our bedroom. We talked about how it would all be better if the children were happier at their schools, if they tried harder to get on with us and with each other, if we all had more space, we wouldn't feel quite so like rats caught in a trap. 'Is that how you feel?' I had asked him. 'Don't you?' he had answered rhetorically. When I mentioned getting a job he argued that it would be best to spend my time finding somewhere better to live. 'When we're settled you could look for something then.' It seemed to make sense but I hadn't missed the point that he was not going to offer me a job on his team. I didn't know then that the project in Spain had fallen through and he had had several subsequent proposals rejected. People who had bought into his ideas and sponsored his projects were not returning his calls.

The highlights of my days were when the postman brought me a letter from David or Maureen or Ted. I would read and re-read their gossip and the memories they gave me of a life that seemed so far away and so long ago. I would write short, non-committal notes about how busy we both were, how the children were doing well, how Carl and I were settling in to life together. I wondered if they realised everything I wrote was a lie.

By Christmas, about three months into our new life, we both knew what a mistake we had made but we were both too stubborn to admit failure. Perhaps Carl was right and moving house would help. It just took a lot longer than I hoped.

I didn't want to go to Hoylake for Charles and Holly's wedding the following Spring. I didn't want the upheaval of taking the children, though they had been specifically invited. I didn't want to watch Holly being unbearably smug as she married my brother, well aware that Carl hadn't once mentioned our getting married. I didn't want Ted to see through the lies of my letters. So I wrote saying we couldn't make it, we were desperately busy, it would be too difficult. He must have known they were just excuses.

Carl and the boys seemed happy enough with the decision, it was only Josie who said rather wistfully that she would like to have gone, she was fond of Uncle Charles and would have liked to have seen Uncle Ted again. I said, at 13, she was far too young to go on her own so she sulked at home.

It was December before we could move into the new house.

"I can't believe it took you a year." Carl said as he carried boxes to the hired van in between shouting at the boys to help a little more.

"It might have taken less if I'd had some help. You were all so picky." My resentment made me shout at everyone. The new house in the village of Hemingford Greys a few miles outside Cambridge, seemed to have everything we needed but Carl refused to buy it in both our names and that made me feel even more insecure. His argument, that I wasn't contributing anything, hardly seemed fair when it was he who had stopped me getting a job, he who had made sure all I had to do with my time was look after the house and the family.

"Christmas is definitely cancelled." I said as we sat around the table for our first meal in the new house. "I can't possibly do all the shopping and cards, and presents in less than a week. It's just all too much."

I hadn't thought life could possibly be so difficult and began to understand what being unsettled really meant. We lived out of boxes for weeks. I didn't know where to shop, we had no routine, every day was a trial, none of us knew where our clothes were, finding anything was impossible, arguments were incessant and became more and more bitter.

And Carl began to spend longer and longer away from home.

I knew I wasn't managing and that made me even more depressed. The children had each other, as they always had. Bill made friends easily at the small village school but Al and Jack kept to themselves and seemed always to be getting into fights. I was called to see the headmistress about their behaviour too often and she didn't accept my excuses that they had had a disrupted childhood and would be fine once they had settled down. Josie was doing well at the local comprehensive, always hard working and conscientious, she reminded me of myself at her age, concentrating on the school work to blot out everything else.

Carl had his work to worry about, even I could recognise that it wasn't going well. He spent less and less time at home, and when he spent my 32nd birthday away I realised he probably had another woman to help him ignore his problems.

It seemed I was the only one who had nothing to keep me sane.

I hadn't made any friends in the village, I didn't want to get involved with the WI or raising money for the church and I had rebuffed all overtures of friendship from neighbours. I had no excuse for being so lonely but that didn't make it any easier to cope with.

Receiving an invitation to Linda Forster's wedding to Ramesh Kambli didn't help at all. Ted's letters had told me how Linda had bought Charles out of the business they had started together and Linda and Ramesh had moved south, to Sevenoaks in Kent, and now they were getting married. There was no question of attending their wedding as it was to be held at his family home in Bombay but the invitation still caused arguments. Carl still made no mention of our getting married.

When Carl was away I left it to Josie to get herself and the boys to school. I had to wait until they had all gone before I could face the mess. When I did get out of bed I would lounge around the house in tracksuit bottoms and a tee-shirt, not knowing where to start to organise the house, the meals and the family. Once a week I would drive the ten miles to the supermarket where I would throw ready made meals, frozen chicken pies, frozen chips and baked beans into the trolley. I soon began to add plastic litre bottles of wine.

If it hadn't been for Josie we all would have starved. After an afternoon's drinking even putting frozen TV dinners in the oven was beyond me. I drank less when Carl was around but when he was away, which seemed to be most of the time, there was nothing to stop me.

It wasn't meant to be like this.

"I need help." I finally plucked up the courage to tell Carl on one of the few evenings he was at home.

"Help? For what?" Carl looked at me in a way that reminded me very much of his father, the man who for most of my life I had thought was my father too.

"The house. The children. Someone just to do some of the housework would make life so much easier."

"Easier? Easier? What could be easier than the life you've got?" The contempt in his voice could not have made his disappointment in me any clearer.

I tried to keep my voice calm. "There's always so much to do. I'm never on top of it. We'll never get straight without some help. It's so hard looking after the house and the children."

"What's hard?" Carl meaningfully looked down at his tray with the remnants of his TV dinner. Then he looked around at the room, cluttered and untidy. He stood up grabbing my arm and pulled me out of the living room and stood me in front of the hall mirror.

"Look at you! Look at yourself! Now tell me what it is that you're doing that takes so much time. You can't even wash your hair, or get dressed, or shop, or clean the house, or help your children with their homework. What is it that takes so much time that you need someone to help you?"

I knew I couldn't answer. I just started to cry. He didn't put his arms round me, he didn't say everything would be alright in the end, he didn't say he loved me. He just said 'you're pathetic' and walked out of the house. I knew he wouldn't be back that night. I sat on the bottom of the stairs and cried until I couldn't cry any more.

I hated being at home all day. I hated trying to run a house. I knew it was filthy and untidy and I hated Carl staying away, hating me. I hated looking after the children, I hated the children, I hated the work they created and I knew they all hated me.

Resenting the children came very easily but disliking Carl, after all those years of believing I loved him, was the oddest feeling. He was not the person I had dreamed of, not the person I thought he was. I didn't think of the possibility that perhaps I wasn't the person he had thought me to be either.

Carl and I had grown up together, living in the same house and spending every minute together for as long as I could remember. All our friends agreed with me that we were a couple, for life. We were until Sunday 19th May 1963 when, for reasons I have never understood, we were told we were brother and sister. Carl fled and I didn't see him again until that Sunday 25th July 1976 when Ted finally told me the truth. For all those 13 years, 2 months and 6 days I had believed that Carl and I would be together in the end. I believed it through everything that happened to me and everything I did. I fell pregnant and was 17 when I married Joe Parry. In the black days of that marriage, as I had children I didn't want and lived a life I hated, I always knew Carl would come to rescue me.

It may have been naïve and simplistic, but we *did* meet again. And he *did* ask me to live with him.

That bit worked out as it should.

79

It was just the 'lived happily ever after' bit that didn't.

After Carl's outburst nothing got easier but I did try harder to keep the house clean, to shop more sensibly and to drink less.

I couldn't make them realise how difficult it was for me. I'd never had to shop or cook in my life, I had had no idea how to gauge what would be needed. Some weeks I threw most of what I had bought away, at others we ran out of everything. When I was married to Joe we had a woman who came to do the cleaning, and Monika had helped every day with the children and it was she who had prepared something for the evenings when we were eating at home. How was I supposed to know how to shop and cook for six people, especially when four of them were uncooperative children who didn't like anything put in front of them. He wouldn't understand that I was honestly doing the best I could.

Through 1980 things just got worse.

Carl was away much of the time though where and with whom he never said and I dared not ask. Al and Jack resented everything as I suppose was only to be expected at their age. They had never settled in the small village school and things were even worse when they moved up to the local comprehensive. They were always in trouble, interested only in fighting and football, and none of the teachers seemed to make any effort with them. The teachers were even worried about Bill. They had no discipline and I had no experience to help me with three boys in their early teens.

I still had occasional letters and cards from the past. Maureen would write asking me to visit, wanting me to tell her more about what I was doing with my time, but mostly her letters were about the minutiae of life in the village. Ted would write occasional but long letters asking how we all were, reminding me of things that had happened in the past and asking about the children. He was concerned about Max who seemed to be losing his grip on reality, wanting only to see Monika who seemed happy to see Charles and Holly and shut out the rest of the world.

I would eventually reply to some of their letters saying that Carl was very busy and doing well, that I had an interesting part time job, that time flew by, that the children were growing up fast, that we were all happy but it would be impossible to get away to visit them.

Some of what I told them was true.

Chapter Thirteen

I wondered whether Carl would remember my 34th birthday, our fourth anniversary, and, if he did, whether he would arrange something special. But he did what he always did when he was around, he came in without any greeting, poured himself a beer and sat down at the kitchen table to read the evening paper. He never looked at me so he didn't mention that I appeared different. I had made a real effort having had my hair cut and styled and bought new clothes but, without looking up from the paper, he just asked 'What's for dinner?'

That he had forgotten the anniversary, or was just ignoring it, made me in an even worse mood than I had been all day.

"I don't know. I haven't made any. I thought you might take me out."

"Why would I do that?"

I poured myself a glass of wine, my first that day, and sat at the other end of the table. It all seemed unnaturally quiet.

"Where are the children?"

"Who knows? I don't. And I don't care. Perhaps they've escaped."

"What's up with you?"

"What do you think?" I wasn't going to make it easy for him. I had made a real effort to look good that evening and I hadn't had a drink all day.

"I have no idea." It was his tone of voice, so like that of Charles, that made me lose my temper.

"Bloody nothing to do with it being my birthday, our anniversary, that is if you can have an anniversary of living together. Bloody nothing to do with that."

He looked up from his paper, neither shocked nor angry, simply weary. I didn't give him a chance to say anything, I carried on, letting off steam, trying to make him realise how unhappy I was.

"I've got absolutely bloody nothing to do all day except see you all off into the world of school and work and then I clear up after you, I do the washing and the cleaning and then I start preparing to mess everything up again by making tea for the children and it's not what I want to do with my life!"

"Well you should have thought about that when you decided to get all maternal again."

"Why did you take us all on?" It was as if I watched the words coming out of my mouth in a bubble, I hadn't meant to bring everything out in the open. When he didn't answer I knew he was trying to find a way to say he regretted it. "You hate all this don't you?" I continued to push him. I know I should have backed off, let him get over whatever it was that had upset him during the day, let myself relax. But I didn't. I ploughed on. "I'm a disappointment aren't I? You wanted something different didn't you? Why did you bother with us at all?"

"Leave then." He spoke softly before adding in his most sarcastic voice "Oh but sorry, I'd forgotten, there are the children." I hated this argument. We had had it many times before. "You can't leave because you have nowhere to go."

"So I'm trapped."

"And I'm stuck with the lot of you."

"At least you get away to work and to your other women."

"Oh shut up."

I knew he would slam the front door behind him and I braced myself for the jarring shock of it.

Perhaps Charles had been right when he'd said I loved a Carl that didn't exist and Carl loved a Susie who probably never had either. I'd told him to bugger off but perhaps he had known us better than I thought. I knew next to nothing of what Carl had done in the years we had been apart. He had graduated brilliantly, advanced his career, built a nationwide reputation as a presenter of historical documentaries on television and the radio and published books about his favourite man, Napoleon. But what else had he done in those years? I knew absolutely nothing and I had never dared ask him.

There is a saying. *Be careful what you wish for lest it come true.* I have no idea where I first heard it but as I sat on that sofa, contemplating the disappointment that was my life, I realised the truth of it. Through all those years married to Joe, then after his death working so hard to make something of myself, I had believed that when I met Carl again everything would be perfect. Now what I had wished for had come true my life felt even worse because I had no dreams left.

I would have to stick it out as long as Carl could.

He was right, as long as the children were around there was nowhere I could go.

On Josie's 16th birthday, Halloween 1980, she came home early in the evening very drunk. As she climbed the stairs helped by a long haired but obviously male companion she announced that since it was now legal for her to have sex she was going to find out what all the fuss was about. She glared at me, daring me to stop her. Carl was away. If I made a fuss and tried to throw the boy out they'd only go somewhere else. It would only be bravado, they were both probably too drunk to do anything anyway. I said nothing. I went back to whatever soap opera was on the television. At least she was experimenting at home not on the sand dunes, in bus shelters and doorways as I had done at her age.

When I tackled her the next morning she spoke in a condescending tone I had never heard her use. 'No mother, we didn't 'do it'. I'm not quite as stupid as you were. Though getting pregnant wouldn't be such a bad idea if it meant I could leave this place. Don't worry. I wouldn't leave the boys.' She made it very clear that morning that she neither liked nor cared for me or Carl but, since we weren't competent, she felt herself to be responsible for looking after her younger brothers. 'I won't leave them until they're old enough to look out for themselves. If I didn't worry about them, make sure they go to school, make sure they get home at night, no one would.'

The six of us lived in the same house but to all intents and purposes we lived separate lives. God knows what the children got up to. Carl and I reached some kind of understanding that enabled us to live together but our lives, like our bodies, barely touched. I knew nothing of what he did, he no longer spoke about his work. He went away for weeks at a time, I didn't know where or why, I just knew he didn't want to tell me anything about what he was doing.

Carl had, like his father, probably never been able to live with only one woman but perhaps, also like his father, he needed the security of his home. He had numerous one night stands and one or more longer term girlfriends but he always came back to us in the end. We bickered and argued as many couples do, but we were just living together until the right moment came to live apart.

One Sunday morning in early January 1982 we were reading the papers, me sprawled on the living room floor, Carl sitting in his armchair, his legs crossed in exactly the same way I had remembered his father sitting, radiating pomposity. Josie was clearing up the breakfast things and the boys were taking advantage of the day without rain to play in the garden.

"Coffee?"

"Thanks." I answered meaninglessly without looking up from the paper.

It was as though neither of us ever had the courage to talk about anything important. As long as we spoke only about day to day things we were safe.

He brought in two coffee mugs and, giving one to me without a word, sat down to continue reading his Telegraph.

When we had first lived together we had discussed all the issues of the day, me always slightly more left wing than Carl. He had argued with me when I had spoken scathingly about President Ford's comments about Eastern Europe but he had listened, even a year later he had treated my views on Mugabe in Rhodesia with some respect, though he had completely disagreed. But after three years any comments I made about the troubles in Northern Ireland or Margaret Thatcher were treated with impatient derision. For some time we had read our papers in silence.

"Good God!" I couldn't help exclaiming a few minutes later.

"What?" Carl was not pleased that his silence had been interrupted.

"It's Max. Max Fischer!"

"There's only one Max. What about him?"

"There's an article about him."

"Well obviously. What's he done now?" Even with sarcasm Carl couldn't completely hide his interest.

"He's contributed loads of money to some charity or other, there's a picture of him presenting a cheque to the patron, some minor royal."

"He'll get his gong."

"That's a bit cynical isn't it?"

"Not for Max. He wants to be 'Sir Maximilian' so he's quite prepared to pay for it."

I read on for a while in silence, saying to myself 'that's not true' 'that's rubbish' at the points where the reporter had misreported Max's history. He was not an Austrian aristocrat disinherited by the Nazis. He was not a man who had worked his way back to prosperity only to spend his wealth on creating employment in the area. He was not a man who had devoted himself to good works after the tragic death of his wife and young daughter.

"This is all complete rubbish. Where do they get this stuff?" I must have spoken out loud as Carl answered me.

"They make it up. 'Fuck the facts get the story'."

"But really this is all so wrong!" I wondered what other people who knew Max would make of the story, if they were reading it. Ted would be amused. How would Maureen feel? And David?

I had had so little to do with these people for years. They had been my friends and I had all but completely shut them out of my life because I could not admit how great a mistake I had made. Perhaps this would be an opportunity to get in touch, to write to David and to Ted and have something to say other than lies about my own life. I drank my, now cold, coffee and gazed out of the window.

"Well I can trump your story of Max." Carl interrupted my thoughts.

"What?" I knew he wasn't going to give his story away as easily as I had given mine. "What is it?"

"Not 'what', 'who'."

"OK *Who* is it?"

"Graham."

"What's the little shit done now?" I didn't like my cousin Graham. I had only ever met him at my mother's funeral when he had shown himself to be crass and rude. But I remembered David had said he was involved with the Indian. I had forgotten how.

"He's dead."

"How did that happen?" I couldn't feel surprise since, from what I had heard about Graham, he was always close to the wrong side of the law.

"An overdose apparently."

"Why do you say 'apparently'?"

"Well they're quite mysterious about it."

"Read."

"Graham Tyler, 30, of Croydon, Surrey, died on Monday. He was jailed in 1977 for the murder of his ex-wife's father and mother Matthew and Mary Eccleston of Toronto, Canada. A registered heroin addict, Tyler appears to have taken an overdose and slashed his wrists with the pen-knife that was found by the body which was discovered at 6am. An enquiry is expected."

"I bet it finds nothing other than that he killed himself."

"There'll be trouble that he got hold of drugs."

"And a knife."

"At least Holly won't have to worry about him any more."

It hadn't occurred to me that Carl could be concerned about what worried Holly. It seemed a long time ago that I had wondered whether there might have been something between them. I had dismissed the possibility. Perhaps I shouldn't have done.

Perhaps I shouldn't have said anything more either.

"Why are you concerned about what worries Holly?"

He must have been surprised at my tone of voice because it was a few moments before he replied, and then, I thought, rather defensively. "She's a good friend."

"Are you fucking her?"

When he didn't answer I repeated the question. "You're sleeping with her aren't you? You fucked her that summer when she was dangling Charles around her little finger. Neither of you could resist the pathetic blonde tart. You and Charles, you're both so fucking stupid." I'm not sure why I was so angry.

"And you're a fucking stupid bitch."

I shouldn't have lost my temper. I knew Carl had had many one night stands and longer relationships since we had been living together, I'm not sure why knowing one was with Holly was particularly hurtful.

"She's conned you just as she conned Charles. All she's after is someone to look after her. As soon as her parents died she married Graham and then when a better bet came along she dumped him. So she's working on you in case it doesn't work out with Charles. She knows which side her bread's buttered."

"She's very well off in her own right." I should have recognised the warning signs in the coldness in his voice. It was the tone even the children respected when he had had enough of their bickering and wanted them to be quiet.

"So if she wasn't after Charles for his money what did she see in him? He's at least ten years older than she is and I bet he's shit in bed. But you're not are you Carl? You're fucking marvellous when you want to be. She's got fed up with Charles and turned to you."

"You are a stupid bitch."

"Don't call me that!" Where Carl's voice was calm and cold I heard mine rise almost hysterically.

"If you don't like being called a bitch don't act like one."

"Who makes me act like one? You! You're always so fucking sanctimonious."

The arguments Carl and I had followed a regular pattern.

Carl would argue 'Whatever you threaten you won't leave me because you've got nowhere to go.' I would reply that I could go wherever I wanted. He would counter 'Well go then, but remember to take your kids with you'. 'How can I do that?' I would say, 'I'm trapped'. Usually after a period of silence I would ask him if he wanted a beer and

I'd go to the fridge and bring two bottles of beer, giving him one I would sit down and we would be OK again, until the next time. I had thought the argument that would lead us to finally split would be over something important; money, the children, his one night stands or my inability to stop moaning about not having a career. I never imagined it would be over Holly.

The argument that day may have started with Holly but it soon spread to include every minor irritation from our time together and the one, over-riding reason I had for all my anger. "I hate you, I hate them. All those fucking children. I never wanted them! I don't want them now. I never did. Why would I want four fucking stupid ignorant brats before I was 21."

I realised Carl was not looking at me, he was looking at the door where Josie was standing watching us with all the superiority of her seventeen years. It seemed for a few moments that she was the adult and we the children.

"Bill's crying." Was all she said.

I got up to go to him.

"He doesn't want *you*."

"For fucks sake he's nearly 13, he's far too fucking old to cry. And if he doesn't want me what the shit are you telling me for?"

I shouldn't have sworn at her. If I could have taken it back I would have done but, once spoken, the words, and all the anger and resentment behind them, were irretrievable.

"I just thought you ought to know." Josie replied with a dignity that neither Carl nor I had shown. Before I could say anything she had turned and gone.

"Well, you stupid, fucking, bitch," He emphasised each word carefully, "that was fucking clever of you." Carl was going to be no help.

"It's all your bloody fault!"

"You're not blaming this one on me!"

"If you hadn't got me upset…"

"You started it…."

It's amazing how childish two adults can be.

After we had snapped at each other for a few minutes we went back to reading our papers, occasionally throwing pointless remarks at each other about being strangers to my children and strangers to each other, and not caring.

After about half an hour I realised there was no other noise in the house.

"I wonder what the kids are up to."

I heard 'little you bloody care' muttered under his breath as I left the room.

They weren't in the garden. I climbed the stairs almost hearing the silence. All the doors to their bedrooms were open but there was no sign of any of them.

"They're not here." I yelled but there was no answer.

I ran down the stairs, a reluctant tinge of worry pressing its way through my anger.

"They're not here." I repeated to Carl.

"I heard you the first time. They probably heard all the nice things you were saying about them…"

"And you…"

"… and decided to leave us alone for a bit. They'll have gone down the village. They'll be OK. Heavens, they're well able to look after themselves while they get over it."

"I'm going out to check anyway."

"Please yourself." I hated it when he said that. He always made it sound like I was being a fool and he was going to great lengths to humour me while I acted in a completely unreasonable fashion.

I noticed the small knot of people as soon as I turned out of the front garden, but it took a while to register that they were in the middle of the road, some standing, some turned away from the crouching figures. I was a lot closer when I realised that they were all surrounding a crumpled red heap that, as I drew nearer, I realised was my youngest son.

Josie was standing staring, an elderly woman's arms around her shoulders.

Jack and Al were being led towards me by a man I recognised as the new landlord of the pub.

The group seemed to stop what they were doing and turn towards me as one.

I felt nothing.

I walked towards them thinking how colourful they were. There was a lot of red and white, part of me realised this was the football team's colours. It was Sunday, the pub team must be playing at home. I walked straight past Jack and Al, registering only the look of fear and guilt on their faces. They must have been larking around. It wasn't my fault. I'd always told them to keep off the road.

A man in a beige overcoat hurried towards me.

"Mrs Witherby?"

I just nodded. Now wasn't the time to say that Carl had never bothered to marry me.

"We've called an ambulance. Edna here is a first-aider and she's doing what she can. The poor little boy just ran into the road."

I now noticed a blue car parked awkwardly against the pavement a few yards beyond the huddle of people, a young man in bright yellow was leaning against the bonnet apparently being sick.

"He's not in pain, Mrs Witherby, he's not conscious so he's not feeling any pain but don't worry, he's still alive, he's breathing. Don't think he's…"

I said nothing as I walked passed the man who I supposed was trying to be kind.

The small crowd parted to make way for me, I thought it rather stage managed and self-conscious.

Bill was lying on the ground, his legs at an unnatural angle, blood seeping through his jeans just above his knees. His eyes were closed, his arms spread eagled above his head. He looked asleep, but not comfortable.

I still felt nothing.

I heard the siren of the approaching ambulance as I walked back towards the house completely certain that I had to get away.

Josie would go to the hospital with Bill and would do a far better job than I would. If Bill died he would never know I wasn't there and if he lived whether I was with him or not would make no difference. I would be no help at all. They were best off without me.

I went through the open door, avoiding contact with Carl and the man in beige as they ran down the path. I walked up the stairs just as I had a few moments earlier, but this time I went into the bedroom and methodically opened drawers choosing which of my clothes I really wanted to take with me. I placed them carefully in a bag. I carried it into the bathroom and calmly took my things from the glass shelves.

I was in no hurry and I was being very deliberate.

I knew what Carl would do when he realised I had gone. He would call Charles and his precious Holly, if she was still with him, and they would look after the children. Ted or Charles would drive down to pick them up. Perhaps he would stay long enough to see how Bill was going to be. In a few days time they would be back in the north, probably where we should have left them all along.

We should never have uprooted them, never have thought we could move them and all be happy. We had taken them away from the cramped terraced cottage where they had lived since their father's death and given them a lovely home with a bedroom each. Instead of the paid nanny who had looked after them since they were young children we had given them two parents. Well it hadn't worked and now they would be going back where they belonged.

I had hated every minute when Carl and I had been separated before. Carl would have known that I'd be staying at Sandhey. I had waited day after day for him to call, but he hadn't. Day after day I waited until I finally accepted he wouldn't call and I'd have to make a life of my own. It wasn't my fault that my new life was a complete failure, a life in which I married Joe, had four children and a breakdown. But through all those years dreams of Carl had never gone away.

I had got what I had wished for and it hadn't worked.

Now, for a second time, I was on my way to a new life. Perhaps I should have been thinking of my children, of Josie, so adult for her years, of Al and Jack, so in need of love and security, but most of all of Bill injured, possibly paralysed, possibly dead.

But I didn't.

I thought of Carl, and of myself.

And I ran, for the second time in my life, to Maureen.

It was the only one place I could have gone.

Chapter Fourteen

It was obvious she knew why I was there and was both disappointed and intrigued to see me, Whatever her feelings she made me feel welcome.

"Your old room is still there, just as you left it, make yourself at home Annie." I loved being called Annie again, it was so much nicer than either Susie or Susannah. "I've missed you dear. You must tell me what you've been up to. You never said anything really in any of your letters and 'love Annie, Carl and the kids' on a Christmas card says nothing at all!"

"It didn't work out."

"Obviously not."

"We didn't really know each other."

"Obviously."

"Not well enough. We didn't really think it through, what we were doing to the kids, why we were moving in together."

"It's always a good idea to make sure your mistakes hurt as few people as possible."

"We did try. We kept going far longer than we might have done. Honestly Maureen, we did try."

"But you didn't succeed and you have run way from your children. Again."

I had left my children the first time as soon as I possibly could have done, the day Joe died. I had run away then, leaving them in the care of Max and Monika and Charles. Just as I had now.

"Well they're back where they want to be." Maureen changed her tone and spoke firmly "Charles and Holly will love having a family."

I didn't want to talk about Holly.

"It's highly likely they won't ever be able to have their own children." Maureen continued. "So sad, she would make a lovely mother."

I could only take it as direct criticism that I hadn't.

"So now she'll have mine she'll be happy?"

"That's very cruel Annie. You can't imagine what it must be like for someone who wants children with the man she loves and can't have them."

There was something in her voice that made me ask "You…?"

"Another time. Not now." I had obviously hit a nerve, Maureen was jumpy and quickly changed the subject. "Anyway, the children will be fine, your conscience can be clear."

I wasn't even going to try to make her understand.

"Carl called a few hours ago. Don't you want to know about Bill?"

"Not particularly. I can't do anything about it can I?"

"I'm going to tell you anyway. He's broken both his legs very badly, apparently the car ran over them. And he's got some very nasty internal injuries."

"But he'll survive and he'll be fine."

"He'll survive but he'll probably…"

"Oh don't say 'he'll probably never walk again' that's so melodramatic."

"But, Annie dear, I'm afraid in this instance true. Carl says they think they won't have to amputate his legs, but it's unlikely he'll ever have any strength in them."

"Surely it's far too soon to know." Perhaps there was the smallest feeling of sorrow for Bill but I quickly remembered to feel nothing.

"There may be a chance, a slim one but a chance, that he may walk with crutches. Whatever happens he'll be spending a long time in hospital. He's is facing a very bleak future."

"He'll be someone else's problem, someone who cares more than I do, who is able to care more than I do."

Maureen had tried her best to get me interested in the fate of my youngest child but she failed. To give her her due she accepted her failure with equanimity.

"You should keep in contact with people better. David has made excuses for you and your uninformative letters. He said you get so involved in your own life you forget there are other people who might be interested in what you're doing and who are doing things you might be interested in. He said it was something you had probably inherited from your grandfather. You will go to see him tomorrow, Annie. I will not allow any excuses."

David had been moved from the hospital to a hospice. He wanted nothing more than to go to sleep and no longer feel the pain, but every time he began to lose consciousness his head jerked back bringing him back to the reality of his agony. I watched this lovely man deteriorate day by day.

Sometimes he seemed quite lucid and reminded me he had kept his promise, he hadn't died before I had come to visit him again. I felt so guilty that I had done nothing in those six years to keep mine.

At times his mind would be wandering and he would ask why there was a cauliflower at the bottom of his bed and whether Edie had taken the eggs out of the airing cupboard. Whenever he spoke he would stare at his hands, trying to flex his fingers, but the misshapen joints barely moved. When he did doze his breathing was shallow, punctuated by involuntary shudders as he experienced a wave of greater pain.

"I'm so sorry. Water..."

I stood up quickly and crossed to the trolley by his chair, angling the straw into his mouth so he could suck up the water. It was not dignified for such a man to have to ask for water like this, sipping through a straw held in place by his grand-daughter because he simply was not able to pick up a glass and do it for himself.

He lifted up his elbow, the most movement he could manage, to indicate that he had had enough.

"I can't talk. Tomorrow, I'll tell you tomorrow. I want you to know. I did try... Wasted..."

He gestured for me to put the straw between his lips again and drank until he was sucking up air.

"I was always told off when I did that." I tried to joke but it was all too sad that this wonderful man had come to this.

I was rewarded with an attempt at a smile. As I stood away he tried to move his hand towards mine, he couldn't grasp it but could only brush across my arm. I took his hand carefully in mine, any touch seemed to give him pain.

"I should have made you ... realise how ... important... he will..."

"What?"

His blue eyes focussed on my face and he spoke with surprising anger. "We tried to ... get you to care... Ted ... your friends ... to get you to care ..."

The effort tired him and he sank back against the pillows and seemed to be going to sleep.

"I do care."

"Not enough." He whispered with difficulty as he let go of my hand. His fingers, for all the pain of his arthritis, had been gripping mine hard.

"I'll see you tomorrow." I bent to kiss him on the cheek. It felt like kissing paper.

The next morning, before I could leave for the hospice, there was a phone call. I was drinking a mug of coffee, leaning against the Aga when Maureen came in and put her arms around me.

"I am so sorry my dear, David has passed on."

I had always wondered why it seemed so difficult for people to say 'he's dead'. There were so many euphemisms that people seem to prefer. I stood awkwardly encompassed by Maureen's arms with the Monty Python sketch revolving in my mind. 'He is a late David, this David is no more, his metabolic processes are history, he's shuffled off this mortal coil, he is an ex-David.'

"He can't have." I said stupidly.

"I'm so sorry." Maureen repeated knowing there was nothing she could say that would help.

I sat down thinking of all the things David had told me, about his childhood, his work, his fears for his family, trying not to think that he was dead. How can so much experience, love, feeling, intelligence, disappear as if it had never existed?

"He was a lovely man, Annie, he had a long and interesting life and I know he was happy those years he had with your grandmother."

"I know. I was just remembering things about him, things he had told me about himself and thinking how sad so much is lost when someone dies without telling their family about themselves."

"As long as he is remembered he is alive. My God that sounds so clichéd!" Maureen put her mug down on the table slowly and deliberately, as if not knowing what to say next but knowing she had to say something. Or perhaps she knew what she had to say but just didn't know how to frame the words.

"He had wanted me to do so much and I had failed him." I was speaking to myself, not really expecting an answer. "He wanted me to find someone he thought would harm us, his family, and I have done nothing."

"What did he ask you to do?" Maureen asked sympathetically.

"He wanted me to find the 'loose cannon'."

"Loose cannon?"

"Years ago, when he was first ill, he told me about some man he thought might harm us."

"What did he say about him?"

There was something about Maureen's question that didn't ring true. She was too interested, it seemed too important for her to know what I knew. 'Not much really' seemed the safest answer and, as she pressed me for more information, I knew I was right to be suspicious.

"Did he say anything about the man?"

It was a long time since I had spent most of my time wondering about Max and David, and his words warning me about the Indian. During those years Maureen had often asked, in a friendly, almost detached, fashion, how I was progressing.

Perhaps she was more involved than I had known.

I wanted to ask her why she was so interested but the phone rang.

After she had put the phone down she looked at me and said, coldly, "That was Charles. Holly has left him. I hope you're proud of yourself."

"Why is that anything to do with me?"

She didn't answer, simply fixing me with a look that showed no friendship, only contempt.

Chapter Fifteen

"Oh shut up Charles." Holly was not in *the* best of moods.

"What have I done now?" Charles was not ready to put up with any of his wife's petulance without fighting back.

"You've done what you always do. You've taken the easy way out."

"What choice have I got? What did you want me to do?" Charles had spent most of the past five years trying to do the right thing but he had felt increasingly between a rock and a hard place. He had been drifting apart from Holly, he knew that, she spent weeks away from him without saying where she was though he knew she was with another man. He hoped he didn't know who that man was.

"Susannah has always had her own way, lived her own life, and left you to pick up the pieces."

There was some truth in what Holly said. Charles had taken some responsibility for his niece and nephews over the years, either because his sister was not well or because she chose not to have anything to do with the children she neither loved nor wanted. Josie had coped better than the boys. There had been a time when she could remember a family with a father and a mother, living together apparently happily. The boys had no such memories, their early years were spent with a nanny who could give them neither the love nor the discipline that energetic, enquiring young boys required.

"I've always thought it was my job...."

"You've loved it. You've loved visiting them and being part of their lives."

"Of course I have."

They sat in silence a few more minutes, the weight of their failure hanging over them.

"You don't need a child of your own do you? Not as long as you have them?" Holly began to speak the unspeakable, put into words the thoughts they both had but could never admit. "It's never been a problem to you has it? Not having children? You've never bothered because you've always had them."

Charles was about to say 'of course it matters, of course I care.' But he knew that there was some truth in what Holly said. Their childlessness mattered much less to him than it did to Holly. He always felt responsibility for Josie, Jack, Al and Bill and had always cared for them as if they were his own.

The one desire Holly had had when she had married Charles five years earlier was to have a baby. She had still been recovering from her disastrous marriage to Graham and a miscarriage but she had been young and the doctors all said it would be only a matter of a short wait before she was pregnant again. And there was no reason, the doctors had said, why any pregnancy should not be brought to a successful conclusion.

Holly didn't believe them.

She knew she had been pregnant at least five times since then. She had been late, she had been tender, she had known she was pregnant. And then a month later she would feel the familiar, nagging pain and know she was not. Any more.

She had gone to a doctor in Liverpool, and one in Oxford where she stayed with Linda's brothers Crispin and Oliver, several in Cambridge where she met up with Carl, and finally one in London. They all said the same thing. There was no reason why she should not conceive and carry till full term. She was the only one who knew they were all wrong.

Through 1977 and 1978 they had tried to have the baby she needed so much. Every month when she realised she had failed she had to get away, back to Crispin in Oxford or Carl in Cambridge. She began meeting Linda's husband in London. With Carl she could relax, he could not father children, he was safe and it was a relief to have the pleasure without the failure. With Crispin and Ramesh she would take her chances. At least she was away from the pressure of temperature charts, and optimal positions which dictated her relationship with Charles.

In that summer of 1976 she had been so relaxed and happy, getting to know Charles, learning to be herself and using her intelligence to earn a living. Charles had looked after her, had shown he loved her, had been supportive and caring. He had loved her and she had loved him in return.

But love was not enough.

For two glorious months in late spring 1980, when the sun shone and the weather was warm, she was pregnant. The doctor confirmed it, she got her National Health Service card saying she qualified for free treatment, and she had a card with her hospital appointments. She walked around Mothercare and bought orange maternity dungarees which she wore despite all her normal clothes still fitting her. She planned for her Christmas baby. She had been born on Christmas Day and she wondered whether this baby would be too.

In the evenings she and Charles would walk to the local pub and she would sip virtuously at an orange juice as he drank his two pints of lager and they would relax with each other. Everything was right with the world. They had overcome the violent death of her mother and father; they had risen above the disaster of her marriage to Graham, his assault on her and his subsequent imprisonment. They were pregnant and they were happy through the spring of 1981, knowing that everything, at last, was turning out right.

"He'll be a Christmas baby, I just feel it." Charles said one morning as they sat drinking their morning tea in bed. He leaned over and patted her stomach, still flat and trim as it had always been. He would have expected her to hold his hand and press it down on her tummy, including him in the changes that were happening to her body. He was surprised when she brushed his hand away without a word.

They listened to the early morning radio, trying to ignore the silence between them. The view from their bed, out through the picture window across the fields to the line of bushes that marked the top of the cliffs, with the river and the hills of Wales beyond, was magnificent and one of the reasons Charles had paid so much money for the house in Caldy.

But neither of them looked at the view that morning. Holly could not bring herself to say why she was so worried and Charles couldn't ask.

"More tea?" Charles broke the uncomfortable silence as the pips for eight o'clock sounded. Neither of them listened as the headlines were read about huge Conservative gains in the local elections. They should have been interested, Charles had worked hard for their local candidates having turned down the opportunity to be one himself. He had felt he couldn't though he had been reminded by many people that his father and his grandfather had both been active in politics. 'Maybe in a year or so' he had said 'the electorate likes man with a family.'.

"Not all fucking women are mothers!' Holly almost shouted at the radio before re-tuning the radio to a music station. "They're always saying women shouldn't work they should stay at home and look after their children. There are two sexes men and mothers. Women without children don't exist. They have no reason to exist. They shouldn't exist. They are a waste of space. They are useless."

Charles realised something was seriously wrong. Why would Holly be so bitter? She was about to be a mother. Wasn't she?

"Are you feeling sick? Can I get you anything?" He asked before he got back into bed beside her.

"No." she answered as if she were miles away. "No. I'm fine."

They sat sipping their mugs of tea, not listening to the radio, not looking out at the wonderful view, not facing up to what was worrying them both.

Eventually Charles spoke. He had rehearsed the words many times in a few minutes. He didn't know how to weight the words, what to say first. All he knew was that he was going to have to say something. Holly was not well.

"You're not all right are you?" he eventually heard himself saying.

Holly didn't answer.

"Holly. Please, darling, what's wrong? I know something is."

Holly put her mug down carefully on the bedside table without speaking.

As she turned to face him he realised for the first time that there were tear streaks down her cheeks.

She didn't speak, she simply pushed the bedclothes away from her and he saw that she was lying in a pool of red.

He went to put his arms around her but she shrugged him away. She just sat looking at him, tears running slowly down her cheeks, and he realised that things would never be the same again.

It was over an hour before she let him move her. He led her into the bathroom and gently took off her tee-shirt, handing her into the shower. She didn't say a word as she stood under the sharp spray turning her face to the fierce jets.

Charles tried not to think what she was feeling. He was grieving too, but he knew his pain couldn't be the same as Holly's.

He didn't want to leave her so he sat on the side of the bath and watched her through the shower screen. She didn't move, she just stood in the water jet, the pink water swirling around her feet.

It was at least ten minutes before she suddenly crumpled, her hands wrapped around her stomach, into a heap on the shower floor. Charles was with her in seconds, feeling the convulsions in her body. He didn't know whether they were pain or sorrow until he heard the whelp she gave as he touched her.

He should have called an ambulance earlier. Holly had been three months pregnant. She was miscarrying. She needed a doctor. He hadn't been thinking of her, only of his own loss.

"We've cleaned her out and there's no infection." The doctor told him showing no understanding or tact. "She'll be ready to try again in a few weeks. Just leave her alone for a month or two."

"But this isn't the first time…" Charles wanted to hear more than platitudes. "Is there an underlying problem of some kind?" If the Doctor wasn't going to be professional he was going to try.

"Oh I doubt it." The doctor replied, not looking at Charles, but seemingly paying attention to a speck of dirt on the sleeve of his white coat. "She's still young isn't she?" Charles was conscious, not for the first time, of the difference in age between himself and Holly, she was 29 and the ten years between them sometimes seemed like 20. He half expected the doctor to ask if she was his daughter.

"She's nearly 30." Charles didn't want to talk to this doctor. He wanted someone sympathetic who would listen to his explanation that Holly had been pregnant several times and had miscarried each time.

"Has she ever had a non spontaneous abortion?" The doctor was blunt. "If that hadn't been done properly it might affect her ability to carry."

A slight movement in the bed indicated Holly may not be asleep, as Charles had thought.

"I was raped." She said matter-of-factly.

"That could have done some damage." The doctor seemed more interested. "Was it violent?"

"What sort of bloody question is that?" Charles was suddenly angry. "What rape isn't? Of course it was violent."

The doctor seemed to think that perhaps he had overstepped the mark. "What I meant was..."

"I think we all know what you meant and I don't think now is the time to discuss it."

"Don't be so fucking pompous Charles. I want to know if I was damaged by what Graham did to me. He certainly wanted to. If he did then I want to know. Then I can stop getting my hopes up every month. I want to know so I can start getting over it. And now is as good a time as any? What do you need to know doctor?"

He seemed to back down when faced with the matter-of-fact tone of Holly's voice. "Perhaps your husband is right, perhaps another time."

"What's wrong with now? Why can't you tell me?" Holly's voice rose as panic and fear and disappointment mingled. "I need to know."

The doctor, a young man whose heart was probably in the right place decided it was time to move on. "I'll come to see you tomorrow, you need some sleep now."

Charles sat by Holly's bed in silence, trying to understand what it would mean to them if Holly couldn't have children. He would be disappointed, of course he would, he had been looking forward to being a father, he had pictured him taking his son to cricket matches, watching him do all the things he had wanted to do himself. Now there wouldn't be a baby. He knew that there would never be a child. And, looking at Holly's back as she ignored him, he knew she knew that too.

"I'm not being silly." Holly sat staring at her hands folded in her lap.

"Yes you are, you know you are." Charles had been very patient in the months since Holly had left hospital. They had had many tests and several consultations that Charles found excruciatingly embarrassing but the resultant diagnosis was that there was no problem and they should 'keep trying'.

"No I'm not. I can't help the way it hurts."

Charles tried to be gentler, more understanding though his patience was running thin. "Look Holly, we've got a lovely life together, this house, everything. We should look at the positives. We have a wonderful life together, it doesn't matter that we don't have children."

"It does."

"A child would change our lives so much, we can enjoy being together can't we? Just the two of us?"

"I thought you wanted a baby as much as I do?"

"Of course I do, you know I do."

"Well then!" Holly's tone implying that there was no more to be said.

"But that doesn't mean it's the end of everything if we don't." Charles persevered, determined that she should not withdraw into her bubble of pain. She did that so often now, refusing to enjoy anything in her life, completely absorbed in her need to conceive and keep a baby. He did not want the familiar argument to end in the same way it always did, with him feeling that he had failed.

As each month passed the regular cycle of hope and despair became part of their lives. They cried together, argued together and reassured each other, they asked each other for forgiveness for blaming where no blame was deserved, appropriate or required.

But Holly spent more time away from her home than in it. She would drive to Cambridge to be with Carl or, when he was away, to Oxford to see Crispin. She knew it wasn't fair going to Crispin because he loved her and had since she could remember. She knew he read more into her visits than she meant but he was kind and gentle and adored her, and she needed someone to love her uncritically.

It was when she lay in bed with Ramesh that she had some small qualms about hurting another person. Linda and Ramesh had been the third couple of the summer of 76. They had met and fallen in love at the same time as she and Charles had got together and Susannah and Carl had been reunited. She didn't really know Susannah so she couldn't feel guilty about sleeping with Carl. But Ramesh was married to Linda who had been her best friend since she had first come to England. Crispin and Carl became habits, but Ramesh was exciting.

That was a proper affair as she didn't always go to London to meet him, he spent time in the Wirral and came to her house when Charles was out. They made love in the same bed she slept in with Charles, in the same sheets, and sometimes within minutes. It was exciting because she knew that if she became pregnant by him it would be obvious that Charles would not be the father. And that didn't matter.

She didn't consider herself to be promiscuous. Meeting and sleeping with four such different men was her only way of coping with the growing knowledge that she would never, ever, have her own child.

In late August 1981 Charles came home from his afternoon walk to an empty house. It was too quiet and too still. No radio played as it always did whether they were home or not. Her car was in the drive but there was no sign of Holly. He walked through the rooms, closing curtains and switching on lights.

He found her in the bedroom.

"I was so sure this time." She cried. "I really thought it was OK this time. I was five days late. I thought it was really it this time."

"I love you." It was the only thing he could say.

"Well I don't know why. I can't give you what you want."

"*I* can't give it to *you*."

"It's just not fair."

"*No one said life should ever be fair.*" Charles remembered what his mother had told him many years before. It was the only time he had ever talked seriously with her. "Holly, my mother told me this and I believed her. No one ever said life should be fair. Don't expect it to be and you won't be so disappointed. Life isn't fair. Life has never been fair and life will never be fair. It's not what life is for. Life is supposed to be unfair. Life is unfair to see what you can cope with. Life will give you all the trials and tribulations you can stand. The worse it gets, the stronger you become and the stronger you become the more is heaped on you because you've shown you can cope."

"Do you really believe that?"

"Yes. Yes I do."

Holly tried to explain to Charles that every month she was losing part of her life. Every month, unstoppable, regular, immutable, unforgiving, irresistible, unchanging, she was being excluded from the fecund world.

"Everyone in the world is pregnant." She said as they walked around the supermarket. Charles, who was the only one listening replied, pedantically, "No. Everyone is not pregnant."

"Well all women seem to be."

He realised that she had not seen the funny side of her comment but he did not see that as the portent of real trouble. He could not catch her eye to smile and make things better. He could not reach her hand to squeeze it.

He followed her as she pushed the trolley, too fast, between the baby foods and the shelves filled with disposable nappies. When they reached the biscuits and the instant coffee she was talking nonsense about how many different sorts of biscuit there were, what sort of biscuit she should get and why one was more expensive than the others. He watched as she pushed the trolley defiantly along the aisle and picked up box after box of tampons. They walked through to the aisle lined with alcohol where a young woman with a toddler and obviously pregnant again was putting plastic bottles of red wine in her trolley."

"You shouldn't be drinking." Charles couldn't stop Holly grabbing the woman's arm and shouting at her. "You don't deserve children. Look at you! Grabbing more wine than you could drink in a month and you're pregnant. You don't deserve it! Why are you pregnant again when you don't deserve *one?* You're not looking after it properly! Look at the food you've bought it's all bad for them, for you, for it!" Charles couldn't stop Holly aiming a fist at the woman's stomach.

"Keep off me! You're mad! Leave me alone! Help!" the woman screamed and people came running.

"This woman! She attacked me! She's mad!"

"I'm not! Holly was screaming. She doesn't deserve to be pregnant! She shouldn't be pregnant it's not fair!"

Charles put his arm round her and pulled her away. "My wife's upset. I'm sorry. No harm done. She didn't actually touch this woman. No harm has been done. Can we go?"

The manager looked at the tearful woman and her husband and the outraged younger woman holding her young son to her. He made a swift judgement that he hoped was right. "OK you two. Leave now, I'll take the trolley you can shop elsewhere. I won't call the police just don't come back."

Charles put his arm round Holly's shoulders and steered her towards the checkout. He couldn't help but see her staring at the 'Parenting' and 'Family' magazines lined up in rows either side of the tills. He manoeuvred her past a woman arguing with her two toddlers who were screaming, bored with shopping.

He felt helpless in the face of such overwhelming odds.

"I'm going for a walk. I'll see you back home." Holly shook off his arm without waiting for his reply and headed along the street, walking quickly and obviously wanting to be alone. He watched her weave her way through the Saturday crowds worried but unable to do anything for her. He thought she was probably ashamed of what she had done and wanted to be alone. She would come home soon, perhaps she would have controlled her pain by then.

Holly walked past the prams, push chairs and baby buggies that were ranged outside the shops. It seemed to her that the pavement was completely blocked by vehicles designed to transport babies. The chemist was crowded, people were walking in and out of the shop, all the prams outside were empty.

The maternity clothes shop wasn't so crowded. She walked through the doors. Smug mothers-to-be filled the shop, smiling shop assistants seemed to enjoy helping their customers choose the clothes that would see them through their last months of being incomplete. The changing rooms were filled with blooming, happy women, radiant in the knowledge that they had succeeded where she had failed.

Holly grabbed several hangers from a display and found an empty changing room. She sat in one, pulling the yellow gingham curtain behind her. She sat in the room and rocked backwards and forwards on the bench. She was remembering a time when she had come to this shop and tried on the orange dungarees.

"Can I help you Madam?" an assistant broke into her thoughts.

"No. No. I don't want any of these. They're too small. Here. Take them." And she thrust the hangers towards the assistant and squeezed passed her out into the shop.

She was a very beautiful little girl, a halo of bright yellow hair, blue eyes, pink cheeks. She looked so happy, gurgling with pleasure as she watched the mobile playing in the air above her head.

She was so beautiful. So perfect.

Holly watched as she played. It seemed to Holly that there were only the two of them in the world. The little girl gradually lost interest in the mobile and, looking around her, began to cry. She had been abandoned, her mother was nowhere to be seen, she was alone. She was perfect and she was alone, and crying.

It was perfectly natural for Holly to reach down and pick the little girl from her pram. She had to give comfort. Holly cuddled the baby, amazed at the quiet gurgle of contentment that soon replaced the cries of fear. The baby settled in Holly's arms as she rocked her, gently 'shushing' her and whispering 'quiet now, everything will be OK'. The contented gurgles continued as Holly gazed down at the perfect face and found her finger enclosed by a perfect tiny fist.

"Is everything all right madam?" She slowly became aware of the assistant's gentle voice. "Do you want to come to the rest room? It's very busy here, your baby may be happier where it's quieter."

Holly didn't think before answering "No, we're fine, thank you. I'll just take her outside for some fresh air." Holly felt calm and in command as she walked though the open doors into the street, the baby held firmly in her arms.

It was easy.

It was wonderful.

Holly walked through the open doors of the shop and placed the baby in one of the empty prams that lined the pavement outside. She quickly tucked her up in the pale pink cellular blanket and pushed the pram down the street, amazed at the way people smiling, moved out of her way, allowing the pram to pass.

Everyone smiled at her as she smiled at everyone. She stopped by one pram and talked to the mother, nonsensical comments about the sex and age of their babies, about hair colour changing and whether to use the new disposable nappies or traditional terries.

She felt she belonged in the world that had rejected her. She had instantly become a member of one of the largest clubs in the world, the club that seemed to be open to everyone, young or old, rich or poor, that seemed so easy for most to join but had been impossible for her.

She walked confidently on, through the streets and into the park, smiling, content, complete.

An hour later she was sitting in a shelter on the promenade, the pram by her side, her hand lightly holding onto the handle. She was staring out watching the incoming tide. The baby was still quiet. Every few minutes Holly stood up and checked the blankets, tucking them closely in around the small body. The baby, Holly had begun calling her Mary after her mother, was so trusting. She picked her up and cuddled her but that made her begin to whimper and soon she was crying.

"Are you hungry my little one? I haven't got any food for you. I'm so sorry."

The cries became more urgent and Holly's feeling of contentment and happiness disintegrated as she realised she couldn't help Mary.

"I'm sorry my little one. Now now, everything will be OK, stop crying Mary please. Stop crying."

She pushed her little finger gently into the baby's mouth and felt the sharp tug of the sucking and the baby was quiet. She was at ease again, she and her baby were content. She began to fall asleep, rocking gently with Mary in her arms.

"Holly. Holly. Can you hear me? Holly."

Charles's arm was around her shoulders. As she raised her eyes to his the look he saw made his chest contract. For one uncontrolled second he thought that this was his wife, and here was his child. But he knew it wasn't so and he shook his head to remove the dangerous thoughts from his head.

"Holly, listen to me. Where did you get the baby? Whose baby is it?" He spoke clearly, trying to get through to her.

Slowly and unwillingly Holly focussed on his face.

"Isn't she beautiful. Her name is Mary."

"But where did she come from?"

"She was alone, she was crying, there wasn't anyone else."

Charles was beginning to realise the enormity of the situation. Holly had stolen someone's baby. There was undoubtedly a frantic woman somewhere in the town desperate for news.

"We've got to get her back to her mother."

Holly, reality dawning, looked at Charles and down at the baby in her arms. "No."

"Yes. Holly Yes. The baby is not yours."

Holly looked up at her husband, defeated. "It hurts so much."

"I know."

Charles took the baby and placed her gently in the pram. "Come on Holly, we must go to the police station."

As they walked along the promenade amongst the crowds on the warm autumn day she couldn't help thinking that they must look like a normal happy couple out for a walk with their new baby. But this time she didn't feel like smiling at any of the people who passed them by.

"Charles I will not keep baling you and your family out." Max Fischer was angry. "You must not put me in a position as awkward as this again."

"We can only say 'thank you' Max. Holly has had such a difficult time. I don't know what came over her."

"Murder I can sort out any day, Charles, as you well know. Theft of babies..."

"A baby."

"... and a pram."

"The woman who lost her pram seemed more upset than the one who had lost her baby."

"I noticed that." Max's voice softened for a moment.

"The woman whose baby Holly 'borrowed' for those few hours seemed to appreciate Holly's pain." Charles had been surprised at how understanding she had been. "At least she said that she did. She talked to Holly for a long time saying how she had tried so hard for a baby for so many years and she understood Holly's need."

"She didn't have to be so understanding." Max had been surprised as well, but had recognised something in the woman. Her name, Claire McNamara, linked her somehow to Kathleen McNamara, and through her to Arnold Donaldson. He didn't know the exact relationship but there had to be one and he knew that Mrs McNamara knew of her connection to Charles. He wondered if Charles had recognised that.

"The holiday we arranged for her and her family in America helped."

"And the police seemed to understand why she didn't want to press charges."

"They were very suspicious but seemed happy enough to be able to record it as a genuine error." Charles had been so relieved that she was going to let Holly come home with him that he hadn't really questioned why the mother had been so helpful.

"The woman with the pram was a little more difficult to pacify." Max felt he had to point that out.

"She seemed OK about it until she heard the name 'Donaldson'."

"Understandable since she was a Parry." Max spoke the name with disdain. "I wonder which one, there were so many."

Charles thought of the brothers and sisters of Joe Parry, his brother in law, the man who had got Susannah pregnant at the age of 16 with the sole aim of marrying into their family to take advantage of their wealth. He knew Glenda Parry, she was the barmaid at the local pub he spent a few comfortable hours in every week. He did not know the others so well. "She's married to a Jim Parry though I don't think they live together any more."

Max responded sharply "We need to know in case they try something in the future. I had to buy her off this time, perhaps she won't be so amenable when she's had time to think, or time to talk to her family who will, no doubt, see their opportunity for the main chance."

Charles realised he had nearly argued with Max and was apparently contrite. "I'm very grateful, Max. We both are."

"I should bloody well hope so."

As Charles drove the five miles home from the police station he realised he knew he could never understand the extent of Holly's pain, just as she would never understand the extent of his. He recognised that afternoon as the end of their marriage. They would stay together, he thought, because they had no alternative but they could never be happy together. There would always be this burden of guilt and loss between them. He felt unutterably sad.

He agreed with his wife.

Life wasn't fair.

When, four months later, Charles had the call from Ted he had known what he had to say. He knew he should ask Holly first but he also knew she would say 'no' and that wasn't the answer he could give.

Susannah's children were alone, she had left them, Bill was desperately ill after an accident. What could he do? He had to say 'yes, of course. I'll look after the children'. He would just have to talk Holly round.

"You can't possibly expect me to look after them." Charles had had an idea of how negative Holly would be when he first mentioned taking on the children but he was unprepared for the vehemence of her response. "I just don't believe how insensitive you are. You know how much I want children. You know I can't have them and so you foist Susannah's bastards on me. I will not do it."

"They aren't bastards, Holly, they are children. Nothing, none of this, is their fault."

She tried to explain to her husband things she thought he should have known. That it was so iniquitous that Susannah had these four children she neither wanted nor loved. That all the wrong people had children. That she was useless and worthless because she couldn't have any children. That every month, when she had to put up with the misery of her period, she resented every other woman in the world.

And now he wanted her to take on Susannah's children.

And he didn't see why she couldn't do it.

"We've got to pick them up tomorrow." He said as they sat in bed drinking their morning tea, the gulf between them immense. For the first years of their marriage they had cuddled together until the tea was cold, then they had intertwined their feet, his warm, hers always cold. Now they lay as if they were strangers.

"No."

"Look Holly, they have nowhere else to go."

Carl had called his half brother the afternoon of Bill's accident as soon as he realised Susannah had left them. Ted had told him to.

"I can't look after them. You and Holly have the space, the time...."

"Time!" Charles couldn't stop himself exclaiming. "You think we have the time? We don't live the life of leisure you obviously imagine." Charles tried to hold his temper in check.

"They're not my children either." Carl was on the defensive, a rare position in relation to Charles.

"But you've effectively been their step-father for what, nearly six years?"

Carl didn't want to admit how little he had had to do with the children since he had taken them and their mother to live with him. He wasn't going to admit how early in that new relationship he had realised he had made a mistake.

"It wouldn't work." Was all he could say in explanation. "I've got to be abroad so much these days."

"That's a feeble excuse Carl, and you know it."

How could Carl say how little he cared about Susannah's children and how much he wanted to be free of all the problems they created? "They need to be back in the north." He tried another approach. "Their friends are there and they know the area. They're lost down here."

"Even after all this time?"

"They never settled."

Charles had tried to read between the lines of what Carl was saying. He knew they would have grown up a lot since he last knew them. He supposed they must be a bit of a handful now they were in their teenage years.

"If we didn't take them what would you do?" Charles asked knowing that they both knew he would eventually say 'yes' but that he wasn't going to make it easy for Carl.

"I don't know, Charles, I really don't know."

"You don't seem very upset about Susannah leaving you."

"It wasn't a surprise." Was all he said, leaving Charles to draw his own conclusions.

"We all have to run away at times. I've done it, Susannah's done it, you're doing it now in your own sort of way."

"Will you take them?"

"We'll be down on Saturday. Can you cope till then?"

"I owe you, Charles."

"You certainly do. And don't think I won't call it in some day."

There was so much to do but first Charles had to persuade Holly to take in another woman's children.

"No." Holly was adamant.

"I've said we will."

"No."

"They have nowhere else to go."

"No. I will not do it."

"You have to. We have to."

"No we don't. Haven't we got enough problems? Not only can't we stand the sight of each other...."

"That's going a bit far isn't it?"

She ignored his interruption "... but my grandparents are ill. I'll have to go over to Canada any time now for goodness knows how long. You're utterly selfish and mad. You've always been stupid about those children, taking on far too much responsibility for them. You think you can be a father to them? You probably can. But I can't, won't, be their mother."

109

"I've said we'll have them."

"Then you won't have me. You look after them. You take them on. If they come here I'm going. If they come here you'll have to look after them yourself."

"OK then. I will."

Charles faced the evening and the next day without thinking too deeply about what he was doing. He watched as Holly packed two bags and he waited to use the phone while she spent time arranging plane tickets. He phoned Monika to ask for her help. He phoned Ted to discuss how best to tackle the problem of schools. He was desperate when he realised Holly was going to sleep that last night in the spare room.

When the Teasmaid went off at 6am he had already been awake for an hour, watching the day break and the world come to life. He had spent the time concentrating on practical things – what time they would have to leave, how long would it take to drive to Hemingford Greys, what route should he take, would the car be big enough for them all, how would the rest of their things be brought up, how would the children react to having their lives uprooted again, how could they get Bill into a hospital nearer home. There were so many practical problems to keep his mind occupied that his thoughts were kept away from the knowledge that this was the last morning of his marriage.

He poured the tea and took a mug in to Holly who was still asleep. He looked down at her remembering the first time he had seen her asleep in bed. She had been in Monika's bedroom and he had been stunned at the sight of her hair on the pillow, her hand up to her face. She had just left her first husband under traumatic circumstances and had been sedated. How that face had changed in such a short time. The long hair was gone, there were dark areas under her eyes and her forehead was wrinkled by a slight frown. He saw something of what their time together had cost her.

He had to take Susannah's children. He had to. But it had lost him Holly. 'Perhaps she would be better off without me,' he thought. 'perhaps she needs a break from me. Time on her own. Time to come to terms with things.'

"Tea?" As he spoke she woke up and for a fleeting moment she looked as if she had forgotten what the day was going to bring, but that moment soon passed and the tenseness returned to her face.

"Thanks." There was no gentleness in her voice as she took hold of the mug.

"We need to leave in about an hour." Charles tried to speak without bitterness. "Can I get you anything?"

"No. Thank you." She was remarkably formal, pulling the sheet up to her shoulders to hide what he had seen, touched, loved so often and so freely. In his awkwardness the only thing he could do was leave without saying anything and shut the door quietly behind him.

They drove to the airport in a silence broken only by occasional practical questions 'What will you do for dollars?' 'Do you have long to wait at Heathrow?' and short, unwilling, answers 'Amex.' 'About 3 hours.'

He dropped her off at the airport bustling with the early morning comings and going.

Did she remember the time she had spent sitting on that piece of pavement when she first arrived as a young teenager in Liverpool with her parents? She hadn't wanted to come to England. What would she have thought if she had known she would marry and make her life there and still be there so many years later? Did she think she was now leaving for good?

Charles wondered where it had all gone wrong as he drove along the concrete roads and headed south. "I'll phone." He had said as she had told him not to park, just to drop and go. "I'll phone tomorrow."

"Do what you like." She had said. "You usually do."

He didn't even know if she had bought a return ticket.

Chapter Sixteen

The night after David's funeral Maureen and I were in reflective mood. So much of the time since David had died had been spent sorting out the practicalities surrounding his death and we hadn't talked properly since that day.

I was surprised by the sharp tones of resentment as she spoke. "You shouldn't have disappeared out of his life so suddenly and for so long."

"I didn't realise time was so short."

"Well you should have done. He was very ill. You knew that. Yet you left us to live your own life. You always do that. There is so much of your mother in you. You didn't even properly answer any of our letters, you said nothing in them that mattered."

"I didn't think anything was changing."

"You didn't think."

Her voice was so full of criticism I had to justify myself. "You think I had any time? I had four teenage children and a man and a house to look after, to feed to clean up after, to shop for. I had no time to myself. No time to do anything I wanted to do. No time to do anything but clean and cook and do the day to day things. When could I sit down and do anything I wanted to do? Anything I would enjoy?" I must have sounded hysterical with so much self-justification and accumulated resentment.

"No time to write a decent letter? No time to pick up the phone and call your grandfather? You can always find time to do something if you thought it important enough. Stop feeling so ruddy sorry for yourself."

"I didn't even have time to do any of the things David asked me to do."

Maureen didn't answer, she waited for me to answer her unspoken question. I could have said 'he wants me to find out if a wartime colleague is still alive' or 'a loose cannon may be trying to ruin the lives of his family and David wants me to protect them from him' or 'Max and David have many secrets I want to find out because it's interesting'. Instead I gave Maureen a detailed answer. "David wanted me to find a man he knew during the war."

112

"Did he give you anything to help you?" I should have realised this was a peculiar question to have asked.

"Not much."

"How are you getting on?"

"I haven't really started. I was going to but ..." I really had no excuse. "... There was never any time."

"Just like there was never any time to write decent letters, or show any interest in your family or people who cared about you?"

"Well it's only been six years. Nothing much has changed has it?"

"You may think that. I'm still here, Ted's still in the Wirral, Monika still runs Max's household, superficially nothing has changed..."

"But?"

"If you look more deeply you will see things are not the same."

"How?"

"Six years has aged us all. Hopes we had had are not coming to fruition. It is becoming, year by year, too late for things to happen that should happen."

Maureen eventually broke the silence that descended after what had nearly been an argument. "Time for bed. We are both weary after a trying time. David is laid to rest and in our tiredness we must not say things we may later regret."

I was going to ask her why, in the years I had known her, she had never acknowledged that she had been David's secretary during the war, that she had been the witness at Max's wedding to Elizabeth, that it was because of her that my mother had met and married her sister's lover. But the atmosphere between us that evening did not allow it. Nor did it in the weeks that followed as, although we lived in the same house, we barely communicated. Perhaps, after those years with Carl, I had forgotten how.

It was difficult to find a job that would pay enough to allow me to give Maureen some rent but wouldn't be too time consuming, I needed to get back to David's tasks. I rather envied men whose manual labouring jobs required little mental effort but were well paid. The local papers were full of jobs that only required strength and a physical presence. Men seemed to earn so much 'painting and decorating', even the 'proper' jobs for men, building, driving delivery vans, security guards were well paid in comparison with the only unskilled job available to women in Surrey, cleaning. I wasn't really qualified to temp. My typing was abysmal and I

113

couldn't do shorthand. Charles and Linda had tried to show me what they did in their business years ago. All that typing onto screens and using strange keyboards with disks all looked completely incomprehensible.

I did do some work in a chemist shop, serving behind the counter. All I had to do all day was press buttons on a till and give the right change. I didn't even have to be nice to people as it was against the company's policy for staff to talk to customers. I stood it for a week. Every evening I was so exhausted from being on my feet all day I couldn't think of doing anything other than sitting in front of the television. And the pay was dreadful.

I worked as a barmaid in the local pub for a week. I got home so late that I was far too tired to do anything until lunchtime the next day and then there was no time to think about anything other than getting ready to be at work by 5. The worst thing about that job was being nice to all and sundry. I've never been much good at pretending to be interested in other people's lives. I couldn't care less whether someone's dog had trampled through someone's vegetable garden and I couldn't even pretend that I cared. At the end of the week the landlord was more than relieved to let me go. 'Not your kind of job I think.' He said as he handed me the pittance that was my wages for the week. 'I've had to deduct something for the breakages and your supper each night.' I didn't argue as I was too pleased not to have to go back for another shift.

"Something will turn up. It usually does." Maureen said as we discussed what would suit me, friendly relationships gradually being re-established. "I wish there was something I could suggest but everything I think of would be too time-consuming. I do understand dear, and don't worry about paying me any rent or anything. How are you getting on with your investigations?"

I didn't want to admit that I was hardly doing anything. It was difficult to know where to start and so the days I spent in the library or up in London were usually spent doing something completely unrelated. David must have been exaggerating the risk, nothing had happened to make me think that Vijay was causing the family grief. I thought his worries must have been the imaginations of a fevered brain.

On the Wednesday evening of my second week working on the till of the local supermarket I was sitting in Maureen's kitchen reading through some of the notes I had made of my conversations with David, trying to see if there was anything to work on, any place to start, any evidence that there was a need to, when the phone rang. I happily put the papers aside and drew myself back from the 1930s.

"Who?" I asked, probably sounding rather vague "Who is that?"

"Linda. Linda Kambli. I married Ramesh, remember? The accountant who loved cricket? Linda Forster as was. I know it's been a while Susannah, but not that long!"

I thought back to that summer six years before. I had been getting to know Carl but Linda had been equally obsessed with Ramesh Kambli. I tried to remember the name David had given me of 'the Indian'. I was sure it wasn't Kambli. I rifled through the notes on the table in front of me. I found them *'Thakersey'* I had written. *Vijay Thakersey.* But still Indian. Could it be possible that there was a relationship between Ramesh Kambli and Vijay Thakersey? It seemed unlikely. Ramesh had been good-looking, intelligent, relatively well off and not in the least threatening. That had been years before anyway, if he was related to David's 'loose end' he didn't seem to be too much of a threat.

"Linda." I tried to sound pleased to hear from her.

"I hope you don't mind my calling." She sounded very formal, very businesslike.

"Not at all." I could play that game too.

"Charles gave me your number. He said to say 'Hello' and tell you that the children are fine. Bill's making good progress though he's still in that hospital near Oswestry."

I didn't want to talk about my children, and most certainly not hear that Bill was still in hospital when it was more than a year since his accident. I was doing my best to forget that I had anything to do with them.

"Good.". It probably wasn't the right thing to say.

"You're not interested are you?"

"Does it sound heartless to say 'no, not particularly'?"

"A bit, but then I've never been in your situation so I can't judge can I?"

"You'd probably be the only one then."

"You sound bitter."

I didn't answer. I was trying to picture Ramesh the accountant. What had he been like? Had he been in any way threatening.

"Look, the reason I called was I was wondering if I could ask, beg actually, for your help."

"You must be really hard up then if you have to call me."

"Well I am actually and I don't mind admitting it, since we're being reasonably honest with each other, that you weren't my first choice. Or even my fourth."

"Running out of options?"

"Somewhat. Can we meet for lunch and I'll explain?"

"I'm working at the moment so that's a bit difficult."

"Oh. You're working? I thought you were looking for something."

Who would have told her that? Carl? Crispin? Maureen? Ted?

"You're talking about offering me work? Then I will. Anything's better than what I've been doing lately. But are you sure I'm the right person? I'm not very good at your machine thingies."

"That's not what I need. Can you make tomorrow?"

"Where? I'm near Leatherhead and you're …"

"Near Sevenoaks. Not that far really."

"We're still married." Linda began as we sat down with our drinks in the old fashioned bar in Godstone. "But only just. He moved out three years ago. He's back in India now. Despite everything he ever said before we were married what he really wanted was a traditional wife."

"Despite everything?"

"Well it was his suggestion we bought Charles and Holly out of the business and moved to Sevenoaks. Then it was really down to me, he worked for a large accountancy firm and was away a lot. So he more or less left me to work all the time and then complained when I did."

Even from my short acquaintance with Linda I knew no one could have thought she would ever have been a 'traditional' wife. He must have had another motive to get involved with her.

"I've got to go out to Bombay to see him. I haven't seen him since he left and I want to make sure he doesn't put a spanner in the works of our divorce. He won't come back here so I've got to go there."

"What about his family? I thought they were all over here. I remember meeting them at the cricket at Old Trafford."

"Some of them lived here but most were just visiting. They were trying to persuade him to marry one of his cousins. He often said that he now understood the value of arranged marriages as his parents couldn't have made a worse choice for him than he had made for himself."

I didn't usually listen to other people's problems with much sympathy but I did listen to Linda because she spoke with absolutely no self pity. It seemed obvious to me that whatever Ramesh had wanted from the marriage he had got quickly.

"It's good to hear that Carl and I weren't the only ones from that summer to have broken up."

"We all have." It took me a while to understand the implications of her reply.

116

"Charles? Charles and Holly? Maureen said something but I thought she was only trying to get at me."

"She left when your brood arrived apparently. She made the excuse that her grandparents in Canada were very ill and needed her, but really it was because Charles was pretty insensitive."

"Never." I couldn't resist the cheap jibe and was rewarded with a small laugh.

"You know Holly couldn't have children don't you? It was too much for her to take yours in when she hadn't come to terms with never being able to have her own."

"Pretty insensitive of him." I agreed. "I suppose Monika's helping him out."

"No. It seems Max has lost patience with your brother, he's asked to be bailed out once too often. He's having a bit of a hard time with your children I gather."

I was happy to hear about Linda's problems but I didn't want to hear about those that should, perhaps, have been mine.

"So we've all broken up."

"Me and Ram, well that's pretty much over, there doesn't seem to be much hope for you and Carl but I do think Holly will come back to Charles."

"I thought you and he…"

"No never, well once, but it as never serious. I'm not his type." She brushed my questions aside "Have you anyone else on the horizon?"

I was surprised at the question but was reminded that Linda was never backwards in coming forwards and would always say what she meant.

"No. I don't think I'm cut out to love anyone but Carl and that didn't work. I so wanted him to marry me and we would live happily ever after but he never asked me."

"And you didn't ask him?"

It hadn't occurred to me.

"Do you think he might be pretty insecure himself? Perhaps he wanted you to make the running, so he couldn't be rejected if he asked you."

"Perhaps. But I didn't so it's history isn't it? Anyway he was having an affair with someone else."

"That doesn't mean he didn't love you."

"How do you make that one out?"

"I think men are different."

"Never!" I used what I hoped was a light sarcastic, disbelieving tone of voice.

"Seriously, take it from one who has twin brothers. They can be completely obsessed with someone, in love with them for life, completely and utterly besotted for years and years and years but still have sex with someone else."

I must have looked interested, and I was because she had spoken with such utter conviction.

"Take my lovely big brother Crispin. He's been in love, and I mean *really* in love, with Holly since the moment he first set eyes on her. He watched as she was obviously infatuated with Carl, then as she went off to university and met Graham, God wasn't he gross! I hated him, everyone hated him yet she still married him. Crispin tried to persuade her not to marry him but still went to their wedding. It tortured him as he watched Holly get more and more unhappy. But he still didn't do anything to tell her how he felt, even when she left Graham and went to stay with Crispin and Oliver in Oxford. Then she went back up north and got involved with Charles. And he still watched. He said nothing, he said the time was never right, as she moved in with Charles and they began to make a life together and then married. They seemed happy. And then he had to watch as she grew unhappier and then she left. But all through this, more than ten years of being in love with Holly, Crispin has had girlfriends. I know he's got at least one he certainly has sex with. I haven't a clue who she is but he sees her often and on a regular basis. But that never stopped him from loving Holly. He still does. He always will."

"But we're not here to discuss the family are we?" I wanted to get the conversation back on track. "However mixed up we are we all muddle through. I thought you called me yesterday to beg my help not talk about family and tell me Carl still loves me even though he has sex with all and sundry."

We both knew that was not what Linda had said but the awkward moment passed as she shifted into business mode.

"Well, yes. I've got to go to India. I don't know how long I'll be there. We got married in Bombay so we've got to see how it's best to divorce there. I've got to persuade him to end the marriage and then we can both move on. While I'm away, it might be two or three weeks, I need someone in the office."

"But I can't use those machines."

"You won't have to. I've got good people but I need someone who I can trust to be in early, leave late and make sure everything is done."

"What would I have to do?"

"Just keep tabs on what's going on, do the wages at the end of the week, deliver work to clients, empty the bins, clean the loos, anything that's necessary to allow all the others to do the jobs they well know how to do."

"Just for a couple of weeks?"

"Well I shouldn't be away longer than that. But if you wanted to carry on doing stuff there's always something. Delivering work, stuffing envelopes. It's not brilliantly interesting but it pays well."

"It sounds better than supermarket checkout clerk."

"Do you want to think about it?"

"Well I would have to travel quite a way." I tried to think of the problems.

"We'd get you a car." That would solve the problem of having to borrow Maureen's.

"Really? That would be brilliant."

"And you'd get a decent hourly rate. I'd have to do it by the hour. Is that OK?"

We were getting down to details as if I had already said 'yes'.

"I'll cover for as many hours as you like when you're away on condition that, when you get back, I can work a few hours as and when."

"That'd work. Sometimes we need loads of people all the time but when we're quiet we wouldn't need you."

"So it would suit us both?"

"Sounds like it."

But nothing turned out quite the way we expected in the weeks that followed.

Chapter Seventeen

Ten days into my stint holding the fort at her office I had a phone call from Linda in India. "Sorry, it's a bit of a bad line but I thought I'd better let you know how it's going."

"What's all that noise?"

"I'll shut the window, it's absolute mayhem outside, millions and millions of black and yellow taxis all hooting their horns and going nowhere."

"Are you staying with the family?"

"No. They didn't want to have anything to do with me. Ram has been very formal and very polite, he arranged this room at the Taj Hotel. It's absolutely fantastic! It's like stepping back 40 years to the days of the Raj with men in turbans everywhere. It's really weird. I've got a lovely room overlooking the harbour. They built it the wrong way round you know. The gardens and swimming pool were supposed to face onto the harbour but they don't. They face back into the teeming hot pale brown streets. Still my room should have looked out over them but it doesn't it looks out over the teeming pale brown harbour instead!"

I laughed gently as I realised she was talking about these pointless things because she didn't want to say what was really on her mind.

"It really is a very, very crowded city. It took ages to drive from the airport. It's only about ten miles but it took over two hours and the millions and millions of people you see absolutely everywhere, walking in the road, squatting at the side of the road doing god knows what…"

"Well you know what!"

"Exactly! And the smell! You just wouldn't believe it! It's absolutely all-pervading. You leave the wonderful air-conditioning of the hotel to go outside and it hits you like you've walked into a very smelly oven, it's completely overwhelming. The funniest thing is that when we arrived at the airport they fumigated *us* in case we were bringing anything into the country! Weird!"

"And Ram?" I had to ask.

"He met me at the airport and his driver brought us to the hotel where he waited while I checked in and then left me. He said he'd be back the next morning for coffee. I don't think he had any idea what I felt like. I was tired out after the flight, I had no idea what to do in the hotel, whether it was safe to go out onto the streets alone or anything. So I stayed in the room and ordered room service. That was weird. They don't just bring a tray and leave it balanced precariously on the bed as they do in England. Oh no! Three bearers bring in a table, fully laid, and a serving trolley and they serve you while you eat! I felt a little underdressed in my jeans and t-shirt but they didn't seem to mind. The manager came up to see me and very carefully called me Mrs Kambli. I got the distinct feeling he knows the family and thinks I'm absolutely not worthy of the name."

"Linda, you've been on the phone for ages. It must be costing a bomb. What did you want me to do?"

"Oh I just called to talk to someone sensible. Ram, or more probably his uncle Vijay, is picking up the tab for the hotel so I'll stay on the phone as long as I can."

Vijay? How common a name was that in India? Could David's loose cannon be Ramesh's uncle? Linda could not know how interested I had become in her conversation.

"Is it getting nasty then? I thought you both wanted to come to some amicable agreement."

"Oh it's fine really. I just don't see why he should get away lightly. Anyway, the next morning, Valentine's Day actually, the phone in my room rang and he said to meet him by the pool. He didn't even want to come to my room and we're still married for God's sake. Anyway I had tried to be a bit more 'memsahibish' by wearing a skirt and headed off for the pool area. Every door was opened by a turbaned attendant, it made me hold my head up higher and my back straighter. Ram was sitting in a large wicker chair, and there were several other men with him. I hadn't been expecting him to come mob-handed. They were his cousins I think. I as only introduced to one, Sandeep. They were there to make sure Ramesh didn't negotiate any of the family fortune away."

"I'm sure it wasn't like that." I wasn't at all sure but it seemed the right thing to say.

"Well I told them I didn't want any of his family's money. All I wanted was the ability to put the last seven years behind me and start again."

"That seems very generous of you." I had to admire Linda's independence, I didn't think it was what I would have done in the circumstances.

"But that wasn't what he wanted. He wanted the business! He

argued that I couldn't have bought Charles out without his financial backing and that he supported me through some of the bad times when the business wasn't making any money so he wanted the business valued and me to pay him three quarters!"

"I don't believe it. He can't do that surely?"

"You can't lend me any money can you?" Before I could answer she had continued swiftly "Only joking."

"You talked him out of it?"

"I told him that I couldn't possibly do that. If I did I would have to ask him for financial support. Either I get the business and don't want anything from him or he gets the business and I get at least £1,500 a month maintenance."

"Thatagirl!"

"Well then he nodded his head and his cousins, or whoever they were, disappeared. He got all chummy and pathetic, saying his family had told him to say that and he knew I wouldn't wear it and not to worry. He didn't want me to have to close the business and he was quite happy to sign the papers as long as I agreed not to have any claims on him or his family. We could probably be divorced before I left the country."

"It's a good thing you didn't have any children, you know, he would have wanted them and it would have been a damned sight more complicated."

"I know. There is that at least. Anyway." She paused dramatically as if what was to follow was the most interesting part of the conversation. "Before he left he gave me a little peck on the cheek and said he had left his driver for me to use for the duration of my stay and that if I wanted anything I should just ask the hotel manager and to put everything on the bill."

"So you're taking him at his word."

"Absolutely. And I'll tell you why." When she paused for breath I heard the phone crackle and thought perhaps the line had gone dead but after a few seconds I realised Linda was crying.

"Are you OK?"

"I'm sorry I just find it very, very funny." She was laughing.

"I thought you were crying."

"No, just finding it all rather funny in a sick sort of way. When I got together with Ram I knew his family were reasonably well off, he was earning good money as an accountant and he seemed educated and, well, quite western in his ways. Well I didn't know the half of it. I've spent a couple of days letting the driver take me to shopping areas and showing me the sites of Bombay. I've spent an afternoon at the Gymkhana Club watching ex-pats playing a very good game of cricket, all very colonial. I'll tell you about that when I get back. I've seen all the sights. Balu, the driver, speaks excellent English and is a very good guide. We had got on famously and I think he felt rather sorry for me in a way. When I wanted to walk on the Maidan, a wonderful stretch of what would be green grass if they had had any rain, completely packed with millions of people playing cricket, surrounded by amazing colonial buildings and statues, he insisted on walking with me and giving me a detailed history of every building. Then he took me to the railway station. Wow! It was absolutely fantastic. I've got loads of photographs. Anyway. Yesterday I asked Balu where *Kambli Sahib* lived. You wouldn't believe it! We parked by the iron gates and I peered in like a naughty schoolgirl. There were gardeners squatting on the lawn cutting the grass blade by blade with scissors! The house, sorry, 'bungalow' was three storeys tall, every storey had a veranda and it was gigantic. It was on the top of one of the hills, Malabar Hill, and the view must have been phenomenal across the bay. Then he took me to Juhu. It's a beach area an hour or so outside the city, where the old airport used to be. The family has three houses there, all on the beach with swimming pools and what seemed like thousands of servants. Susannah, let me tell you, they are rich, with a capital R. Apparently the Kambli family live with their uncle and cousins. They have such a silly surname, it sounds more English than Indian, Thakersey."

It was all I could do to stop myself interrupting Linda. I tried to keep listening while my mind took in what she was saying. Ramesh was Vijay's nephew. I had not only found that Vijay was alive but had found a link with our family. Not perhaps the dangerous connection David had been concerned about, divorce was hardly the disaster it was for my parents 25 years earlier, but a connection nonetheless.

I concentrated back on what Linda had to say.

"Ram and his mother, she's the one who we met at Old Trafford in 1976, well they live with her brother Vijay Thakersey who is the head of the family and his children, the oldest is Sandeep who is sort of taking over from his father as head of the family. Vijay lived in Europe for a long time and is the one who started the family business and rules everyone with a rod of iron."

It was a few moments before I realised Linda had stopped talking. I had to say something. "And Ram never let on his family were rich?"

"Nope. Never. We got Christmas cards and birthday presents from his family but they never helped us when money was tight. I realised they were comfortable, possibly even well off, but mega-rich! No. I never realised. Balu told me they are one of the richest, most famous and most important families in India."

"Surely he's exaggerating."

"He seemed quite proud of it. Apparently although they are basically accountants they are also investors."

"They must have invested in something pretty worthwhile."

"Films. They invested in films. Bollywood they call it. They make more films than Hollywood and Italy put together. Balu waxed lyrical about the actors and actresses who owed their fame and fortune to Sandeep Thakersey and his uncle, even though they are always behind the scenes they rake it in. You wouldn't believe how popular films are over here. Millions go every night. There are cinemas everywhere, and enormous billboards. Films and cricket, they obsess millions upon millions of people."

"Are you going to change your demands then? Tell Ramesh you want some money as well as his signature on a piece of paper."

"No. That hasn't changed. I just feel very sorry for him. All those years we had together and he didn't let on. I think what really happened was he did fall in love with me, but his family wanted him to marry someone else, keep it all in the family."

I wasn't going to tell her that I believed the only reason he got involved with her was to be closer to our family, and his motive certainly wasn't love.

"Perhaps if I'd had children they would have relented, but I think they put endless pressure on him for marrying an English woman and that overcame any feelings he may still have for me. He's bowing in to his family. I don't like that. It shows he's a bit weak and I'm quite happy giving up on him and trying to find someone stronger. Balu is picking me up tomorrow and we're going to the court."

"Good luck."

"What's to be lucky about. Divorce is divorce isn't it? We both want to be free of the marriage, free to start again. It's a win win situation."

"Phone me if you need anything."

"Thanks for listening. I'm going down to the bar now, enjoy a bit of luxury while I can."

In the traffic jam trying to get off the part of the M25 that was finished and head off down Reigate Hill to the A25 I tried to make sense of what was happening. Linda was an innocent pawn in whatever game it was the Kambli-Thakersey family was playing. Perhaps she was just too closely connected with our family, and too easy a target, for Vijay to ignore. She was putting a brave face on it but I wondered how I would cope; a foreign country, no friends, a strange hotel, thousands of miles from friends and home. She must be more upset than she was letting on. I had to admire her.

That evening Maureen was making conversation as the atmosphere between us was still tense. She had said one evening that there were so many things about me that reminded me of my mother and I don't think she was being complimentary.

She asked whether I had heard from Linda.

"She's fine. She's finding out so much about Ramesh. He's part of a large family and they are very, very rich. She has been shown round all their houses." That wasn't really a lie though I can understand that Maureen may have got an idea different from the truth. "She hasn't met any of the family but she's heard a lot about them."

As I ate my supper I rambled on repeating much of what Linda had told me I noticed a change in Maureen.

"Are you alright?" I had to ask as she put her knife and fork down on her plate and stopped eating.

"This isn't quite agreeing with me. I think I'll retire. I've been feeling a little under the weather today it's just catching up with me." As I cleared away and did the washing up I had no reason to think that Maureen's sudden indisposition was due to anything I might have said.

I was in the office early the next day, deciding to beat the road-work jams by leaving at 6am. The phone rang at 7.30.

"Oh Susannah, thank God you're in. I really had to speak to someone before my flight."

"You're at the airport?"

"No, Balu is picking me up in half an hour."

"That's all a bit of a rush isn't it?"

"It has to be. My passport won't be valid after tomorrow."

"What on earth are you talking about?"

"I am not, will not be, indeed never have been, Linda Kambli."

I felt like an idiot repeating "Linda, what are you talking about?"

"The bastard, the utter conniving cheating bastard didn't want a divorce…"

"But…"

"He hadn't applied to the court for a divorce. He had applied for a 'Civil Annulment Decree'."

"An annulment? How can he do that?"

"The marriage is void, it never happened, because, and I quote 'Miss Forster's unwillingness or inability to accede to the petitioner's right to a family. It was entirely Miss Forster's decision, against all the wishes and arguments of the petitioner, not to have children'. They kept calling me 'Miss Forster', over and over as if I didn't know what my name had been."

"But..."

"Apparently it is absolutely the law. It means I have never been married. Of course we talked about having children, he always said it would be OK later, when the business ran itself. He never, never, said it was a problem."

"It's the family isn't it? They wanted the annulment. If you'd been divorced you might always have some call on them or their money, you would be a loose end."

"That's exactly it! Now I'm nothing. I feel so... so..."

"And to them a loose end might become a loose cannon. Say you got divorced and found out, next week, that you were pregnant? You would claim he was the father..."

"I haven't..."

"He would argue he wasn't and it would all get very messy. This way you were never part of their family, never, in any way, possibly, their responsibility."

"Oh shit shit shit."

I thought perhaps being practical would help.

"What time does your plane get in? Do you want me to meet you?"

"I don't know. No. Don't worry about me. I'll see you in the office on Monday. I've got to go. See you Monday."

And the phone went dead.

I looked around the office at all the references to 'Linda Kambli'. Linda hadn't kept her maiden name when she had married Ram. She had, unusually for the 1980s, worked under her married name. I began to realise how difficult this was going to be. The company registration, bank accounts, everything would have to be changed. What would happen to her house, her mortgage?

And at every turn she would have to explain why. I couldn't begin to think of all the implications for her.

So I called Ted, the only person I knew would help.

Chapter Eighteen

"Susannah, how lovely to hear from you after all this time." He sounded genuinely pleased but I had to speak quickly to dispel any ideas he might have had that I was calling about the children.

"Ted it's about Linda."

"What about Linda?"

"She's just called from India. I think she'll need your advice."

I gave him a brief explanation of what had happened in the past two weeks.

"You're right she will need some advice, and support. I can't believe it of Ramesh, he seemed such a nice young man."

"Well he's turned out a total shit. It was obviously his family that made him do it, but he didn't have to go along with it. Does it have to stand? Is it legal in this country?"

"I can't say it's something I've come across before but I will make some enquiries. When does she get back?"

"She said she would be in the office on Monday."

"Would she see me then do you think, if I came down?"

"I'm sure she would. Come down on Sunday and stay with us." Ted must have known I was staying with Maureen, they were frequently in touch and it seemed a reasonable assumption to make.

"Do you think I could? I'll call Maureen and if she agrees I'll see you on Sunday."

Linda had always closed the office early on a Friday, and all the staff loved having longer weekends, they told me that just two hours on a Friday afternoon meant that they could 'get ahead with things' and therefore enjoy Saturday and Sunday more. Driving home on the pre-rush hour roads I thought how lucky I was not to have to wheel a trolley round a supermarket buying plastic meat in polystyrene trays wrapped in cellophane. Maureen and I took it in turns on a Saturday morning to walk up and down the small village high street buying meat in a butcher's, vegetables in a greengrocers, bread in the bakers, tea, flour, spices in a grocers shop and cleaning materials in the ironmongery. I wondered for how long that would be possible, already there were signs that the local shops were losing business to the big supermarket that had opened in the town.

Maureen and I were enjoying an early evening drink. "I am so looking forward to seeing Ted. I was trying to remember when we last met. It would have been at your mother's funeral, or was it Charles's wedding I can't remember if he was there or not. Still, it will be nice to see him and catch up."

"You like him very much, don't you?" Maureen was easier to talk to than she had been for months.

"I've known him for a very long time." Again Maureen succeeded in not directly answering a straight question.

"He was always very good to you and to your brother Charles, and to the children. There isn't a member of your family that doesn't owe a lot of their happiness to Ted."

"Yet I never thought of him as happy, but how does an unhappy person do so much to improve other people's lives?"

"He's not so much unhappy as lonely, I think, but he gets a great deal of satisfaction from his work. He's done very well over the years, Max couldn't do without him. He set out with nothing and I think he believes that was an advantage, all the people he knew who were born into money needed his help. He believes that he has been the privileged one, having the satisfaction of knowing that everything he has he has earned, he owes nothing to anyone."

"He had Max's help."

"Ah. Max."

"You don't like him do you?"

"No."

"You know about his history? Where he came from. And why?"

"I know the story he tells, the public Max. You know I would have told you if I had known anything to help your search."

She obviously didn't know how much David had told me. But why would she lie?

She ended the conversation. "Another drink?"

When she came back from the bar and placed glasses on the table she changed the subject. "Now for the weekend. Let's get it all sorted. First the shopping."

I was looking forward to seeing Ted so much. It wasn't just because he was going to help Linda, it certainly wasn't that he would bring

128

information about the children. I supposed it was because he was something solid and unchanging in my life. He had genuinely wanted me to be happy with Carl, and, unlike Charles, he hadn't been cynical or pessimistic about our chances, at least if he had been he hadn't shown it.

I don't know what I was expecting. I always remembered Ted in a comfortable checked shirt, usually worn with a paisley cravat, and grey trousers and that is how I always thought of him, so I was a little shocked to see him in denims with a red and white striped shirt and navy blue sweater.

"Ted!" I gave him a rather self-conscious hug.

Was it me getting older or Ted's new image, but I saw Ted through completely new eyes.

He looked very nice, almost attractive.

This was 1983. I was 36 years old. Ted was in his 60s. There was nearly 30 years between us. He had been like a father to me, cheering me up when I was depressed, giving me somewhere to live when I had nowhere, finding solutions to most of the problems in my life.

"What's with this new image?"

"Hello you too." He hugged me back and kept an arm draped over my shoulder as we walked down the path and into the house. "And I forgive you for never answering any of the questions I asked in my letters. I realise how difficult it must have been for you." Ted had always been on my side, giving me the benefit of any doubt about my behaviour.

Maureen had been looking forward to Ted's visit as much as I had but I was surprised to see a fleeting look of distaste when Ted and I walked into the house together.

"Hello Maureen, it's good to see you again." I saw her relax and smile as he put his hands on her shoulders and kissed her cheek.

We sat down around the fire where the logs were glowing red, giving out not just a feeling of warmth but of welcome and we went through all the pleasantries about his journey, what the roads were like, how much easier it will be when they get all the M25 open; and the weather, how cold it was after such a mild January, how lucky it was that the snow we'd had earlier in the month had cleared.

"But you didn't bring me all the way down here just to talk about the weather did you?" He asked, and as he turned towards me I noticed the reason for the difference in his appearance.

"You've grown your hair."

"So I have!" he twiddled some of his grey hair around his fingers "Josie said I should change my image, whatever that means. Just before

Christmas she made me go shopping with her and she took me into establishments I would never have dreamed of entering. She said if I fitted into the clothes then I should wear them. I suppose spending a lot of time with the youngsters made me realise how old I was becoming."

"You spend a lot of time with them?"

"Certainly, and they are great fun. Even young Bill gets us all laughing. You've missed such a lot Susannah, you really have." Before I could interrupt to justify myself he continued "But I respect your decision. If you weren't meant to be a mother then there's no point in forcing it. That's what Josie says anyway and I am absolutely certain she means it."

"What about Charles? Isn't he around?" I realised that I had no idea what arrangements had been put in place for my children.

"Holly hasn't come back even though she is in England. I believe she has other irons in the fire. Charles is devastated by the break-up and it's likely they will be divorced soon. Since she left there has been all sorts of gossip which has been very hurtful. You know he and Holly worked with Linda for a while, before she bought them out and moved south, well there were rumours that Holly got a little too close to Linda's husband."

"Ted. I'm ashamed of you passing on idle gossip." Maureen did seem genuinely shocked.

I had little doubt that Holly would have had an affair with Ramesh, she was a tart who would sleep with anyone, but my immediate fear was at how close Ramesh Kambli seemed to have got to the family. I could only guess at his motives.

For the first time I thought that, perhaps, David had been right and I should have been more on my guard.

"I should hate to see them divorce," Ted continued "but unfortunately these days no relationship seems to be taken as seriously as it should." Realising he was straying onto tricky ground he changed tack. "Do you want to hear about your children Susannah? If not I won't say anything other than to say they are doing fine. All of them, even young Bill."

"You see Bill?"

"Charles and I take it in turns to drive down to the hospital. Sometimes Al and Jack come, sometimes they don't but Josie always does so, yes, I spend a lot of time with them every weekend. And then we meet up during the week. Josie has decided to study Law and has been picking my brains. You know that despite all the disruptions in her education she takes her A-levels next summer. She'll do well that one."

I thought of saying 'despite having Joe for a father and me for a mother' but thought better of it.

"I've been helping Al and Jack as well. They find school work more difficult and need nudging even to turn up at school every day, but I have my spies and know pretty much what they are up to. They got into a bit of trouble, in with a bad crowd, when they first came back up north but it didn't take long to show them the error of their ways."

I realised how little I knew about my family.

"Am I odd that I don't care? Is it unnatural?"

Ted looked thoughtful for a few moments, as if trying to decide whether to say anything in front of Maureen, but obviously decided that there was no reason not to be honest.

"My dear Susannah, or Annie I believe I should be calling you, I am probably one of the very few people who understand how you feel about your children. Remember I knew Joe and I know the circumstances under which these poor young things came into the world. Maureen, don't look so shocked. I know that Susannah conceived Josie at a time when she was desperately unhappy. Joe wanted to marry into the rich Donaldson family, Susannah was used. Once he had achieved the respectability and opportunity of working for me, he abused any love Susannah may have had for him. You must remember that, just as Alicia was reminded of the circumstances of Susannah's conception every time she saw her daughter, so Annie is reminded of that awful period of her life every time she looks at her children. She has never had any reason to love them. Annie, I completely understand." He reached over and took my hand, squeezing it with affection. I would have cried if I hadn't noticed the look of distaste in Maureen's eyes.

"Does Josie know this?" I asked, worrying possibly for the first time what my daughter thought of me.

"I have told her what she needs to know. She may also be more wary about men than many of her generation."

"You seem to get on well together."

"She is a very nice young lady, tending to be a bit bossy like her mother and grandmother but, just like them, an absolute charmer."

His affection for our family was tangible and I noticed a look of censure cross Maureen's face.

"Despite everything Charles needs some help." Ted surprised me. It all sounded as though they were getting on fine and I said so.

"He needs some time to himself. He didn't realise what he was doing when he took the children on. Monika's getting on and has been less able to be helpful, so we found him a young Norwegian girl to help with the children but it didn't work out. There's been a succession of au pairs but no one at all satisfactory. He's holding together, that's all."

When Charles and I had been children it had been a succession of nannies, now it was au pairs, but I didn't fail to notice the parallel.

"And Holly knows all this but still hasn't come back."

"No. I believe as soon as the divorce is finalised she will be marrying again."

"Not another sucker?"

"However much I tend to agree with you, it is not for me to say." I didn't notice how pointedly he changed the subject. "Actually, a plan was rather forming in my mind as I drove down this morning. I didn't have much time on Friday to look into Linda's problems but I did do a little searching. Let me ask you some questions about her. Do you mind?"

I was more than happy to abandon the subject of my brother and my children.

"I just need to get an idea of her life. I did go to see Linda's parents yesterday to see if, by any chance Linda had confided in them but I'd like another view of things."

"I've only known her a few weeks. She called out of the blue to get some help with the business while she was away."

"Didn't that seem odd when you hardly knew each other. You would hardly have been her first choice."

"No, fifth I think, at least, she admitted as much."

"She didn't tell you why the others she had asked had said no, why there was no one in the office already who could take over?"

"No, now you come to mention it she didn't."

"Were you busy while she was away?"

"You mean the office? Not particularly, there were things to do most days but the phone didn't ring very often. It all seemed pretty regular stuff."

"What about bills?"

"How do you mean?"

"Were there many? What sort of bills were there? Did you get any people ringing up asking for money?"

I began to realise what he was getting at. "Do you mean were there any signs she was in trouble? I don't think so. There were lots of bills but I assumed that was because it was a business." I had noticed that most of the post was made up of demands for payment but there had been cheques to bank as well. "Money came in as well. And before you ask, I didn't see any bank statements and if any had come in I wouldn't have opened them." I noticed Maureen's disbelieving look. Anyway, she's lent me a car. She can't be in trouble if she's got a car to give away."

"She recently had to sack her office manager. I suppose the Metro was hers."

"Why did she have to get rid of her? Who was it? No one said anything about anyone leaving."

Ted's questions began to make other, small, things fall into place. Linda had said she had had to borrow a lot of money to buy Charles out of the business. Even I knew interest rates were high and likely to get higher. And it seemed obvious, now, that she had brought someone in from the outside to keep an eye on the office because she didn't trust the people there not to snoop around the books while she was away.

"The business is in trouble isn't it?"

"I don't know. I'm not just being discreet. I won't know until I've spoken to her tomorrow. I'll be able to see then if my plan is a sensible one. Now let's enjoy the evening, can I take you both out to dinner somewhere?"

As we were washing up the breakfast things together the next morning comfortably chatting about nothing Ted suggested we drive separately to Sevenoaks. I was rather disappointed as I had been looking forward to an hour or so with him. But he was adamant. Linda would need some time in the office to catch up on what she had missed while she was away; she might not know he was coming, she might not have spoken to her parents. I would have to arrive first and explain to her. He would follow on an hour or so later.

It was only as I drove carefully down the icy ramp onto the M25 at the top of Reigate Hill that I realised it probably meant he was expecting that I would have to leave the Metro there and he would drive me home.

When I arrived the lights were on and Linda was already in the office, working her way through the carefully labelled piles of paper. It was only because of what Ted had said the day before that I realised how large the bills pile was.

"Coffee?"

She nodded.

When I brought the mugs into her office and sat down she looked up and I realised she had been crying.

"Problems?"

Again she nodded. "I probably should have said something before

I left but I couldn't think of anything until I had got it sorted. With Ram I mean. But it only gets worse."

"You can't do all this on your own." I wasn't sure what I meant by 'all this'. "It's an awful lot to deal with, you're tired out from your trip, angry and hurt by what Ram has done and now you're faced with what must seem like a brick wall of problems." I paused, but since she said nothing, I continued. "When we spoke on Friday I was worried about you, I don't know you well enough to know how you would cope but you sounded very upset, frightened and in need of support. So I rang Ted."

She looked up and it was difficult to read the emotions on her face. "Ted?"

"Well he's a solicitor, he might be able to understand your options better than anyone else we know."

"Probably."

"Anyway he'll be here in a few minutes."

"Here?"

"Yes, he stayed with me and Maureen last night. He drove down yesterday. He wants to help."

I wasn't prepared for her bursting into tears, folding her arms on the desk in front of her, bending her head onto them and sobbing uncontrollably.

I was never any good with emotions and so I got up and closed the door to her office behind me.

"Is Linda OK?" Asked Debbie, one of the girls I had been sharing an office with for the past fortnight, but who seemed to like me as little as I liked her.

"She's tired after her trip. Where's Ivy?"

"She's not in today. There isn't any work anyway."

"Is there nothing that needs finishing?"

"Nothing."

"Then you'd better have the day off too."

"But I came in. I want paying for half a day, I can't do anything else now. I should get a day's money. That's what would be fair."

"All right then. I'll make sure you get paid for the full day but you'd better catch up by doing double the normal amount of work tomorrow."

"I always work hard." She sounded so defensive I knew she was lying.

I answered her silently 'probably not, your gravy train is coming to an end' as she put on her coat and left the office as quickly as she possibly could.

The office seemed remarkably quiet and empty for 9 o'clock on a Monday morning. It hadn't occurred to me during my two weeks in that office that it should have been bustling with activity if it were to make a living for all the people employed, and for Linda.

The post arrived and as I opened the envelopes it seemed obvious that the sum of the bills was far greater than the value of the cheques. More ominously there was a letter from a firm I knew to be one of Linda's main regular clients. It was a very pleasant letter, full of thanks for all the hard work done in the past but saying they were purchasing their own equipment and wouldn't need the services of a bureau after the end of March. 'Nice of them to give a month's notice'. I think I spoke out loud. I went into the small kitchen and watched the kettle as it boiled, listening to the silence. What Ted had said seemed very true.

I took two more mugs into her office without knocking. She was standing by the window, looking out on the busy High Street.

"You know, Susannah, I have always thought I would be a success, that this business would grow and I would be, if not rich, then comfortable. But it's all over isn't it?"

Before I could answer the bell rang and I went to welcome Ted.

Perhaps he would be able to help Linda.

Someone had to.

Chapter Nineteen

Linda was still in her office with Ted when the phone rang. I answered it, wondering what would be the best thing to say if someone wanted some work done, perhaps I shouldn't have sent Debbie home.

"I've got a bit of a problem." The voice at the end of the phone seemed foreign and rather theatrical but since it didn't seem to be sensible to turn work away I agreed to go straight round to the paper mill some miles outside the town. As I tried to follow the directions, driving through small villages and between orchards fields full of lines of poles, I was hoping the client wouldn't see through me and realise how little I knew about what I would be talking about. Perhaps I should have had a word with Linda before leaving the office unattended and driving out to meet a possible new client.

"Thank you for coming at such short notice."

I tried to listen carefully about the details of what he needed, nodding in appropriate places, but it was quite difficult to concentrate. He had a smooth voice with a strong Australian or New Zealand accent, I could never tell the difference. After he had given me a large envelope stuffed with pieces of paper with the request that the first draft of his report be available by Wednesday he asked if I had time for a quick lunch.

"There's a pub just down the road, it won't prejudice getting the work done will it?"

I think he was flirting with me but I didn't really hesitate before accepting. "I can't see an hour making much difference." The work couldn't be started until the following morning anyway, with Linda tied up with Ted and the girls given the day off.

I followed his silver BMW through the narrow lanes, I was pleased he was ahead of me because he would come across any cars coming in the opposite direction first. He drove far faster than I wanted to and I spent the time worried about losing sight of him. It was a relief to see the car eventually slow down and pull into a pub car park.

The time went quickly and without any embarrassing silences. His name was Jonathan Smith 'No really' he had added swiftly. He was 40 years old, not only currently unattached but had never been married, was a management consultant who was normally based in London but was to work at the paper mill for a few weeks. He only knew about this pub because he was staying there during the week. He normally lived in a flat in Connaught Square.

I told him far less about myself, but that didn't seem to be a problem as he seemed quite happy to talk about himself, his parents' farm in New Zealand, why he had decided to come to England three years earlier 'to see if I can hack it'.

When I asked what he did in his spare time he laughed 'you've never met a management consultant have you? There is no such thing as spare time.' Though it seemed he did do quite a bit other than work. He had a pilot's licence and shared ownership of a plane with his flat mate. He went to concerts, 'pop, classical, anyone and anything as long as it's the best in its field.' He travelled. 'We have to go over to the States every few months but I'm gradually working my way round the capitals of Europe.' And he read. 'Science fiction, war, fantasy, anything as long as it's not too clichéd.'

At the end of the lunch I felt I knew everything there was to know about him.

"Look, I'd better be getting back to the office. I'll call you tomorrow to say how we're getting on and hopefully the first draft will be ready on Wednesday."

"Wednesday lunch? Here? Bring the script with you and then we can go back to the mill afterwards to go through it."

I couldn't see a reason why I shouldn't accept and set off back to the office feeling excited and looking forward to Wednesday. A mood that was completely shattered after ten minutes with Linda and Ted.

"Where've you been?" Linda asked shortly.

"A man rang, I had to go to talk about some work."

"Couldn't you have left a note? We had no idea where you were. The office was empty, where are the others? Ivy? Debbie?"

"I sent them home, I didn't want them asking questions about why you were in a long meeting with Ted. I wouldn't have known how to answer."

"What about the work?"

"Apart from this," I waved the envelope in my hand "there isn't any."

She was silenced by that, and I thought she would break down but she pulled herself together and took the envelope from me.

"That's a big firm, how come they want us to do anything? They must have the resources themselves." It seemed like she was going to add something but thought better of it.

I explained about the mill and that it was not going to be a regular client. "He'll be back in London in a few weeks, he just wanted this put onto disk now. We were the only people with the same machines they have."

It had seemed a plausible explanation.

"Well at least I did something right, getting the right machines." She sounded very down again.

"You did a lot right, Linda, you just didn't have much support." Ted put his arm around her shoulder in an attempt to comfort her.

I was unprepared for how I felt. Part of me realised he was just being the nice man he had always been, part of me was irritated that he showed such interest in someone else's feelings. All my life Ted had been my comforter and his arm had been around my shoulders when I had needed comfort. Linda wasn't even family.

"Susannah and I will help in every way we can, won't we?" Ted must have noticed a change in my attitude and shot me a warning look.

"Of course, anything I can do." I said, perhaps a little unconvincingly.

"Now you go home Linda, get some sleep, and we'll be back tomorrow morning."

"I can't go home, I'll never sleep. I'll stay and do this," she gestured to the envelope still in her hand, "Is there anything I need to know?" she asked me.

"Nothing that can't be said in a few minutes."

"I'll wait and drive you home, Susannah, I think the Metro had better stay here."

Ten minutes later I as sitting beside Ted as he drove us down the hill towards the motorway.

"Not a bad time of the day to be setting out." He sounded ill at ease, almost nervous.

"At least it's not snowing." I wasn't sure whether to ask about his day with Linda or not. Eventually he answered my unasked question.

"Linda has decided to close the business down."

I waited for Ted to continue, biting back the comment that at least I wasn't the only failure around.

"It's the only way I'm afraid. She's put everything into it but it's just not going to work. That kind of business seems to have run its course, her clients are getting their own word processors. I feel very sad because

I feel responsible for her setting it up."

"I thought it was Charles's way of getting a proper job." My brother hadn't had to work, he had enough money from Max to live comfortably off the interest and he earned something writing and talking about birds, but in 1975 he had decided he needed to do something more and he and Linda had gone into business together, employing Holly. I hadn't realised Ted had been involved from the beginning. Perhaps I should have done. It wasn't that I felt possessive about Ted, I was just feeling that he seemed to have helped everyone except me.

"Certainly, but they really put a lot into it. But when Charles married Holly they decided it wouldn't be wise to work together, and they always thought they would have a family, so Ram bought them out and they closed the office in Hoylake and Linda opened up down here on her own. It appears, however, that Kambli didn't do it through the goodness of his heart, it was very much a business arrangement. He arranged a loan in Linda's name which has been repaid only from the business. Kambli put nothing in and with interest rates rising it has meant too much of the profit was going to the bank."

"I would have thought he'd have helped her out. He must have been earning good money."

"And there was family money too."

"But he just left her to sink or swim?"

"It seems so. She's been trying to pay back the loan through years of some of the highest interest rates. When she took out the loan they were 5 or 6% since then they have been as high as 16. It was crippling."

"But Ramesh could have paid it all back, he could have cleared it completely. Linda said his family are seriously rich."

"But he chose not to. He put her into a position where she had to work all the hours there were and then left her saying she spent too much time working."

"I don't understand how he could do that." I said the words that were expected of me though I was thinking that this must have been part of Vijay's plan.

"Neither does she."

"Couldn't she have gone to Charles? Her parents?"

"And admit her failure? Admit that her husband wouldn't help her? I don't think so."

"Perhaps not. But why did she keep on the staff? And the office, that can't have been cheap to run."

"She answered that, I asked the same questions and I have to say I agree with her reasoning. She said 'success breeds success, if you look down at heel no one will give you any business'. No one would trust a one-man band so she had to have staff. I don't think she was wrong, and it would have been successful if she hadn't had that crippling debt."

"Which was Ramesh's fault."

"I'm not sure I'd go that far. But he didn't help."

"So she's going to lose her business as well as her husband."

"I'm afraid so."

I looked out of the window at the passing fields while Ted concentrated on his driving. When my father, that is the man who brought me up as his daughter, had gone bankrupt it had had a catastrophic effect on the family. I had been 12. My world was changed completely. One day we lived in a large house with people to look after us, the next we'd moved to a cramped semi-detached where we had to do everything for ourselves. I hoped Linda would be more resilient than my father who had never recovered from losing his money, even though he had had the support of the woman he loved and who loved him. Linda would be on her own.

"What about the annulment? Is there any way that can be reversed? Linda was OK about divorce, in fact she was looking forward to getting her freedom back, but an annulment? What are the implications of that?" I tried to sound concerned and understanding, it was obviously what Ted wanted me to feel.

"Well first and foremost she has to change her name back to Forster in absolutely everything. If she had been divorced she could have kept her married name but not now."

"What about her house?"

"His. I'm afraid she really is in a bit of a spot. There was a letter delivered today giving her notice to quit by the end of the month."

"That's unnecessary." Perhaps Ted's concern was because of the seriousness of Linda's position, not because he felt any personal responsibility for her.

"I've spent some time this morning talking to the Kambli solicitors in London and they are adamant there has never been a marriage. They are insistent that she must leave as he wants the house for one of his cousins. She has to be out by the end of the month."

Ramesh wasn't just being harsh, he was being vindictive. How did this all help Vijay get back at David? I recognised that Linda had been practically part of the family when they had first met, she was Charles's good friend and business partner, so it must be the whole of our extended family he wanted to wound. I felt a shudder of apprehension. If he would go to these lengths to harm Linda how much more would he hurt a closer member of our family?

"Isn't there anything you can do?"

"She doesn't want me to. She said that now she realises what he is really like she wants to put her life with him behind her. She wants to start afresh as soon as possible."

"With nothing?"

"As you say, she's going to have to start again but she isn't starting quite from scratch, she has some of the most important assets in the world."

"What's that? She has no money, no home, no work?"

"She has family."

"She would never go back to her parents for help, and she'd never ask her brothers either."

"They will always support her, I mean give her moral support not financial assistance. She would never accept that, you're quite right. But, perhaps more importantly, she also has friends. Her friends can make her accept their help because they can make it impossible for her to refuse."

"I don't understand."

"She'll be helping others. She won't be being helped. I think it's all going to work out quite well."

"How…"

"We'll have to go over this later. Here we are, home."

I was left to mull over what Ted had said while we went through the evening routine of an early evening drink before cooking and eating dinner. Nothing was said about the events of the day until the washing up had been done.

"Well, I've been patient. How did it go?" Maureen asked as she sat down in front of the fire.

Neither Ted nor I immediately answered. We looked at each other to see who was going to answer and I nodded to him. How different our relationship was now, we were almost equals. I watched him carefully as he spoke, recognising the mannerisms and tones of voice that had been so familiar, and that I had taken so much for granted. Had I felt jealousy that 'my friend' was so concerned about Linda? Was I attracted to him in a way I would never have thought possible? Whatever the feeling was it was completely different from anything I had anticipated.

141

"I'm not going to tell you the tale of Linda's woes and the problems caused by Ramesh's actions and those of his family. I will tell you the solutions."

When neither Maureen nor I interrupted him he continued. "In summary Linda has, as of the end of this week, no husband, no home and no business. I am going to ask Susannah, sorry, 'Annie'..." he turned towards me, "I like that name by the way, it suits you, it's softer somehow, gentler than Susannah," I tried not to feel so pleased. "I'm going to ask Annie to help me here. There will be work to complete, administration to be done as the business winds up and I am hoping she will agree to spend two or three weeks looking after the office." He looked at me questioningly and I was surprised to feel flattered that Ted had been thinking of me while working out Linda's problems. "We really need you to help. My plan won't work without you."

I nodded assent.

"I will tell you all that you have to do, as long as you can make sure all contracts are fulfilled and all clients understand the circumstances. We don't want to let any one of them down and we need to get in all the money from creditors we possibly can. You say there was a new client today?"

"It won't be a long term thing, he's just here for a few weeks before going back to London, but I'm sure we can get quite a lot done in the time, and I quoted our highest rate, he's used to London prices."

"March Quarter Day will be the day the office shuts, so you'll have quite a bit to do in that time. Will you help?"

"Of course." I answered, basking in the glow of Ted's approving smile.

"Linda will be coming north with me on Friday." I think, by the mischievous look on his face, Ted knew this would surprise both Maureen and I. "The school holidays begin next week." I began to realise what Ted had planned.

"You mean...?"

"Yes, Charles is getting desperate and Linda is the ideal person. She is going to stay with Charles and look after the children."

"But..."

"They got over any possible attraction years ago, so there won't be any embarrassment. Everybody's happy."

I caught a look between Ted and Maureen, a comfortable, knowing look. It annoyed me.

"What if I don't want her to look after my children? I have to ask

142

the question, though I know I have given away most of my rights." I didn't mean my voice to sound so bitter and resentful.

"I think you have answered your own question, my dear." Maureen answered for Ted. "Charles has obviously been doing his best against all the odds. I think this is a brilliant solution. The children can only gain."

"That's what Charles thinks. He knows he can't do it all on his own with a succession of au pairs. It's not fair on him to expect it."

"You've spoken to him?"

"Yes, this afternoon. He is relieved and very, very grateful though obviously shocked and disappointed at the circumstances."

"If he hadn't married Holly he wouldn't have sold his share of the business, Linda wouldn't have had to take out the loan, she wouldn't be in such a mess." As I spoke I heard the words and how they would sound, not only harsh but also childish.

From basking in the warm glow of Ted's approval I felt that I was letting him down, not quite measuring up to some invisible standard that he had expected of me. "I don't think it's fair to blame him for that."

"I wasn't. I was blaming Holly."

"That isn't exactly logical either."

"What are you worrying about, Annie?" Maureen noticed the change in my mood.

"I'm not sure."

"You don't want to look after them, you've made that very clear. Allow Charles to judge what will be good for them. He's known them longer and better than anyone." There was a criticism in her voice that I couldn't help reacting to.

"Meaning I should know them better?"

I don't know why I seemed to be heading for an argument. It was almost as if I was watching myself winding myself up to say things I didn't mean just to get some reaction. I have no idea why I was doing it.

"No one is condemning you."

"Yes you are! You both are! "

"We're just trying to do what's best for everyone."

"Because I've made such a mess of everything!"

"No. Because there are problems to be solved." I could see both Maureen and Ted exchanging glances of exasperation as Maureen spoke harshly. "That is something you have never been good at recognising, other people's problems."

Something from a conversation with Maureen came to mind *"Nothing has changed, Ted's still in the Wirral, I'm still here."* The things in

143

Maureen's life that had always made her sad... her failure to have the child of the man she loved... It was all so obvious. Maureen was in love with Ted.

There was nothing I could do to stop myself. "You're saying I've failed. You're saying I've let everyone down. Well I don't want Linda looking after my children. I don't want her anywhere near them."

"Susannah..." Ted was looking at me with such disappointment. I couldn't stand any more and got up.

"I don't want to talk about it any more. I'm going to bed."

"I'm sorry you feel this way. We'll talk about it in the morning. Perhaps, when you've had a few minutes mature," Maureen emphasised the word and I felt again like a child being told off for something I didn't do. "mature," she repeated sounding so like her sister, my step-mother, I couldn't bear it, "reflection you may realise how like the old Susannah you are being, and how unlike the new Annie." She was enjoying making the most of my stupidity.

I could have realised how silly I was being, I could have relaxed, apologised and sat down again, the atmosphere restored to conviviality, my relationship with Ted not soured.

I could have. I didn't.

I walked out of the room and went to bed. As I left there was a look of smug satisfaction on Maureen's face as she turned to pour Ted another cup of coffee.

The next morning at breakfast Ted asked, in a very formal way, whether I had slept well and whether I had had a chance to think about whether I would help Linda. Maureen busied herself at the Aga.

"Thanks, not really, I'm sorry about last night. I must have been tired, there's so much to think about, so many decisions to be made."

"Apology accepted but it's a shame we couldn't talk about it last night, there isn't much time to get everything sorted out and the extra hours would have been useful." Ted's disapproval and disappointment were manifest in the lack of warmth in his voice.

"Have you changed your mind about the children?" Maureen seemed equally distant. It was as if they were ganging up on me.

"Do I have a choice?" I couldn't help the reluctance in my voice, my determination to be generous and co-operative evaporating with every word Maureen spoke.

"Of course you do, though I can't think of one that would solve so many problems." Maureen smiled at Ted. She seemed to want to try to smooth the atmosphere but only succeeded in making me feel less part of the arrangement. It seemed as though they were combined together against me. "I do think you could be more gracious about it."

I ate my toast and drank my coffee whilst Maureen and Ted talked about other things.

"We'd better be going. There's a busy day ahead." Ted stacked the plates and carried them to the sink.

I realised he was offering an olive branch so I grabbed the drying up cloth and stood next to him as he washed and I dried. It reminded me of the times we had performed the same, and the reverse, roles whilst I had lived with him after Joe had died and when we were both looking after my mother. But there was something dividing us now that there hadn't been the day before.

I couldn't help feeling that something important had been lost.

"Have you had a chance to think sensibly about Linda?" He asked with little preamble as he manoeuvred the car through the narrow streets of the village towards the main road.

I had thought most of the night about it and could think of no good reason to object. I hadn't meant to make such a fuss the night before, it was just that they had really annoyed me and words I didn't mean came out of my mouth. I had done that all the time when arguing with Carl, I would get myself into a position and just carry on as if it wasn't me doing the talking. I would say things I knew to be best left unsaid. It was probably a brilliant idea that the children, especially Josie, would get a mother figure in their lives and I realised that would never be me. I just didn't like it that Ted and Maureen knew that too.

"I'm really sorry about last night. I don't know why I was so silly. It's a brilliant idea. It'll be the best thing for the children, and for Charles." I tried to recover some of the ground I had lost with Ted. I so wanted him to think well of me.

"I'm glad you've come round to the idea. We wouldn't have done it without your approval you know. Despite everything you are their mother."

This time I didn't rise to the implied criticism. Perhaps it was that Maureen wasn't there revelling in my discomfort.

"I'm more worried about what you expect me to do down here. You'll have to tell me everything that needs doing. I'll get it all done, Ted, you can rely on me."

"I know, but sometimes you do make it rather difficult. In that you are just like your mother."

He reached over and patted my hand. Perhaps we were friends again.

As we entered the office the door was unlocked, the lights on and there was the clatter of the printer.

"You look dreadful." I couldn't help the exclamation. Linda did, indeed, look tired and drawn.

"Thanks."

"Let me get you some coffee."

"God no! I've had so much bloody coffee my blood must be brown."

"Have you been here all night?"

"I said I'd get this stuff done." She indicated the envelope Jonathan had given me the previous lunchtime.

"You've done it?"

"Of course."

"But there was a couple of days work there."

"It's surprising how much you can get done when the phone isn't ringing and you're not worried about what everyone else is up to." She was trying to sound cheerful. "I quite enjoyed it."

"I can't ring him now and tell him it's done, he'll expect this service all the time."

"I thought it was only a one off."

"It is, but there'll be amendments." I hastily added 'his not yours' when I saw the look on her face as she tore the paper out of the printer and began splitting the long continuous sheet into separate pages.

Ted came in from the kitchen with the coffee.

"Come on girls, time to sit down and make some plans. Are you up to it Linda?"

She nodded. "As ready as I'll ever be."

We sat whilst Ted talked and I made lists. We had another mug of coffee as I made notes around all the items on those lists. By lunchtime we had the next three weeks mapped out, what had to be done and when. And I would be on my own. Ted had to go to London the next day and Linda had only two days to pack up her home and move to her new life.

Chapter Twenty

There seemed to be a great deal to do in the winding up of a business but none of it was difficult, it would just need method and organisation. I did all that was required in the next three weeks which I spent either in the office or with Jonathan.

I had met him, as arranged, for lunch on that first Wednesday and he had given the work hardly a glance. "Come on, I can look at that later, let's have a drink."

After lunch he did talk very briefly about the work. "It looks good, you've done a great job but I will need to look at it." I didn't correct his assumption that it was I who had done the work. "Can you come back tomorrow to pick up my changes?"

After that I had to meet him again to give him back the corrected sheets.

"Back to London for a day or two." He answered when I asked what he was going to do at the weekend. "But I'll be back next Tuesday. Lunch?"

I had been wondering why he only ever asked me to lunch and not after work in the evening.

"Sorry, Tuesday I've got appointments during the day." I tried to manoeuvre an evening date. Linda and Ted had left for the north and I was left with Maureen who seemed to have changed since Ted's visit. It was like living with my step-mother and I didn't enjoy it. "How about after work? Are you still staying at that pub? I could come round and meet you there."

"A bit risky isn't it? My territory and that sort of thing? You never know what might happen."

He was being very obvious, but then so, I suppose, was I.

Despite it being my second wedding Jonathan wanted to make it a really big event.

He drew up a guest list that seemed to comprise mostly his family and colleagues at work, none of whom I knew.

"I'm not sure they would enjoy the day." He argued when I gave him a list of people I wanted to invite. "It certainly won't be a suitable event for children."

I had told him very early on in our relationship that I had children from my first marriage. 'They don't live with me.' I had said, rather defensively. 'Then we don't need to worry about them do we?' he had answered without looking up from reading his paper.

"It's not an event it's my wedding." He ignored my objections. "What about other members of my family, my friends?"

"I don't think so. You always said you had no friends and you don't get on with your family do you? No? Then we won't invite any of them."

"But …"

"No buts Susannah." He had decided 'Susannah' had more style than 'Annie'.

"My side of the church is going to be very empty."

He didn't pick up on the doubt in my voice. "Richard and Nicholas are ushers, they'll distribute people evenly, regardless of whether they're 'yours' or 'mine'." He was adamant and there were times when he used a tone of voice I could just not argue with.

"There won't be any of 'mine' will there?" I muttered under my breath.

All the arrangements for the ceremony were out of my hands. We had to have the marriage ceremony itself in a Register Office but Jonathan planned a big blessing ceremony in a fashionable central London church.

"I'm not having my family come half way round the world simply to stand in a dingy office for ten minutes."

"Well they don't have to come half way round the world do they?" I asked, perhaps unwisely.

He gave me a withering look. "Of course they'll come to my wedding. It would look very odd if they didn't"

"But no one in my family is invited."

"That's different." I thought at the time he meant that my parents were dead but as the wedding approached and I saw what it was turning into I realised he saw it as *his* wedding. *He* was on view to his work colleagues and superiors. I was simply a necessary extra.

I took no part in the decision of venue for the reception. The wife of a friend of his was a barrister and had agreed to sponsor Jonathan to have his reception in Middle Temple. I had soon learned that there was never anything unostentatious or cheap about Jonathan.

"Just sort out some wonderful outfits and leave the rest to me." He had said when I had asked what he was planning, who was going to pay for it and whether I would have any say at all in the arrangements for my wedding day. He did, after something of a discussion, allow me to choose which theatre we all went to on the evening after the Register Office ceremony.

He didn't even let me in on the secret of where he was taking me for our honeymoon.

"You've got to tell me or I won't know what to take with me."

"OK it'll be hot. You'll need formal clothes and casual ones. A bit of everything really."

"That's no good! That tells me nothing at all." I tried to get him to tell me where we were going but he was adamant.

"It's a surprise. You'll love it."

It was when he said that the solution was for me to only bring underwear, he would organise everything else, that I began to feel I was losing control not only of my wedding but of my whole life.

There were times when I thought, perhaps, I had made a mistake when I had accepted Jonathan's proposal.

It had all happened so fast. It was after only a couple of meetings that we were taking every opportunity to make love, on the office floor, in his car in pub car parks, and, as it grew warmer, on a blanket on the ground in the woods that surrounded the mill.

"Is that it then?" I had asked, trying not to sound too unhappy when, on the last Friday in March, he said he wasn't coming back to Kent the next week and he had told me what I already knew, that I would have no reason to return to Sevenoaks anyway.

"Between us? It's certainly the end of the beginning, not necessarily the beginning of the end."

"You're teasing me. I don't like that."

"Well, you could marry me?"

It had been as casual as that, and I had answered in the same tone "I could, couldn't I?"

From then on it was out of my hands.

I had told Maureen the week after the proposal as I packed my bags to move out. Her reaction was ambiguous.

"If you're sure this is the right thing to do then I'm happy for you but you hardly know the man. Bring him here for dinner. Let me meet him."

"I'll try." I didn't hold up much hope that Jonathan would want to spend an evening with Maureen.

149

"I'll ask him."

"It shouldn't be a question of having to ask him, Annie dear, you should be able to tell him that it is expected of him and he should want to know the people who are important to you."

I did ask him and he was dismissive. 'What on earth would we talk about?' he had said 'I don't know her.' When I countered that he expected me to talk to all his colleagues and friends, people I didn't know, he just said that that was different.

"It's difficult, Maureen, he works such long hours and he's so busy." I gave the only excuse I could think of when I telephoned.

"He would make the time if he wanted to." She answered coldly.

"It isn't like that." I replied in rather feeble fashion.

"Well I hope you'll be very happy." She seemed doubtful but perhaps a little relieved that she had done her duty and I was off her hands.

I suppose he had swept me off my feet. He showed me a lifestyle I had never dreamed existed. Dinner parties, theatre, shopping on his credit card, all became quite normal. It took very little time for me to get very used to not having to worry about money or what to do in the evenings. Through the summer of 1983 as all the arrangements that had to be made were being made by other people my job was to be where and when Jonathan needed me to socialise with his colleagues, to have sex with and, very soon, to clean his flat and do his ironing. My promise to David, again, forgotten as I lived my busy life. In any case apart from Ramesh's treatment of Linda I had heard of nothing that could possibly be considered a threat to anyone in the family.

The wedding date was set for my 37th birthday, the 1st September.

I thought back to some of my birthdays and could think of none that had been particularly happy. There had been my second birthday party when everyone had caught Whooping Cough and Max's daughter had died. All the way through my childhood it had marked the end of summer and the beginning of school. Seven years earlier, my 30th birthday, had been full of the hope that Carl and I would be together and we would enjoy our family life in Cambridge but that hadn't been the best thing I had ever done. Now I was marrying Jonathan. Was that going to be just as stupid an idea? I was beginning to think so but, again, I had painted myself into a corner. So many arrangements had been made, so many people were committed to long journeys, it would be impossible to pull out now. And anyway. I loved Jonathan. Didn't I.

My job was to be Jonathan's wife, my career was to support his.

On the frequent occasions he was away working in America or Newcastle or Blackpool one or other of his colleagues would come round every evening to take me out to dinner, or to the theatre. He said he didn't want me to be lonely but I began to think he just wanted to know what I was doing at all times. I lost contact, again, with all the people who should have mattered in my life.

I spent the days shopping, whiling away the hours in a health club or at the hairdresser with the wives and girlfriends of Jonathan's colleagues. I became one of those women I had always previously despised 'a lady who lunched'.

If anything my doubts increased as the wedding approached, I couldn't call it off this late, could I? His family's tickets were booked, all the arrangements were in place.

There was only one place I could have run and that was to Maureen and I didn't think I would have much of a welcome if I turned up with my tail between my legs saying I had made a dreadful mistake. Again.

Perhaps I should have done.

Somehow I got through the two wedding days, the Register Office on the last day of August and then the big ceremony the next day. I hated every minute of both days. They were not what I would have chosen if I had been given any say whatsoever

It was two days spent in taxis between airports and hotels, dressing for one event, rushing home to change for another. I felt as if I was a spectator or had somehow strayed into someone else's life as I knew so few people who ate the food Jonathan had chosen and listened to the music he thought his bosses would enjoy.

It all felt so wrong.

Sitting alone at the top table after the meal inaccurately called the 'wedding breakfast', I watched Jonathan laughing and joking with his colleagues. They weren't friends. We had no friends. I had soon realised that all the men and women who worked for that management consultancy firm would stab each other in the back as soon as talk to each other. Only a few of each year's intake would be promoted and those who weren't were unceremoniously told to find some other way of making a living. Every conversation they held, everything they did in their lives was geared to getting through to the next year, up one step of the career ladder that was everything to them. I also learned that promotion wasn't so much about how good they were at their work as what sort of person they were. I watched Jonathan as he talked to his colleagues and their wives and I realised why he had married me. He had to have a wife to have a chance to make it to the next level, with the decision being made in late September the timing was perfect. This whole pantomime of a wedding was to establish him as Partner Material. I was simply a means to that end.

"You look a little lonely up here. Where's your gorgeous husband?" I tried to focus on the woman, somewhat younger than me, who had sat down in Jonathan's vacant seat. "Where are you going on your honeymoon? Susannah?" I just wanted her to go away yet I couldn't make a scene. That wouldn't do at all.

"I don't know. It's a surprise."

"He hasn't told you? How on earth did you know what clothes to pack?"

"I didn't. He did it."

She laughed in a rather forced manner "Jonny has always been a complete control freak." I had never heard anyone call him Jonny. But then I had only known him six months. For all I knew he had lived for years with this woman who called him 'Jonny' and who seemed to know him far better than I did.

"I bet I know where he's taking you." She carried on talking, oblivious to the absence of any encouragement. "It'll either be Amsterdam, he loves Amsterdam, or India. Yes, I'd bet on India. It'll be somewhere he can easily get hold of stuff. We all went to Amsterdam last year and were OK with the coffee shops and the cannabis bars but Jonny wanted more and he always found it. I'm sure he'll tell you about it. We all had such a great time. Jonny was with Flic then, he's told you about Felicity hasn't he? No? Oh he will. They worked together and were very close, but she didn't make the cut last year. I think she's in Hong Kong now working for a bank or something. It doesn't matter. He was never going to get serious with her. He needed someone from outside the firm. Anyway, where was I? Oh yes the honeymoon. I'd bet on India because there he'll get everything he needs if you know what I mean."

I didn't like her false laughter or the tone of her voice and I had absolutely no idea what she meant.

She was right though, the honeymoon was in India.

Chapter Twenty-One

I found out as we sat in the aircraft and the captain came over the intercom to announce the destination. Jonathan had managed to get me aboard without seeing any signs of the final destination. 'Welcome aboard this flight to Bombay'.

"Are you surprised?"

He seemed genuinely disappointed when I said flatly 'Not really'.

The flight was a long one but we had the VIP treatment in First Class. I remembered what Linda had said, about de-fumigation, the noise, the heat and the crowds. I had hoped the surprise would be a good one, a safari perhaps, a luxury resort in the Caribbean or a villa in Tuscany. I had not expected one of the dirtiest, noisiest, poorest cities in the world. Perhaps I shouldn't have been surprised.

Despite my tiredness and disappointment the drive from the airport was exciting. The air conditioned limousine was everything you could expect in luxury. After what seemed like hours driving through the colour brown with more people, cars, black and yellow taxis than I had ever imagined we began to drive past lush green squares, beautiful red and white buildings and through cool, tree lined streets.

We pulled up outside a building I knew immediately was the Taj Mahal Hotel. This was where Linda had been staying when she phoned me only a few months before. I wondered at the coincidence.

But then, I told myself, I don't believe in coincidence.

The Manager said something to Jonathan I didn't hear then my husband gestured for me to follow him. He didn't head for the lift, instead he crossed the wide foyer and walked through doors which were, as Linda had described, opened by a pair of turbaned attendants. Jonathan strode along the wide corridor and it became obvious he had been here before and knew exactly where he was going. Without checking whether I was behind him he turned sharply to the left and instead of the small room I had been half expecting there was a staircase.

I stood and looked at it, Jonathan had paused at the bottom.

"Magnificent isn't it."

I wasn't in the right mood to take in its beauty. I did not want to climb how many flights of stairs, however magnificent they were. I wanted to have a shower, lie down and rest after two emotional days and a long journey.

"For Pete's sake Jonathan, I'm tired. Why bring me this way? What was wrong with the lift?"

"I thought you'd like to see the staircase, reach the rooms the same way people did for a hundred years."

"I just want to get out of these clothes and sleep."

He seemed disappointed in me, but for once I didn't care.

I followed him up the stairs, watching as he paused briefly to talk to a man walking down. A short way down the corridor on the third floor we turned right into our room. It was furnished in an old fashioned way with heavy rosewood furniture and rich silk fabrics. The view from the seat in the bow window was across the brown water of the harbour, a large arch which I knew to be The Gateway of India, was just visible to the left. Despite the fact that this wasn't the blue Caribbean or the wide expanse of the Serengeti I had to admit it had its own sort of beauty.

I was prepared to relax. I sat in the window seat and waited for Jonathan to come over to me, gently remove my clothes, lead me to the shower and wash me down, then lead me back to the bedroom and make long, leisurely and satisfying love to me. Whatever his motives, and whatever my misgivings about our marriage we had usually enjoyed sex together and this would be our first time as husband and wife.

But although he walked over to the bed he ignored me, instead lifting the phone and speaking a few words in what seemed to be the local language.

"You speak Hindi?" I asked, surprised out of my expectations.

"*Muje Urdu aatee hay.*" It seemed to be some sort of answer to my question.

"There's a lot about you I don't know isn't there?"

He didn't answer me directly, he just said I should have a shower and then spend some time walking around the hotel. He had things to do.

"What about clothes?"

"They're in the closets."

I opened the wardrobe and the drawers in the unit in the dressing room and found them filled with enough clothes to last for weeks.

"Have a shower, change, go and walk round the hotel, do some shopping. I need some time on my own."

It was not what I expected my new husband to say.

I found my way to the pool, and sat down wearily in what were possibly the same wicker seats Linda had sat in six months before as she heard her husband and his family tell her she had never had a marriage.

It was all so strange. Inside the walls of the hotel and the high fence, there were servants, there was water, food, cleanliness. I hadn't realised how cooling the sound of the splashing water of the small fountains could be as I concentrated on the refreshing sound they made. Squatting on the grass were boys cutting the grass with what looked like scissors, blade by blade just as Linda had described. I walked aimlessly along the wide corridors of the hotel. There were western shops with shoes that perhaps a fraction of one percent of the population of the city could afford, there were clothes that someone must have taken a month to make, earning a minute fraction of their value. I looked at a montage of photographs of the rich and famous that had stayed at the hotel, and wondered whether any of them had seen anything other than this air-conditioned convenience store, an oasis of western consumerism in the desert that was the poverty of the city.

I hated it.

I walked through the doors. They opened for me as if they were automatic but really through the attentiveness of the attendants. The heat hit me like a wall and I was in the real world with its dirt, noise, stench and overwhelming heat. Very carefully I crossed the road and headed for the large archway, the Gateway of India.

"*Baksheesh baksheesh*" the beggars repeated monotonously with their hands held weakly out in front of them. They seemed to be everywhere. Thin children dressed in ragged and dirty saris with babies balanced on their hips pursed their hands to their lips as if pretending to eat non-existent food. '*Baksheesh*'. A boy, no older than five, his legs tied up around his neck, propelled himself on a wheeled board. '*Taxi munta? Taxi?*'

"No. No." I repeated over and over to everyone who approached me. But I was determined not to go back to the hotel. I knew this wasn't the real India but it was a damned sight more India than the hotel.

I walked along to the arch and read the inscriptions redolent of empire and imperialism, I watched the multitudes piling into pleasure boats to take trips around the harbour, to their islands. There were so many boats I could hardly see the water. And people, so many people.

I turned away from the archway and walked towards a green roundabout, wishing I'd thought to wear shoes that didn't hurt my feet every step I took on the hot, uneven pavement. There were shops, barely the size of the doorways of shops in London. And everywhere there were children, with babies on their hips, mouthing '*baksheesh*'. Always behind the beggars' cries was the noise of cars breaking and accelerating and the incessant hooting of horns.

I walked for a long time on pavements that were so potholed as to be almost impassable. I needed something to take my mind off the knowledge that was overwhelming me, that in marrying Jonathan I had made a terrible mistake. I took my life in my hands crossing wide streets one minute clear the next filled with a mass of anarchic traffic as I headed for an area of green. I didn't know what to expect when I reached it, peace perhaps, a respite from the incessant noise and the tides of people who all seemed to be rushing somewhere. If I had been expecting something like a London park I was to be disappointed. There was as much mayhem as in the streets. Tens upon tens of wickets were marked out, all surrounded by their own group of fielders. Thousands of people were playing cricket. I thought of the village cricket pitch where I had spent so many Sunday afternoons watching my father play. The players there had worn perfect whites and there was never any noise apart from the polite murmur of 'shot' or the ripple of embarrassed applause as a wicket was taken or a boundary scored. That was the cricket I had known, this was something completely different. This was a mêlée of men and boys of all ages in their normal clothes, shouting at each other. The wickets, bats and balls seemed to be anything that could serve the purpose. There appeared to be no set teams, any number of fielders were placed in any positions and most seemed to be playing in more than one game, occasionally turning to face a different group. Everyone seemed to be taking it all extremely seriously, shouting instructions to everyone and anyone who cared to listen.

This was so completely different from any cricket I had known that I sat down on an empty patch of ground. When I reached out instinctively to stop a ball that came my way I smiled at the young man as I threw it to him and was pleased to get a broad, red-toothed smile in return. That young boy seemed to me to be the only person I had enjoyed meeting in months.

I don't know how long I sat watching but when eventually I stood up I realised how painful my feet were. They were not used to such uneven streets in such heat. I walked gingerly to the road and held my hand out hoping that a taxi would stop, there seemed to be enough of them.

"Taj Hotel" I said with a confidence I did not feel and was relieved to find that the driver seemed to know where I meant. As we drove back through the teeming streets I wondered what I would do to pay him. I had no money. But, feeling very much as if I were part of the world of the Raj, I assumed that the hotel would sort it out.

I was dusty and somewhat bedraggled when I limped bare-footed into our suite, looking forward to the air conditioning and the wonderful shower.

"Well Susannah. There you are, I was wondering where you had got to."

"I went for a walk."

"You shouldn't have."

"Well I did. It was very interesting."

"Here." He went to hand me a cigarette.

"You know I don't smoke. Neither do you."

"Tobacco. No, I don't smoke tobacco but this…" he took a long drag of what I assumed was a joint but exhaled very little smoke. "This is different."

"Where did you get it?"

"I have my contacts." He said mysteriously as he took another long drag before stubbing out the minute remnants in the ashtray on his bedside table.

"Don't be so prissy, Susannah, relax, enjoy."

I had seen him drunk, I had seen him very drunk, but I had never seen him when his eyes were such intense bright marbles. But his mind was dull and uncomprehending.

"Here."

He reached over and took a small packet out of the pocket of his jacket and teased out a brown sliver from a cube the size of a sugar lump.

I turned away from him.

Drugs. Whatever it was I didn't want to know. I heard small noises that could have been anything and when I turned around he was lying back, a small pipe in his hands, smoke rising from the bowl as he exhaled.

"That's real good stuff." He said approvingly.

"What is it? Where did you get it?"

He took another long draw from the pipe and handed it towards me.

"No!" I turned away. I didn't know how to react or what to do.

"You must have done this sometime." I shook my head "You're a big girl. Try some." I shook my head again. "Please yourself bitch."

After a few moments I turned around. He was masturbating as he smoked, bringing himself to a climax in a very short time, giggling absurdly as he watched the small fountain of ejaculate. He stared at me as he handled himself, defying me to object.

157

"Relax, we're not in England now. We can do what we like."

He had obviously been doing exactly that since I had left the room an hour or more earlier.

I went into the bathroom, locked the door and tried to forget what my husband was doing. I decided to try to forget he was my husband.

When, after half an hour I went back into the room he was lying asleep on the enormous bed. I pulled the covers over him with something approaching disgust and sat at the table by the window looking out at the teeming world wondering what on earth I had done and why on earth I had done it.

I was interrupted by the room bell which was followed immediately by the noise of the servants bringing in the tea table with great ceremony. I acted the part of the aloof and distant memsahib as Jonathan woke up and spoke briefly in words I could hardly hear let alone understand. I said nothing to him, there was nothing I wanted to say, as I poured the tea, buttered the scones and ignored the pile of tiny triangular cucumber sandwiches.

"We must talk."

I couldn't disagree and he seemed more in control of himself than he had been an hour or so earlier.

"I haven't been entirely honest with you."

I gave him what I hoped was a withering look of sarcastic disbelief.

"There is a lot you don't know …"

He paused as if waiting for me to say something but I stayed staring out from the window seat over the harbour. It was late in the afternoon and the sea front was crowded, but then I supposed it was crowded throughout the day and the night.

"You're over-reacting Susannah, everyone does drugs, everyone. I really didn't think I'd have to tell you that. How do you think we work so hard, such long hours, and still stay out half the night taking you girls to dinner and the theatre?"

"I didn't know."

"Well you should have done." He answered me in a parody of my own voice. "Why is it such a big deal?"

"It's illegal." Even to me it sounded feeble.

"Have you never done anything illegal? Oh come off it woman, relax. Once you've had some you'll feel better."

"No! I don't want any! I'm not having any! Go away!"

He had rolled a cigarette and put it between his lips to light it and walked over to me, grabbing my arm and trying to force the joint into my mouth.

"No!" I tried to speak without opening my mouth. I kept my lips pursed together and I realised how idiotic I must have looked and sounded.

"You will take a drag Susie. You will." He knew I hated being called Susie. He only did it to annoy me.

With my mouth and eyes tight shut and my arms flailing like a windmill to keep him away from me I heard crockery crashing to the floor.

"Do you know how stupid you look?"

I hadn't realised he was standing a few feet away. I started to cry. I was tired and I was disappointed. I was so angry with myself for having been taken in by his charm.

"You really are a naïve little bitch."

Apart from Susie, the one word I hated to be called was bitch.

I picked up the first thing I could lay my hands on, a heavy glass ashtray, and threw it with all the force I could in his direction.

It hit him on his arm. He made no effort to catch it and it clattered against the wall, falling to the ground without shattering.

"You are very, very stupid." He spoke slowly and deliberately as if what he said was a matter of fact.

I charged across the room and tried to hit him with clenched fists. I really wanted to hurt him for having made such a fool of me.

My fist connected with the side of his face just as his hand slapped out at me. I obviously hadn't hurt him as much as he had hurt me and it was in no way a fair contest.

Nothing that had ever happened in my life prepared me for what followed. None of the dreadful times with Joe, nor the experimental affairs I had while in Sussex, prepared me for what Jonathan did to me in the next few minutes. It was obvious that he felt nothing for me. He couldn't have inflicted the pain in such a cold-blooded and methodical way if he had cared at all. When he had finished humiliating me he dressed slowly and left, not even bothering to close the door behind him.

I ran a bath and lay in it, watching the colours of my skin change as the bruises began to show. Was there anything that he had said or done in the past six months that would have warned me? I could think of nothing. He had been charming and generous, polite and attentive. He had made love carefully and considerately. He was right. I was a naïve fool.

Eventually I pulled myself out of the bath and walked, rather shakily, to the mirror. I stood with my head bowed, staring at the black

159

and white floor before plucking up the courage to look up and into the mirror.

Now I knew I would be spending my honeymoon in this suite, venturing outside only with a scarf to cover my face.

I soaked the thick white cotton flannel in cold water and winced as I gingerly pressed it onto my face. What had I done to deserve this? This should have been the happiest day, the first day of my married life. Instead I felt as I had so many times before in my life; defeated, a failure, lost and lonely.

I thought of picking up the phone and calling … who? I had failed with Joe, I had failed with Carl. I couldn't fail again. I had to put up with it. I just had to.

Somehow.

That evening Jonathan and I were served room service. I stayed in the bathroom as the meal was delivered and Jonathan requested the bearers leave us alone. I'm sure he made some ribald comment as I heard the tone of his voice and the bearers' stifled laughter.

We ate in silence.

What was there for either of us to say?

As we were finishing the meal the room bell rang.

I got up, preparing to go into the bathroom, assuming it was the bearers come to clear away our meal.

"Oh no Susie, you must stay and meet my guest. He has come specially to see you. I am sure you will be delighted to see him. He is an old friend of yours."

The last time I had seen Ramesh he had been sitting with Linda on the sea wall of Sandhey in September 1976.

"Good evening Susannah. Welcome to my country."

He must have noticed the bruising on my face and neck, and on my arms but he said nothing. "I am so pleased to see you again after what, almost exactly seven years? So much time, so much 'water under the bridge'. I hate that saying, It is so very English with its implication that the water is moving, that it is fresh and new, that every moment brings something different. In my country water under the bridge would be stagnant, foul and stinking."

"Hello Ramesh." I didn't want to say any more.

"Jonathan, my good friend, your memsahib isn't very impressed is she?" Did you appreciate my wedding gift to you?"

"I did, but my wife didn't. She disapproves."

Very deliberately he took something out of his pocket and went over to the table by the window.

"Something you may not have had before, Jonny. Very good. Very special."

Soon the air was filled with a sweet sickly smoke and they were talking quickly in a language I did not understand.

"Why?" I asked a simple question. They both turned towards me. They seemed to have forgotten I was there.

While I had been watching them I had been thinking.

That I had not put two and two together annoyed me almost as much as everything else that had happened to me in the past few weeks.

Why had Jonathan called Linda's firm to do his work? Certainly she was in the phone directory, but nowhere near the top of the list. He must have known who he was calling.

I began to think of some of the things I had told Jonathan in those early weeks. I had not been discreet. Why would I be? I could not possibly have known he knew the people I had talked about and was passing all the secrets I shared with him straight back to Ramesh. How he must have loved hearing of the pain he was causing.

I was looking at Ramesh. I was looking into the clear brown eyes that Linda had once loved. There was so much cold dislike in them.

"Why have you gone to so much trouble?" I repeated my question.

"Shall I tell her now?" He asked Jonathan.

"Why not? I suspect any hopes of a long and happy union have already been dashed." They laughed together, as if recognising a shared joke.

Ramesh sat down, crossing his legs precisely and dusting an imaginary speck of dust from his neatly pressed chinos.

"My father was dead before I was born and my mother lived with his family as is our custom. We do not abandon family members as you do. She was lucky we were not so traditional a family as to require her to go *sati*. My uncle returned with tales of how he had been cheated, how he had been rich but had been cheated by the man he called *voh aadmee* 'that man'. '*Voh aadmee*' was responsible for so much. My family deserved a prosperity that 'that man' had stolen from us."

"But he didn't earn anything! He stole it!" I couldn't believe Ramesh had such a simplistic view of his family.

But he continued, ignoring me. "My uncle's wealth had been taken from him, he returned with nothing. We had all expected better. My aunts told me it was my job to go to England and find *voh aadmee* and repay him

161

for what he had done to our family. So that is what I have done. I found David McKennah and I found the people he cared for. One by one I have done my best to ruin your lives. I think I have done quite well. Your cousin Graham as a very willing tool, he and that fascist friend of his. Your friend Linda was gullible and forward. You were easy to flatter, so easy to fool, so trusting and malleable. Carl's work hasn't been going so well has it? Such a shame. Your beautiful homosexual brother and his wife no longer have any trust or love between them. Your children … Yes I think I have done quite well and I will go on as long as your family gains from what it stole from my uncle."

"You are being ridiculous, none of us gained from your family."

He again ignored my interruption and I realised that he had other motives as he spoke animatedly and with such arrogance.

"When I first met Linda she was demure and yet ambitious, she wanted to make a success of business, she did not seem interested in anything else. The women I had been introduced to with a view to marriage had all been simpering and shy. Linda had a mind of her own and I found that attractive. But you argued with the men as if you were our equals, you talked loudly and you swore. I watched you all that summer and I learned to hate you. I don't mean dislike. I mean hate. I was determined that you would all learn what it was like to have to work for people's good opinion. You showed your bodies to anyone. Only whores, the girls of the cages, do that to catch the attention of a man. You were no better. You were older and had been married, you were a mother, yet you ignored your children, you threw yourself at a man who was as close as a brother. You should have had more respect for yourself. And the beautiful Holly. She had been abused, she was unhappy, she should have known to keep herself to herself, but she didn't. She had sex with your brother while she was still married to another man. And then she married him but continued to have sex with me, many times, even in her own bed, sometimes minutes before her husband would take her too. She would still be moist from me and he flattered himself that he thought he was arousing her!"

He paused, provocatively uncrossing his legs and sitting with them splayed apart, his erection clear for anyone who cared to look. I didn't rise to his bait, waiting silently for him to continue.

"You all need to be taught a lesson. All through that summer I listened to you and your friends. I was acceptable because I knew about cricket! Have you any idea how humiliating that is? You never had to apologise for your whiteness, for the colour of your skin. You never had

162

to try to be something that you weren't because you were already what other people aspired to. You were all confident in your ability to do exactly as you chose. You were all shameless, decadent, disgusting. You had so much confidence in your god-given right to be where you were in society. You were all so smug and self-satisfied. None of you realised what it was like for others to fight for the right to be considered equal. You did not know what it was like to have to be perfect in order to be average. I had to be so clever, so polite, so perfect in every way just to be accepted. You would never have to do that."

Ramesh sat back in his chair, silent, pleased with himself, still aroused. Jonathan was not listening, he had lost interest some time before and sat smoking in a world of his own.

Since some response seemed necessary and I was not going to rise to this invective I spoke quietly and simply. "Why did you want to hurt us so much?"

"Because my family has had to start from nothing when we should have had wealth and it was your grandfather's fault. He stole my birthright. He, and his family, must be made to pay."

"What good will that do?"

"Haven't I just told you? Don't you understand?"

"What you have said is all a load of sanctimonious bullshit."

"I think I've been very successful." Ramesh's voice had changed. It was charming, ingratiating, almost apologetic. "Not one of you is happy."

I must have given him the impression I was defeated, that he had shocked and distressed me into silent acceptance because Ramesh then went too far. Whether it was the drugs and his feeling of superiority that made him feel invincible, or his belief that I knew far less than I did, he began to give away more information than he should have done.

"I went to see Graham Tyler before he died." That was how he had got hold of the drugs in prison. It seemed so very long ago that Carl had read me the report from his Sunday newspaper but it was only 18 months. "He gave me this."

When I looked at the contents of the envelope I knew Graham would not have given that to anyone willingly. Perhaps it had been the price he paid for the drugs that would kill him.

There were several sheets of paper, closely written with names David McKennah, Elizabeth Moreton, Maximilian Fischer. I recognised most of them. There were dates and a number of addresses. I was surprised to see the address of our flat in London, but the writing was older and obviously written years before I had moved in with Jonathan.

I looked across at my husband. He was asleep. I looked back at the papers in my hand. I knew Ramesh would take it back from me, he was taunting me with knowledge he suspected I would want, so I tried to memorise as much as I could whilst unconvincingly feigning a lack of interest.

"Why did you go to see Graham?"

"I was curious. You were all too interested in your love affairs to see what was in front of you. Holly had been married to Graham. She was divorcing him. He was an inconvenience and he was removed. I wondered at the power of someone who could do that. I asked questions and got answers, perhaps no one thought I was important enough to have the truth hidden from me. Graham had been blackmailing the great Max Fischer and I knew why. The other person in the plot was Holly's fascist father, another man who was conveniently disposed of."

"He died in a car crash. He was drunk!"

"Convenient wasn't it? Graham was on to something. He knew much, much more than he told me at the time."

"You met him?"

"Oh yes. We spent quite a lot of time together. But you wouldn't have known, you were all so involved in your own little romances and Graham and I were invisible, unimportant because of our class and colour."

I knew that wasn't fair but couldn't think of anything to say that wouldn't sound like self-justification and I didn't see why I should explain myself to this man.

"I wouldn't have thought you were obvious friends."

As we talked I was trying to commit as much of the contents of those tantalising sheets of paper as I could to my, thankfully good, memory. Did Ramesh think I knew nothing of his uncle or was he testing me?

"We had a lot in common."

I suspected that was a hatred of Max. Graham must have felt himself very lucky to meet up with Ramesh to help him with his plans. He wouldn't have known he was out of his depth and that Ramesh was a great deal more clever and his desire for revenge went a great deal deeper.

"Mine I think." Ramesh held his hand out for the papers I was still holding. "Don't be silly and think you can keep them."

Every day of the two weeks that was supposed to have been my honeymoon was spent with Ramesh. He showed us round the city, he took us on drives into the mountains and kept us company on the yachts he arranged to sail us across the harbour to the islands with the caves. We never mentioned the documents he had briefly shown me, he never mentioned Max or his uncle, he didn't offer to introduce us to his family or take us to his home or beach hut. It seemed that he didn't want to let me out of his sight. It was almost that he didn't trust what I might get up to if left alone for an hour.

I framed questions in my mind as he drove with us to the Juhu Airport for our flight home 'You never mention your uncle' or 'What a shame we haven't had the opportunity to meet your uncle?'.

I never did ask him and wondered what he would have done if I had.

In the few hours on the plane returning to England Jonathan and I reached an agreement. I wouldn't leave him, I would act the dutiful wife and support him in his career as he, and his colleagues, expected me to. We would live together in his flat but I would have my own room. He wouldn't bother me and I would ask no questions about his life. In return he would allow me to live my life as I wanted.

The previous January I had needed a job that allowed me time to do my research, I had had no knowledge of where to start finding Vijay and no means of paying for anything. Now, in late September, I had a man to pay the bills and knew who and where Vijay was. I just didn't know how to approach him, and what to approach him with. I sat back in the comfort of the first class seat thinking that, whatever it had cost, I had achieved some of the things David has asked of me.

It was as I looked out over the seemingly endless mountainous deserts of Pakistan, Afghanistan and Iran that I thought of my situation in another way. We were vulnerable now in a way we never had been when David had been alive. David had ensured that Max had some reason to protect Charles and I and our families. Whatever Vijay or Ramesh had planned in the past we had had an umbrella of security around us. Since David had died Max had no reason, nor perhaps any inclination, to honour his commitment. Since David had died the bad luck in our family had accelerated.

Why hadn't Ramesh done anything about his marriage in the three years since he had left Linda? Why had he chosen this year to ruin her? Why had Ramesh involved Jonathan this year to wreck any chances I may have had of happiness. Maureen had certainly changed in her attitude towards me.

Ramesh had succeeded in disrupting Linda's life, and mine, but was disruption going to be enough for him? He would wreak his revenge through our humiliation, he would ensure we ended with nothing, neither money, nor social standing, nor self-respect. One by one he would pick us off. For so many years I had thought that there was no threat to our family.

I had thought David was over-dramatic and had not realised that the world had moved on.

I had been wrong.

My interest in David and Max's past was no longer academic. I had to find more about them and about Vijay. I had, somehow, to find a way to get him off our family's back. And I had to do it all without Jonathan having an idea because everything I did, everywhere I went, would be reported back.

Linda had done this journey in despair at the knowledge that her marriage had been annulled. I would have given anything to have been in the same position. I believed I had grounds for divorce already, if not annulment.

But, again, I had nowhere to go.

If only I hadn't forfeited my friendship with Maureen and with Ted. But I had.

I had run away from them once too often.

Chapter Twenty-Two

"Are you ready for this?" Ted asked Linda as he helped her into the car and she took one last look at the house that had been her home in one of the better roads of Sevenoaks.

Linda nodded. She couldn't bring herself to speak without showing how upset she really was; her marriage, her work, the life as she knew it, were all ending. "Somehow I feel like someone in a Victorian novel, you know the poor family member heading off for life as a governess."

"Anyone less like a governess would be difficult to imagine." Ted joked, but added more seriously when he realised she meant it "You are helping Charles far more than he is helping you. You could go anywhere, do anything. With your skills and experience you could move to London, get a job, enjoy yourself."

"Still, I'll be looking after Susannah's children, the 'surrogate mother'."

"Charles is desperate, Linda. He's had them for over six months and he's at his wits end. He is so grateful to you. Don't think it is an unequal relationship at all. He won't be your boss, he won't be employing you."

"But he'll pay for all my living expenses, he'll probably give me pocket money, I'll be living in his house. I've got nothing."

"You'll be saving his life! He really is at the end of his tether. He changed when Holly left him, he was happy with her, he loved her very much."

"You're talking in the past tense."

"She hurt him. Badly. Its changed him. They had been through a lot together and he believed they had enough love to see them through but it seemed he did and she didn't."

"What had they been through? I thought they were fine, money, each other, a lovely house?"

"They couldn't have children."

Linda didn't have any understanding of what that could mean.

"Why would that be a problem?"

"Holly had a real need. You must realise that. She was desperate. Perhaps it was because she had lost her parents. You've always had loving parents, loving brothers. Have you ever felt alone, really alone?

Have you ever felt that there seems no reason to live if you can't pass something of yourself on to another generation?"

Linda had no answer. She had always had her parents. She hadn't been as close to them since she had gone to live in the south, but she had known they would always be there to help her. If she had ever asked. Crispin and Oliver would have killed Ram if they had known what he had done to their little sister. They would love her and look after her. If she asked them. She realised that what Ted said was true. She had never felt alone. She had never felt, even now, that she had to dig herself out of a problem because she was the only person who could. She had never had a problem that was *her* fault, *her* problem to solve.

"Whose fault was it? Their not having a baby I mean."

It was a question Ted had wondered himself and to which he had never achieved a satisfactory answer.

"I don't know."

"You must have *some* idea?"

"Probably hers. After what Graham did to her. That's my guess. So she felt very guilty that she couldn't give Charles the son he probably never let her forget he wanted."

"Still lots of couples never have children, they seem to manage."

"But Holly couldn't manage. She wanted a baby so much she stole one."

"What!"

"She stole a baby, she wanted one so much she imagined it was hers."

"How long for?"

"A few hours."

"What happened?" Linda was amazed. It seemed such a helpless thing to do. No one could steal a baby and get away with it for long.

"She was outside a shop, she just wheeled it away in a pram."

"But they caught her?"

"A few hours later. Charles found her on the promenade, acting in every way as if the child were hers. I think she almost believed she could keep it."

"I never heard anything, there wasn't anything in the papers was there? There usually is."

"It was all kept quiet, the mother was compensated..."

"Max. Max sorted it didn't he?"

"Yes. How did you guess?"

"Max could sort anything. He sorted Graham. He's probably sorted a lot of things I've never heard about. He's such a secretive man, I bet he could sort absolutely anything."

Ted didn't have anything to say to Linda on the topic and drove in silence for a few miles until Linda's curiosity got the better of her and she continued to ask questions about Charles and Holly.

"They seemed happy at their wedding."

"So they should do! If you can't be happy on your wedding day when can you? They were happy for a while, but sometimes it seemed they were living on a knife-edge. The simplest of things would send Holly into fits of depression and sometimes her behaviour was very odd. She gave up working because she thought it would improve her chances of becoming pregnant and she resented Charles for continuing to work. She … she saw other men, probably from quite early in her marriage. I think she was very unhappy. The deaths of her parents and her disaster with Graham must have affected her far more deeply than any of us ever imagined. Ramesh spent a lot of time with her…"

"Ram?"

"Yes, he came up north very regularly. There was gossip in the town of seeing him and Holly together."

"I should have known shouldn't I?"

"I only know his visits unsettled Holly and she and Charles would always argue when he left."

"So Holly and Ramesh had an affair? Though it wouldn't have been an affair would it? Since we weren't married." Linda couldn't help sounding bitter. "Perhaps she wanted a baby so much it wouldn't have mattered to her who the father was. Perhaps she wanted the baby for herself, not for Charles at all."

"That's very harsh."

"But it would explain why she left him. She knew as soon as they had a brood of a family Charles wouldn't try so hard, wouldn't mind so much and it would never happen for her. She never wanted *Charles's* child, she just wanted her own baby."

After a period, when Ted seemed to be concentrating hard on his driving but was really wondering how Linda could be so perceptive, he admitted. "You know Linda, on all counts you are probably absolutely right."

Linda thought about those early days when they had bought Charles out of the business and she had worked so hard to keep it going. She couldn't remember if Ramesh had ever said anything about Holly or Charles, or visiting them. She realised she probably wouldn't have noticed if he was having an affair because she was working so many hours and thinking of nothing but the business. How much else hadn't she seen when she had been concentrating on her work? What life would she have lived if she had never had her own business, never spent so much of her energy, practically all of her energy, worrying about work, clients, cash flow, staff, VAT, paying tax, getting everything perfect all the time? What things had happened to her family and the people who had been her friends while she had been worrying about making the tiniest mistake? It had only been a few years but she had done nothing but work all that time. She and Ramesh had never had a holiday together, he had always spent several weeks in Mumbai with his family each summer but she had stayed looking after the office. She hadn't made any friends in the town; the only people she knew were her employees or her clients. She had lost touch with all the good friends she had had, including Holly,

And she hadn't even made a success of the business.

She caught her breath, stifling a sob of self pity.

"Are you OK?" Ted asked, looking sideways at his passenger as she turned away from him and stared out of the window.

Ted thought it best to give Linda some silence so he turned back to concentrate on the road, remembering other times he had made this journey through the Midlands. He always avoided the motorways if he had the time so that he could remember past journeys, when there hadn't been so much traffic, when he hadn't known what he wanted to do with his life.

It was only 13 years since he had driven Alicia back home to the Wirral that last time. He had driven this route, avoiding main roads and large towns, to show Alicia the English countryside for the last time. They had both known she would never do a journey like this again. He had been 50 years old, the best and most useful years of his life behind him.

It had been Alicia's dying so young that had made him realise that if he didn't do something there would be no footprint of his on the planet when he died. He understood Holly's need more than she, or anyone, could possibly imagine. He knew he was too old to marry and have children. Even if he found someone to marry they would be too old for motherhood. So he knew he had to live through others, help them, make them remember him with fondness. He didn't believe in life after death, he wasn't religious in any traditional way. He believed that the only life after death there could possibly be would be in people's thoughts. If he could do something good for people, something they would remember him by, then that would be the best he could expect.

This rather passive view of life came to an end four years after Alicia had died.

He had fallen in love. Again.

He had loved Alicia since the earliest days when she had appeared in his office in Liverpool, heavily pregnant, in the manipulative control of her husband. He had felt sorry for her and then he had loved her. He had tried to do his best by her the few times they met after she had finally left her family, but he hadn't always done well. It was only when she was dying and had nowhere else to go and no-one else to help her that she had fallen back on him and had called him 'friend'.

When she died he had been bereft. But not as bereft as he had thought he should have been. The funeral had been a trial, but perhaps for the wrong reasons. 'If,' he had told himself 'I really loved Alicia, shouldn't I be feeling more?' He had expected physical pain, but had felt none. Instead he had been fascinated by the manoeuvrings of Max, Maureen and David as they acted out the myth that they did not know each other. When life returned to normal he had expected time to fall heavily around him without Alicia, but it didn't. He began to understand what he had actually felt for Alicia was not love in any physical sense, he didn't imagine making love with her, lying with her in his arms, synchronising his breathing with hers through the night.

He reserved those thoughts for someone else.

It had been a surprise when he realised he was lying in bed before sleep came imagining someone else in his bed, imagining what they would be doing together. He had pushed the thoughts away as being totally inappropriate. But however hard he tried, the thoughts had not gone away.

And he had stood back from them while Alicia's children grew up, fell in love, made mistakes and were hurt. To have become involved would have been too painful.

"Are they divorced?" Linda's voice jolted him back to the present. It took him a few moments to realise that he must have driven for some miles without being aware of anything other than the thoughts in his head.

"In process though it's very complicated I think."

"You think? Aren't you dealing with it?"

"No. Charles wanted someone else. He said I was too good a friend to know all the murky details but I think it was because there was more to it than he ever wanted me to know."

"Is she in Canada?"

"No. She came back when her grandparents died and left her millions. She left Toronto as soon as she could. I don't think she ever came to terms with who her father was and what he had done."

"Who was he?"

Ted realised he had said too much. "Just not who she thought he was."

But Linda's interest wasn't Matthew Ecclestone, it was Holly. "Where is she now?"

"Oxford." then he quickly corrected himself "At least I think so. She travels a lot."

"Crispin never said."

"He wouldn't. He still loves her just as he did years ago."

"That's sad."

"It is always sad when people love each other and haven't quite realised it."

"You sound like that comes from the heart."

"I have loved."

"I'm sure you have Ted, you're a very nice man, didn't she love you as well?"

"They. I don't think either of them loved me, love me. Not in that way."

"That's sad."

"Yes. Now let's change the subject."

"How are the children?" It seemed the sensible thing to ask though Ted wasn't entirely sure what she meant. He didn't think she was asking after their health, he realised she was asking how they were as people, and he did his best to give her a sensible answer.

"Josie's great. She tries to look after the others, keep them under control. I think she's always been the only discipline in their lives, the only continuity."

"How old is she now?"

"17, a very grown up 17. Sometimes she seems like she's about 30."

"What about Al and Jack?"

"They need to be part of a family. They need a strong and loving adult hand. Josie does her best but she is, after all, only their sister."

"They must be 15 or 16?"

"Not quite. Jack's 14, 15 in August, and it's Al's 14th birthday on Tuesday."

"They're pretty close to each other."

"Yes. Al was premature but still there were the two within a year."

"Why?"

"That's a long story. Susannah didn't choose that. She didn't want any of them, that's the shame of it. She got sucked into it and Joe was what today I would happily call a complete shit, but it was a different world then."

"How about Bill?"

"Bill's still in the hospital."

"But it's been months since the accident."

"Just over a year."

"Will he ever come out?"

"Oh yes. He could have been at home last month but they thought it best to keep him in when things were, how should I put it, a little unsettled. He can't walk and probably never will, but he's mobile in his chair. He's very good in it actually, he wants to play sport in it. I can't see that somehow, but if anyone can it will be Bill. He's a bright boy, quick, clever, and surprisingly completely without any self pity."

"You like him."

"He's a lovely boy, you'll like him too."

"Do you want to bring him home now I'm there?"

"Yes. There's no point in denying it, I hope you will be able to bring the children back together. I think you will be the making of them all. You will take responsibility from Josie and let her have her childhood back, if only for a couple of years. You'll have to work with the boys, they are not far from being delinquents but I suppose they are not beyond redemption and they'll love to have Bill back. You see, Linda, you have a lot to do."

"And I'm the one to do it?"

"Yes. And..."

"Charles?"

"Yes, Charles has had a dreadful time, you might be able to help him, make him enjoy life again."

"Alicia was one of the people you loved wasn't she? That's why you want her children to be happy."

Ted didn't answer.

"I'll take that as a 'yes' then, but who's the other one, the other one you have loved?"

He didn't answer that question either and much of the rest of the journey was spent in an almost comfortable silence

"Here we are."

Ted drew up outside the house that was to be her home. Somehow she had expected it to be like Sandhey, prominent and grand. It was a perfectly normal large detached, fairly modern, house in a row of other large detached, perfectly normal houses. It wasn't what she had expected, though if anyone had asked her what she had been expecting she probably couldn't have told them.

Charles answered the door and opened his arms to give her a hug.

"Hello saviour!"

She hugged him back, unable to say anything but grateful for the obvious warmth and genuineness of his welcome.

"Here, leave your cases," he had glanced at the overloaded rear of Ted's car, "let me show you the house. I think there's a room that you'll like but we're all rather crowded so there's not much choice. If we have to move we'll have to move, we'll have to talk about it when you've had a chance to settle. I thought there'd be so much space but I hadn't realised how much room four youngsters take up."

As Charles talked Linda looked around her.

"The children have pretty much taken over haven't they?"

"Josie and I do what we can but it's a losing battle I'm afraid."

"When will they be in?"

"God knows! I don't seem to see much of them. They come home to sleep but..."

"Charles! They're 14 and you don't know where they are?"

"They're down on the promenade in West Kirby most of the time. People who see them let me know. They're not getting into much trouble, well not serious trouble. They hang around with a crowd of other kids and I know one or two of the fathers. They're perfectly respectable families for the most part."

"For the most part?" Linda quoted back at him.

"Well the ones I know of anyway. The world has changed, people mix more than they did when we were young."

"I'm not saying they shouldn't *mix* Charles, just you ought to keep a good eye on who it is they're mixing with. I'm sure it'll be the same here as in Sevenoaks, there are bad sorts around, alcohol, drugs, that sort of thing."

"I'm sure all they get up to is kicking a ball around on the beach."

"I'm sure they get up to a hell of a lot more than that!"

"Oh." Charles was so obviously out of his depth in looking after Susannah's children and Linda began to realise the scale of what he, and now she, had taken on.

"Where's Josie?"

"She's gone to the cinema."

"On her own?"

"No. She has made one or two friends, I don't think there's a special boyfriend but she goes out quite a bit at the weekends."

"Have you met any of them?"

Charles was beginning to realise that he hadn't known anything about how to look after children. It had never occurred to him to encourage her to bring any of her friends home. "I didn't think to suggest it."

For the past six months, since he had driven into the empty drive of the empty house with his fractious passengers, he had realised how badly prepared he was for what he had taken on.

His childhood had given him no clue to what parenting should be. His mother had left when he was young but he and his sister had been brought up by a succession of nannies even when she had lived at home. His father had had nothing to do with their upbringing. The children themselves had never had a father figure until those few years living with Carl and Charles couldn't believe he had known much about being a father either.

"Where do I put these?"

Ted appeared with several bags and cases.

"In here, if the room's OK with you Linda?"

Linda walked into a smallish bedroom, sparsely if adequately furnished, and went straight to the window. She looked out at the view across the back garden to the distant Welsh hills.

Although she replied 'Fine. Thanks' she wondered where she was going to stash the contents of the bags and cases she had hurriedly packed. Charles must have read her thoughts, or he must have noticed the slight hint of panic in the way she glanced around the room, because he was smiling as he walked to the door in the wall near the window and opened it "Here's your bathroom and..." he walked into the room so Linda followed, "and through this door is another room, you could use it as a sitting room or move the bed in if you prefer it."

"This house is like Dr Who's tardis." Linda smiled, "It doesn't look much from the outside but it's gigantic inside!"

Charles smiled back at her, an open almost childlike smile, that Ted realised was the first he had seen from Charles for some time.

"Look you two must be tired after the drive, let me fix you something. Spag bog be OK? I've got some serviceable wine and then you can tackle unpacking in the morning.

"I'll leave you two to it." Ted thought it best to let them get to know each other again. "I'll pop over in the morning. I was going down to see Bill tomorrow anyway, shall we all go? We could take two cars." When he saw the agreement in Charles and Linda's faces he continued "I'll get here at 10, make sure the tribe is ready."

"I will." Linda had already taken charge.

Chapter Twenty-Three

They took longer over their spaghetti than either of them had expected.

Instead of his usual rushed meal Charles found himself lingering over the wine and twiddling the remaining strands of pasta round the tines of his fork. Conversation had been easy, their old friendship returning unforced. He had told Linda everything about his break up with Holly, some of which Ted had told her but a lot he hadn't. He knew about her affairs, he had accepted them and would never have thrown her out because of them. Linda nodded and commiserated in the right moments, making Charles remember how much he had always liked her. Then she had told him about her life since they had parted company and she found it easy to tell him the thoughts she had only just formulated in the car on the journey up. How afraid she was that she had wasted the last years of her life by working so hard, when she should have been keeping in touch with friends and family. Charles encouraged her, told her not to blame herself for anything, she had plenty of time to make contact with everyone now.

She had always liked the feelings of security Charles seemed to give those around him. She couldn't understand what Holly's problem had been.

They were still talking around the table when they heard the key in the door and Josie's voice 'Hello! I'm back!"

"Hi Josie." Linda said brightly.

"Oh Linda, Hello." It was almost as if she had forgotten Linda was coming to live with them but she remembered her manners and politely asked if she had had a good journey.

In the short time since Linda had accepted her new role she had wondered how she was going to approach being surrogate step-mother to Susannah's children and had already decided on her tactics. She was going to treat them exactly as she had those people who had worked for her over the years of the business. She would never talk down to them, they would be her equals as long as there were no decisions to be taken, at which point she would be the boss and democracy wouldn't come into it. She might, if necessary, share some of the decisions with Charles before the children knew there was a choice.

"Hello Josie, nice to see you again. I had a good trip thank you. How was the film?"

Josie picked up a glass from the draining board and sat down at the table, reaching over to the wine bottle. She noticed Linda's look and said, rather defensively, "I am nearly 18 you know. I am allowed to drink."

"I didn't say you weren't. It's just that..."

"You can't just come and live here and tell me what to do! It's not fair. I'm an adult now and you can't tell me what I can and can't do."

"Josie." Charles said in a warning tone, trying to intercede in what he thought was going to be a dangerous argument as boundaries between Josie and Linda were being established.

"Josie, all I was going to say was ..."

"I know what you were going to say, you were going to say I shouldn't be drinking wine 'at my age' well I'm old enough and it's my choice anyway."

"So you say, Josie, but there's one thing no one can do."

"What's that?" Josie was still defiant, though sensing somehow that she was on weak ground.

"No one can drink from an empty bottle. I was going to suggest you got another from the rack, this one's finished." And she smiled, not condescending, not as an adult would to a child, but the smile of someone who was making friends. Josie smiled ruefully, "Sorry. I didn't mean to go all stroppy."

"Friends?"

"Friends."

Charles's smile was one of relief.

The three sat round the table talking about what Josie wanted to do when she left school at the end of the year. Charles realised that whenever he spoke to Josie it was always about the boys, he had never asked her what she wanted to do, how she was getting on, whether she needed any help keeping up with all the work that would be required for her exams. It hadn't even occurred to him before he heard Linda talking that Josie had moved schools in her most important exam year.

"I moved schools for my final year too." Linda told Josie how her parents had moved house and she had had to start at a new school in the final year before her A-levels. "I met up with ..." she was about to say how she had met Holly and made friends with her and how they had worked for those exams together. Perhaps talking about Holly wasn't the most tactful thing to do but Charles had picked up on the overriding honesty of the evening.

"Holly." He finished for her. "Linda and Holly met up and were the greatest of friends for a while."

"We went to university together."

"I'm not going to university."

"Why not?"

"I want to go to work properly, learn on the job."

"You want to go into the law. Ted told me."

"Yes. I really want to stand up in court and persuade people of the truth by argument."

"You want to be an actress!"

"Same thing, but better paid."

"How are you going to do that without a degree?"

Josie didn't answer. She couldn't. She couldn't explain that she didn't want to do what her mother had done. She wanted to work, experience the world, be a good lawyer because she has seen something of life before she committed herself to a possibly rarefied life in her chosen profession. Her grandfather had been a lawyer, Ted had told her. Ted was a lawyer. She wanted to help people like Ted did, but she was going to be able to do it better because she will have done other things first. She just said 'I'll do other things first'.

"You'll find everything easier with good exams though. Are you going to do well?"

"Yes."

"In everything?"

"Yes."

"Then we won't worry about you unless you ask us to." Linda said, continuing quickly "The person we should worry about is Bill. We must get him home. Paper? Biro? Tell me what we need to do to the house to get Bill home."

The list included ramps, a bedroom downstairs (or a lift), changing the heights of the door handles, removing various doors and they were just tackling the need to buy a van or larger car that could take the wheelchair when they heard Al and Jack at the door. It was well past midnight.

They were expecting to find the house dark and quiet and had wandered into the kitchen without seeing the lights were on until it was too late. They looked guiltily at each other expecting an argument.

The strange woman looked up towards them as if it were perfectly natural for them to come in at midnight.

"What haven't we thought of?"

Jack took the lead, as he always did. "Dunno whatcha talking about."

Linda ignored the slurred words and the wilful rudeness.

"We're making a list of all the things we need to do to the house before Bill can come home."

"But he's sick."

"Not so sick that he can't be home."

"What have you got so far?" Jack asked in a more normal, less argumentative tone and Linda handed over the pad.

"Can you make us all some coffee Al? Please?"

Unused to being asked to do anything Al did as Linda had suggested.

Half an hour later Charles sat back and watched the miracle Linda had wrought. As Jack and Al were discussing how they would build the ramps and make all the adjustments that they had listed, Josie was noting down the materials they mentioned. Every few minutes Linda asked Charles a question about whether something was possible or not. Time wasn't important. The fact that they should all have been in bed hours ago, that the boys should have been told off for coming in so late, that Linda hadn't even started to unpack and must be exhausted all threaded their way through his mind but looking at the group he realised, for the first time since they had come to live with him, they seemed almost to be a family.

"They don't want you to come home until Social Services have checked everything back at the house, and they won't let it be a weekend anyway." Charles explained to Bill as soon as all they were all settled in the inhospitable room that was the only one available for visitors. "There wouldn't be any back up if anything goes wrong'."

"What's going to go wrong?" Bill asked "I've done everything they've asked me to, they know I'm not going to get any better until I have the next op and that can't be for another year or more. They don't want me in here all that time."

"They've got to come and check where you'll be living, whether we're OK to look after you. All that stuff." Jack joined in.

"They're coming at the end of next week and once they realise we won't be locking you in a cupboard."

"Or starving you to death because you're so useless..."

"They'll say you can come home."

"It's not quite like that. They have to check that there's nothing dangerous in the house and that it's as suitable for a wheelchair as we can get it." Ted injected a serious note into the conversation.

"I think we all knew that." Jack said with the pitying voice he reserved for all adults who did not understand their sense of humour.

"Of course you did." Ted acknowledged. "It's just that I didn't want the nurses to hear what we really had planned for him." The dangerous moment passed as the boys giggled. 'Sometimes' Linda thought 'they seem so grown up and at others they are really very young children after all. I'll have to be careful.'

"I don't mind what you do as long as I'm out of this place." Bill's supposedly light-hearted comment was tinged with a bitterness that Linda was not alone in recognising.

"It'll take a while to sort everything out." Linda was business-like and Bill liked that. He was fed up with people skirting round the problems that would arise from having a boy in a wheelchair at home.

"And I'll need ramps if there are any steps."

"We know! We've made a list." Al sounded pleased with himself as he took the pieces of paper out of his pocket and read them out.

When he had finished Linda asked Bill if there was anything they had forgotten.

"I don't know." He answered, "I don't know what the house is like." Linda only then realised that Bill had never seen the house that was to be his home. "Haven't they shown you any photos?"

She turned to Al "Haven't you brought any photos to show Bill? No? Well you should have done."

"Josie..."

"It's not up to Josie to do everything. You're perfectly able to think of these things yourself."

It was probably the first time anyone had expected Al to be responsible for anything in all his 14 years.

Al and Jack then explained to their young brother what they had planned to do to make life easier for him once he was home and Charles and Ted sat back as the four youngsters chatted around diagrams on Linda's notepad.

"Is it home?" Charles heard Bill ask at one point. "Yeah." Jack had replied, "Yeah, it's all right." On hearing this exchange Charles had glanced across at Linda who had moved away to talk to one of the nurses. She caught his eye and smiled at him and then at the boys and back at him. He realised she still had the talent he had noticed when they had worked together of holding one conversation but being aware of everything else that was going on in her immediate vicinity.

When she came back to sit with them she had a sheet of paper the nurse had given her. "We've just got to make sure all these things are taken care of."

They worked through their list and the one the nurse had given Linda and smiled with satisfaction when they realised they had covered everything.

"We're bloody brilliant." Al shouted in triumph. Jack nudged him in the ribs and they both looked to Linda to see if he was going to be in trouble for swearing but it was Bill who warned his brothers. "They don't like shouting in the hospital, it upsets people." And the moment passed when Linda's control might have been questioned.

When the bell for the end of the visiting hour rang they left Bill saying they would be back next week to pick him up.

"Can't wait." Bill said as Linda gave him a hug.

"Neither can we." Jack spoke for them all.

Linda had driven down with Ted and Josie. Linda, sitting in the back, had listened to the easy conversation between the young woman and the older man. She was again struck by how much younger Ted seemed. 'Perhaps it's me getting older' she thought 'but he doesn't really seem old enough to be my dad any more.' The radio was playing pop music, not the talks and discussions she would have expected. Ted seemed to be a bit of a chameleon, adjusting his manner to suit whoever he was talking to whilst managing to be relaxed and easy with everyone. She used the opportunity to learn more about Josie.

She listened to a serious young woman who was well spoken, polite and with a dry sense of humour, who teased and allowed herself to be teased in an easy going way. It was obvious that the two knew each other well and liked each other. Apart from relationships between parents and their children she had never seen a friendship between the generations at close hand before. They talked easily, as equals. She realised that that was why the friendship worked, it was that, friendship, not an adult who knew better and a youngster who knew nothing. She took the lesson to heart and wondered, briefly, whether that was exactly what Ted had expected of her when he had suggested she travel with Josie in his car and had deliberately settled her in the back. She thought perhaps Ted had also had something in mind when he had insisted she drive the boys home in Charles's car. 'I need to talk to Charles so he's got to come with me' he had said as if it was the most natural arrangement.

She knew she now had two hours in which the relationship between Al, Jack and herself would be settled; what she said or did would define their future relationships however well they appeared to have started.

She fiddled with the keys as she watched the boys walking several yards ahead of her through the car park. They were very close in age and were so alike that some people thought them to be twins. 'Heaven help anyone who tries to play one off against the other' she thought, they were an inseparable team. And now they, together, would look after Bill. She knew, also, that her first test would be immediate. They would argue about who was to sit with her in the front, pretend to fight about it. She could almost hear them talking about it as they walked towards the car.

"Right now, both of you in the back." She said firmly as she unlocked the driver's door. "And I'll tell you why. I've never driven this

181

car before, I have no idea how it works and where all the knobs and switches are so what I don't want is some eager beaver pointing things out to me as I go. If I can't find something or I switch the windscreen wipers on instead of the indicators I don't want any helpful fingers doing the right thing. So in the back. Both of you. Now."

She could hear what they said, as long as the radio wasn't on too loud, and they had to listen carefully to hear what she was saying to them. She congratulated herself on a small success.

She let them laugh at her for not finding reverse to get out of the parking spot and let them hear her berate Charles for not backing in to make it easier for her. She was careful not to swear, though she felt like it. She asked them directions, though she was pretty sure she knew the way.

When Jack asked, rather tentatively, if she could tune the radio to get the football results she agreed and listened to their 'oohs' and 'aahs' as the results came through.

"What team do you support?" she asked when the programme had finished. And the rest of the journey was spent as they told her, with great enthusiasm, that there really was only one team and she listened as they talked, seemingly quite knowledgeably, about its progress through the year. They didn't seem to notice when she stalled the car as she drove through the centre of Chester, if they did they didn't say anything, and they didn't laugh when, for the third time, she set off the windscreen wipers instead of the indicator. All in all, she thought as she drove into the drive and parked alongside Ted's car, the journey could have been a lot worse.

The next few days were a whirlwind of activity. She drove the boys down to the local D-I-Y store to buy all the items that they had listed, and she bought some pot plants as well. She had noticed how empty the house had felt without flowers or greenery. She told Jack and Al to choose the oddest plants they could find and, although they had pretended to be bored by the whole idea, had selected pots with such a variety of colours and sizes she wondered what Charles would say when they took them home. Even if she had to put them all in her own room it was worth it to hear the boys arguing with each other about which was the weirdest.

"Do you want to do anything with your rooms?"

"Could we paint them?" Al asked tentatively. "I've never liked it, it's so yuccy."

"On one condition."

"What's that?"

"You don't paint them black."

"Purple?"

"Two conditions."

Tins of red and white paint were piled into the trolley.

"Won't Uncle Charles mind?" Al spoke tentatively though Linda wasn't sure whether he really cared.

"He won't have to." Jack was the stronger of the two, but still caught Linda's eye to check whether he was going too far.

"I'm sure he won't as long as you only paint your own rooms and don't make too much of a mess and clear up after yourselves and don't..."

"OK OK We get it." The signals that Linda had sent to Jack, passed on to Al were accepted. As long as they were sensible they could, within reason, do as they wanted.

Linda organised who was going to do what in the days leading up to the visit from Social Services and Bill's return and the schedule she wrote out and pinned to the kitchen wall was going to be difficult to follow. Everyone would have to pull their weight and the fall back position of bringing in a local handy man would have been considered an admission of failure by everyone.

When they got home and were talking about what they had planned Charles remembered a book that Holly had given him and which he had never thought to open, a book on D-I-Y detailing with diagrams and pictures even the most basic of techniques. He couldn't remember why Holly had given it to him, after what argument and in what circumstances, but he was glad she had as they pored over the step by step instructions. He exerted his authority by insisting Linda and the boys stick to the instructions and follow them religiously to learn the best practices and not get into bad habits. Josie took over the kitchen and fed them the continuous stream of tea and coffee that she said was the essential part of being an English workman. Whenever they found they didn't have the right tools Linda went off with either Jack or Al to buy them.

"It's amazing what five people can do in a week when they set their minds to it." Charles sat at the head of the kitchen table with Jack and Al on one side and Josie and Linda on the other. "Well done everyone." The woman from the Social Services had just left and had shaken Charles's hand rather too firmly for his comfort, saying it all looked satisfactory. She could see no reason not to recommend that their young son could come back home.

"How can anyone with that amount of power get it so wrong?" Linda asked anyone who cared to answer. "She had no idea what she was talking about, she probably didn't even have the right notes. 'your son' indeed!"

"All that matters is that the room was OK..."

"More than OK it looks brilliant!" Al was really pleased with finishing touches he had put to what had been a very boring dining room, and was now a riot of red and white.

"...and the house didn't have any booby traps at wheelchair height..."

"and all the ramps and handles were all in place." Charles finished his sentence firmly.

"Does that mean we can bring Bill back tomorrow?"

"That's what she said."

So the family was to be complete again.

"You've worked a minor miracle Linda." Charles said as he settled down to the familiar drive. "I can hardly recognise the boys. They didn't moan and argue with each other and everyone else. And I didn't hear them swear much either."

"They just needed someone to trust them, give them responsibility, not treat them like delinquents." Noticing the hurt look on Charles's face she hurried on "I'm not saying you did."

"No. You're right, I probably acted like I was expecting them to be a problem."

"And Josie always treated them like the little brothers they were."

"But are no longer."

"Let's hope they keep up with this new attitude, it's only been a week and they had a project that interested them."

"It kept them away from that crowd they've been running with. I think they're a bit younger than the others and I'm sure they get up to all kinds of things they shouldn't. There's two I've heard of that we need to worry about, Pod and Brickie. I've heard Jack and Al talking about them in tones of great respect but I shouldn't think there's anything respectable about them at all."

"Have you ever met any of them? Ever talked to them? Found out what they're really like?"

"No. They've never been near the house. They all hang out down the prom or around the bandstand, it's where the town louts have always congregated."

"That's not what you said the other day."

"I didn't want to worry you."

"We're going to have to wean them away."

"We can't let them take Bill down there."

"Don't worry. I'll think of something. We can't let the miracle fail can we?"

It was Bill himself who gave them the answer. As he wheeled himself along the long corridor of the hospital for the last time for at least a year he began to speed up, pushing his hands down fiercely on the rims around the wheels, propelling himself ever faster along the corridor. Just as Linda and Charles thought he would be through the doors and into the road he turned sharply around and headed back towards them.

"I want to do sport." He said with such determination. "I'm not just going to sit and do embroidery or woodwork, if I'm stuck in this thing I'm going to enjoy it. Jack and Al will help me won't they?"

"We all will."

"Bill Parry, athlete."

"It'll be hard."

"But it'll be worth it."

Josie helped her youngest brother write letters to Stoke Mandeville Hospital to see what he could do. She found them very helpful and was amazed at the amount of work being done to make life in a wheelchair much more than just basket-weaving.

"Are we talking about a team game?" Bill was asked by the sympathetic woman on the other end of the phone and they had established what disability group he qualified for.

"I hadn't thought of it as 'qualifying'."

"Well are you an amputee?" Bill was amazed at how down to earth people could be.

"No. I've got both legs it's just that they don't work." He decided to take the same realistic approach.

"Are you visually impaired?"

"No. I've got bloody good eyesight," he said, possibly too aggressively though the woman at the end of the phone didn't seem to mind, "and there's nothing wrong with my hearing either." He added pointedly, aware of a shuffling behind the door as Al and Jack jostled to hear what was going on.

"Have you cerebral palsy?"

"No, I'm just wheelchair bound because I ran out in front of a car and it hit me, broke both my legs and my back, severed bits of my spinal cord that are necessary for control of my legs and that's it."

"Wheelchair then. That gives you a lot of choice. Do you like team games or are you an individual player."

"Individual I think."

"Well there's archery, power-lifting, shooting, table tennis, bowls..."

"I like the idea of archery."

"There's a target for you as well. Sorry, no pun intended, but there is something good to aim at." Bill heard her giggling in the background.

"Very funny but what do you mean?"

"The 1984 Paralympic Games might be a bit soon if you're just taking it up but there's always 1988 in Seoul."

"Wow, that would be something!"

"It's always a good thing to have a target, if it turns out to be a bit high or you don't like it, there'll always be something else."

The next weekend Linda drove Josie and Bill down to Buckinghamshire.

"I loved it." He spoke enthusiastically as they reported the events of their day away to Charles.

"Will it be OK? I mean everything will be terribly expensive. It'll be an awful lot of money to buy good equipment and to get good training."

"Of course." Charles wore a smug smile. "I'd be delighted but you've got to be sure. You'll have to join a club and do it properly."

"I will."

"Can we do it too?" Jack spoke for his elder brother.

Charles made a show of looking doubtful.

"Honestly. We'll do it seriously." Al joined in.

"Bill says we're too weak, his arms are strong because of the wheelchair but we'd train."

"And the best thing is that we would all compete against each other."

"And we could set up the target thing in the garden and practice every day."

"It means we can all do it together."

Charles was smiling broadly, as was Linda. "Well that's good because I've arranged for us all to go to Thornton Hough next Wednesday to see the club there, Neston Bowmen they're called and you'll get all the training and help you need."

Charles was amazed when Bill manoeuvred his chair close to his chair and reached up to hug him. "Thanks. I mean it. Really. Thanks."

Chapter Twenty-Four

"Max has been burgled."

"I wondered who it was on the phone." Linda had her back to Charles and couldn't see the look on his face. "You were a long time. Was it bad?"

"Pretty bad. Apparently Monika heard something and went downstairs to investigate and they hit out at her. She's OK but badly shaken."

"Should I go round? Is there anything I can do?" Linda spoke as she wiped her hands on the dishcloth and went to turn around. She was shocked at the vehemence of Charles's tone.

"No. Absolutely not."

"Why not? What's happened?"

In the five months since Linda had returned to the Wirral and had taken over the reins of the Donaldson household she and Charles had been regular, if infrequent, visitors to Sandhey. She didn't quite know what to make of the middle aged lady who lived with Max. Monika had always been friendly towards her when they had all spent time at Sandhey in 1975 and 1976 when she and Charles were working together to build up their business but her attitude was very different now. 'She thinks Holly left you because of me' she had suggested to Charles as they left after a particularly frosty tea. He had argued Monika must have known there were months between Holly's going to Canada and her arrival but once the idea had been planted in his mind he thought she was probably right. If Monika thought they were living together as man and wife, which she obviously did, that would explain her attitude and the distance she put between them.

Charles had always been close to Monika, he had once believed that he loved her and would look after her all his life, but he had met Holly and realised what love should be. As he had courted Holly he had noticed similarities between her and Monika. There was a possibility they were related. In one of his more perceptive moments he understood that her anger at no longer having Holly close would have turned Monika against him. He understood, also, that she would be poisoning Max's mind against them as his greetings were now rarely friendly. He was just beginning to realise how much had changed when Holly left him.

"What's happened?" Linda repeated unable to even hazard a guess why Charles should look so angry.

"Max thinks it was the boys."

"What!"

"Max accused Jack and Al of being involved in the robbery."

"But why? What could possibly make him think something like that?"

"Monika said she heard one of the robbers talking, he called one of the others 'Pod'. She is prepared to say our boys were with him."

"Oh dear."

"Not 'Oh dear' at all. Even if one of the little bastards was Pod and another was Brickie why would that mean Jack and Al were involved? They haven't hung around with them at for months now. Why would they be involved now?"

"They couldn't be."

"Of course not." Charles was absolute in his confidence.

"But Max thinks they are?"

"Yes. Monika said they were and so he was very sure. He was very rude."

"What on earth did you say?"

"I told him he was wrong. Quite strongly actually. I told him he was a prejudiced suspicious old man who didn't know what he was talking about."

"Oh dear."

"Actually I said a lot more. He was being so unfair. He hasn't bothered to understand how they've taken responsibility for Bill and how much time they spend with him. He just hasn't bothered to get to know them. As far as he's concerned they're Parry scum. That's what he called them 'Parry scum'. I could hear Monika in the background saying I should never have taken them on, if I'd not taken them on Holly would still be … well she'd still be here. I was so angry with both of them. I probably said a lot of things I shouldn't." Charles finished rather lamely.

"You were right to defend them." Linda put her arm on Charles's shoulder to comfort him. "Did he say what was taken?"

"Not really, not in much detail, pictures, books. Nothing of real value he said."

"I didn't think Max has anything 'of no real value' in the house."

"I didn't believe him either."

"Anyway they don't seem the things an opportunist thief would take, especially lads, surely they'd take the television and things they could easily sell? Why would they take pictures?"

"I wondered that too. There's a lot more to it than just a couple of youngsters trying to make a few quid for nothing."

"Did you say that to Max as well."

"I did, but he was adamant. He kept repeating that Jack and Al had to be involved. He's calling in the police. He still has a lot of influence with them." Charles wasn't going to worry Linda by telling her how much influence he knew Max had, not only with the police, but with less visible powers behind normal law and order enforcement.

"How did you leave it?"

"Not very well I'm afraid. He reminded me of certain obligations I had towards him and he said I must hand them back to their family and the police will deal with them."

"But they had nothing to do with it! Hasn't he *any* sense of justice? He'd condemn them without even checking the facts?" Linda was incredulous and angrily defensive of the children. "I'm going round. I've got to tell him he's wrong. He's being *so* unfair, *so* ... Oh I can't find the words. *Surely* he must understand you can't condemn people without any evidence, no trial, no opportunity to prove their innocence?"

"I don't think that would be a good idea. He included you in the exodus. You were to go away and leave me in peace so Holly will return and we will all be together again. Monika has influenced him about many things, the children, you, me, us all. She hates us therefore now so does Max."

"The man is senile."

"I pretty much told him that too."

Max had been unambiguous. Charles must return the children to their proper family. He must send Linda packing. He must affect a reconciliation with Holly. Only then would he be accepted back into the family. Charles was to make a choice between loyalty to Max, his friend and protector for many years, the man who had supplied him with the funds to establish himself and enjoy his life the way he had wanted to, or loyalty to Linda and the children.

Charles had found the decision surprisingly easy.

"Isn't there anything we can do? We've got to just sit here waiting for the police to call and take the boys away?"

"Police? What's going on?" Bill had wheeled himself into the kitchen.

Linda and Charles looked at each other and Linda pursed her lips, shrugging, trying to say that they must be open and not try to hide anything. So Charles told him the bare bones. Although he trusted his belief in Al and Jack some words of corroboration from Bill might remove any worries he might have had. "Someone has had their house broken into and they think Jack and Al are involved somehow."

"That's ridiculous."

"That's what I said."

"When did this happen?"

"Late last night."

"Well it couldn't have been them. We were all here weren't we? Playing space invaders."

"It might have been some friends of theirs."

"Who?"

"Pod."

"Oh him. They haven't seen him for ages, nor Brickie. We don't have time to hang around them any more. We decided ages ago that we didn't much like them. Al said he was afraid of them and once they tried to push me over. There was a bit of a ruck and we haven't seen them since."

"When was that?"

"Ages ago. May. June. Early in the summer anyway."

"And you haven't seen them since?"

"No. Wouldn't want to. Who did they rob anyway?"

"Sandhey. Max and Monika."

"That figures." Bill knew from the expressions on their faces that neither Charles nor Linda was prepared for his answer.

"Go on." Charles spoke firmly.

Bill had spoken without thinking. Now he would have to explain that he had been wondering about why the smartly dressed man had spent so much time with the gang, and what he had really been after.

"Just after I came home we saw Pod and Brickie around, we saw them in the street when we were going to the gym. It was good because then they just didn't think that I was there and could hear them. They never looked me in the eye and just talked above my head, probably believing that I couldn't see and was deaf and dumb as well." There was such unfamiliar bitterness in his voice that made Linda think it wasn't only Pod and Brickie who had acted like that. "Anyway I wasn't deaf and I wasn't blind though I could play dumb when it suited me." Linda and Charles looked at each other wondering what else he saw and heard. "There was this funny bloke who turned up now and again. He seemed too old and too well off to have anything to do with them. He wasn't fuzz, I mean police, he wasn't anything like that. He was coloured, you know Pakistani or something." Linda shuddered and Charles made an involuntary protective movement putting an arm on her shoulders. "He gave them money sometimes, said he'd tell them when he was ready to make them earn it. I reckoned it was drugs and they were getting stuff for him but I soon realised it was the other way round. He was giving them money *and* drugs. He wanted them for something."

"Why are you telling us this now?"

"I saw him. The man. The Paki or whatever he is. He was here yesterday."

Linda shuddered. "Apart from being coloured was there anything else about him?" she asked very deliberately. "Was his hair long or short? What was he wearing? Did he speak well or with a heavy accent? Did you ever hear his name?" She knew who it was, so did Charles, but they needed confirmation to extinguish any hope that they might have been mistaken.

"He was quite tall, but shorter than Charles. He spoke well, you wouldn't have known he wasn't English. He was well dressed, jeans but they were smart ..."

"And pressed with a clear crease down the front." Linda finished for him.

"Yes. How did you know?"

"I just know."

Charles looked down at Linda who had gone very pale. "Bill, can you leave us for a few minutes? Don't tell your brothers for the moment. Don't worry, we'll tell them everything later. No secrets. We promise."

Bill skilfully turned his chair and left the room, closing the door behind him.

"Do you think he'll tell Al and Jack?" Linda tried to put off the moment she would have to accept that the man who had been her husband had been so close, had possibly spied on her, had watched her and was doing his best to destroy any happiness she had achieved.

"Of course he will. But it doesn't matter." Charles understood her reluctance to face up to the inevitable but knew the name had to be spoken. "I wonder what Ramesh is up to?"

"Why can't he leave me alone?" Linda was close to tears, the pain of humiliation surfacing. It had probably not been buried too deeply.

"Forgive me but I don't think it is you he's after. He's undoubtedly behind the robbery and he will have told them exactly what to take and they will have given him what they stole. His interest in the family goes far beyond you, I'm afraid."

"So he has some pictures and books. So what? Why?"

"He actually has probably got a lot more. Pod and Brickie got into Max's safe, they didn't break in, they didn't force the lock, they knew the combination. Max said I was the only other person to know it and they must have heard it from me. They didn't steal anything, they put a piece of paper inside which contained a message Max really did not want to get."

"A note?"

"He didn't say what it was, or who it was from. He just said it proved someone he hoped was dead was not."

"But why has Ramesh gone to such lengths to do that?"

"I haven't a clue, but I bet we'll find out one day."

In the years that followed Charles thought many times about the last time he saw Max, every time he tried to explain to himself where it had all gone so wrong.

They had been friends for years. Max had made Charles his heir, had always treated him as his son. Whatever it was he wanted to do with his life, whether it was writing and broadcasting about birds or setting up a business with Linda or marrying Holly, Max had always encouraged him. Their friendship had been tested at times, Max had secrets he wanted to disclose to no one and gradually Charles had learned some of them. Every time he had learned something there had been a temporary cooling in their friendship but, until the week after the robbery, their relationship had always been strong enough to survive.

There had been no knock on the door, the police had not come to arrest the boys or even question them, but equally Charles hadn't made any move to break up his home. Ten days after the robbery, during which time Linda's nerve had been stretched to breaking point, Charles had driven to Sandhey determined to convince Max of Al and Jack's innocence. He had to tell Max how Ramesh was involved and find out if Max could tell him why.

Monika was silent as she had let Charles into the house, she didn't welcome him with a smile and a kiss on both cheeks as she always had, even in recent months. She had nodded towards Max's study and Charles had taken that as an instruction.

They were never anything other than polite but it became increasingly obvious to Charles that Max was to be persuaded of nothing. Charles was a married man. Holly might return. Linda had to go, as did the children. Holly must be given the opportunity to return. It was insufferable to him and to Monika that Charles's obduracy had led to their loss of Holly. Max's anger was quiet and Charles knew it was genuinely felt but couldn't help wondering at the extent to which Monika had influenced Max's thinking.

Charles had stood up when it seemed the conversation could not go any further. He had proffered his hand in a final gesture of mutual respect but Max had ignored it. "There will be many things you will regret in your life Charles. I'm very afraid that this conversation will be one of the worst mistakes you will ever make."

Charles always remembered the words as Max never made idle

threats. People who crossed him or harmed people he loved had been imprisoned on what Charles knew were false charges, had died in what Charles knew had not been accidents or had simply disappeared.

"In choosing that scum and that woman over your responsibilities and your history you have turned your back on me so I turn my back on you." And he did.

As Charles drove out of the gates of Sandhey, turning left to take the long straight road that ran alongside the golf course Charles was aware that this was the last time he would make this journey as long as Max lived. He would have to leave the town where he had lived all his life. His house would be sold, he would repay Max the money he had given him on his 21st birthday.

Max had made him choose, and he had made his decision.

"What about the bowmen?"

"There'll be other clubs, other groups to join."

"But we've all been getting on so well, and we've got so many friends there."

"You'll make other friends. And you'll probably meet up with them at competitions anyway."

The thought of leaving when they had been making such good progress had worried both Charles and Linda. They explained something of the reasons, leaving the children in no doubt that there was no choice. Once they realised the move was going to happen they all joined enthusiastically in the discussions about where they would go.

"Somewhere nice..."

"With a choice of cinemas, I'm fed up with only having one flea pit."

"The house has got to have a large garden, we've got to be able to set up the bosses and backstop netting."

"We've got to work out where the house is going to be first."

"This is impossible. We could go anywhere."

"It's always more difficult to make a decision when there's absolutely no restriction."

"Well let's start listing things we want and things we don't." Ever the organiser, Linda firmly drew a line down the middle of a sheet of paper. "Right. Seaside? OK. No. we've done that and we want something completely different. Countryside or Town? OK. Town in the middle of countryside, or city? OK. Not city. North or South? OK. South."

It was Josie who achieved some focus in the discussion. "I'm going to be working in London. If you were within commuting distance

I could live at home and that would be cheaper."

"Great that's 40 miles from London, near a railway station."

"House prices will be cheap there then." Charles could just be heard to mutter. He was not used to thinking about money and the knowledge that he would have to borrow to move to a house large enough for everyone in the most expensive area in the country did not make him comfortable.

Living with Holly, he had never even thought that the income from his investments wouldn't be enough to support them. The house was bought and paid for and their needs hadn't been great. But things had changed since he had the children and there had been months when his expenditure was greater than his income. He wanted to pay Max back, at least something of what he had been given. He didn't like the prospect of having to spend more of his capital in buying a new house, reducing his income at the same time as his expenditure was likely to go through the roof. For the first time in his life, there was a need to think about, if not yet worry about, money. He was very conscious that the high interest rates that had caused Linda so many problems had been good for him.

His depressing turn of thoughts was interrupted by Linda.

"I know exactly where we should go." She blurted out, surprising herself with the certainty. "We should go back to Kent."

Charles looked at her as if to ask how she could want to do that so she continued rapidly "No problem. Look, I'm going to have to do something, bring in some money, and there I know people who will help me do that. I know which are the best areas and which wouldn't be good at all. It would be an awful risk to go somewhere completely new where we didn't know anything. If we all moved to Kent we'd have a head start."

"It makes sense in a funny sort of way." Charles sounded doubtful.

"Look, Ramesh is thousands of miles away."

"Except when he's here."

"Exactly. It doesn't matter where I am does it?"

And so, on the day that Susannah and Jonathan Smith returned from their honeymoon in India, it was decided that her brother's disparate family would move south.

Charles never saw Max again.

Chapter Twenty-Five

"Susannah where the bloody hell are you?"

Jonathan was home.

"In here."

I was sitting at my desk working at the Personal Computer that had been my Christmas present to myself. In the two weeks since Jonathan had returned to work after the long Christmas and New Year break, I had been transferring all the information I had accumulated over the previous years from my old fashioned word processor to my new machine. It had taken two weeks but I had everything I had learned in a well labelled series of files in documents and spreadsheets in carefully organised directories. In the year since the wedding I had re-focussed on David, Max and Vijay and as 1985 began I was busy planning the next stage of my investigations. I would have plenty of time now as the Christmas round of socialising was over and I would not be required to be Jonathan's 'wife' for some time.

"I've got news for you." Jonathan was slurring his words.

"Yes?" I probably sounded as irritated as I felt at being interrupted. "Anything I might be remotely interested in?"

"Probably."

"Terrific."

"In fact, darling girl, it might be the best news I have ever given you." Jonathan's sarcastic use of endearments always annoyed me.

"When have you ever given me good news?"

"I've been fired."

"Now that *is* good news."

"No notice. No nothing. Just no job!" He laughed and I realised he was drunk, or stoned, or both.

I wasn't going to ask what happened, I would wait for him to tell me in his own good time. He would eventually tell me if he wanted to and it only made him happier if I asked, so I waited for him to explain.

"Pissed. I was pissed. I told the fuckers what they could do with their fucking job. They said I wasn't going to make Partner. They couldn't even wait 'til fucking September. They said I was 'unreliable' so I told

195

them where they could stick their fucking job. I went to the pub and went back and told them what they could fucking do. And they told me to fuck off. Well no, they didn't actually," he giggled inanely "they told me never to darken their door again, 'begone' they said, 'leave, go, disappear, depart!' So I fucked off." And he stumbled against the settee and fell to the floor.

I didn't try to help him. I was thinking what his news meant for me. Our arrangement had only been for as long as he had the prospect of making partner, as long as he needed a wife for respectability. I had played my side of the bargain and had attended all the dinner parties and sporting events, operas and gallery openings that were part of the process of proving that Jonathan was the 'right sort of person' to be offered a partnership. I thought all along it was a lost cause but I went along with it so long as I had a place to live, someone to pay my credit card bills and the time to learn about David, Vijay and Max. Now I could divorce him, I had grounds enough, he would go back to New Zealand and I would be free to take up my own life again.

At times I had let myself imagine what life would have been like if I had stayed with Carl. I wondered where he was, what he was doing, who he was with. What if we ever got together again? I had changed, perhaps I was readier now than I had ever been for a relationship with him. In moments of self-knowledge, perhaps too rare, I realised that he had tried to make a go of it, at least, at first. It was me that had failed, literally miserably, to make his life better. He still appeared, albeit infrequently, on obscure television programmes, his media career seemingly in decline. In the libraries I would look under indexes for 'Carl Witherby' to find that he hadn't published anything recently.

I hadn't heard from the children, Linda or Charles, and there hadn't even been a card from Maureen or from Ted the previous Christmas. I had made a point of writing them bright, optimistic letters, when I had got back from India. I had hoped Ted at least would have seen through the bravado and realised how much I wanted to hear from him. It had only been two years but it seemed forever since we had all been in touch.

I made two mugs of coffee and gave one to Jonathan who had calmed down a bit.

"Here, drink this, we need to talk."

Although he said 'Yes, dear.' I knew he wasn't really hearing anything I said.

"When are you going then?"

He looked mystified. "Going? Whatchamean 'going'?"

"You'll be going back to NZ."

He stood up, as if to go out of the door. "Of course. Gotta go home." When he got to the door, one hand on the handle he turned back "Can't. Can't go home." He looked at me and laughed "Gotta pack first. Can't go home without packing. Pack pack pack pack pack." He stumbled across the corridor and fumbled with his keys to lock his room. He turned round and held the keys out towards me grinning childishly. "Help Jonny?"

I took the keys from him and went into my husband's bedroom for the first time since the day before we were married. It was a very different me who, 16 months earlier, had left to meet his family at the airport, before going directly to the register office. The morning we had arrived back from India he had emptied all my things from the drawers and wardrobes and thrown them out onto the corridor and I had been happy to move into the spare room. The next Saturday a man came round with a tool box to fit a lock on Jonathan's room so that even had I wanted to go in I couldn't.

It was a mess. There were t-shirts socks and underpants on the floor, his work suits were on hangers but not in the cupboard, they were suspended from the curtain rails. I couldn't believe that a man, so fastidious in so many ways, could live in such a way. But then, I reasoned, he had hardly spent any time here.

I went to open the cupboard but Jonathan stumbled to block the door in a melodramatic fashion. "Thou shalt not pass!" and when I turned to go out of the room without argument he moved away asking in his hurt, boyish voice "Don't you want to see?" I knew if I moved towards him he would block the door again and laugh at my optimism so I carried on towards the door. "All my little secrets? Aren't you the teensiest weensiest bit curious?"

"No."

"Well I'm going to show you anyway!" He shouted as if he had won a great victory. "Here!" He had slid the cupboard door open and picked up a carrier bag which he threw vaguely in my direction. "There you are!" It seemed that that effort was all he could make as he collapsed on the floor. "Stupid bitch." He looked up at me and around the room as if he had never seen it before and passed out.

I took the bag and went to my room.

It was full of envelopes. Most were addressed to me but at an address I did not recognise. The various handwritings were familiar, the dates on the postmarks regular throughout the previous months.

Another packet, held together with a blue elastic band, were all the letters I had written and given to him to post.

I put the bag in a holdall along with some clothes. I packed the papers I knew I couldn't do without into my briefcase. I took the disk out of my new computer and poured the remainder of my coffee into the drives. I glanced swiftly around the flat to make sure I had everything that I really needed and left.

I took a taxi to The Savoy. Without a second glance the concierge took my briefcase and holdall and ushered me into the foyer. In jeans and sweatshirt I was not dressed as their usual guests were but the hotel's staff were well trained.

Giving them a credit card I decided that Jonathan was going to have a surprise when he read his next statement, a river suite at the Savoy is not cheap. Nor was the limousine the hotel had arranged which waited patiently that afternoon outside various exclusive shops in Knightsbridge, Bond Street and Piccadilly.

With a roomful of shopping bags I finally sat down in my suite, with a room service meal and bottle of good wine, to read the letters that Jonathan had kept from me.

I didn't recognise the address they had been sent to, I didn't know anyone in Wimbledon. Perhaps one of Jonathan's colleagues had agreed to have my post go to his address, perhaps Jonathan had another flat, another life. God knows he spent enough time away he could have had a mistress or even another wife and children for all I knew. Perhaps I was just the 'work wife'. I thought the best thing was to sort the letters into chronological order as far as I could read the postmarks.

The earliest were from when I had only been with Jonathan for a few weeks. He must have planned from the very beginning to isolate me from my friends and family. He would have been in touch with Ramesh all that time, taking his instructions. That birthday, 1983, I hadn't really expected many cards, especially with the wedding, but I had been upset not to get one from Ted or Maureen. When we had got back from our honeymoon and I had mentioned in passing that there were no birthday cards waiting for me, he had poured some more wine and asked me sarcastically if he wasn't enough for me.

I opened an envelope which had a birthday card in it, signed *With love always,* Maureen. Inserted in the card was a note in Ted's recognisably neat handwriting.

My dear Annie, or are you Susannah again?
This is just a short note to wish you both all the luck in the world.

Don't lose touch, always remember that, whatever you may think, you are very dear to a lot of people.

There were Christmas cards postmarked 1983. I recognised Ted's writing and read another note.

I am so disappointed you haven't been in touch, perhaps life is too hectic.

Write when you get a chance

With my love.

Ted

I had sent them cards. I had written. It was so unfair that they thought I hadn't.

There were others, from Linda and Charles, and scribbled notes from Josie and the boys. They would think I hadn't wanted to keep in touch with them. I hated people thinking badly of me, especially when it wasn't my fault.

All those years with Carl I hadn't replied to letters as I should have done. These, however, were letters I had never had the opportunity to read and would have opened and replied to enthusiastically if I had ever known of their existence.

None of the letters were addressed to 'Susannah Smith', they were all to me as 'Donaldson'.

They could never have been sent wedding invitations. He had been working with Ramesh to isolate me from them all from the very beginning and I had gone along with it.

It seemed very important to talk to someone, to explain that it wasn't my fault that I hadn't been in touch, that they mustn't think badly of me; that I needed them. I picked up the phone and dialled Maureen's number, I didn't even have to look it up.

There was no reply.

I tried Ted's number.

The voice that answered was unfamiliar.

"Ted?"

"I'm afraid not. You must have the wrong number."

I repeated the number I had dialled.

"That's my number. Perhaps you're calling a previous occupant. I've only been here a few months."

"Have you got a forwarding address? A new number?"

"Sorry, no." The man's voice was pleasant, with a noticeable, but not unpleasant, Merseyside accent.

"Sorry to have bothered you."

I tried Maureen's number again. Again no reply.

I tried Ted's office. I knew there would be no one there at this time of night but thought there might be an answering machine. There was no reply. I went to my address book and checked the number. I had remembered it wrongly and with my sense of panic barely in check I dialled again. That number was unobtainable. I tried directory enquiries. 'No, there is no company of that name listed in Liverpool. And no there is no Mr Edward Mottram either.'

It was my fault, but I had cut myself off from these people I had loved and who had loved me and now I couldn't re-connect. I clenched my fists and gave way to tears.

When I began to think again, rather than just feel loneliness and fear, I looked down at the address book in my hand. My thumb was keeping it open in the Ms. *Mottram, McKennah, McNamara*, and *Me*. There was the phone number of the flat and it made me think of Jonathan, passed out on his bedroom floor.

But that had been several hours ago. He would be awake now, aware that I had gone. He would have sobered up and would check my room, he would see that I had taken many of my things. His first instinct wouldn't be regret or pain, it would be to stop the credit cards and tell the bank not to honour any of my cheques. Could he have done it already?

In five minutes I was at a cash machine withdrawing £100. My relief was enormous when it gave me both the money and the card back. I had visited four more machines, gradually increasing the sum requested, before one didn't return my card. I was not unhappy, I had enough cash to see me through a few weeks and it seemed Jonathan had not managed to put a stop on anything. If I checked out early in the morning I should be OK. On my way through the foyer at the hotel I asked the concierge to arrange a first class return rail ticket.

I had to go back to Hoylake.

Chapter Twenty-Six

The following afternoon I was in a taxi being driven from Liverpool Lime Street station through the Mersey tunnel, the streets of Birkenhead, over the sandstone of Bidston Hill and across the Wirral to Hoylake I wondered whether my mother had felt this much of a stranger when she had returned.

I checked in at the hotel and in the fading light of the January day I made the once familiar walk down the long straight road by the golf course towards Sandhey. Instead of turning into the drive I carried on down the slipway and onto the sandstone rocks.

I stood for some minutes looking out over the wet sands towards Hilbre Island, those sands where I should have drowned over 20 years before. There were a few hardy people throwing sticks for golden retrievers in the blustery winds coming off the Irish Sea in late January. It was the same time of year as my mother's funeral. If she had lived she would have been a pensioner now, 65. I found it difficult to picture her, let alone imagine what she would have been like had she lived. She had only just managed 50. She would have been 44 when she had come to my first wedding. The reception was held in the garden behind the wall I was now leaning on. Weddings, funerals and birthday parties, they all seemed to have been held in this garden, such was the control Max had over our family's life.

'*The past is a foreign country; they do things differently there*'. Where did that come from? I stared across the sands, hearing the hauntingly familiar cry of the gulls. What is it about being in a particular place that brings such obscure memories flooding back so clearly?

I rang the doorbell of Sandhey. Looking around me as I waited for the door to be answered I was pulled out of my reflective mood. The windows were badly in need of repair and decoration, the pebbledash was cracked and splitting away from the walls, exposing brickwork. Even the garden, usually so neat in its winter hibernation, seemed unusually neglected and unkempt.

Monika finally answered the door. It was more than eight years since she had stood on this doorstep waving me and the children off as we left with Carl to start our new life. I know I had aged in those years, but where Monika had seemed a young woman when I last saw her she was now an old one. Middle age had passed her by. She would be in her 50s yet she seemed 20 years older, as old as Edith had been when I had last seen her.

Her first words 'we aren't expecting visitors, you should have telephoned' were hardly welcoming but she did eventually move aside to let me in. As I took off my coat I looked around at the hallway I had known so well. I remembered brushing the stair carpet on my hands and knees hoping every minute that Carl would ring. That would have been 1963. Minutes passed and I was still alone in the hall. I walked around the walls, under the stairs, remembering standing with David looking at the Schiele and holding the conversation that had been the beginning of so much for me.

But the picture wasn't there.

I had only a few moments to look around and realise that all the walls were practically bare, all the original paintings now replaced by small, cheaply framed photographs of Max with a variety of famous people before Monika ushered me into the drawing room.

They may exist in the traditionally accepted sense of ethereal beings with lives of their own but my understanding of ghosts is what I saw as I walked into Max's presence.

Standing by the fireplace was the ghost of Charles, looking disapproving, as he had done the evening of our mother's funeral; Maureen stood by the drinks cabinet and Ted was sitting in the chair by the fireplace. There were other figures, Graham, Edith, I could almost see us all in this room still holding the same taut conversations as we had that evening.

For a few fractions of a second we were all here, just as we had been years ago.

"We were not expecting you." Max asked, he was nearly 80 but I was still surprised at how old he looked.

"Sir Max disapproves of surprises."

"*Sir* Max?" I asked remembering my argument with Carl.

"*Sir* Max." Monika replied with emphasis. Max's efforts with giving to charity and political parties must have paid off. I had missed the announcement.

"I'm sorry I didn't know I was coming until yesterday."

I didn't like to add that I thought they might have been pleased to see me, but perhaps it had been thoughtless of me. There was no warmth in their welcome, though Max was impeccably polite. We sat drinking tea, making conversation in a detached way. I looked at the bare bookshelves and the walls empty of the valued pictures of the past.

"You live in London?"

"Yes, I have been living in London." I qualified my answer. Now wasn't the time to explain my changed circumstances. I didn't even know if they knew I had been married. I was saying nothing that was unnecessary, it would only lead to awkward questions. But I saw my opportunity.

"Yes, Uncle Max." I was not going to call him 'Sir'. "I have been living in a flat in Connaught Square."

I didn't imagine the change in his expression, though slight it was detectable. I continued unnaturally cheerily. "It's a lovely old building with many original features such as the cornices and the fireplaces. It's not one of those flats that has been recently developed. I understand the block belonged to the government for many years and they've only just started selling bits off. My room had a lovely view, I could almost see the park."

He understood what I was trying to tell him.

"Look, I have a photograph here…" I rummaged in my bag.

"I don't think so." Max waved his hand dismissively. But he knew I knew.

"I've enjoyed living in London, it's been so easy to go to museums and art galleries, I've grown quite fond of some early 20th Century artists. You had some lovely examples here didn't you? I didn't see them in the hall?" Perhaps I was pushing him too hard.

"They've been put away for safe keeping." Monika answered firmly.

"Have you seen your brother?" Max asked, perhaps trying to change the subject.

"I haven't seen him for years."

"But don't you live close by?"

I thought he must be confused. "I've lived in the south for years now, Max."

"He never writes."

Why would he write? Perhaps they had fallen out. Perhaps Max had finally seen through Charles and their long friendship had finally petered out.

"He was an ungrateful, spiteful boy." I had never known Monika say anything critical of Charles. "You don't want to know where he is, Sir Max. Remember, you don't have anything to do with him. Not since he

203

took up with that woman and those delinquents." She looked at me defiantly as we both knew she was talking about my children.

Max lapsed into the self-pitying memories of the old. "He did change. He was a good, thoughtful, boy. He was no trouble at all and then he changed …" His voice tailed off and, obviously deciding not to share his thoughts and he sat quietly sipping his tea, with Monika fussing about him in case he spilt the hot liquid and burned himself.

"You must go soon." She said without warmth. "Sir Max is getting tired." I had once been her 'little girl' and she my 'nanny'. But that was a long time ago and we hadn't spoken as friends for years. "You will want to be at the station before it gets dark."

Max interrupted her with something of his old authority. "No, Monika, I want to talk to Susannah and I'm well able to speak for myself."

Monika did not like the reprimand and hurried to tidy away the tea tray and the biscuits. In the old days there would always have been sandwiches and small cakes for tea, even when there were no visitors 'just in case anyone pops in.' Times were obviously harder.

"Susannah. Please, follow me."

Max's study had always been out of bounds. I could remember being in the room only twice in my life and this was the first time I had been invited in.

He walked steadily, if slowly, around his desk and sat down, gesturing for me to sit in the armchair by the fireplace. "Well, young, lady, you have been doing some investigating." He chuckled, it was a strange sound and I wondered whether it was going to turn into a cough but he cleared his throat and continued, not expecting me to answer. "I am not surprised, indeed I am delighted that you show an interest in your family. And you are quite correct, I am familiar with Connaught Square."

"Can you answer a question that has been worrying me?"

"I will try, though much of what you want to know is written down in these papers, locked away in this drawer until I die."

"Why?"

"Is that your question? Or are you asking me why I don't want people to read my papers until I am gone. That is easy to answer; because it will hurt."

"You've never worried about hurting people in the past have you?"

"That is both unfair and untrue. I have done everything in my power not to hurt people."

"Where do I begin? The people whose valuables you stole before the war?"

He was unapologetic. "They would have been stolen anyway."

"But you made no effort after the war to return them to their owners."

"They would have been dead."

"You used all that wealth to live a life of luxury. Didn't you feel in the least guilty?"

"I was guilty only of one thing, Susannah, I survived. That is where my guilt lies. I have survived where millions didn't."

"And what about Graham? And Holly's father?"

"What about them?"

"When they became inconvenient you managed to have them removed."

"I have friends in powerful places who were kind enough to help."

"I wouldn't call David a 'friend', would you?"

Max hesitated, perhaps wondering how much I knew and whether I was bluffing. "He is dead. I need not call him anything."

We paused in our sparring and I looked at the empty grate.

"What was your question?" Max asked after a few moments of uncomfortable silence.

"Where has all your money gone?" It was not the question he had been expecting. "Max, it's obvious. The house and garden are falling apart, they need money spending on them, repairs that would have been done automatically have been neglected. The paintings have gone, they're not 'in safe keeping' are they? They've been sold or stolen haven't they? Where has all the money gone because its gone hasn't it?"

"I have enough to live out my life."

"What about Monika?"

"She will be provided for."

"What about the others, they all expect something of your millions."

"Including you Susannah?"

"No. Not including me." He seemed to accept what I said.

"The money was never mine."

"I know." He looked up from the table where he had been doodling on the large sheet of blue blotting paper as I continued. "As long as you looked after David's family." He continued doodling to hide his interest in how much I had found out. "But then you stopped spending it on Alicia's children."

"You had no need of it."

"You didn't give it all to charity, did you? How much of it was stolen? How many of your paintings, you art, your silver, you wine? You used what you could, you used what was available, but the rest was stolen. Who stole it? Do you know? Do you care?"

"It was your delinquent children. They stole it." There was something in the way he half looked up towards me that made me realise he knew that was a lie.

"No they didn't. It was someone else? Someone you knew?" I was persistent.

He was saying nothing. I decided to change tack.

"Did losing all your wealth salve your guilty conscience?"

"I am guilty of nothing. I have done no harm. I have done nothing that hundreds of others have not also done. I have nothing to be guilty about."

"But little to be proud of either."

Max's face broke slowly into an unconvincing smile. "It is amusing." His tone was conversational rather than confrontational but he was not relaxed.

"What is?"

"How like your mother you are. She was an intelligent woman, very beautiful and very talented but she was no good with men. You are argumentative and strong. Men don't like that. Are you married? I see no ring on your finger but there is the mark where one has been. You see I notice these things, just because I am old don't think I can't see. Your mother chose her men unwisely. Arnold was never going to be a good husband to her. Me? I was never going to give her security or standing in society. Ted? Now he would have been good for your mother. He was steadfast and honest but she never looked at him as anything other than a shoulder to lean on. Now you, you wasted so much of your young life on Witherby, then Parry, now this latest man, a weak man and a disaster too? You think you are the strong one, I think so too, so find someone who is even stronger than you, someone who is steady and secure, someone who loves you for who you are not who you think you are. If you are not careful you will be like your mother and not find that special one. You will not find him unless you keep your eyes open. Your mother lived her life with her eyes shut. Make sure you do not do the same."

He was a different man from the one who had been sipping tea under the eagle gaze of Monika. He seemed to be speaking caring words but there was no sympathy in them. He sounded bitter. "Take care or you will miss him. You cannot go through this life without your soul mate."

"That sounds like you feel you have."

I wondered if I had gone too far. He stood up and lit the fire in the grate. He seemed to be settling in to talk for some time.

"Perhaps I have nothing to lose by explaining…"

"Justifying…"

"That, perhaps."

"I was married to a woman I never slept with. I have made love to many women, your mother included, but I have only once been in love."

He went to a small table and poured two glasses of a brown liquid from a decanter. His voice steadier. "You see whoever stole everything from me didn't know what he was looking for. This…" he held the decanter in the air "…is absolutely priceless. It was owned by the Princess Sophie, only daughter of Franz, Archduke of Austria, Prince Imperial of Austria, Prince Royal of Hungary and Bohemia."

"The one who was assassinated in 1914?" I was stunned as Max nodded.

"They took so much but they did not take everything."

As he sat down in the other armchair by the fire that was beginning to give off some heat he handed me a glass.

"I was a young man. I was misguided, my priorities were wrong and I missed the opportunity of a lifetime. It has cost me, believe me, it has cost me very dear."

"Was she in Vienna? Your lady?"

"She was."

"What was her name?"

"Without the whole story, it makes no sense."

Chapter Twenty-Seven

Max Fischer's life was never going to be an easy one.

He was born into a lower middle class family at the beginning of 1906, the second child of elderly parents. His father was a shop keeper. The family, a relatively prosperous one, was well respected in the small town a few miles from Vienna. His sister Ingrid was ten years older than Max and had left home when she married Johannes in 1915. They had been introduced by a mutual friend and although her parents were not satisfied with the marriage, they knew that with the war there would be fewer suitable men and Ingrid seemed happy enough with the prospect of life as a farmer's wife. It wasn't long before she had two young sons to keep her busy as the seasons and the years passed.

Once a year after harvest Ingrid packed two bags and took the boys, Matthieu and August, to spend a week with her family in the city. In 1927 her visit was later than usual as there had been a general strike and violence in Vienna with many protesters and policemen killed. It was thought by many that there would be a revolution and Johannes forbade her to go until the city had quietened down. In previous years her visit had been in July or August but it was late September when she walked with her brother through the parks of the Prater towards the giant Ferris wheel while he told her excitedly of the change in his circumstances. No longer would he be a poverty stricken student living beyond his means, he had found a sponsor.

"It was an accident. I was just walking along the street. Everyone knew there was going to be trouble but we thought it would be concentrated in a few streets, the usual places."

"This would be the 'we' that spends all your time drinking and womanising." Ingrid said disapprovingly, but Max ignored her.

"On that Friday it was dreadful. There had been a trial and the city was alive with rumours, apparently the perpetrators had not been found guilty though everyone who had thought about it knew them to be as guilty as..."

"I don't understand politics."

"There were people on street corners making speeches supporting a general strike, word got around quickly and there were groups of people demonstrating, some were more violent than others, one set fire to the Palace of Justice. It seemed like a revolution. The police came on the streets and started shooting, the demonstrators shot back, people were being killed all over the city. The bar filled with young men with wounds of varying degrees of seriousness but all bringing news, more or less accurate, of what was happening in the city. I left the bar to see what was happening."

"Were you drunk?"

"Of course not. Well, maybe, but no more than was usual."

"You should have gone home. What would have happened to our parents if you had got yourself killed? You were very reckless." Ingrid's made her disapproval obvious.

"People were saying history was being made and I wanted to see it." Max knew he could justify his actions. "So I went out into the streets. I was stopped by a group of thugs who were going to hurt me but I talked my way out of danger, they heard my accent, they realised I wasn't a toff and they let me go."

"But you always speak so well now, you have no accent at all."

"I can revert to the old ways of speaking, Ingrid, I have to be a chameleon, changing my voice for the different people I meet. I can be well-spoken when I have to be but equally, I can be as common as you like if it suits."

"That is dreadful Maxi, you will lose sight of who you really are if you do that."

"Of course I won't. I will always be me."

"You still should have gone home."

"But I didn't, I carried on through the streets towards the Rathaus, I saw more and more groups of thugs. As I passed some university buildings I saw a man in a dark blue coat. He was holding his hat in both hands in front of his chest, as if it would protect him against the screaming and swearing pack that seemed to be baiting him. I thought they were going to kill him, he thought they were going to kill him. I waded in, speaking in my working class accent, saying they were mistaken, this was a good man, a friend to my poor family, they should let him go. I grabbed the man's arm and pulled him after me. I was perhaps too rough but we got away."

"You were very foolish Maxi, you could have been killed twice in a few minutes." Ingrid was torn between horror at her brother's actions and admiration of his bravery and quick thinking.

"I'm sure there was no real threat. They seemed dangerous but most of the people that night were killed by the police."

"Oh no! That's not true!"

"It is. Still we must not discuss politics I know Johannes' views and they are not my own. He will talk to August and Mattieu and fill their heads with that dangerous right wing nonsense."

"I'm sure I don't understand. I am just pleased you weren't harmed. What did you do with the man?"

"I took him into a bar, it wasn't a very clean bar but he bought us both several drinks to help us get over our shock. He said his name was Münz. I explained who I was and that I was studying at the university to be a lawyer but I was worried that I would never make a success of my career as it was always difficult for someone without the right connections, however clever, to get a position in the right kind of firm."

"You should not have been so forward, Max."

"I realised I had been very lucky with the man I had saved."

"Why was that?"

"He asked me questions about myself and my family. 'Did I have any dependents?' 'Did I support my parents?' I said 'No, of course I didn't. I was a young man, my parents, though not rich were well enough off for their needs and wishes'."

"What did he say to that?"

"He was very particular about that. 'A young man setting himself up in life should be unencumbered of women, be they wives or mothers', it seemed very important to him."

"So you told him you were young and free and what did he do?"

"We had had three or four drinks when he delved into his pocket and drew out a card. 'We will meet at my offices at 11 on Monday morning. He said he thought I was an ambitious young man who will work hard and do well."

"So you went to his offices on the Monday at 11?"

"Of course."

"And..."

"There he agreed to support me at the university until I pass all my examinations, another three years. He has been very generous."

"And what must you do in return?"

"I saved his life Ingrid. What more can I do for him?"

When Max saw Ingrid two years later he was less forthcoming about Mr Münz when she asked her brother how his career was progressing.

"Do you see Mr Münz very often?"

"I work in his offices once a month. It's very interesting work."

"Does he ask you to do anything else?"

"He has instructed me to learn English."

"English? What do you need to speak that language for? Is it political?" Even Ingrid in the rural west of the country knew of the changes that were happening in her country. She knew that no one had settled down after the Great War. Even her husband Johannes, who had not read a newspaper for years, now listened regularly to the wireless in the bar in the village. He said it would not be long before there was a war between the socialists and the industrialists. She didn't see how the English would be involved.

"It is a difficult language but interesting."

Max had become an invaluable part of the team that met every weekend at the Münz offices. They spent their time tracking down records, accumulating details of assets, searching for papers, birth, marriage and death certificates, drawing up family trees. Mr Münz wanted to know everything about everyone who was anyone in the city. And the team grew in experience and expertise.

It had taken only a few weeks before Max realised his role on the team. Some of the areas that had to be explored were in the parts of the city where the accents he could adopt would allow him to obtain information that none of the others could hope to gather.

It wasn't that he had saved Mr Münz, it was how he had saved him that had given him his chance.

It took him only a little longer to realise how this work could be turned to his own advantage. He had realised that many of the people they were documenting, indeed most of them, were Jewish. The accent he could so easily adopt was the one of a lower middle class Jewish shopkeeper, the precise accent of his grandfather.

In July 1929 Max's conversations with Ingrid were not of his English lessons or of his weekends working in the Münz offices, it was of his girlfriend.

"But didn't Mr Münz insist on no women, no girlfriends, no encumbrances?"

"She's beautiful but I'm not going to get tied down."

"Make sure you don't. At your age you must simply stay with your friends, in a group."

"Safety in numbers?"

"How did you meet her?"

"She's the daughter of one of the men who work at the weekends. She's very respectable."

"I've no doubt she is." Whenever the question of respectability or class came into the conversation between Ingrid and Max there was always awkwardness. They were both aware of the difference in status between a small-holder's wife in the west of the country and a prosperous shopkeeper in a town not too far from the capital.

"Her father speaks very good English and is helping me speak it well too."

"Well you are 23 years old now, you know what's best for yourself."

"I think so."

"I hope so."

In 1930 Max needed to handle his sister Ingrid very carefully.

"I can't possibly take her."

"You have to Ingrid, I have no other choice."

"You don't have a choice? It seems to me that it is I who have no choice."

"You've always wanted a daughter."

Ingrid's two sons took after their father in too many ways. He had often spoken of her wish that one of her children had been a daughter, a daughter would help her around the house. Johannes had his two sons to help him with the animals and in the fields. She had no one.

"If you don't take her she'll end up in an orphanage."

"So? She is an orphan. Her mother doesn't want her and her father can't look after her."

"Her parents have told me I must take responsibility next week. The baby will be a month old. Any longer with her mother and they say she won't want to give her up. There's no one else but you."

"What does Mr Münz say?"

"Mr Münz has been very kind to me. He's given me a second chance, as long as I get someone to look after the child and I continue to have no responsibilities. He says soon it will be too dangerous to have responsibilities. There will be a war and young men must be free to do what young men in war must do. 'You must only have yourself to worry about' he said."

"He'll always be good to you because you saved his life."

"And I mean to repay him for his kindness to me."

"Johannes will want money. He will want it to be made worth his while."

"I will send money."

"You will *bring* money. With a baby to look after I won't be able to visit the city for a while."

"I'll visit you, I promise. And I will bring your husband money."

"It is agreed then. I will take your daughter back with me.

Ingrid broke the silence that descended between them as they both contemplated something of the future the little girl would have. "What did he mean? About war?"

"He is convinced there'll be a war. Maybe not next year, maybe not for a few years but before too long. You must be prepared to leave

212

the farm at short notice. But there will be a time. I'll get word to you when you have to leave."

"You think it will come to that. Leaving the country? Running away?"

"Of course it will."

Ingrid looked at her brother uncomprehendingly.

He answered her unspoken question in one word "Grandfather."

That was all he had to say to make her remember to be frightened and they were quiet again.

This time it was Max' turn to break the silence, changing the subject back to his daughter. "The child, I didn't mean it to happen."

"Of course you didn't."

"We enjoyed each other's company. We talked about everything, you know, about religion and history, art and music and books. We talked a lot about books."

"Obviously you didn't just talk."

"We loved each other."

"Of course you did."

"Mr Münz has told me never to see her again. I have no more chances. I won't see her I'll always love her and I will never forget her."

"What is her name? You've never told me."

"Monika. Her name is Monika."

Chapter Twenty-Eight

Max poured us another drink from the beautiful decanter.

"You know more about me than anyone alive Susannah, does everything you have learned make you like me more or less?"

It was an odd question.

"It's not a question of 'like'. I want to 'understand'. You have had such an interesting life it would be a shame if the story wasn't told." Perhaps he had told me his story to deflect me from asking about David. I was not going to let him.

"You talk of the time before the war, before you met David and before you became one of his Fishermen."

"You have been doing your homework."

"David told me quite a lot before he died, I have been learning more since."

"Come back tomorrow. I'm tired now"

"I wanted to ask you about Vijay Thakersey?" I pressed him but Max appeared undisturbed at hearing the name. "You know he was behind your burglary don't you?"

"Vijay was behind a lot of things. I am tired. Come back tomorrow." I was dismissed.

Monika was waiting for us in the sitting room. She stood up as if impatient to see me gone.

I aimed an air kiss on either side of Monika's face, making sure no contact was made, and we said goodbye.

She could not know she was Max's daughter.

Walking back up the long straight road towards my hotel I looked across at the lights of the houses on the other side of the golf course. I picked out Millcourt, my home when I was a child and which had been since divided into flats. Ted had lived there for many years. But he had now left it too and I didn't know where he was. I wondered if the new occupant would have an address, perhaps he would give it to me if I asked him in person.

Standing at the door of Millcourt I looked at the array of bells. There was a new name on the label to Ted's old flat but I couldn't read the name on the sodden piece of card. I rang the bell anyway.

I could hardly hear the man's voice which crackled through the door phone so I briefly explained that I used to live in his flat and that I had first lived there when it had been an undivided house. The voice changed, he sounded young and enthusiastic. "Oh I'd love to hear about it then, come on up."

The buzzer went and the door clicked open.

As I was ushered into the living room I remembered my mother, another ghost, sitting in the window seat. I hadn't realised how much it would affect me to see this room again, it had barely changed. In that window seat I had sat listening hour after hour as she had recorded and re-recorded a song and a poem that were played at her funeral so soon afterwards. I could hear her voice *I'll see you again, whenever Spring breaks through again*. She had been sitting in that window seat when I had read my step-mother's death notice to her on the morning she died. Five years later I had been sitting there when Ted had told me so many things I had not known. 'It took far too long,' he once said, 'I should have told you earlier. Truth can be painful and shocking, people run away from it but it catches up with them in the end.' But he did tell me how my parents had lied to me to protect themselves. Perhaps he should have let that truth stay buried.

The young man offered me a cup of tea "or perhaps a glass of wine? It must be very cold out there."

I accepted the wine and watched as he walked across the room. I was not too old to appreciate the looks and body of this young man in his dark blue jeans and grey wool polo-necked sweater.

"I'm sorry, I don't know your name, I couldn't read it on the bell."

He didn't answer immediately, instead establishing who I was. "You're the lady who called for Ted Mottram, yesterday, on the phone? I recognise your voice."

"Yes. That was me."

"I'm Jim, James Parry, just call me Jim."

I barely heard what he was saying, I assumed he was asking me my name and I answered "Susan…" I cut off before the end, wondering briefly if he noticed, I couldn't say Susannah. Just in case.

Parry. He was a Parry. I looked at him again and saw the same nose and blond hair. Parry was not an uncommon name in this part of the world but I realised he was one of *the* Parrys. I knew Joe had brothers but I had barely met them, Joe had made sure we mixed in different circles as he tried to distance himself from the fishermen and casual labourers that made up most of his family. This young man must be the son of one of them, the family resemblance was too striking for him not to be. Yet he seemed respectable enough.

Jim handed me a glass of red wine and indicated for me to sit. I couldn't fault his manners.

He sat opposite me and began the conversation easily, "You said you used to live here?"

So I told him. Little by little I explained how my parents had moved here during the war, how we had left when I was in my early teens, how this room had been part of the nursery suite, how I had spent so much time here with my brother and another boy who I believed was a sort of cousin. Jim listened as I described the house and the garden as it had been then. I tried not to look at him, he was so very like what I would have liked Joe to be.

"And then I came back to live here after it had been divided into flats." I found it easy to tell Jim about those months, I think I probably told him more than I needed to. I had given too many hints about my life and Jim had put them together.

"Your name isn't Susan is it? It's Susannah." He was standing with his back to me, opening another bottle of wine, I couldn't see his face and I didn't know him well enough to interpret the inflexion of his voice. Was he curious, or triumphant?

"Yes. I'm Susannah, Joe was my husband." There was no point in lying.

"I thought you must be. When Gran knew it was a flat in this house I was buying she told me all about you, none of it was very flattering. That was the first I knew that Uncle Joe had been married. It's been fascinating listening to your side of the story."

"Have I told you so much?"

"Enough to know you a bit I think. Would you like to stay for supper?"

All that evening we talked. Jim knew names and would ask who the people were and how they fitted into the family, and it was only a matter of time before he had produced a large sheet of paper and some felt tipped pens and was encouraging me to draw a family tree.

As I drew the complicated network of lines and names I surprised myself by telling Jim details I never thought I could speak freely about. But I didn't put everything on that diagram. There were some things Jim had no right to know.

It was nearly midnight when I realised the time.

"I've got to go, good grief I had no idea it was so late."

"Stay."

It would have been so easy to agree, so easy to stay in the warm and open another bottle of wine. It would have been so easy to be undressed and made love to by this strangely attractive man, because that was what he wanted to do.

But, attractive as he was, I had known him for only a few hours. I was the older by at least fifteen years and for the first three years of his life I had been his aunt. Two years ago these things probably wouldn't have mattered and I would have stayed. But now they did and for the first time in my life I didn't sleep with someone because it wouldn't have been right.

My hotel room was cold, made even colder by the sound of the wind. It was beginning to blow fiercely and I remembered nights spent at Sandhey when such a wind blew. I wondered how many members of the Parry family were members of the lifeboat crew, whether Jim would be getting a message to leave the warmth of his flat and go out onto the sea. I hoped no one was stupid enough to put others at risk by being out in the storm.

The progress I'd made with Max didn't compensate for my sense of loneliness. What good would it be to learn all about Max if my life was still a mess?

Soul searching wasn't something I usually went in for but that night I spent time looking at my life as if it were someone else's. I didn't like what I saw.

For so long I had blamed others for ruining my life. Charles, my mother, my father and Kathleen had all stopped me from being with Carl. No one had stopped me marrying Joe and that had ruined my chances of a career. It was all someone else's fault. But Jonathan, who could I blame him on? Ramesh? Ramesh had only put me in the position to make such a mistake. No one had made me marry him.

Now I was really alone. Ted, Charles, my children had all moved, Max had made that clear, but where to? I went back to the carrier bag of letters and read them all carefully. There was nothing in them to give an address, postmarks were unclear.

It was time to take some responsibility for myself. In a way I was glad Maureen hadn't been in as I would simply have run back to her and, despite everything, she would have welcomed me back and saved me from making any decisions. But I would have loved to have found Ted.

He would have helped me. Just as he always had.

I didn't go back to see Max the next day.

As I sat in the freezing cold dining room drinking a miserable, obviously instant, coffee and looking at the worst egg and bacon I had seen for some time when an apologetic waitress came in with an envelope. Inside were a bundle of papers and a letter.

Susannah,

Perhaps I have to admit to not having been entirely honest with you. On the morning after your mother's funeral I had a long talk with David Redhead.

We had thought to use Carl but for all his success he is not as bright as you and we felt he would have been too condemnatory. That morning we decided you would be the one and we sought to prepare you. It would be necessary to give you the correct background so you could understand why we did what we did so you would not judge us too harshly. Maureen was reminded of her obligations to us. I knew her husband during the war, he was a good chap but died before he could really be of any use to us. Our talk yesterday proved to me that we made the right decision, though it has taken far longer than we had thought. You will use the enclosed papers to help complete your work. We hoped you would find Vijay Thakersey before he had a chance to wreak any havoc on the family but it is too late for that. But it is still necessary for you to find him to convince him that we did not betray him. Another generation will suffer if you don't.

On another, more personal, matter. Your mother would be saddened that you haven't found the man who will make you happy. She despaired of Charles, she had no understanding of him whatsoever, perhaps he was too like his father, perhaps it was because she blamed him for many things, but she worried about you. 'She will cling to the wrong people, she will need men but, like me, she will never find the right one.' Find that 'right man' Susannah. The right man is strong and he is patient. He loves you and he is waiting for you to find him. This man is not Carl Witherby.

Maximilian

Do not judge us too harshly for things we could not know.

"Who brought this?" I had finally managed to attract the attention of the waitress thinking that only a day earlier I had been at the Savoy, my every need anticipated and the breakfast faultless.

"An old man dropped it into reception. I thought he was a tramp he was that dishevelled."

"An old man? Did he say anything?"

"I dunno I didn't talk to him. Do you want me to ask?"

"That would be very helpful." I hoped there wasn't too much sarcasm in my voice.

She came back a few minutes later.

"The man said to give it to the beautiful lady from London. He didn't seem to know your name."

Perhaps now I would know where to start. Perhaps now, finally, if it wasn't too late, I would do what David had wanted me to do.

I did not appreciate Max's comments about my life. It was far more important for me to find a place to live and a way of earning some money, to divorce Jonathan and learn to cope with having no friends and no family.

As the taxi driver drove me back across the Wirral to Lime Street Station everything that I owned was in his car. There were two brand new suitcases packed with, possibly technically stolen, clothes; my two briefcases containing all my research material and computer disks. In my handbag was about £1,500 in cash, I had destroyed all my credit and bank cards, they were all Jonathan's.

I was going to start again.

But this time Annie Donaldson was going to do things right.

Chapter Twenty-Nine

I rented a flat in south London, near enough to get to the libraries, galleries and auction houses but far enough out of the city to be affordable. I wrote short articles which I submitted to local newspapers, regional magazines and the small cheques soon added up, £50 here, £100 there until I could buy my own computer. I wrote short stories which were accepted for some of the lower circulation women's magazines. The theme of all my work was the generation that grew up between the wars. It was something I was learning more and more about. I even did some teaching, tutoring in the evenings to help the children of over-anxious parents enjoy reading and learning about words.

I had nothing in common with my flat mate Caroline, a young teacher at the local comprehensive. She had an active social life and seemed to spend practically every evening out. I wondered when she managed to do any marking or lesson planning, activities I had always thought teachers had to do in their spare time. At least she was away for long periods during her holidays and I had the flat to myself. She had a regular boyfriend who frequently stayed with her.

After several weeks I had had enough of feeling that neither Caroline nor he recognised that it wasn't *their* flat. They would sit on the settee entwined, touching each other as if I didn't exist and in the mornings he would wander around the flat in his underpants. When I tackled them about their behaviour I was rewarded with a withering look 'We didn't think you'd notice, you're old enough to be our mother.'

It hurt to realise they were right.

That made me wonder about my own children. Josie would be coming up to her 21st birthday, the boys all in their late teens. Even Bill would be 16, the same age I was when I was pregnant with Josie. They would all have grown up in the three years since Cambridge. I had rarely wondered about their lives but what Caroline had said struck a chord and I began to think of them more, of Maureen and of Ted. I had vanished, again, from their lives. What, if anything, did they ever think of me?

Most of my time was spent working on Max's inventories. He had given me page upon page of lists. All the items he knew to have been brought to England by David's Fishermen. Tracking down items in arts sales over the past few years was easier than I had thought it might be, but was time consuming. It was more difficult to persuade museums and art galleries to provide lists of the items they had in their cellars and storage facilities. They admitted quite readily that only a small percentage of their complete catalogue was ever on display and that many items were on loan to government ministries, embassies around the world and even, in exceptional circumstances, individuals. Whenever I was able to match an item to Max's inventories and identify, as far as possible, where it had been since the 1930s the details were entered on my spreadsheet and I quietly celebrated another piece in the jigsaw. Somehow something must connect to Vijay.

The details on some items such as Princess Sophie's decanter, were very easy to complete. Everything that had been in Max's column now had a question mark against them. Nothing that had been Max's had showed up since the burglary in any of the sales catalogues I had seen.

But there were successes. I traced three Fabergé eggs which had been brought over by Max. They were sold at Christie's in London in 1983 by a member of the House of Lords to an American. The sum paid astonished me and I wondered how his Lordship had explained the provenance of eggs and how he had proved his ownership. I felt like I was really achieving something and it was most satisfying, little successes buoyed me up through the days when the only contact I had with anyone was a letter in the post from Jonathan's lawyers.

He had not been happy with my assault on his credit card the day I had left him but he had accepted it and had not asked me to repay anything. I could not have done anyway.

I was glad Ted was not acting for me, there was much I would not want him to have known.

I hated telling my solicitor so many details about my life but she seemed to think the divorce would be quite straightforward. I had come into the marriage with nothing and would leave with as much as she could extract on my behalf. I had told her I didn't care what I got, I just wanted my freedom and that was more important than regular maintenance payments or a lump sum. She seemed to think I could get quite a substantial sum. Jonathan had earned a great deal of money when we were married, had property and assets, and she seemed to think I was entitled to a reasonable share. "It won't be half or even a third but we should get 15%, maybe 20 if we're lucky."

"Even though we were only married a few months?"

"Absolutely, it was his unreasonable behaviour that brought the marriage to its premature end wasn't it?"

"Absolutely." I had confirmed. There were few things about my marriage that I did not tell her. "I really was not prepared for marriage to a drug addict. He had never indicated before the honeymoon that he had ever taken drugs. I wouldn't have had anything to do with him if I had known."

"The court will like that. A woman, widowed so young, wanting another chance of happiness, you had such a shock so early in your marriage, yet you persevered, you didn't leave him immediately, you tried to make it work."

I had agreed with a slight nod of my head, as if words would have been too difficult.

"It'll play very well. I think we might get more than the 20."

Ted's approach would have been completely different. He would have looked at both sides of the argument and I couldn't see him believing my word quite so readily. He wouldn't have taken some of the excesses of my statements at their face value, but Miss James asked me more questions, leading me to greater detail of my husband's depravities. I found myself exaggerating his friendship with Ramesh, hinting at a relationship that might have been rather more intimate than perhaps it should have been.

"Excellent!" Miss James had exclaimed, "We don't have to actually say that they were lovers, we can just gently hint at it. Worth an extra 5% I would expect. "Wonderful."

I couldn't imagine Ted even accepting the possibility let alone using it to my advantage.

Chapter Thirty

I wasn't really concentrating when I answered the phone, it was late and I was tired and cold. It was just a year since I had moved to the flat and that fact had depressed me. Caroline had gone to her room with whoever she was with that week. I lost count of the different men she had brought back since she broke up with the one I had always thought of as 'Pants'. She would make perfunctory introductions as we had an awkward cup of coffee together before they disappeared to her room. Some names I heard, Ian, Alan, Stuart, Pete, Malcolm; others I never knew. They were usually gone early the following morning and very few ever appeared a second time.

"Hello." I had said, expecting to have to talk to one of Caroline's men.

"Susie?"

"Who?" I didn't want to recognise the voice.

"Susie is that you?"

"Who's that?"

"It's Carl, is that you Susie? Have I got the right number?"

"Carl?"

"I've found you! Thank God for that! Where have you been? What have you been up to? Why haven't you been in touch with anyone? Oh Susie is that really you?"

"Carl?"

"Stop saying that! We have all been so worried about you. Where are you? Can I come to see you?"

"What are you talking about?"

"We haven't known where you've been for years. How are you? Say something."

I couldn't answer. I couldn't believe Carl had found me and was on the other end of the phone.

"Yes, Carl. It's me."

"How are you? Susie? Please talk to me."

"Hello Carl. What do you want me to say?"

"Are you OK? That's the most important thing. Are you OK?"

"Of course I'm all right. Why wouldn't I be?"

"Susie, we haven't heard from you for years, the children have sent cards that have been returned, we've written and had no reply we're all worrying about you. It's like you disappeared off the face of the earth."

"I'm here."

"Where's here?"

"You phoned me. You must know."

"I got your number from the man at the library."

"What?"

"I saw you. The other day. You were at the British Library and I watched you."

"You didn't come up and talk to me?"

He didn't answer directly. "You were engrossed, I watched you and you were the Susie I knew all those years ago, you were concentrating, oblivious to everything and anybody else. I recognised you immediately, you've lost weight, it suits you, and you've cut your hair, that suits you too. I watched you working, and I wanted to go over to you."

"Why didn't you?"

"You looked so untouchable, so confident, so different."

"You were afraid of me?"

"Yes. Susie, that's it. I was afraid you would tell me to piss off."

"Why would I do that?"

"Susie, please, can we meet? Can I talk to you face to face? Please?"

I thought about it for a few seconds.

"Why not?"

"Where are you? I know you're somewhere in London, your phone number told me that but I haven't a clue where."

"How did you get my number?"

"The chap at the Library. I said I fancied you. He was very sympathetic. He said he had seen you over the months and you were always on your own, you never spoke to anyone, you always looked so serious and so lonely. He took pity on you."

"He shouldn't have given you my number."

"No. But he did. Let's meet. Please."

"OK." I couldn't believe how I felt. For so much of my life Carl asking me to meet up with him would have sent me into every sort of joy. Now I wasn't so sure. But there was so much history.

"I know this isn't going to make any sense at all but how about tea at the Savoy?"

"I'd like that. That would be quite special. Is there any particular reason?"

"No. I just thought it would be somewhere we wouldn't lose control. We will be polite and distant. Probably better than somewhere where we can actually be ourselves."

I understood exactly what he meant.

I spent a great deal of time getting ready the next day. I bought a suit that I thought might be considered sufficiently smart. It was late February, cold and wet, but I was determined to be sophisticated and professional. I wanted Carl to see what he had been missing. I made sure I had my briefcase with me when I took the train into town. I wanted to make sure Carl saw me as a professional woman. It may have been stupid but it was very important that he didn't think I was the wreck of a Susie who had lived with him. But I remembered Max's words '...find the man who will make you happy ... this is not Carl.'

"Susie, you look wonderful."

Carl stood up and kissed me on both cheeks. We were both being incredibly civilised.

"Good to see you Carl."

"Delighted to welcome you Mr Witherby." Carl was obviously a regular, the waiter seemed to know him well. "Afternoon tea for two?" Carl nodded in agreement and I realised how at home he was in this world.

"Do you come here often?"

"Pretty much. It's close to Bush House and I'm doing a lot with the World Service now, also for what you get it's actually a very cheap meal."

I enjoyed the tea, the pianist played a medley of songs that were all about summer. I liked that, there was a certain light irony bearing in mind the February weather outside. Somehow 'Summertime and the living is easy' sounded even better when you knew it was miserable outside.

Sitting in the warm lounge of the hotel drinking tea from perfect pink and white tea cups meant that the real world didn't exist. After biting into one of the beautifully manicured cucumber sandwiches I nearly choked.

"Are you OK? What's the matter?"

"Nothing. Sorry." I couldn't tell Carl I was remembering tea served in the room at the Taj Mahal Hotel on the first day of my honeymoon.

"I was just thinking about the title for an article 'My Life in Cucumber Sandwiches', it might be quite fun."

We didn't really talk much, perhaps we were both shy and a little unsure of ourselves. A man came up and shook Carl's hand muttering something about needing to keep in touch and appreciating his last series. So people did still know about Carl.

"Allow me to introduce Susannah Donaldson." Carl said to the man. It hadn't occurred to Carl that I might not be 'Donaldson' any more and it didn't occur to me to correct his error.

"Delighted." The man said, taking my proffered hand and brushing it briefly against his lips.

Carl and the man exchanged a few words which I couldn't really hear, and wasn't really trying to. And he left.

"What are you up to then?" Carl finally asked a personal question that had to be answered.

"I'm researching a book." It seemed like a reasonable answer.

Carl's question was also perfectly reasonable. "What about?"

Should I answer honestly? Should I lie and say something completely innocuous or should I answer truthfully and get Carl on my side perhaps? There wasn't really any choice. I was never a good liar. I chose the easier option, not mentioning Max. "It's about my grandfather."

I was surprised at his immediate response "Can I help?"

"I'm doing very well on my own thank you." I couldn't help the bitter defensiveness in my tone.

"I wasn't saying you weren't."

"Sorry, I know. I'm just so used to people thinking I'm a complete idiot."

"I mean it. I would love to help if I can."

But I was defensive. "Tell me about your work, what are you up to these days?" The awkward moment passed and we talked comfortably as we drank several pots of tea. The time flew by.

"Time for a cocktail I think. Come on Susie. Let's go up to the American Bar."

I followed him up the stairs and along the corridor to the American Bar. Again he seemed well known.

"Can I tell you about the first time I came to this place?" And he told me of my mother's birthday, how he had treated her to a night of luxury, how he had led her into this very bar and how people had admired the woman who was my mother. "We drank here, we ate in the River Room, we talked and she was very beautiful."

I remembered something David had said, the night after my mother's funeral, the first time he had really spoken to us and admitted who he was. He had said he had seen his daughter, at the Savoy, 'with a beautiful young man'. I felt the goose pimples rising on my arm as I realised that that young man must have been Carl. That was the evening he was talking about and David had been eating here too. I felt inordinately sad that they had not realised who they really were, and had not sealed the circle.

"You slept together didn't you?" I had asked the question before I knew whether I wanted him to answer or not.

"Yes. I slept with Alicia. It wasn't planned, it wasn't anything either of us had worked towards. We danced together, she sang and it just happened."

"It doesn't matter." I sipped at the Martini in the triangular glass and tried to imagine Carl here, at this exact spot at the bar, with my mother how many years earlier?

"It was 1967. November 29th 1967."

"Her birthday."

"Yes it was her 47th birthday and also her 26th wedding anniversary, or at least it would have been if she and Arnold hadn't divorced."

"And you were…"

"21"

"Why…"

"Why did I do it? Simple. She was like you. I wanted to sleep with you, I wanted to be with you, and she was so like you. That and the fact that she asked me to."

There was nothing I could say so I nodded towards the bartender for another Martini.

"Not that long ago really."

"A lifetime."

The tea that had become cocktails became dinner.

"Don't tell me this was the table you sat at with my mother." I ventured as we sat looking at the menus.

"No. Not quite. It was that table, in the corner" And he indicated a table three away from ours over his shoulder. I stared at the table imagining Carl, 21 years old, with my mother. She wouldn't have been that much older than I was now. Ghosts. I could see them at the table and the echoes of it were almost tangible. David was sitting at the table just behind them. These were the tables, this was the setting. I almost felt them sitting in their designated places. I so wanted to tell David to talk to them. I so wanted to tell my mother that her father was sitting just six feet away. They were really there. It was so clear to me, so vivid.

The food was excellent, the wine too. We talked about everything and anything. We both knew what was going to happen, there had been an inevitability about it since his phone call. Without his saying anything

227

I knew he had a room, I knew he had known I would stay. And it didn't matter. As we drank the coffee looking out over the river and the lights reflecting in the water I knew that I would wake up to look out over that view. I knew that my mother had done just the same years before. And I knew that I would have absolutely no regrets.

"Can we do this again?" He asked the question tentatively, but not without confidence that he knew my answer would be 'yes'. Carl was standing by the window, his white towelling robe not completely disguising his nakedness. I was sitting up in the large bed, the lovely linen sheets pulled up around my neck.

"I don't see why not." I answered with theatrical nonchalance.

"Susie, seriously, was that a one off or are we going to do this properly?"

"Do what properly?"

"You know. Be lovers, whatever. Have an affair."

"Why? Are you married?" It hadn't occurred to me to ask. He didn't wear a ring but then why would he? Of course he was married. By saying nothing he gave me his answer. "I don't suppose you thought to tell me?" I made myself sound nonchalant.

Carl had not changed. I had always thought of him as the perfect man, the knight in shining armour who would rescue me from all my pain and loneliness. But I had always known underneath everything he was weak. He had loved me but he had slept with countless women. He had slept with my mother. God knows who else had had the pleasure, and it was a pleasure, of being made love to by Carl. Of course he would be unfaithful to his wife. I was just so happy that I was the 'other woman' not the betrayed one, so very happy that tables were turning. Max had been absolutely right.

"Does it make a difference? It would never have worked if we'd got married Susie, really it wouldn't, but do you want to know anything about her?"

"No and No. I absolutely don't care." Perhaps I should have pressed him, asked the name of the woman I was betraying, but I didn't.

In the first months I never saw him anywhere but at the Savoy. We would meet in the bar and eat in the restaurant overlooking the river. We would share a bath and the bed and then the shower and the bed again with no suggestion of responsibility or guilt. I never worried about leaving him after our nights together because I knew he would be there the next week and strangely it wouldn't have mattered if he hadn't been.

Early in the summer Carl asked me to help with a project he was working on.

"Could you come to my office? We need to talk about you helping with the research. Your expertise would be very welcome on the team."

I was flattered, and intrigued. I didn't even mind that the invitation was a few years late.

"OK."

Our affair lasted all through the spring and the summer. I was working with Carl and his team on my 40th birthday and I thought he had forgotten. When he shepherded us all into the pub at the end of the road where their small office was I realised he hadn't. I woke up on the office floor the next morning, under a blanket that someone must have draped over me and remembering nothing about the evening before.

"Coffee?" Carl was in the small corner of the office we called the kitchen.

"Was I out of order? Do I have to apologise to everyone?"

"You were sweet, a little maudlin but sweet. They loved you. No you don't have to apologise to anyone. Except me that is."

"Why?"

"You were too pissed to make love."

Carl had introduced me to colleagues as an 'old and dear friend, almost a sister'. After that night I felt sure the rest of the team must have known that was not quite the case but nothing was ever said.

It was a perfect time. But as with all perfect times it had to come to an end.

Carl asked me to go to lunch with him one day when I was working in the library rather than in the office. He seemed tense and unusually quiet as we walked in silence to a small Italian restaurant I had never been to before. I went to tuck my hand into the crook of his arm, as I frequently did when we were walking together, but he shrugged me away.

"What is it?" As I asked I knew what the answer would be.

"I think we've been found out."

"Your wife?"

"She's left me. Do you want me to tell you about her?"

"Not particularly but if you need to."

"I need to."

And he talked. We hardly touched our bowls of pasta.

He had married Holly.

"I thought you would have married the woman you were fucking all the time we were together." I couldn't help the bitterness in my voice but I was determined that he would not know how angry I was that he had married Holly. He loved me but couldn't live with me, he had never asked me to marry him in the years we were together. But he had asked Holly.

"No. Most women started sleeping with me because they felt sorry for me. I had such a shitty home life, what with all those children that weren't mine and a clingy woman who just wanted to marry me for security." He was angry as well but less good at hiding his emotion.

Ignoring the reference to 'most women' I pushed home my advantage. "So you married a clingy woman who only wanted to marry you for security."

"Holly isn't clingy."

I simply raised my eyebrow in disbelief. "But she is rich."

"That's a cheap point."

It probably was, but the way he reacted made me think I had hit on his real reason.

"But you still fuck around." Was I sounding hurt?

"Only with you." Was he being disingenuous?

"I'm supposed to believe that?"

"It's true."

"No it absolutely is not true. You fuck around with anyone and everybody. You're just like your father. You couldn't be faithful to any one single person to save your life." Although I spoke quietly, not wanting the people in the tables around us to hear, there was bitterness in my voice.

"Are we arguing?"

"Probably."

We were quite for a while, both concentrating, ridiculously, on the plates of pasta in front of us.

"Anyway, Holly has found out about us."

"Us?"

"Well she knows I'm having an affair."

"Does she know it's me?" I couldn't believe he had told her about me.

He hedged around being honest, as he had so often done in the past. "She knows I'm seeing someone regularly, and spending the night with them."

"Does she mind?"

"Of course she fucking minds! She's fucking divorcing me." Heads turned towards us, there were disapproving stares before people turned back to their meals and their conversations.

230

"Divorce? That's a bit dangerous isn't it? I mean she has loads more money than you. You could take her to the cleaners." I tried to sound as cynical as possible.

"It's not like that."

"I bet it isn't. No divorce 'isn't like that'. She'll cling on tooth and nail to everything."

"She's naming you."

"Naming me?" I looked at Carl, long and hard. "*Naming* me? You told her my *name*? You told her it was *me*?"

"I had to. She guessed. She asked directly 'It's Susannah isn't it?' I had to say yes."

"God you're weak."

"Probably. Anyway she's naming you as correspondent. It's just that she doesn't know your address."

"I don't believe you! You want this divorce don't you? You want the excuse, the reason, me? But you don't know my address! That's beautiful! That's absolutely fucking beautiful. How about 'Care of The Savoy'? No? That won't do? Oh Carl you are so bloody weak."

I started laughing. It was so perfect. I looked closely at him across the table and wondered if I was really seeing him for the first time, this man I had loved forever. I realised the truth of what Ted had said ten years earlier, Carl needed me more than I needed him. I don't know how and in what exact ways but he needed me. Slowly, over the years, the tables had turned and I was now the strong one. I was almost sorry for him. "You're afraid I won't tell you."

"I wondered."

"You mustn't tell anyone else. Not Charles nor Linda. None of them. I'll get back in touch when I need to. Not before."

"Even if I wanted to I couldn't. We have nothing to do with them for pretty obvious reasons. I wouldn't know how to contact them to save my life."

I reached down into my bag and pulled out my Filofax. Tearing a page out of it I wrote my full name and address handed it to him across the table.

"Susannah *Smith*?"

"You're not the only one who got married." I knew I was completely in control and enjoyed the power of the moment.

"You never said." He sounded like a little boy, resentful that someone had something he had wanted.

"You never asked."

I spoke matter-of-factly "Married on my birthday 1983 divorced October 1985. The two years of my marriage netted me the flat in Connaught Square and a six figure sum in the bank. My solicitor was worth every penny of her fees. Apparently Mr Smith, that was my ex, was happy to pay anything so that his parents wouldn't learn of his homosexuality. I hadn't known he was that way inclined but it didn't matter, we hadn't had sex since almost before we were married. I've sold the flat and banked the ridiculous sum it raised. So, you see," I ended with a hint of triumph "you have a rich wife and a rich mistress, both of whom you are about to lose."

We ate what we could of the cold pasta in silence.

"I'll finish this project at home and so there's no need to meet in the office. Then we'll have a bit of a gap. Call me when you want another job done, but we can't work together all the time. It'll be difficult when the guys find out what's been going on, we'll have a bit of a break until they've all left and you're breaking in a new little team."

"That makes sense." He seemed pleased that someone was making difficult decisions for him. "What about..." he parked his fork on the plate and wiped his mouth with the napkin. "... the other stuff?"

"I wouldn't mind one last night."

"No reason why not."

"Saturday? It's the 29th of November." I wanted to lay that ghost. The opportunity appealed to my sense of history.

We met as usual in the American Bar and ate, as usual, in the River Restaurant, but this time we had the corner table. We both knew why. In every way it was exactly the same as the thirty or so meetings we had had through the past months. But knowing this was the last time we would be together as lovers gave the evening a special edge. From now on we would just be friends.

I looked over my shoulder at the table behind, half expecting David to be sitting there watching us.

At the end of the meal Carl lifted his glass towards mine, "Happy birthday Alicia."

I lifted mine and touched it to his. "Happy birthday Mother. She would have been 66. It's impossible to think of her that old. You know you never remembered my birthday or our anniversary. Have you any idea how much that hurt?"

He emptied the glass and signalled to the waiter for another. We sat in silence as the new bottle was opened with due ceremony and our old glasses were removed from the table to be replaced with clean new ones.

He lifted the new glass towards me, and I lifted mine to his and they touched. "Happy Anniversary Alicia and Arnold." We were being forgiving on this last night.

"Happy Anniversary." He replied. "How many years would it have been?"

"She married on her 21st birthday so 45."

"You know my mother and he were together long before he married your mother don't you?"

"I've never really thought about it."

"Well I have. There's so much we don't know but what I do know is that my father loved my mother. He couldn't have known they were brother and sister. I will never believe he knew that. I believe he loved her but was told not to marry her so he married Alicia. I believe he never loved your mother, that was a marriage of convenience. As soon as he could he married my mother. He wouldn't have done if he'd known they were brother and sister."

"After all these years it still hurts."

"Of course it hurts. It's the most important thing in my life."

"Oh Carl. You should have forgotten all this years ago."

"How could I? How can I? It's where I come from. It's me."

"Carl. You are you. Not your parents, or your grandparents. *You* are what *you* make of *you*."

"No, Susie, That's where we're different. You have managed to do that, to separate yourself from your parents...

"That's because I never really knew them."

"... but I can't. I've tried. Every day I've tried not to be my father's son, my grandfather's grandson. I've tried and I've never managed it. Every time I do something I see Arnold or Kathleen in it. I see the fact of their incest. There is no way I can get away from it. Ever. I've tried and I can't."

I listened to the pain in his voice. It was real and it went very, very deep. He had spoken quietly and deliberately, no one could have heard what he was saying or how much it hurt him. Ted had told me how much it hurt him and I hadn't helped.

"I'm sorry Susie, but I can never forget what they were. It's not you, it's not anything that you have done, it's me. I can never, ever, forget that I should never have been born. I can't forget it. It is as much part of me as ..." he held out his hand to me "... this, my hand. I can't chop it off, I can't get rid of it. It is part of me. I am dirty, I am tainted, I am the child of incest."

For so many years I had thought that incest was not so bad. All the years I had thought Carl was my brother and I hadn't cared, all I had wanted was to be with him, but he had cared about incest. He knew what it really meant. I felt so sorry that I hadn't understood him years ago.

"You tried." I spoke gently, I hoped gently enough. "You really tried Carl, you took us on, you looked after us those years in Cambridge, you really tried."

The waiter came and cleared the table, running a stupid little roller over the tablecloth to get rid of any crumbs. What he made of our earnest, quiet conversation I don't know. Perhaps he didn't hear much of it.

"I didn't try hard enough to help did I? Ted told me you needed me more than I needed you but I never believed him. I should have done shouldn't I? All the time it was you who needed someone to build confidence and I thought it was you who was there to help me."

I looked at Carl. His hair, always long as if this were still the 1960s tied behind his neck in a pony tail, was turning grey. His eyes, so blue and so deep were set in a face that I realised I had never really known.

"We'll always be friends won't we?"

"Absolutely always."

"You'll always come to me when there is absolutely no one else and you need help won't you?"

"Absolutely always."

We finished the rest of the bottle in silence, looking out over the lights reflected in the river.

At six o'clock the next morning, when we had spent our last night together, Carl stood in the window. I looked at his naked body knowing this really was the last time I would see him like this. I got out of bed and stood next to him, he put his arm around me and I leant my body against his.

"Whatever happened to 'Happy Ever After'?" He asked wistfully.

"Or of life ever being fair?"

Chapter Thirty-One

Christmas 1986 was a particularly bad time. The weather was dire and I watched too much television and drank too much wine. On Christmas Day the Fred Astaire and Ginger Rogers film lasted a bottle and when it finished I sat on the sofa feeling very sorry for myself reflecting on the year. I wasn't looking forward to 1987.

On New Year's Eve I could stand being on my own no longer and called Maureen's number.

I didn't recognise the voice that answered, it was a man's voice but not Ted. I could hear laughter and music in the background, almost like a party.

"Is Maureen in?"

"Who? Sorry. It's a bit difficult to hear, hang on a moment while I close the door." I heard footsteps on Maureen's wooden floor, and could even picture the mat which muffled the man's footsteps for a few seconds as he walked to the door. It was so familiar to me, the corridor with the phone, the furniture in the room behind the now closed door. I pictured myself sitting with Ted and Maureen around the fire in that room. Who were these people? Had Maureen moved? Were these new occupants? So many thoughts went through my head as the man came back to the phone.

"Sorry about that, I couldn't hear you. Who was it you wanted?"

"Maureen. Maureen Sheldon. Does she still live at this number?"

"Oh Maureen! Yes, Shall I tell her who's calling?" The man was very polite, very well spoken. I decided he had a lovely voice.

"Annie. Can you tell her it's Annie."

"Hang on a sec." The name seemed to mean nothing to the young man but I heard the silence after he had opened the door and announced "Maureen, there's a lady called Annie on the phone for you." After a few moments I recognised Linda's voice. "Did you say 'Annie'?" She did not seemed pleased.

"Yes. Why? Is there a problem?" The young man seemed worried that he hadn't just put the phone down. "Should I have hung up?"

There was a period of quiet, even the music had stopped.

Then I heard Ted's voice "I'll go."

I listened to his footsteps on the bare boards, then muffled by the rug. I could picture him approaching the phone. I shouldn't have called. I was expecting to speak to Maureen, I was expecting her to be alone, as I was. I wasn't expecting her to be having a family gathering; a gathering of my family. Linda was there, was Charles? If there were there perhaps that well-spoken, polite young man was my son. Who else was there? Josie? Did she have a boyfriend? Did the boys have girlfriends? So many thoughts in such a short time. And I had no idea what I was going to say.

"Annie? Susannah? Is that you?"

"Hello Ted. Happy New Year." I tried to sound casual.

"Oh Annie, it is so good to hear your voice." He sounded as if the weight of years was lifting from him. "How are you? Where are you?"

I responded in kind, happy and relaxed. "I'm fine. I've missed you."

"We've all missed you Susannah. Where are you? There's so much to say. Give me your phone number, your address. Don't hang up." He sounded frantic at the prospect. I was flattered and relieved.

"I wasn't going to." It was so good to hear the familiar reassurance in his voice. I was crying as I recited my phone number.

"You're in London?" He said recognising the dialling code.

"You sound surprised."

"We thought you were in New Zealand."

"Why would you think that?"

"Never mind now. Can I come to see you? Tomorrow? I can't come now I've had a few glasses of wine."

"It's probably not a good idea to drive on New Year's Eve anyway." I couldn't believe I was holding a perfectly normal conversation.

"No. Where are you? I'll come tomorrow morning."

I gave him the address.

"Do you need directions?"

"I'll find it."

I couldn't think of anything else to say and I didn't want to hang up. Ted must have heard me sniffling into a tissue.

"Annie, it really is lovely to hear from you. Thank you for calling. It couldn't have been easy."

Still I couldn't say anything. Four years seemed a very long time.

"I'll see you tomorrow. Don't worry about a thing."

The phone went dead and I sat on the floor looking at the phone in my hand and I cried.

The next morning I spent more time cleaning the flat ready for my visitor.

After the divorce I didn't need to stay in the flat. I had hated its dingy decoration and incongruous assortment of furniture. It was always cold and I didn't like Caroline and her endless stream of one-night-stands. But since it was convenient I had asked her to leave. The landlord agreed that I could live rent free for a year if I paid for a complete refurbishment. He got a very good bargain but I had a flat that suited me. As I tidied and hoovered around I wondered what Ted would make of it, a very well appointed flat in a very dingy area.

I worried about what to wear and changed several times, finally settling on a pair or camel slacks and a grey polo neck sweater. I looked critically in the mirror and wondered what changes Ted would see. I had lost weight. I had grey in my hair, which needed cutting. It was important that Ted approved of what he saw.

I didn't know what time he would arrive and at 10.30 I was standing in the window watching for a car. I didn't know what car he had, perhaps still the Rover he had driven me to Sevenoaks in four years before. There wasn't much traffic and the time passed very slowly. It was past 11 when a sports car pulled into the parking area that had once been the front garden of the house.

I hardly recognised him. Where I had aged ten years in the past four Ted was ten years younger.

I stood outside the door and listened as he ran up the stairs two at a time.

"Annie! Oh Annie!" He put his arms around me and hugged me so hard I had to ask him to let me breathe.

"Oh sorry, I'm hurting you! But it is so very good to see you."

"We'd better go in."

After the initial hugs and when I had wiped away my tears we settled down with mugs of coffee. There had been many times in my life when I hadn't seen Ted for years on end and we had always taken up where we had left off. When I went back to Hoylake after my four years at Sussex conversation hadn't been stilted or strained between us. We had stood together in the garden of Sandhey and talked as if we had seen each other every day. There had been no awkwardness or embarrassment. But when he had come to Linda's rescue and stayed those few days with Maureen things had got a bit awkward and now I didn't know what to say to this man who had been my friend all my life.

And it seemed he didn't know what to say to me either.

We fell back on polite conversation. 'Was the drive up OK?' 'Did you find it easily?' 'I wonder what the year will bring.'

It was that last question that Ted picked up on.

"You weren't at the New Year's Party in 1976 were you?"' He didn't wait for an answer before continuing, "No, you didn't get back until that summer did you? Charles decided to have a New Year's Party funnily enough with Linda. They had just started the business. It was an odd do. It was the day Holly ran away from her husband and probably the day Charles fell in love with her. Funny how things work out isn't it?"

I just managed to say 'No, I hadn't been there' when he continued rather lamely. "There's so much that's happened in the past few years, there's so much to tell you. But what about you? When did you get back from New Zealand?" His voice had changed, it had less energy and seemed guarded.

"I've never been there."

He gave me a funny look.

"But the postcards you sent?"

"I've never been to New Zealand." I repeated rather lamely. "When was I supposed to be there?"

"You weren't?"

"No."

"Why did you say you were?"

"I didn't"

"But…"

"Tell me what you think I've been up to these past years." I knew Jonathan had been devious and had lied about our lives, I wondered how far he had gone.

"We got a card from you, a couple of weeks after you left Maureen's, saying you'd gone to New Zealand with that man you'd met in Sevenoaks."

"Jonathan."

"That's it. You said you'd decided to start a new life there. You said that your life in England was a mess and that you loved this man and were going to New Zealand to live with him and his family but if we wanted to write to you there was an address in south London we could send letters to and they would be forwarded to you."

"In Wimbledon?"

"Yes SW19."

"I have never been there."

"Then how…?"

"Jonathan." I spoke with what I hoped was sufficient coldness. "He must have sent them, or got his family to, someone. It wasn't me. He tried to cut me off from all my friends."

"What have you been doing? Where have you been?"

"I've been in London, most of the time."

"Oh Susie, what did that man do?"

"He tried to separate me from you all, but he couldn't could he? Not in the end." I kissed him on the cheek and he put his hand on mine, squeezed it, and did not let it go.

"No Susie, he couldn't."

I caught his eye and smiled. "We've got a lot of catching up to do. Haven't we?" And we began to relax.

"You tell me first." There would be time enough to tell him of my disastrous marriage and successful divorce, of the progress I had made with learning about the long, rather convoluted, relationship between Max and David and my search for Vijay.

Now was the time to hear about my children.

I listened to Ted without interruption for over an hour. I had wondered at Linda's ability to work with my children, I had shuddered with her when hearing of the influence of Ramesh, I had actually felt sorry for Charles and the misunderstanding of Max and the misanthropy of Monika. But more than anything I had felt admiration for Josie and Bill and affection for their brothers.

Ted paused frequently as he had told me how my children had grown through what the past years had thrown at them expecting me, I suspect, to ask specific questions about them. But I had not interrupted him.

"Don't you want to know how they've got on down here? How well they've done? You should be very proud of them all. Josie has as good an analytical brain as I've seen in any young person I've worked with over the years. She did exactly what she said she would do. She has worked while studying and has experienced life. She's had a few good relationships and some terrible ones, but has put all the bad ones down to experience and learned from them. You'll like her. She is very like you were at her age. She's a very attractive young woman in every possible way."

I was aware of the indirect compliment and felt myself blushing.

"Bill is the spectacular one. He travels all over the country…"

"In a wheelchair?"

"Absolutely. He competes all over the country. He does very well. Jack and Al drive him wherever he wants to go though he's always complaining that more should be done for sport for the 'dis-tinctively-abled' as he describes it."

"Al and Jack *drive?*

"Yes. Strangely enough they both passed their tests first time. I didn't think they would but Charles made sure they had plenty of proper lessons and didn't pick up his bad habits."

"What do they do with the rest of their time?"

"They're not academic like their sister but they're all still at school. Jack's in his final year, he lost a lot of time in their various moves, but oddly enough they have great plans for when they leave. They're dab hands at carpentry and decorating, that time sorting out the house for Bill had a lasting effect, and they already make good money in the holidays doing all sorts of handy-man type things. Charles was very sensible making sure they had the best tools and a good grounding in technique. They're starting their own business next year. Linda's doing the administration for them. Sevenoaks is a good area, there will be no end of work for them if they turn up when they say they will and do what they are paid to do."

"Will Bill be able to help?"

"Absolutely, that's the great thing. He already does during the holidays. It really is the best thing for them. They would hate to have proper jobs, working for other people, being told what to do all the time."

"I didn't think I'd be interested in what they were doing."

"But you are?"

"Surprisingly so. And what about you? Have you joined the exodus to the south?"

"I followed very shortly after Charles left. Max changed. He sold the business and let us all go."

"He *fired* you?"

"Made us redundant."

"How *could* he after all those years?"

"Very easily. I told you. He changed."

"That would explain why I couldn't find the firm in the phone book and all your numbers were unobtainable."

"So you did try to contact us?"

"Eventually."

"After the big break-in Max became positively paranoid, he seemed petrified that someone was coming to get him. He never went out of the house, never allowed visitors…"

"I visited him."

"When?" Ted was surprised.

"In January a couple of years ago. January '85"

"How was he?"

"Rude, secretive to start with but I was able to break through. You see I knew stuff about him and I told him something of what I knew. He told me a lot, some I knew some I didn't. You see David asked me to do something which meant I have had to learn about Max and his colleagues, and what they got up to before during and after the war. I'm some of the way through it but have so, so much more to do."

"Anything you're going to tell me?"

"Not yet. Just like there're things you know that you're not telling me!"

"Susannah, seriously, we've talked about everyone but you. What are you doing in this flat? What happened to you? Why did you go silent and lose contact with all your friends."

It was not going to be easy to answer and there would have been a time when I wouldn't have been able to be so honest, I would have put a rosy gloss on my actions and painted myself as the victim of circumstances and malevolence. But I had grown up.

"I made a mistake."

"I never thought I'd hear you say that."

"It was a bad one. I got married." I couldn't help noticing the effect this had on him. "And then I got divorced."

"I'm sorry to hear that." He didn't sound it.

"It was the best thing to happen. I had what people in glossy magazines call 'a good divorce'. I took him to the cleaners."

"Then why this?" Ted looked around him. "There's nothing wrong with the flat, but the area leaves a lot to be desired."

"Inertia I suppose. I didn't want to move to anything larger. I had luxury when I was married, and there didn't seem much point in buying a house just for me when I'm not here very often. I've travelled a lot, it's been easy I suppose."

"And the spoils of your divorce?"

"In the bank. I know you don't approve, and I wouldn't normally, but he really was a manipulative little shit. It seems that he had been effectively 'hired' by Linda's Ramesh to marry me and make me unhappy."

"Ramesh?"

"That's why I found the bit about Ramesh being behind Max's

robbery quite frightening. Somehow his role in this jigsaw puzzle is a getting more and more significant. When exactly was that robbery?"

"1983, August 1983."

"When in August? What date?"

"Is it important?"

"Yes."

"It was towards the end of the month, the 24th, 25th perhaps."

"And according to Bill he saw Ramesh the day before so that's the 23rd or 24th."

"Ish. Why? Is this important?"

"I've got a horrible feeling the robbery was my fault."

I began to explain about the wedding, about my knowing beforehand that it was a mistake but not being strong enough to stop it. I gave Ted an edited version of the honeymoon in Mumbai but I did include the fact that we had met Ramesh. I had to admit that everything I had ever told Jonathan about Max and his wealth had been passed to Ramesh.

"You couldn't have known."

Things were beginning to fall into place. I couldn't talk to Ted about it, not until I had all the pieces of the jigsaw together. So I changed the subject.

"Anyway, what are you doing now? Are you retired? Enjoying a well-deserved life of leisure?"

"Actually I'm teaching. Not full time, a few hours a week here and a few hours there."

"Who? What?" It was a relief to talk about everyday life and forget, for the time being, the threat posed by Vijay's nephew.

"Don't sound so surprised. Officially I'm teaching general studies to sixth form students but unofficially anything and everything they want to talk about. It's great fun. Josie got me the job really. She circled the advertisement in the paper and left it lying around the house. Then she phoned for an application form and made me sign the form she had filled in. The only thing she didn't do was attend the interview, though she did drive me there to make sure I didn't abscond."

"You said 'around the house'?"

"She lives with me, boards really. She felt it was time to leave Charles and Linda, quite rightly, she's nearly 21, but she couldn't afford somewhere of her own and she didn't want to share with strangers. I've got plenty of room and so it works really well."

"Another generation of the family you've lived with, grandmother,

mother and now daughter."

"And grand-son."

"What?" It took me a few moments to realise the implications of what Ted had said.

"You know I said she had some pretty dreadful relationships, well one of them produced a rather permanent reminder."

"Josie's had a baby?"

"Yes, my dear, you are a grandmother. He's a lovely little boy, just six weeks old now"

"Oh my God! What's his name? Is he OK?" I could hardly bring myself to ask, but felt it was the expected thing.

"Andrew is a beautiful baby, well behaved and perfect."

"Andrew. Was that what the father was called?"

"Probably, though she's never actually said who the father was."

"Didn't she want to, you know…"

Ted knew what I meant. He had helped me years ago when I couldn't face yet another pregnancy.

"No. She didn't want an abortion. She talked it over with all of us and we all agreed to support her. She has no shortage of babysitters and no shortage of shoulders to cry on when she gets depressed, which isn't very often. She's sure she's made the right decision."

"Are you?"

"Yes. Yes I am."

"Wow. This is an awful lot to take in for one morning."

"So you'd better pack your bags, Annie my dear, you're coming home with me. How much of all this is yours? We can come back to sort out what you can't fit in the car some other time."

"Pretty much everything, and the rent is sorted for a few months."

"Let's go. I don't care how beautiful this flat is you're not living here a day longer, it's a dreadful area, God knows what people get up to on the street outside."

"I never notice."

I turned to Ted and was surprised to see the intense way he was looking at me.

"Where are you taking me?"

"I'm taking you to Maureen's."

So for the third time in my life I was running to Maureen.

Though this time it didn't feel like I was running away *from* anything, rather I was running *to* something.

What that was I did not know.

Chapter Thirty-Two

"Won't Maureen have a problem with me, I mean I wasn't very nice when I left her last time?"

"She is very, very happy to have you. All that is forgotten." Ted answered, I hadn't been aware I had spoken out loud. Ted's voice was again unruffled and convincing.

"You were so sure I'd come back?"

"I hoped you would." I was aware that he had said 'I' not 'we' and wondered how difficult the next days would be.

"I'll have to meet the children again, and get to know them."

"They may not like that idea for a bit." Ted's voice changed, no longer calming and confident he had to admit that that part of my return would be more difficult.

"They don't know me."

"No I mean they may not like the idea of you living so close to them. They've grown up without you and have thought that you never considered them part of your life so they may not like you trying to be their mother again."

"I wouldn't try! They're far too old to need one." I was beginning to realise the scale of the problems I would be facing.

Maureen was welcoming, as Ted said she would be, accepting me back with no questions and no recriminations. Whatever she may have thought she said nothing.

Most days I walked the mile to the railway station from the cottage in the morning and returned, after the main rush hour, to walk back to a warm welcome and a friendly chat. Maureen, as ever, seemed interested in what I was doing but I only told her about the work I was doing for Carl's company. It seemed somehow too difficult to ask her about her work with David and I didn't want to jeopardise what friendship she was offering me.

I didn't see much of the children, or indeed my grandchild. Ted thought it best that they carried on in much the same way as they always had and got used to the idea that they knew where their mother was, even if she was not, and never could be, a part of their lives.

Ted was a frequent and welcome visitor at the cottage, often he was there when I got back from London and it was a very rare weekend that he did not spend Sunday with us. At the end of August he surprised us with his decision to have a party to celebrate my birthday.

He had got together with the children and they had all decided it was the right time to get the family together again and there was no saying no to him. 'I think we're all ready for it now'.

As I was fastening my seat belt for the hour's drive Maureen, who had insisted upon driving, asked "Do you mind if I ask you some questions? I feel that there are things I need to know." I wondered what she was talking about, she had had so many opportunities in the past months to question me about my work, the stupidity of my marriage to Jonathan Smith, how I felt about Carl.

"Can I ask you when you started to see or think of Ted as anything other than a parent-substitute?"

I had no idea what she was talking about.

"Pardon?"

"When did you realise you were in love with him?"

It took a while to think of anything to say and my answer wasn't satisfactory.

"I don't think I am."

"You never were any good at judging your own feelings, or those of others." I was surprised at the hardness in her voice.

"He's always been a friend, a good friend, always there to help when I needed it. He was always there to talk to."

"He loves you very much you know."

I wasn't sure what she was getting at. I decided to take what she said at its face value and not worry about anything deeper.

"I know, he's always been there for me, since I was a little girl."

"He has loved you for a long time."

What was she saying? I remembered the look I had caught on Ted's face when he had picked me up from the flat at New Year. Had he wanted to hold me? Had it been more than just 'the old friend of the family' who had sat holding my hand and talking to me for hours? Perhaps I had almost thought of him as something more than an old friend in those few days when he had been rescuing Linda.

Maureen concentrated on her driving for a few moments, negotiating a roundabout and heading down towards the motorway.

"Let me tell you something. Before the war, when I was young, I watched my sister in love with Arnold Donaldson, her brother. She loved him, she belittled herself for him. My mother and I, we knew she was George's daughter, but we said nothing. My mother always said it would be to cut our noses off to spite our faces. I should have argued with her. I very much regret that I didn't. My sister wasted her life loving the wrong man. She had his son, she married him in the end, but he never made her happy."

I had never thought about Carl's mother, my step-mother, as anything other than a witch. I had never thought of her as a woman who was lonely and who loved an insignificant man. I tried to remember the quote from long ago English lessons, something about *'loving not wisely but too well'*. I had hated Kathleen, as her sister talked to me I realised that I had never, not for one moment, tried to understand her.

Maureen continued, it was as if she was thinking aloud and that she had almost forgotten I was in the car. "I fell in love with the wrong man too. Only he was wrong not because he didn't love me and I didn't love him, Dick Shelton was the wrong man because he was a pilot and we met at the beginning of the war. We were married for just under a year before he was shot down. The first I heard was one of my letters returned unopened with a pencil note in the top left hand corner 'Posted Missing'. It was a year later that I received an official letter saying he had been confirmed as being a prisoner of war."

She didn't seem to be aware that I was in the car.

"His plane had been shot down but he had baled out. They looked after him well until his burns healed and then he was put in a camp. I wrote so many letters to him but I never knew if he got them, I never received any from him. Just before the end of the war I heard he had been killed. The Allies bombed his camp as they advanced through Europe." I had heard that such things happened, though I had no idea whether it was true or not. Judging from the intensity in Maureen's voice I believed her. "It was hushed up, of course, but so many of those men who had put up with years as prisoners and who were just about to be freed to go home to their families were killed by our own side. It was never acknowledged and they said he had been killed whilst trying to escape. He wouldn't have done that. None of them would have done that. Not when they all knew the war was about to end."

I was beginning to worry for our safety. Maureen was so involved in telling me about Dick Shelton that she could not have been concentrating on her driving. "He was killed by our own bombers. I'll never forgive them for that. They all knew it was happening and they ignored it, they said it was enemy propaganda, that no camps were bombed, but they were. They killed so many of those lovely, patient, brave young boys who had been shot down then lived out the war waiting for rescue. They killed him, they killed Dick, they knew it and they never said 'sorry'." That's why I had to do what I did. I had to do something in revenge. She was quieter for a few moments and I thought perhaps she was concentrating again on her driving. "I loved the wrong person because he didn't come home to me."

"But you fell in love again." I don't think she heard me.

"I wasn't like Elizabeth, poor lucky Elizabeth. Unlike Elizabeth I was not pregnant. I was able to forget the man who had been my husband for five years but whom I had only been with for such a short time. I was able, if not to forget him, to live with the knowledge that he was dead. That was something Elizabeth never understood, she could never do that. My widowhood freed me. Perhaps it would have been a difficult marriage had he survived the war. Perhaps his experiences in the camp and my very different ones working through the war would have meant we had grown apart. Many wartime marriages would have been disasters had the partners lived. Alicia's was. Many others would have been. Perhaps mine would have been. Maybe we couldn't have lived together for 30 or 40 years. But I think we would have been happy. That's why it was their fault. That's why I had to stop them ruining him. They couldn't kill him but they wanted to ruin him, sending him home with nothing. After all he'd been through. It wasn't right. So I helped him."

"You fell in love with someone else?" I tried again, hoping that if I could get through to her she might realise how badly she was driving.

"Yes I fell in love again." She had heard me but she was still talking as if from another time. "I fell for another most unsuitable man. He was beautiful, brave and clever. He was older than me, he made me feel safe and cherished. But he had to leave me. He had to go back to his own country. He wasn't English you see. I had to help him. I loved him but I had to let him go. They were going to take everything from him, leave him with nothing after all he had done. I made sure he didn't leave with nothing."

Was she talking about Vijay? She had to be.

"I had to let him go and I thought I would never feel the same about anyone again. I waited."

Maureen turned towards me concentrating on me.

Not looking at the road.

"I waited for years. I thought he must be dead, if he had been alive he would have got in touch with me."

"You were living in Hoylake? Friends with my mother?" Somehow I had to get her to break out of the past and concentrate on the road.

"Yes. I had gone home after the war. But he would have known how to contact me. He would have found me." She sounded desperate.

"Of course he would." I said trying to keep the panic from my voice as she nearly didn't break in time to avoid the car in front.

"I allowed myself to fall in love again. I loved a man, the complete opposite of my lover in every way. He was my age, he was English, he wasn't exciting or mysterious. And he did not love me. He has never acknowledged how I feel about him, in 40 years he has never even mentioned it."

It could only be Ted. I remembered her saying something like 'nothing has changed, Ted's still in the Wirral and I'm still here'. But he didn't feel the same.

"Then you told me Vijay is alive. There was no reason why he couldn't have contacted me but he didn't. Why had he made his life without me? Whey had he never told me he was alive?"

How much I didn't know about the lives of the people close to me. But then perhaps I had never looked closely enough.

"You loved the wrong ones too." Still she wasn't concentrating on her driving, half turning towards me every few seconds.

"Me?" I looked back at the road, trying to make her do the same.

"Your first husband, what was his name?"

"Joe." I was staring straight ahead, trying not to engage with her, hoping she would concentrate again on driving as we headed up the slip road towards the motorway. I was relieved when her head turned back towards the road though she didn't relax the intensity of her conversation. "He was never going to make you happy. And Carl. You and he are too alike. You are both selfish." Out of the corner of my eye I saw she had turned towards me again. I was determined not to look at her hoping she would concentrate on the driving. "You needed a solid, reliable person, someone older, wiser, who would have told you what to do and how to do it." I didn't answer, hoping that the conversation was over as we joined the unforgiving traffic on the busy motorway.

Maureen positioned the car in the inside lane and drove steadily at a conservative 60 mph. I tried to concentrate on the woods and fields that we passed but could only try to work out what it was Maureen was

248

trying to tell me. She had loved the wrong people all her life, she thought I had too.

I glanced across at her and saw something in her face I had never seen before. There was a determination, a single-mindedness in her eyes. There was also a great sadness. Her voice was completely different when she spoke again, no longer passionate it was almost as if a switch had been turned. She spoke quietly, with resignation.

"It's not a problem Annie darling. Being 'in love with' someone is very different from loving them. I have loved Ted for nearly 40 years. I have watched him be obsessed with your mother and then, with hardly a blink of his eye fall in love with you. He shouldn't have done that. That wasn't fair."

It was all I could do not to take the wheel and steer towards the hard shoulder and stop the car.

"Don't feel sorry for me Annie dear, I knew a long time ago that I would never have him. He had plenty of opportunities. He is fond of me but only as one is fond of an old sofa. I am comfortable, and undemanding." There was resignation in her voice, but also anger. "He stayed with me many times when he was visiting your mother. But then he was so obsessed with her I felt sorry for him. I don't think she ever thought of him romantically for a moment. He was simply another person to be used to make her life more comfortable. I longed to tell him that he was looking in the wrong direction, that I would make him happy if only he would let me. Then he whisked her away up north to die. We kept in touch while you were studying but we didn't meet for years. Then at your graduation he fell in love with you."

"Sorry?" I thought I hadn't heard her correctly. I was trying to take in what she was saying , but she chose to interpret my word of enquiry as one of apology.

"Don't be, my dear. What you have to understand is that when you love someone you want them to be happy. They must be happy. Ted must be happy. But if that happiness is with you ..." She sounded sad and so defeated but at the same time defiant and proud. "He will be happy, but not..."

I thought I heard the last words *"with Alicia's daughter"* but I will never be sure.

That was it.

The car was travelling too slowly. I only realised at the last moment that as she had talked she was driving more and more slowly and had strayed across to the outside lane. The lorries and the vans wanted to go faster.

Maureen had been distracted, she had been looking at me instead of the road ahead and behind. I'm not sure whether she ever noticed the vehicle that slammed into the back of the car, pushing us into the central reservation from where we rebounded into the impatient traffic.

I clutched at the steering wheel and I suppose I must have screamed as I waited for the impact I could not prevent and into which I intuitively relaxed.

I looked at the grass, uncomprehending. It was brown, individual stems stood up in front of my eyes. I was lying face down. I hurt. I couldn't tell where I hurt, I just hurt. I tried to focus on the blades of grass in front of me but all I could feel was pain. Was this the pain my mother had felt, her back broken in the car crash that had changed her life? Was this how Bill had felt when he had been hit by the car? Was this complete absence of anything else in the world but pain what they, too, had felt?

I don't know how long I lay there until the silence was broken by the sound of sirens.

'My name is Jenny. I'm a paramedic. Can you hear me?' I think I was shouting, I have no idea what I would have been saying. 'My name is Jenny. I'm a paramedic. Can you hear me? My name is Jenny, I'm a paramedic, listen to me. What is your name?' 'My name?' 'Your name, darling, what is your name? Can you hear me?' I managed to mouth my name though whether any sound came out I don't know. 'Annie.' 'Annie? Can you tell me where it hurts?' She sounded relieved that I could at least try to speak. 'Bloody everywhere.' I tried to say. 'Don't move for a moment Annie, we just need to check you out.' She didn't need to tell me not to move I couldn't have. 'Maureen?' I tried to ask. 'Your friend? Don't you worry about her, she's being well looked after.' But I knew she was dead. I had seen her, she was leaning on the steering wheel and her eyes were open, her arms held out in front of her. Jenny said nothing other than to repeat that Maureen was 'being looked after'. 'Here, I'm giving you something for the pain. Everything will be alright. Just stay still Annie. Annie?' 'She's dead. Oh shit it hurts.' Jenny pulled the needle out and spoke into her radio. I couldn't hear what she was saying, I wasn't listening. Maureen was dead. I tried to move to look up at her, she deserved that. She deserved someone to look over her as she lay dead in that car and the noise of the traffic began to flow again. The edge of the pain began to soften as the injection began to take effect, the blades of grass slipped out of focus.

The image of Maureen blurred and was never seen again.

Chapter Thirty-Three

'Cuts and bruises' was the description of my injuries, nothing was broken, there would be no permanent damage. It didn't seem fair when Maureen was dead but I knew that never again would I hear the words 'only cuts and bruises' and think that the victim had got off lightly.

Despite her death being sudden and so unexpected Ted had found an envelope in the top drawer of her desk marked *'To be opened upon my demise'*. One sheet of paper listed all the people who would be important in the event of her death, her solicitor, particular friends and family members who should be contacted with details of her funeral. Another sheet described her wishes for her funeral, listing the music to be played and the poems to be read. I was surprised that there was a request for Ted to play my mother's tape, the same tape of her singing and reciting poems that had been played at her own funeral. I hadn't imagined it could still exist. I had listened to her re-recording that poem until it was, to her ears, perfect. *There's a breathless hush in the close tonight, Ten to make and the match to win"* and singing, again and again Noël Coward's words *I'll see you again, whenever Spring breaks through again,* until she felt it was as good as it was ever going to be. Only Ted and I, the two who had also been at that funeral 16 years before, could possibly understand the significance as we sat together in the church.

I had looked for some clue as to when she had made these notes and sealed the envelope. There was no date but the address for Ted was Greensand Hill. I didn't know exactly how long he had lived there but it was not long. There was no mention of me. Perhaps she had made the notes because it was the sensible thing for her to do, she was, after all, in her late 60s. I had never thought of her as being 'an old woman' but I supposed she must have thought herself one at times.

I really hoped Maureen had not done anything deliberately to hurt herself. Or me.

The church was not full but it was not embarrassingly empty. Most of the congregation were friends of Maureen's from the village. Maureen had requested bright colours for her funeral, apparently she had talked of it to Ted when they had both been at my mother's funeral. She didn't want people to be sombre in blacks and greys, so there were many bright hats and ties in the late summer sunshine.

Carl didn't attend the service though I know Ted had written to him with a copy of the notice he had put in the Telegraph. Charles and Linda were at the church, with Josie and little Andrew but they didn't come back to the cottage afterwards. I think they had told Bill, Al and Jack to stay at home, wary of us all meeting for the first time on such an occasion. I couldn't believe they would be so petty, the day was about Maureen and what she had meant to all of us, not about family differences, however long-standing and significant.

I threw the roses I had picked from her garden that morning onto Maureen's coffin concentrating on the brass nameplate with the words *Maureen Shelton 1918 – 1987* as they were lost forever under handfuls of soil.

It wasn't long before everyone had made their excuses and left Ted and I alone to tidy up. We would be back in a few days to clear all her things, there was no one else to do it. In the meantime I would be staying with Ted and my daughter. I wasn't ready to be on my own, especially in the emptiness of Maureen's house.

"You're quiet." Ted said as I dried the dishes he was washing and put them away in the familiar cupboards.

"It's been a long day."

"And an emotional one."

"Were you ever in love with her? Maureen I mean?" I had to ask.

"No." He didn't seem surprised at the question and weighed his answer carefully. "I can truthfully say that I never was in love with Maureen."

"Not even a little bit?"

"No, never, not even a little bit."

"But you knew she was in love with you."

"Yes, I'm afraid it was difficult to ignore at times. It was never spoken about. I just knew and she knew I knew and because I didn't say anything she knew the answer."

"How sad."

"I think she was sad for much of her life. She had many friends, just look how many turned out today, but none that were really close, that she could confide in. Alicia was too flighty and self-centred to be interested in anybody else, David had been her boss…"

"You knew?"

"Yes, of course, it wasn't a secret. She worked for him at the Ministry during the war. I think they tried to find jobs for people whose husbands were missing or in P-o-W camps. She was his secretary." As I listened to Ted talking about Maureen's war work I realised that he had no idea of what David's work had really been. "I think it was all pretty mundane stuff, supplies or some such."

Or perhaps he knew and wasn't letting on.

He lifted his soapy arms from the washing up bowl and pursed his lips, drew a breath and sighed deeply. "She had no one she could confide in, no real friends, so I think she was really quite lonely at times. Which is why," his voice brightened up "that is why she loved having you to stay."

"There was so much she could have told me if I had thought to ask, known to ask."

"Maybe she has." He said gently as he put his arm around my shoulders and held me gently to him and I cried tears of pain, frustration and tiredness. "Come on, you're tired. You've done far too much today and you're still not well. We'll come back next week. There'll be plenty of time to finish clearing up then."

So I left the cottage to drive past the scene of the accident to Greensand Hill, where I would finally meet my daughter and try to make some sort of sense about everything.

It was mid October before I felt up to going back to the cottage but we were finally setting off, after a quick drink at the Fox to allow the rush hour on the M25 to clear.

Ted and I had soon got into the habit of spending an hour or so every evening in the pub a short walk from Greensand Hill, it gave Josie some private time with Andrew. We usually got home in time for the Archers but enjoyed the company of the varied group of farmers, professionals and self employed who congregated at six o'clock in the comfortable, old-fashioned bar.

"They say there's going to be a bit of a blow tonight."

"Someone's said a hurricane's on the way."

"You don't get hurricanes in this part of the world."

"Well bloody strong winds then."

"No way. It'll all blow over…."

"Ho ho ho."

"It'll all be a storm in a teacup…"

"Ho ho ho."

"Any more jokes about wind?"

"You're having a laugh aren't you?"

Half listening to the conversation going on around us Ted and I planned the evening. We had put off going back to Maureen's cottage for too long, every time Ted had suggested it I had found a reason not to. 'We've got to go together, I can't do it on my own.' he said patiently. 'We'll wait until you're ready.' And now I was ready.

Since the day of the accident I had watched Ted, trying to read what he was thinking, how he was looking at me. I never saw anything but friendly concern. Apart from the one time when he had taken my arm at the funeral as my mother's voice rang out through the packed church he had done nothing that could be misunderstood. We had spent a lot of time together and had talked without tension or embarrassment about many things. He had never given any indication that he felt the way Maureen had told me he did.

"Quick, drink up, we'd better be on our way if we're going to get there."

"What do you think about the weather forecast?" I asked as we drove through the woods down to the main road. Ted turned on the news and we listened in silence. "Nothing about an impending storm. We'll be fine." He took his hand off the wheel and squeezed my knee in a familiar gesture of reassurance.

"Please..." I couldn't keep the panic out of my voice and he replaced his hand on the steering wheel.

As we passed Greensand Hill I thought of Josie and Andrew, how good she had been about my coming to live with them, how understanding she had been of the interloper in the household that she had largely run. She had been absolutely wonderful. 'As long as you baby-sit whenever I ask I don't mind one bit' she had said. I was enjoying spending time with my grandson. He was beautiful and I realised what I had missed by being such a bad mother to my own children. Josie put me to shame. In the previous month I had renewed my acquaintance with Jack, Al and Bill, neither Charles nor Linda had wanted to see me. The boys often visited their sister and we had established a relationship that ignored the fact that I was their mother. They had offered to stay with Josie and Andrew while Ted and I were away. 'You never know what might happen in a big empty house isolated in the dark woods.' Al had teased their sister. 'They may be bears' Jack added 'or wolves' Bill completed the argument and Josie had laughingly agreed. She hadn't had a night alone since Andrew was born.

It was still light when we pulled up outside the empty cottage after a trouble free journey. It was warm inside the house as we had left the Aga on, thinking we would be back much sooner, but there was a pile of post on the doormat and the house felt unlived in and unloved.

"We should have come sooner." Ted spoke aloud what I had been thinking.

I put the jumble of envelopes on the kitchen table and went round the house switching on lights and closing curtains. I hesitated outside the room that had been Maureen's bedroom but took a deep breath and opened the door, striding across the small room to the windows and pulled the curtains shut with two brisk movements.

I was going to hate the next two days.

"Come on, we'll have a bite to eat at the pub and then come back to sort this lot." Ted had read my mood and realised that sitting in the house without a little bit of Dutch courage would be impossible.

We missed the 9 o'clock news but we caught the end of the weather forecast which now was talking about 'very high wind speeds expected along the south coast'.

"Force 9 or 10 is bad isn't it?" I asked.

"It won't get that bad inland, look they say it will go up the Straits of Dover. I wouldn't want to be on a cross channel ferry but we'll be fine here."

"And the children?"

"They'll be fine."

"Can we listen to a later forecast? If you think about it every one we've heard has got worse and worse."

"You know something Annie?"

"What?"

"For the first time in my life I'm listening to you being worried about your children."

"What the hell was that?" I sat up in bed, aware I was shouting and rigid with fear at the noise outside. There had been a gigantic crash, as if a bomb had gone off or a lorry had driven into the front of the cottage. A number of alarms were sounding discordantly adding to the chaos. I got up out of the bed I had slept in over the years and put on my dressing gown and bumped into Ted who was on the landing.

"What's happening?" I screamed trying to make myself heard. "What's going on?"

"I think it's that hurricane that wasn't going to happen."

We went from room to room together, checking windows and

seeing what damage had been done to the house. The noise of the wind and the alarms was horrendous.

"Can you see anything?"

"Nothing."

"Can you hear the phone?"

At that moment the lights went out but Ted turned on the torch he had in his hand, it was a dim beam but at least there was some light as we felt our way down the narrow stairs.

I found the phone and picked up the receiver. I could hardly hear the voice at the other end of the line.

"Mum? Mum?" It was Josie.

I could never remember her calling me Mum. And she sounded very upset.

"Yes darling." I don't think I had ever called her that in her life. "What is it? Are you alright? Are you all alright?" I realised I was shouting to make myself heard. She shouted back "No. Oh Mum! Everything's falling apart! There's trees down everywhere! Jack went out to see what was happening and came back with his crash helmet on so many tiles were flying off the roof! And the big tree's down! There's branches in the…"

"Josie! Josie! Are you there? Oh Ted. The phones gone dead. There's trees down, tiles off the roof. Oh Ted what can we *do*?"

"We're not going anywhere in this, all we can do is listen to the radio."

"What time is it?"

"Two thirty."

"Do you want a coffee?"

So we sat in the dark kitchen and listened to the transistor radio. Ted twiddled the knob backwards and forwards to find anything that was talking about the storm.

"Do you think they'll be alright?"

"The house is well built."

"But they're surrounded by millions of trees and trees are coming down all over the place."

"I'd be worried if they were on the coast, or at the top of the hill, but they're not, they're protected. They'll be fine. They're probably all sitting round the kitchen table drinking coffee listening to the radio. Just as we are."

"I hope the boys aren't stupid enough to try to go outside again. It sounds like it's getting worse."

There was nothing we could do but drink coffee, listen to the noise and the crackling radio which Ted continually retuned to try to find out what was happening.

It was a long night.

When the shipping forecast came on the radio just before 6 o'clock we listened in awe at the storm warnings and coastal reports. I knew next to nothing about the sea, despite having been born and brought up in a coastal town. Hoylake had been, as my brother Charles used to say, 'Orpington on Sea', a suburb of Liverpool first and foremost, not a real coastal town. But even I knew Force 7 was pretty bad, but they were talking about 'Gusting Hurricane Force 12'.

"They said there wouldn't be a hurricane." I complained.

"'Hurricane force' doesn't mean a Hurricane it just means very, very strong." Ted was being pedantic.

"How strong? What does 'hurricane force 12' do?"

It was beginning to get light and there was enough for Ted to find the books that Maureen had used to complete her crosswords. "This one will have it in." He thumbed through the index and found the pages he wanted. "It doesn't say what Hurricane force does." He sounded disappointed but carried on reading. "*Force 11, Violent storm, Very rarely experienced, accompanied by widespread damage.*"

"What does 'widespread damage' mean?"

"Well Force 10 says *seldom experienced inland, trees uprooted, considerable structural damage.* We definitely had that." Looking outside as the day began to establish itself we could begin to see the mess that had been the garden. "Force 9 says *slight structural damage occurs, chimney-pots and slates removed.* That must be what that is." He pointed towards a pile of bricks in the middle of the lawn.

"What about Force 8?" I asked.

"*Breaks twigs off trees, generally impedes progress.*"

We both laughed. In the middle of the lawn was a complete tree, on its side, surrounded by bricks and slates, the remains of someone's garden furniture. "I recognise that," I said somewhat hysterically, "that belongs to the pub. We were sitting on that last night. It should be 100 yards away."

"So should that." Ted pointed to the door of the red phone box, caught up in branches leaning against what was left of the garden hedge.

"Oh my God."

Ted took my hand and we walked through the house and opened the front door. The wind was nothing like as bad as it had been but we watched as tree branches, dustbins and rubbish were blown down the lane.

Ted shut the door. "Come back in, Annie. Let's get back to that radio."

'Under no circumstances should you attempt to travel anywhere.'

'There are no trains or buses, many roads are blocked.'

'The area around Sevenoaks has been particularly badly hit.'

"Sevenoaks! Ted! They say Sevenoaks is *particularly badly hit*. Should we call the police?"

"They'll be inundated."

"What about Charles? Linda?" Surely they wouldn't continue their feud against me under these circumstances. "We can try them to see if they know what's going on?"

"I'll try, I doubt they'd be asleep." He picked up the phone and dialled. I noticed he knew the number without looking it up.

"No. There's nothing. Just number unobtainable."

There was nothing that could give either of us peace of mind. There was a continuous stream of warnings, not to go out on the roads, not to venture out of houses while trees, chimneys, roof slates were likely to fall at any time, not to try to get to work. "They're all telling us what *not* to do. What *can* we do? And *please* don't say have another cup of coffee."

"Thank goodness for the Aga. Eggs, bacon, sausage and tomato. Just what we need to start the day."

I opened the cold box we had brought with us and began to cook breakfast.

"We've got to try to get back, Ted."

"I don't think we should. We should stay listening to the radio. Then, later, we can try. If you want to."

"Of course I want to. God knows what's happened to them all. What are you smiling at?"

"I know it's not nice, worrying, but really they will be fine and it's wonderful to see you caring."

"Of course I care."

"No 'of course' about it. You spent a large part of your life not caring."

"And a lot of the rest of it caring for the wrong people."

I couldn't begin to interpret the look he gave me before he changed the subject.

"There's nothing you can do for a few hours, get some rest because once we get going, oh yes, we'll try at lunchtime, of course we will, you'll need all the energy you have."

So as the last of the storm died down I lay in the bed that had once been mine and tried to relax to the sound of Ray Moore on Radio 2 telling no one in south eastern England to attempt to leave their homes.

It was just past 12 when we put our bags back in the car and settled in for the unknown.

"We'll come back as soon as we can." He said as he tuned the radio into a station that was talking about travel and the weather. "I've made the house as secure as I can and spoken to the neighbours, they'll keep an eye on the place but we'll get back as soon as we can."

He reached over and put his hand on mine. "Everything will be fine. Trust me."

And I did.

"So far so good." Ted said as we drove slowly up the main street of the village, our usual route, and out onto the deserted main road. Although we had to zig zag to avoid fallen trees we managed to reach the final roundabout before the motorway. The road there was completely blocked so we had to turn towards the town centre. There was simply no alternative if we weren't to turn back, and we weren't going to do that.

"This is a one way street."

"I know."

"And we're going the wrong way."

"I'm following that chap in front, he seems to know where he's going."

"He might be going home."

"In which case we'll join him."

Ted concentrated on following the car in front. The zig-zagging stopped as we neared the centre of the town where there were fewer trees. But by now we were the centre car in a convoy of five and entering the pedestrian precinct.

"This is ridiculous."

"But look, there's the road to the motorway."

"But we've got to drive down these *steps*!"

"That didn't do the suspension any good. Still here we are, clear road to the motorway."

There was nothing on the slip road to say the motorway was closed but I was very worried. There seemed so little other traffic. Were we the only ones stupid enough to be out ignoring all the warnings? We crept along never faster than 20 miles an hour, often considerably slower.

There was so much debris. Every few yards there would be a carpet of leaves and twigs, branches, even large trees, but we managed to get through to the Reigate turn off where we were flagged down by the police cars parked across the carriageway.

"You can't go any further I'm afraid. Sir. Madam."

"But we've got to get to Westerham, my children, my grandson." I was so tense from the journey and disappointed not to have got those extra few miles that I was nearly in tears.

"Sorry madam, but the road is completely shut. You could try the A25, though I think you'll be lucky to get through. You'll get close to the town but they want the roads clear for the police and emergency vehicles."

"Emergency? Are people hurt? Are people injured?"

"I'm afraid so madam, there are tens of thousands of trees down, many onto houses and there have been injuries. Haven't you been watching the news? Listening to the radio?"

"They don't go into much detail."

"It's not the town that's worst hit, it's the hills around. It'll be some time before any of those people get out."

"What about helicopters? Can't you get to them like that?"

"There are hundreds of people trapped by the trees, People are cutting roads through, now the wind has dropped and people are they're walking through."

"But my son's in a wheelchair, my grand-son's only a few weeks old. How are *they* going to cope?" I don't care what impression I gave I wanted them to help, and if they thought it was only a woman, her baby and crippled husband in the house I didn't care.

The young policeman looked concerned, I tried not to catch Ted's eye but out of the corner of my eye I thought I saw him trying not to smile.

"Give me the details and I'll get onto the radio."

A few minutes later, after he had muttered urgently into his radio, the young policeman said "Follow me. I'll escort you as far as I can. I won't be able to take you into Kent but I can get you to the border."

"Why were you smiling back there?" I asked Ted as we followed the police car off the motorway and down Reigate Hill.

"It's just that you're like a lioness trying to protect her cubs, but those cubs are pretty grown up and have been looking after themselves for years. I have far more confidence in them than you do, I suppose it's because I don't think of them as children. You still do, but they are as grown up as you and me. Whoops!" He interrupted himself as we turned sharply to the right, following the police car through someone's drive. It was a very large house with an in and out drive, which was handy as there were a number of trees blocking the main road exactly half way between the entrance and the exit. "Neat!"

"Where do you get expressions like that?"

"From your daughter."

It took a long time to get to Westerham and as we got closer our worries increased. We had thought Surrey was bad, but as we travelled eastwards the devastation was getting worse and worse. Our police escort stopped short of the town. The young officer got out of the car and wished us luck. We thanked him saying we hoped he wouldn't get into trouble. "No one really knows what anyone's doing today. I hope your daughter is OK and your grandson."

We drove the final few miles in awed silence, it seemed that nothing had been untouched by the wind, every house, every garden, was affected. We reached Brasted and at the point where we should have turned right off the main road to head up the hill there was a 'Road Closed' sign. It was completely redundant because no one could have thought for one moment that they could drive up the lane, it was as if the cables and trees had been woven together in an impenetrable three dimensional tapestry.

"I'll try the pub." Ted did a three point turn in the road where usually there was so much traffic that such a manoeuvre would have been unthinkable and drove back to the White Hart where the car park was full of pick up trucks and four wheel drives.

We were welcomed as if from another planet, the lady behind the bar handed us all drinks.

"On the house, if you'll just tell us what it's like in the outside world." There was no electricity here either and they had been relying on a barely audible transistor radio for any news.

"Is everyone alright on the hill?"

"We've heard from the Fox," she said "well not actually *from* the Fox, *about* it."

"As far as we can tell. They're all using a car-phone, it's the only contact anyone has. There're hundreds of men working with chain saws to clear the lane, they've even got the army involved."

"Has anyone heard from Josie?" Ted asked.

"No. Sorry. There's that many trees down in the drive."

We were only half a mile from the house but today it might well have been a hundred miles.

"Will they be OK?"

"There's no reason why not. We haven't heard of any problems. Well here's your answer…" She pointed to the door.

"Jack!"

"Ted?" He sounded shocked and relieved. "Mum?"

He couldn't help but show his surprise as I got up and gave him a relieved hug.

"How is everyone? Josie?"

"Everyone's fine. Tired, no shattered, but we're all OK. Andrew slept through the lot."

"How did you get here?"

"Down the lane, crawling over and under the trees. The chainsaws are making a bit of headway but it'll take days. You wouldn't believe it up there. It's like all the trees were matchsticks and someone's just tipped the box out. It's unbelievable."

"Are you sure everyone's OK? We've been so worried."

"We're OK but we haven't got much food. We've no milk and so I came down to see if I could get some, anything really. We were only expecting to be there last night. They say we won't be able to get through with a car for three or four days."

"Three or four days!"

"You can't believe what it's like up there."

"We'll get some food, there must be some in town, and then we'll all carry it back."

"I don't think you'll find much in the shops, everyone's clearing the shelves." A man sitting at the bar with a shopping basket interrupted our conversation, "I've been into town and this is all I could get." He pointed out a single bottle of water and some packet cheese.

"No bread?"

"Nothing, the shelves were cleared."

"What are we going to do?"

"There'll be stuff tomorrow, we've only got to get through today."

"I'm so stupid, Ted, we both are. We could have got everything we could possibly have needed in the village and brought it with us. We just didn't think."

"Why would we? We couldn't have known it was like this."

"We'd still have to carry it up the hill and it was difficult enough coming down hill not carrying anything."

"We'll have to try."

We sat in the bar sipping at the beer, Ted making a list of what we would need for two or three days for six people and a baby and how we could possibly, even if we managed to buy anything, get it up the hill.

"Come on Jack," Ted suddenly stood up, "come with me, no, Annie, you stay here. We'll be back in an hour or so."

It was the middle of the afternoon already, it might be dark before they got back and then we had to walk two miles up the hill, a difficult enough walk even without the hundreds of fallen trees it looked like we would have to negotiate.

I watched Jack leave with Ted and sat down at a corner table by the fireplace. I didn't know any of the men and women standing around the bar sharing their experiences of the night before. I picked up the menu that was on the table and read the brief history of the pub that was printed on the back. *The White Hart* ... *The Pub of the Few* ... There was a picture of a blackout screen with chalked signatures *Dickie* ... *Brian*... *Michael* ... *Tony* ... *Jimmy* ... Elizabeth had sat here, under this low beamed ceiling and had waited for Jimbo. David had sat down with her and had told her what she had already known. I was too tired to cry so I just thought as hard as I could about them both, trying to connect with them across the gulf of 45 years.

Just over an hour later Ted and Jack came back grinning and excited.

"Come on, we're setting off up the hill. But first, here, put these on."

They had thought of everything, even a pair of decent walking shoes for me, the ones I was wearing would obviously have been completely useless. Outside they handed me an anorak, a pair of gloves and a rucksack which clattered as I manhandled it over my shoulders. When they had helped me prepare myself for the trek each of them put on an identical anorak and hoisted vast rucksacks, at least twice the size of the one they had given me, onto their backs.

"It looks like we're heading off into the Himalayan foothills. I hope you've got the..." and as Ted silently held up a white slab "...Kendal Mint Cake." We laughed together. It was a wonderful feeling.

I caught Jack's eye and he grinned, "Here, put this in your sack" we might not get there by dark.

Ted was suddenly very serious, "It's not going to be easy, Jack's told me what it was like for him coming down, going up's going to be hard work."

"And Ted's worried about you Mum, he thinks you're not really OK after the accident. But I'll help. Don't struggle on, tell me when you need a rest." I couldn't believe this thoughtful young man was the same Jack who had made my life such a misery in Cambridge.

"It will probably be dark anyway before we get to the end of the drive."

I saw Jack and Ted exchange a look, I realised they were both thinking I would not be able to make it. I was going to show them.

We started off up the lane, Jack in front, Ted in the rear and me in the middle. At first it was quite easy going and I wondered what all the fuss was about, there was a relatively clear path along the middle of the road. There were twigs and leaves covering the tarmac and they were slippery from the rain which was still falling and I was very grateful for the anorak and the gloves. The cut trunks of trees littered the side of the road, but as we walked the clear road got narrower and narrower until every yard became a struggle.

When we turned a small bend we reached as far as the chainsaws had reached in a day.

We were maybe 100 yards up the lane.

It had taken them a day and we had hardly started. Ahead, in the gathering dark, there was a haphazard tapestry of trunks, branches and cables. Everything suddenly seemed overwhelming; the storm, the disruption, the implications of all this damage, what it was doing to so many people's lives suddenly seemed immeasurably vast. I just sat down staring at the mud and leaf covered tarmac.

"Come on Annie. We can do it." Ted saw the tears in my eyes and knew encouragement was all I needed.

"Come on Mum."

I thought, for the second time that day, that my children calling me 'Mum' was one of the most wonderful things I had ever heard.

"Here we go then!" I clambered over the first trunk and slithered down the other side. "What are you two waiting for?"

We struggled up the lane, pushing through the branches, hoisting each other over the trunks, pulling branches and cables out of the way for the others, squeezing through narrow gaps. As it got darker Ted turned on his torch. "Let's just use one for as long as we can, you never know how long they're going to have to last us." Jack nodded seriously in agreement. Two men together, facing up to whatever the elements could throw at us. Somehow we kept going until we reached the drive. It seemed to have taken hours and we were exhausted when we turned to face the final hundred yards to the house.

"There's no lights." I should really have known better but I was exhausted and was worried about what we would find. The effort of actually getting back to the house had kept that out of my mind all the way up the hill. Now we were almost home I began to worry.

"Nearly there. I cleared some of the drive this morning, Al and Bill were going to do what they could during the day."

"Bill?" I couldn't help asking.

"His chair was really useful. Once we cut stuff he could carry it out of the way. His arms are really strong, he's much stronger than either of us. They'll have cleared most of the drive, only a few yards to go."

"Look, there's a light."

"Hey! Jack! Is that you?" We heard the relief in Al's voice.

"Yeah! And I've got company." Jack yelled back to his brothers.

We stumbled towards the light, thankful not to have to climb any more. As we neared the house Ted shone his torch upwards.

"Oh my good God!"

The large cedar tree that had occupied most of the front lawn had fallen onto the house. It was leaning against what was left of the front gable of the roof, its branches poking through what should have been windows.

"Where..? Are you..? What...?" I knew I should be calm and collected but so many thoughts came to my mind at once.

"When we're inside we can find out everything." Ted took off my rucksack and slung it over his shoulder, he put his arm around my waist and almost carried me the last few yards into the house. A few minutes later we were sitting around the table in the kitchen, the candlelight flickering, the bread and cheese a feast.

"We had to turn the Aga off."

"A tree's fallen on the oil tank."

"We didn't know whether it was safe or not."

"So we thought we'd better turn it off."

"You did absolutely the right thing."

"So we cut up some of the branches."

"There are a few around."

"Ho ho."

"And lit the fire."

"But it smoked."

"I told them the wood was too wet and too green."

"But we found some dry stuff in the shed."

"Well actually it *was* the shed."

"Well anyway we found some dry stuff and made a fire."

"We didn't burn it all."

"We kept some. Just in case."

Everyone around the table was talking twenty to the dozen and we carried on talking for most of the evening about what we had all gone through the night before. As I listened to Ted and my children I realised how happy I was.

Scared, bewildered, exhausted.

But happy.

Chapter Thirty-Four

It took a week before we had returned to something like normality after the storm. It was two days after we had returned to the house before the men with JCBs and chainsaws reached us. It wasn't possible to leave in a car for another day and we still hadn't got the electricity back before Ted said we must get back to Maureen's cottage.

We'll just go for the day, we won't stay. We'll go over and make a start." He said at breakfast on the Tuesday after the storm. "The longer we leave it the more difficult it will be."

"And there'll be a lot of clearing up to do."

Ted and I walked down the lane, rucksacks on our backs, to retrieve the car which was still parked at the White Hart. We had no opportunity to talk as all our efforts were spent avoiding slipping on the debris of a thousand trees but we had no need to talk; simple glances were enough to communicate and once in the car we were concentrating on our worries about the task ahead.

The cottage looked forlorn as we pulled up. The village had been cleared of much of the detritus of the storm, but the gardens looked as if bombs had hit the area.

While Ted sorted everything that could be burned from the garden and lit a bonfire, I started looking through Maureen's things. In the first black sack I put the contents of her dressing table and drawers, her wardrobe was neat and tidy and I looked at the clothes on the hangers and decided they were all suitable for the charity shop and carried them down to the car. They all looked perfectly clean and there were still dry cleaning labels on some, attached with small safety pins. I stripped her bed and put the sheets and blankets in a second black sack for burning. There were still creases in the sheets, it was almost as if they had only been slept in the once. I was surprised that there was nothing in her laundry basket, there were no dirty clothes anywhere.

I went down to the kitchen and checked the larder. There were very few tins and bottles but what there were I packed into a box to give to the church. The fridge was empty apart from the remains of the milk Ted and I had brought the previous week. I hadn't noticed then that there was so little food in the house, no half used packs of cheese or butter, no unopened packs of food ready for eating.

It was almost as if the house had been cleared already.

I took the black sacks out to Ted who was tending the bonfire, handing him a cup of tea.

"That's all?" he asked.

"Everything's so neat and tidy. Unnaturally so."

"You're thinking it's almost as if she knew aren't you?"

"Or…"

"Don't say it Annie. Don't even think it."

Despite what Ted said, I couldn't help but think 'it'.

I stayed with Ted, helping him pile branches of ever increasing size on the bonfire. I didn't like to say that I was worried about going back inside the over-organised and uncomfortably tidy house. We watched the black sacks melt, and the clothes inside disintegrate in the heat.

I stood back and watched Ted working on the bonfire, prodding at bits of wood and plastic, intent on the flames.

How long had I known this man but how many times had I really looked at him? Had I ever *really* looked at him, had I ever *really* seen him at all? I watched his movements, his arms and his back, the slight shake of his head as he successfully moved a large log into position. His hands, why had I never noticed how long and tapered his fingers were, tucking some of his hair behind an ear. Some would say his hair was too long for a man of his age but it suited him. There was something very, I tried to find the word to describe him, strong, physical, about his back and his arms, with his shirt sleeves rolled up to his elbows, as he turned to pick up some more fuel for the fire.

"Is there much else?" Ted turned towards me and I hoped he hadn't noticed that I had been staring at him for some time.

"I haven't touched the dining room and her desk."

"I'll be with you when this has died down a bit. If there's anything you don't want to look at leave it to one side."

"I think she knew. Either she knew or…."

"Annie. I told you. No."

But we both thought it. I know I did, and from the look in Ted's eyes, he thought it too. I didn't just *think* it, I *knew* it. Maureen had tried to kill us both when she had driven me along the M25. I don't know why. I would never be able to prove it, but I was as sure as I could be, and it made me wary of what I was going to find in the papers that she would have left.

I opened one of the twenty or thirty identical brown notebooks, randomly picking a page about half way through. I had no idea when it had been written.

Heard from Ted. It is so very hard not to say anything but to say anything would be a waste of valuable breath.

I flicked through a few pages and read more.

David is dangerous because he is so charming. He knows what he's doing but he never lets other people in on his plans, you have to guess and usually you will guess wrong."

Maureen had known so much all along and I had never had the chance to ask her. Perhaps that was one of the many things I had done to upset her.

There were pages in the diaries she had kept during the war devoted to details of bombing raids, travel difficulties, and worries about her husband, though these were surprisingly few and far between. I noted the mentions of her sister, Kathleen, and trips to the Wirral.

I couldn't resist reading the entry for 1st September 1946, the day I was born.

Poor Alicia. We were watching the cricket when she started. A was going to let her go to the nursing home alone. Ted took her. No one should ever have to carry a child conceived by rape to full term, it is not right, it can never be right but A will never know and will bring up the brat as his own. At least she has a friend in me – at least until she learns Kathleen is my sister. Sometimes it is good that I was married, what relationship has Maureen Shelton to Kathleen McNamara?

So she had known from the very beginning that Carl and I weren't related by blood. Somehow it didn't matter any more. Flicking back through one of the diaries I caught another entry in January 1946.

V at the flat. I don't know what I would do without him and his support.

I didn't note which book it was in as I wanted to read more about my mother and was flicking through book after book looking for a reference to 'Alicia'.

Alicia wrote today, she wants to find a house, live here in Surrey, She will be broke but I will do my best.

A few pages later Maureen's patience was obviously being sorely tried.

Kathleen says Arnold has money troubles, but surely he's got enough to support Alicia. Maybe not. He's giving her £100 a month, I've told her that's nothing. If only V were here, he'd help. She wants money, far more money than I have any idea she might get. God I hope Max knows what he's doing.

The implications of what I was reading did not sink in. If I had been reading more carefully I would have known exactly what they were but I had noticed the word 'Carl' and concentrated on that.

This young man Carl. What a shame he has no idea of our history, mine and his. Really he is very naïve and weak. If Susannah falls for his story I feel it won't last long and she will be the lesser for it. He is a self centred, self important person. I hope that she manages to extract herself from her obsession with him. He is not worth the trouble.

There were so many books of handwritten notes. I opened another at random.

They're going to stop him at Aden, take everything he has. But I've arranged…

I didn't have a chance to turn over the page and read more as Ted asked "How are you doing?"

I would have to take all these books with me. I pushed them hurriedly into one of the black sacks and hoped Ted didn't see anything furtive in my movement.

"Just diaries. I haven't found a will or anything like that." I tried to divert Ted from the contents of the bag, perhaps he would think they weren't important.

"Her will? Of course." He answered as if I had given him an idea he had never had. "Annie. Never mind." His voice had changed and I looked up to see him staring at me in a way I found impossible to interpret.

"Here. I think I've found her will." I handed him the envelope.

He read it quickly without telling me what the contents were. "This seems in order. Oh dear."

"What is it?"

"She's left everything to me. The house, everything. Oh dear. I can't possibly…"

I took the single sheet from him and read.

And finally, Ted, you have my memories, my hopes, my dreams, my wasted opportunities, my sincere and complete wishes that you find happiness."

"She really loved you didn't she?"

"I rather think she did."

"And to Josie, my diaries. May she make sense of them, understand them, learn about her family from them."

"She never expected me to survive did she? She hasn't left anything to me. When was the will signed?"

Ted didn't answer, he simply held up a piece of notepaper that had been tucked into the envelope with the will.

"Oh Annie." He said, distraught, as I grabbed the paper from his hands.

"Goodbye Ted, I am not in the least sorry that at last it is all over. I could not

have deserved you, if I had I would have won something more than just your affection years ago. I hope I have succeeded in taking her with me because if I didn't deserve you she surely doesn't either. If she still exists, perhaps standing by you as you read this, you must both know that you can never be together. I know you want her Ted, and I have watched her growing to want you. But you will never find happiness with your daughter, the daughter you forced into Alicia."

I looked at him, no words would come. Maureen was saying that Ted was the man who had raped my mother. Ted was my father.

"It is *not* true." He spoke quietly as if disappointed that I could possibly believe what I had read. "It is not *true*. Annie. She is *lying*. It is *not true*."

I really couldn't think.

Maureen had killed herself. She had tried to kill me. And the reason she gave was that Ted, the man she had loved for years, was my father and loved me in a way he should not.

She had tried to tell me. I remembered parts of that last conversation we had had in the car. I tried to remember the details. Why had she always welcomed me to her house? Was that just to keep an eye on me? If I was with her I couldn't be with Ted. I tried to think back years to when I had first met Jonathan. Had she encouraged me? Had she said anything to push me in his direction? She had been like a mother to me, I had always thought she was far more like a mother to me than my own.

"Annie, look at me. *It… is… not… true."*

"Why would she lie? What reason on earth did she have to lie?"

"To separate us. Annie Can't you see? It was her insurance. In case you survived. In case there was ever a chance we would be together."

"But…" I couldn't think what to say. Ted had always been my friend, I had always loved him as a friend. He had always been part of my life, my *'parent substitute'* Maureen had said.

He stood more stiffly, more uncomfortably than I had ever seen him.

"Believe me, Annie, please. You must believe me. This is a *lie*. I'll have any test you like. It is absolutely not true."

He sounded so convincing but I couldn't speak.

"Talk to me Annie. Please." He sounded desperate. "Are you all right Annie? Please, say something."

"I think I'd better go."

"Don't. Annie, please you must believe me. This is *absolutely not true.*"

But I wasn't listening.

I picked up the black sack, turned and ran away.

Chapter Thirty-Five

I made a pact with fate as I headed for the station. If the taxi was there I would use it, if it wasn't I would walk back to the pub and wait for Ted to finish and listen to his explanation of what had been written on that piece of paper. Even as I turned the corner of the lane, bringing the station forecourt into view I wasn't sure whether or not I wanted the cab to be there. I walked for at least 20 steps staring at the ground, not daring to look. I still can't remember whether I was pleased or not to see the silver car with its driver waiting patiently for the next London train. How could I have been so deceived by Ted? I had thought he cared for me, I even wondered if I was falling in love with him. And all along it was he who had raped my mother. It would explain why he had looked after us so carefully. Josie and the boys were *his* grandchildren. Of course he would want to take care of them.

"It's rather a long trip I'm afraid." I warned the driver as I got into the taxi, still giving fate the opportunity to keep me here, send me back to the pub to wait for Ted.

"No worries, love, where to?"

He didn't blink when I said 'Westerham', he simply looked sympathetic. "Got family involved in the hurricane?"

"Something like that."

As we drove away I wondered what Ted would do when I didn't come back to him. He'd sit and have a drink, perhaps, thinking I had gone for a walk. After a few minutes he would ask at the pub if anyone had seen me. When told 'no' he would begin to worry, he'd go back to the cottage to see if I was there, he'd go back to the pub. Then, and only then, would he really begin to worry. He'd try to think what I would do.

I reckoned I had about two hours start on him.

The taxi drove at a steady pace and I settled in the back to think what I could do. I obviously had to go back to Greensand Hill to pick up my disks, my notes, some clothes, my passport. Luckily most of my things were still packed from my move from the cottage.

That seemed a lifetime ago.

In many ways it was.

I tried to put what had just happened out of my mind. I could not let myself think about Ted and what Maureen had written. I couldn't think about all the diaries I had in black plastic sack on the seat next to me. I had to just concentrate on what I was going to do in the next hour. Then I would worry about the next hour. And then the next.

The boys had gone back to Charles and Linda so Josie was the only person I would have to avoid. I asked the taxi to wait at the end of the drive while I walked to the house. It was quiet, there was no sign of Josie and Andrew. I let myself in and went straight to my room. I threw some clothes into a bag and picked up my briefcase.

I could hardly see for tears trying to focus my mind on what I could do now.

I would find Vijay and ask him why he wanted to hurt our family so much. For years now not one of us had been happy.

I had to go to India.

And at least in India I wouldn't have to think about Ted.

"Are you all right dear? Is everything OK?" The taxi driver looked concerned, my bags and tears seemed to indicate tragedy.

"I'm fine. Can you take me to London?" I couldn't face seeing if any trains were running. "The Savoy."

"It's going to be a lot of money."

"That's OK. Can we just get on our way?" I had been too long in the house and I didn't want anyone to come back, I didn't want Josie to look accusingly at me, or Ted to look disappointed.

As we drove down the lane I prayed we wouldn't meet Ted's MG coming up the hill. I couldn't face that.

We drove the hour it took to get to London in silence apart from the familiar tunes playing on the car radio. Every one had a meaning. I *will always love you* brought tears to my eyes and I tried not to listen to the lyrics but some of the songs were so familiar that the words just came into my head anyway. All of them seemed to be about leaving, loving, losing. We had hardly reached Bromley before I asked the taxi drive to turn the radio off.

I was really not sure I was doing the right thing.

But then what else was there I could do?

As the car drove me towards Heathrow two days later it would have been very easy to dwell on the four years since I had flown to India under such different circumstances but I was determined to be positive. I was not going to stay at the Taj so, since the Kambli family had a house in Juhu, a beach resort to the north of the city, American Express booked me a room in a hotel there. They were surprised there was a room at such short notice.

But every time I thought of something positive Ted came back into my mind.

Only when I was checking in my luggage did I realise something significant was missing. Maureen's diaries. They had been in the taxi as I had been driven up to London.

I had eight hours on the plane to do nothing but worry about the diaries.

I tried to think of other things, questioning everything I had always believed.

It was Ted who had told me I was not Arnold Donaldson's child, it was Ted who had told me I was free to love Carl as we did not share a father, it was Ted who had told me I was conceived when my mother was raped. I had never wondered who my real father was.

It had never seemed to matter.

I had never had any reason to disbelieve what Ted had told me that summer's evening in 1976 and I had never known anyone else well enough to ask them if what Ted had said was true. Everyone who might have known was dead. Except Max. And Ted.

I tried not to believe Ted could have harmed my mother. They had been friends, she wouldn't have been gone to live with him in her dying months if he had done that to her.

But maybe they had had an affair, maybe it hadn't been rape at all, maybe my mother had wanted to be made love to by Ted.

Just as I did.

I didn't know what to think.

I only knew that I loved Ted and really did not want him to be my father.

And Maureen's diaries would have told me more. But I had left them behind on the seat of a taxi that I would never be able to trace.

I had left them on the seat.

I couldn't believe I could have been so stupid.

Chapter Thirty-Six

Twenty hours after leaving the Savoy I was sitting in the garden of my luxurious room watching the waves crash onto the beach. The sun was setting, the red band leading straight across the Arabian Sea from it to me. The perfect red circle, so much larger than ever it was in England, dropped gradually under the horizon. Sunset here, where would it be sunrise? I tried to remember the time zones and not think about the black sack on a taxi's back seat, or now in a dustbin or on a tip.

I was woken by the phone ringing.

"Mrs Smith?" The voice was Indian but the accent was perfect middle class English. He didn't talk like a member of the hotel's staff, there was too much authority in his voice. "Or should I say Mrs Parry? Miss Donaldson?"

"Who are you? Ramesh? Is that you?"

"My name is not Ramesh."

"Then how do you know my names, my history?"

"We knew you were coming. We have contacts at the High Commission, we have been waiting for you."

"Who's 'we'?"

"My family."

"Are you a Kambli or a Thakersey? Are you related to Ramesh? Vijay? I want to meet Vijay I have so much I need to tell him."

"There are many questions to ask and to answer. You have been very busy since you were in our city last. We want to know what you know, then we can tell you what you don't."

"You mean you want to *help* me?"

"You've got this far. You deserve to reach your goal."

"Do you know what that is?"

"Better than you do yourself." He waited for that to sink in before asking, very politely whether I would like to join him for a drink in the hotel bar at noon the following day. I accepted his invitation knowing that I had no alternative but to do so.

I opened the drawer in the bedside table and picked out the telephone directory. I hadn't really expected to find a Vijay Thakersey or even Ramesh Kambli. And I didn't.

I turned on the television and watched the amazing ham acting and stylised singing of an old film *Love in Tokyo*. The colours, the music and the story all seemed completely over the top and for the hour I was watching it I forgot about England, the storm, the children and Ted.

But then there was a news programme. It was in English but not in an English that was easy to follow or understand. There was film of an old man getting into a large white limousine, the caption read *Vijay Thakersey*. I couldn't understand what the news story was about but it had something to do with films and a new deal that had been signed. I looked at the three younger men with him and wondered if I would be meeting one of them the next day.

I picked up the phone. "Is it possible to call England?"

"I'm afraid not, Memsahib, if you give me the number I will phone you when we have got through. Sometimes it is easier than others, but with the World Cup there are no lines available."

"The World Cup?"

"The cricket Memsahib. You mean you did not know? You were lucky to get the room here. It was only because of the High Commission in London, they said it was very important that you have a room in this hotel."

"Should I call you Annie or Susannah?" The good looking, well dressed man sat next to me in the bar. I recognised him from the news bulletin the previous evening.

"Susannah." I replied, Annie reminded me too much of Ted and Maureen, then added "Thanks" hurriedly in case he thought I was being short with him.

"And I am Sandeep."

"How do you do Sandeep? Do I assume your family name is Thakersey?"

He nodded in assent.

"I feel like we should get to know each other well, Susannah, my grandfather knew your grandfather very well."

"So I understand." I didn't want Sandeep to feel he had the upper hand in this conversation. "Do I have to thank you for ensuring I had a room in this lovely hotel despite the World Cup?"

He dipped his head in acknowledgement. "We felt it was time to talk to you and since you seemed to want to talk to us, well, we were not going to make it difficult for you."

"I suppose you want me to tell you what I know."

"No. It is not like that at all. You must understand that my grandfather and I never approved of what Ramesh did. We never wished harm to you or your family. It was Ramesh who felt the need for vengeance and who tried to bring ruin to my grandfather's friends."

"You don't like Ramesh?" I asked tentatively.

"He is a cousin. I would not say we had to like each other. I have no respect for him nor he for me. He breaks the law as if law doesn't apply to him. He is neither a nice nor a respectable man."

"And you are? Respectable? Nice?"

"I hope you will find me so."

"Can you tell me about your grandfather? I know something about him but, obviously, not enough."

"Of course. I am here to make you welcome and to do as you wish."

It was not the first contact with the Thakersey family I had expected.

"You must understand that my grandfather had a difficult time in England. He did not fit in with society, there was a lot of civil unrest at the time and Englishmen were not willing to welcome foreigners in their midst. He was an educated man who did not appreciate being treated as if he were of a lower caste. But he was a determined man, he would not return to his family with his tail between his legs. So he did what he was best able to do. He read the quality newspapers of the day and he wrote letters. Every day he would write a letter to The Times about some issue of the day, many were published. One day he received a note requesting his attendance at an office in a small street situated off Whitehall, of course he went. There he met Mr David Redhead who told him perhaps he could be of assistance to the mother country.

"My grandfather, however, was disappointed and shocked by the tone of the meeting. Instead of a request for service, which he would have been happy to comply with, Mr Redhead showed no respect, insisting that my grandfather was in his debt since, if he did not do as Mr Redhead instructed he would be deported. It was obvious that Mr Redhead knew a great deal about my grandfather's life as he threatened him with exposure as a fraud.

"My grandfather was a qualified lawyer but he had exaggerated his experience and qualifications to obtain work in London, a situation which Mr Redhead made very plain he was aware of. My grandfather understood he had little choice but to do as Mr Redhead instructed. He had gone to the meeting full of hope and enthusiasm for his mother country, he left disillusioned because what he had been told he must do to stay in the country was to lie, to cheat and to steal."

I had listened intrigued as Sandeep filled in some of the jigsaw pieces for me. What I resented, and I had had to keep myself from interrupting, was his view of David as a blackmailer. I tried to redress the imbalance of his view.

"But David, Mr Redhead, had to recruit the best people for the job."

I was surprised by his reaction.

"Your grandfather was not a 'nice' man. The operation he ran was not 'nice'."

"He was only doing what he had to do."

"You still don't understand do you? In that first year Mr Redhead recruited 15 men and women. If they didn't want to do what they were asked to do, or they tried and failed, the result was still the same." He paused seemingly reluctant to spell everything out. It was as if he felt I should have understood. I wasn't deliberately trying not to understand, it was just that where Sandeep was leading me was to a view of David I could not recognise. "My grandfather's test was to kidnap a brilliant young scientist from the University in Göttingen. They wanted him in England, or if not that then at least not working for Germany. My grandfather was to bring him to England and if he couldn't he was to kill him. He managed to drug the scientist and transport him into France but there were difficulties, I don't know exactly what happened but he tried to escape, my grandfather killed him. If he hadn't my grandfather was in no doubt he himself would have been killed.

"David couldn't…"

But Sandeep ignored my interruption.

"There was a lady my grandfather knew of, she was an aristocrat, she flew an aeroplane which was unheard of for a woman at the time. She failed in the task your grandfather had set her and her aeroplane crashed."

"You can't know that that was my grandfather's fault!"

"He admitted it. He told the others that it would happen the day before it did."

I couldn't believe this was the David I had known.

"There was another man, a man from the east of London, his name was Ian. He failed in his task and his body was found many weeks after he disappeared, tied in chains and dumped in the River Thames. There was a girl, a working class girl from the north of England who had been recruited because her father was German and she spoke the language perfectly. She failed and she was found burned to death in her flat which had apparently caught fire when she had failed to turn off a gas fire. There was…"

"You've made your point." I wondered for a few moments how much of this could be true. I had found out none of these things, focussed as I was on the merchandise the fishermen had imported. Sandeep was telling me I had been looking in entirely the wrong direction.

But then I had been doing what David had wanted me to do.

"This is all irrelevant, my grandfather and the successful candidates worked through the 1930s doing as they were told."

"But they didn't did they? They did what they were told but they also kept stuff for themselves. They all siphoned off quite a lot for themselves."

"Ah yes. The inventory."

"You know about that?"

"Of course. We have followed your investigations. My grandfather and I have wanted you to succeed When we knew you were researching Max's inventory we knew you would discover that artefacts were traceable to my grandfather."

"But I never found any proof of that. I looked, I was looking for anything that could link anything to Vijay. I never found anything."

"We were hoping you would be able to prove that he had not been exiled with nothing. We needed the proof to persuade Ramesh."

"I don't understand."

"There is no reason why you should. Ramesh believes that your family owes us a great debt. He believes your family stole our wealth and left his uncle to start with nothing. We have told him he is wrong and in the old days he would have done what his elders told him but he is a hothead. He decided upon a vendetta against your family and for many years now he has done what he could to cause you pain and distress. I believe he has been involved with far more than that, with burglary, murder, drugs. Our family has important business here in India, we are influential and powerful. Ramesh's exploits are putting our business at risk. Quite simply, our word is not good enough, we need proof that Ramesh is wrong and then perhaps he will stop his illegal activities. That Ramesh will not believe his uncle's word is a cause of great distress to him. If you hadn't come here of your own accord we would have brought you here because you must have found the proof we need to stop Ramesh doing what he has been doing. There must be something in your work."

All this time I had thought Vijay was the cause of Ramesh's actions. Perhaps, after all we were on the same side.

"Can you give a message to your grandfather?"

"Of course."

"Please tell him that Maureen is dead."

"That is sad. He has spoken of her. She was a good friend to him."

"She died in a car crash a few weeks ago. She was talking of him just before it happened."

"They were different times. My grandfather could love a woman of a different culture but he could never marry her. Marriage was in the hands of the fates and the family. He may have loved this woman but he could never marry her if he ever wished to return to his family."

He took the drinks from the silver tray proffered by the bearer and handed one to me.

"In 1947 my grandfather had a choice to make. He could stay in England and marry or he could return to India. He could not do both and he knew what was happening as our country faced Independence. Your government rushed through the arrangements, it all happened too quickly and my grandfather had to make a difficult decision under great pressure. He chose his family and his country over the love of a woman. He always believed he was right to do so even though he knew how much he had hurt her. He will be sorry to hear of her death."

"He did well though, didn't he? When he came back to India."

"The process of Independence was difficult. But he saw that there would be many opportunities for a family with wealth and power. The old order would be destroyed, it would take some time for the British to leave but then there would be immense opportunities. The Americans came in for some years, through the 1960s, but eventually they, too, left us to run our own country. My grandfather spent a decade building up resources and capital, working out what would be the best way to make his families fortune in this new world. He started producing films in 1963. He hired the most beautiful young women, the best looking young men and it didn't matter whether they could sing or act because their voices were always dubbed by the man and women with the best voices. He had seen a film *Singing in the Rain* and his idea came from that. He added a great deal of colour and excitement, making sure the simplest language was used so the largest number of people could understand the simple, melodramatic plots. He had success after success. He bought cinemas then cinema chains, he became very powerful and very rich."

"Bollywood."

"As you say, Bollywood. It would not have existed in the way it does if it hadn't been for my grandfather. And Ramesh is risking all this for his misguided anger against your family. We know he has been involved in drugs and burglaries and even, we suspect, murder. He has put the good name of our family at considerable risk, simply because he will not believe what is the truth. The truth, we know, is that your family helped our grandfather, they did not cheat him. We must prove this to Ramesh, then and only then will he leave your family in peace and our family can get on with our business."

"And you think I have the proof."

"Somewhere in all the work you have done you must have the proof, items you cannot trace but which we know of, anything that can prove that Ramesh is wrong. We need him to be wrong. We *both* need him to be wrong."

"If I have what you're looking for I haven't recognised it."

"You must look again, you must look through all your computer disks, your writings and notes and you must find proof."

"Why is it so important now?"

"Cinema has had its best day, the world of television is opening up. Satellite communications will give us great power but if there is the slightest stain on our reputation we will lose these valuable contracts. We cannot take the risk."

"And if I don't find proof?"

"You are the only person who can."

"Sandeep?"

"Susannah?"

"I will need a computer."

I went back to my room wondering whether Sandeep had been entirely honest and half expecting to find my room ransacked and all my papers and notebooks gone, but the room was exactly as I had left it. I poured some soda water from the fridge and squeezed two sectors of lime into it, thinking all the time about how to find what Sandeep and Vijay Thakersey needed.

I didn't want to think about David as a ruthless, almost evil, man. I didn't want to be aware that some of the things I thought I knew, the lives I thought I had unravelled, were not complete pictures. All these years I had believed Ramesh was acting on Vijay's orders. It had never occurred to me that he might be what David had said his uncle was, a loose cannon. Perhaps you never can learn everything about another person.

There was a knock on the door and a man in the white uniform of the hotel wheeled a trolley into my room with a computer that was more up to date than the one I had left back at Ted's. He was followed by a man in a smart grey suit.

"I am to check that this is compatible with your requirements. You are to see if your disks can be used."

I looked at the machine, oddly incongruous in this environment. "It looks absolutely fine. Thank you."

"Mr Sandeep has asked me to wait while you check. Please memsahib, if you would be so kind."

It was a very polite order.

The attendant had plugged in the machine and I looked around for the on-off switch, I was not familiar with this make or model but hopefully, once I could see what programs it had loaded onto it, I would be on more familiar ground. It seemed an age as we waited for the screen to light up. I sat down and was relieved to see displayed a neatly organised menu listing available programs. The machine had been well set up and it was obvious at one glance I would have everything I could possibly need but I put my disk in the drive and gave the instruction for the machine to access it. It worked.

I looked up at the man in the suit and smiled. "Perfect."

They left, closing the door carefully behind themselves. I would not have been surprised if I had heard the sound of a key turning in the lock but there was none and I realised I was being paranoid. My room opened through a wide French window onto the open garden and the beach beyond, it was hardly the prison I had fleetingly imagined myself to be in.

An hour later there was another knock on the door and a different attendant entered with another trolley, this time laden with bowls of fruit, plates of sandwiches and bottles of water.

Frustrated and tired after several hours of concentration, I turned away from the computer and worked my way through Max's notes and my hand written records of conversations with David. I could find nothing. How could I prove that Vijay had not been empty handed on his escape? How could I prove that Maureen, or Max or even David had helped him leave? At the end of a fruitless afternoon I took a break as the sun was setting and sat out on the veranda with a glass of water. I wondered how much time Sandeep would give me.

Sitting alone and feeling conspicuous in the dining room later that evening I was wondering what it was that I had missed when Sandeep appeared, politely excused himself and sat down opposite me.

"How are you progressing?" He asked without preamble.

"Progressing." I answered trying not to give anything away.

"I have spoken with the manager and we have arranged for you to move to a much better room."

"But I am quite comfortable, it's a lovely room." I didn't like the feeling that I was being moved to an upper floor, away from the garden. Neither did I like the idea of all my personal things being moved without my being there to supervise.

"It is our best suite, my grandfather has arranged it especially. You will be much more comfortable. You are our honoured guest and as such you must have the best room in our hotel."

As soon as I walked into the room I realised why I had been moved. It was truly luxurious, with a large balcony overlooking the sea. But it wasn't the luxury that caught my eye. It was one of a group of pictures on the wall above the bed.

The last time I had seen it had been in the dark hall at Sandhey and I had been talking to David.

Max's Schiele.

I sat on the bed and stared at the drawing I had first really looked at the day after my mother's funeral. It had been stolen from Max in the burglary in which Ramesh was undoubtedly involved. It now graced the wall of this wonderful room. I noticed behind the drawings there was a lighter patch of wall, as if a larger picture had occupied the space until very recently. They had put them up specially for me.

I had had lists of all the artefacts that were known to have been run by the fishermen and I had identified where the vast majority had been within the past 20 years. But nothing I had found could be in any way attributable to Vijay.

Perhaps I had been working in the wrong direction.

I should have focussed on Maureen. She would have known what David did, she was in love with Vijay, she would have helped him. All I had to do was prove it. It was only a week before that I had sat at her desk and leafed through her diaries as Ted had tended the bonfire but it seemed like a lifetime. There had been so much to take in. My realisation that I loved Ted, that Maureen had tried to kill me and that Maureen had known so much that she had never told me as she tried to protect the man she loved. And that Ted was my father.

I sat on the enormous bed and cried.

I cried because it was not fair that I had realised I loved him minutes before he was taken away from me, because it was not fair that I was thousands of miles from home, that I had no home, that I was alone, that I had lost all those people who had been my family and friends.

I cried because I had made such a mess of everything.

I remembered something I had glimpsed in one of Maureen's diaries. *All the answers are there for her to find but neither her eyes nor her mind is open.* I had assumed I had known what it was I was looking for but I had been focussing on the wrong thing.

As the image of Ted tending the bonfire came to my mind I realised that that was true of so many things in my life.

I had wasted years of my life fascinated by the wrong men, then so much of my time concentrated on the wrong research. Everything I had explored over the past years had been for nothing. All the hours I had spent researching and reading had been for nothing. I looked up at the Schiele thinking that the only item I had found that could be traced to India had been stolen from Max. The only use all that information could possibly have was if I could prove that some of it was here, in India, and had been brought here by Vijay in 1947 with David's approval.

The proof for Sandeep wouldn't be in the lists of merchandise, it would be in Maureen's diaries. I had been so careless, so stupid, even when I had been reading those I had focussed on the unimportant trivia of my own life.

Vijay's proof would be in Maureen's diaries.

And I had lost them.

I looked at the picture that Ted must have passed a hundred times when it was on the wall in Sandhey. I thought of him from the Sandhey days. He had seemed like an old man in his grey flannel trousers, tweed jackets and paisley ties. He had seemed as old as Max though, even in 1976, he would have only been in his 50s. Now I was in my 40s that didn't seem so old at all. He had seemed years younger when we had spent the time driving backwards and forwards to Sevenoaks to help Linda, dressed in blue jeans and a red sweater. When he'd come to pick me up from the flat in south London he had seemed even nearer me in age. Perhaps it was just me getting older.

Then in the light of the bonfire I knew I not only loved him but wanted him.

Less than an hour after that realisation I had heard what Maureen had written. Ted was my father. It was Ted who had raped my mother.

But he had denied it.

Who could I believe?

If Ted had raped her why had she let him take her to the nursing home to give birth to me, why were they such friends in those end days, why had they spent so much time enjoying each other's company? The only answer was that he hadn't raped her. He could be my father but they had loved each other. It hadn't been rape, it had been an affair.

It was the only arrangement that made any sense.

But I loved him now.

And not as a daughter should love her father.

I looked at the phone. I could pick up the receiver and ask the operator to call him. I wanted more than anything to hear his voice. What he had said *could* have been true.

If Maureen had loved him and hated me that much she *could* have left that note as insurance that Ted and I would never be together. He had seemed genuinely devastated by the contents. Perhaps I should have given him more of a chance to explain.

Tears don't solve anything, but they help to relieve tension and so I cried.

I wanted to run away. But where can the runaway run?

I had not truly faced up to anything in my life but now, with nowhere to go, I had to.

I had run away from everyone except myself.

I was the one person I could never leave behind.

Chapter Thirty-Seven

The knock on the door woke me up. I quickly checked that I was decent, I was getting used to the way the attendants walked straight in after the briefest of knocks. I was lying on the top of the bed still fully clothed. I must have fallen asleep looking at the Schiele feeling lonely and afraid.

The knock was repeated. Whoever it was seemed to be waiting politely for me to open the door.

I walked stiffly across the room and opened the door.

"Ted!"

"Hello Annie." We just stood there for a few long seconds. "Can I come in?"

"Oh Ted." I opened the door wide and he walked through. He shrugged his shoulders and slipped his hurricane rucksack off his shoulders.

"Travelling light?" I tried to sound light-hearted.

"Annie. Why did you run away from me?" He was coming straight to the point. "I thought you'd go for a walk, come back and we could talk about it. I *know* you care for me. I *know* we have a lot to talk about. Why did you believe Maureen's note? Why couldn't you believe me?"

"I always run away Ted. You know that."

"Stop it. Stop acting as if you don't care."

I stood looking at him, still half asleep, knowing my eyes were tight and puffy from all the tears.

"Please Annie."

"Please what?"

He stood in the middle of the floor, his arms hanging by his side. "Please say you're pleased to see me."

He looked so confused and bewildered. "Oh God." He said, as if defeated by something. "I've made a mistake haven't I? I should have waited for you to come home. We would have talked then, I know we would have done, but I couldn't stand it, Annie. I couldn't bear being in that house and you weren't there."

"How did you know where to find me?" I tried to sound cold and unwelcoming. I didn't want him to know how very pleased I was to see him.

"Two days ago a taxi driver came to the house. He was looking for the 'lovely lady who was very upset' who he'd taken to the Savoy last week. You had left something in his cab and he thought he ought to return it to you. He was sorry it had taken so long but he didn't often come out this far. It was the black plastic bag of Maureen's diaries."

"You've got them?"

"Yes. Is it important?"

"Just a bit."

"So I knew you'd gone to the Savoy. Josie told me to follow. She insisted. She said I would never forgive myself, nor would she, if I didn't. So I threw some things into this," he gestured to the rucksack on the floor, "and your lovely taxi driver took me straight back up to London. I lied to the accounts people at the hotel and they showed me your bill. Indian High Commission, American Express, all those things you put on your bill, it was quite simple really."

"You've really got Maureen's diaries?"

"All of them, just as you left them."

I had the diaries, and I knew they held the answer.

It was awkward and it was difficult but we managed to spend the afternoon talking of other things. I explained something of why I was in a luxurious suite in one of Bombay's most expensive hotels with a desk covered in papers and a computer.

"I've got to do something. Finish stuff off."

"Can I help?"

"No." It sounded ruder than I had meant to be, "Sorry. I just mean it's something I've got to do."

"If I can't help with that..." he nodded towards the desk and the computer, "I can keep you company. Can't I?"

"Yes. Yes that would be nice."

So he stayed.

That evening we stood on the balcony enjoying the drinks that had been served with the excellent Italian meal. The sun was going down

"You know it will be sunrise in Florida." Ted said and didn't understand why I laughed.

"What have I said now?" he asked.

"Nothing."

I was trying so hard not to love him.

The hotel obviously knew of Ted's appearance as the dinner trolley that evening was laid for two. We ate in uncomfortable silence.

"I'll sleep on the settee. It'll be more comfortable than the plane anyway."

We edged around each other for the rest of the evening. We had lived in the same flat before but this was very different. He was gathering spare pillows from the wardrobe and towels from the bathroom when he stopped in the middle of the floor and dropped everything he had in his arms.

"For God's sake what is it Ted?" I was worried and uncertain and he looked dreadful.

"Sit down." Ted had regained something of his normal composure. I sat down at the irresistible authority in his voice.

He pulled up a chair and placed it deliberately on the floor about three feet in front of me.

"I think it's best we talk." He spoke firmly but gently. It was the tone of voice I remembered when he had talked to my mother.

"You must understand that what Maureen wrote in that note was not true. You must believe me. You are absolutely *not* my daughter. I did *not* rape Alicia. In all the time I knew her I never so much as kissed her."

I tried to believe him.

"It is so, so important that you listen to me."

"OK" I said, reluctantly and sulkily.

"There are things you must understand."

"OK" I repeated torn between wanting to understand and not wanting to hear.

"Are you listening? It is so very important." He repeated.

"OK"

"From the day I first saw your mother I wanted to care for her. She seemed weak and unhappy and needed a friend, but I was being paid to look out for her. It was not something I'm particularly proud of but your grandfather had arranged for me to report back to him everything she did. I always tried to be her friend, Annie, you must believe I was never, ever, anything other than a friend."

I so wanted to believe him.

"Alright Annie. I've told you the truth. If you don't want to believe me so be it. I'll stay tonight and get the first plane back tomorrow. I'm sorry. I shouldn't have put you in this position."

"Why did you then?" It was churlish and childish. I did not mean to be so cruel.

"Because I love you. I couldn't let you believe those things. They are wrong."

So Ted slept that night on the settee and I in the enormous bed. I could hear his breathing. I'm not sure either of us slept much.

"Are you awake?" I asked as the sky began to lighten and the sounds of the hotel awakening around us filtered into the room.

"I am Annie."

"Can we talk?" There must have been something conciliatory in my voice because he seemed more relaxed when he answered "I'll make some tea first. You have the bathroom."

"What about Maureen?" I asked him as we were sitting on the balcony, cups of tea in hand looking out over the already crowded beach.

"I never realised that Maureen felt so strongly about me. I had known her and her family since before the war but apart from concern for your mother we had nothing in common. I knew she was fond of me but if I'd known the strength of her feelings I would never have confided in her."

"What about?"

"About how I felt about you."

"Oh."

We drank our tea in silence watching the beach vendors plying their trades, young boys carrying large billy cans, women with baskets of fruit on their head and a man leading a string of camels.

"How did you feel about me?" Eventually I couldn't help asking.

"It was at your graduation party. We were standing on the terrace at Sandhey, drinking champagne I seem to remember and there was something so completely new about you. I watched you when you left me to talk to someone else, and I couldn't keep from watching you."

"You said I was like my mother." I was remembering the afternoon.

"Your mother was a very attractive woman too. But there was always something about Alicia that was hard. She used people, she used me I know. I don't think you do, not deliberately anyway. There's something about you that was vulnerable, I wanted to hold you safe. From that day of your graduation party I wanted it to be me you loved."

"But it was you that brought me and Carl together."

"I had to. If I hadn't you would always have wondered about him, always hankered after him, wondering 'what if'. It was the best thing I ever did. It really was. I couldn't lose really could I?"

"How do you mean?"

"If you were happy with Carl I would be happy because you were happy. If you discovered that Carl was not for you after all then I would have another opportunity, someday. Without your discovering that you weren't going to find lasting happiness with Carl I would never have had that chance."

I had to think about that. Could I care about anyone enough to ever have been that patient, that selfless? "I was pretty single minded about him wasn't I?"

"Completely. Remember the morning your mother died? You read your step-mother's obituary and your thoughts were only for Carl. You didn't care how your mother felt, there was only excitement that you knew how to contact Carl. I remembered that when we were drinking champagne at your graduation party five years later."

"It was Carl or nothing. I had always wanted to be with him. I never looked at anyone else, I never even thought about anybody else."

"You were both young. I watched you go away and I watched your obsession with him."

Ted held out his hand towards me but I couldn't take it. He put it back on his lap, finishing in a resigned voice, "I have known how I felt ever since your graduation party. I haven't changed. I won't change whatever you think of me."

I didn't know whether I was disappointed or not. Some part of me wanted Ted to have known he loved me all my life but even I realised that would not only have been ridiculous it would have been dangerous. He was 26 years older than I was. He would have been 36 when I was 10, 42 before I was 16. It would have been obscene if he had seen me in any other way than as a caring adult for a child.

"So it wasn't until my graduation party?"

"No."

"Why didn't you say anything then?"

"Would I have got anywhere? Would you have even thought twice about me as anyone other than your old Uncle Ted?"

"So four days later you called Carl to come and be with me, and you watched all summer as we grew closer and then you watched as we drove to Cambridge sure that this was what was meant to be."

"I couldn't stop you going with Carl. I knew it was wrong, it would be too much for you, learning to live with Carl and learning to look after the children at the same time. I thought you should have done one thing or the other, not both."

"I thought it would all be OK. I had always thought that getting together with Carl would make everything right."

"I did talk to Carl, before you left. I told him to take care of you, never hurt you, look after you because you were more vulnerable, less hard-skinned than anyone thought. I gave him a bit of a lecture really and he didn't take it very well."

"I can imagine."

"He told me to mind my own business, though not quite as politely as that. Charles argued with him as well, saying he should let you have some time to get to know the children before foisting a step-father on them. That was when Charles and I became really worried because…" Ted stopped talking in mid sentence as if he decided against saying what he had been about to say, so I finished his sentence for him.

"… you both knew he had no intention of marrying me."

"That certainly, but more importantly we knew he was incapable of being faithful. It is a trait he inherited from his father that both Charles and I knew would hurt you desperately. Through that summer I felt responsible, I had brought you to Carl and I wondered if I hadn't done it for selfish reasons. Perhaps I had offered you up for years of unhappiness simply so you would come to me in the end. Perhaps my motives were very, very suspect. On the one hand I desperately wanted you to be happy, but on the other I wanted you to be happy *with me*. I made it my business to find out a little more about what he had been up to in the years we had had little contact with him. What I found out I didn't like."

The perfunctory knock on the door was followed by the bearer with breakfast and the moment was broken.

"I'd better get to work. I've got to…" I nodded towards the computer and the black sack filled with Maureen's diaries.

"Are you sure you want me to go?"

He sounded so resigned.

I knew I didn't want him to go but wasn't sure how to ask him to stay.

"I could sleep on the settee, it was very comfortable actually, and I don't like the idea of leaving you alone here. I don't need to know what you're up to, but I could be here when you need company."

We slipped into an easy routine. I would work through the diaries during the day while Ted sat on the balcony listening to the cricket on the radio. Together we ate the meals which were wheeled into the suite three times a day and whenever I needed a break we would sit on the balcony and look out over the idyllic beach. It was only as the evenings came to an end that there was any awkwardness, as I retreated to the large bed and Ted settled down on the settee.

"You must be very tired." He said after the end of the fourth day. We talked generally about what I was doing, never straying onto what we probably both recognised was dangerous territory. "But I think I'm getting somewhere." I noticed his sharp glance of relief.

By the fourteenth book I had built up a picture of layers of betrayal and fear between every surviving member of the Fishermen section.

An hour later I was reading through one of the many brown books filled with Maureen's closely written script. With Ted sitting on the balcony I was happy. It was an unusual feeling and it made the reading more poignant. I didn't skip a word as I tried to find out everything Maureen could so easily have told me, if she had wanted to. I was able to fill in so many of the gaps David and Max had left in what they had told me. I read on, lunch was bought on a trolley, I carried on reading. Ted was silent, letting me concentrate on what I had to do.

As I read I put markers in the diary at every reference I could find to Vijay, noting on a computer spreadsheet the book number, page number and short description. The methodology acquired over the past twenty years had not, after all, been wasted.

It was a curious and novel intimacy. We were using the same bathroom, we were aware of each others presence by swift glances but we avoided any contact that was not strictly necessary. The suite was a large one, it was almost as if, when Sandeep had moved me from the room below, he had known I would have company. I just couldn't help the feeling that we were in a luxurious kind of detention, and that there would be no opportunity to leave until I found what Vijay and Sandeep needed.

On the evening of the fifth day we were eating our dinner, reading the UK papers that we were being supplied with. England seemed so far away as I turned the flimsy airmail paper.

"The Schiele."

"Sorry?" I hadn't been concentrating and wasn't sure I had heard Ted.

"Max's Schiele. Annie..."

As I always did, I interrupted. "It's a long story, Ramesh arranged for them to be stolen from Max. Graham and Sandeep were involved..."

"But Annie," For once Ted interrupted me.

"Two of those Schieles are not Max's. I've never seen them before."

"But that's impossible! Unless..."

"Yes?"

"I've got to get back to work!" With renewed energy and a sudden sense of purpose I looked back through my files. I looked back through Maureen's diaries and, as it was beginning to get dark on the evening of the sixth day I shouted out in triumph "I've found it!"

Chapter Thirty-Eight

"What?" Ted had been dozing.

"She had it all along."

"What?"

"The proof!" I started talking fast and furiously, pointing to pages in the diaries, picking up other volumes, half showing him the words on the pages. "Maureen was devastated when he told her he would be leaving for India without her. She told David of Vijay's plans. David wanted to confiscate everything but she persuaded him not to, they arranged to allow him most of what he had. But Max thought that David had betrayed Vijay and would do the same to him. It's all here."

"I have no idea what you are talking about."

"We need to see Vijay and Sandeep. I've got what they need to control Ramesh." I waved one of Maureen's diaries triumphantly at Ted. "It's all here!" I rushed over to him, just remembering to stop before getting too close.

"Don't call them straight away, Annie, get it all together, organise it properly. Don't rush."

"But we can go home. They can't keep us…" I started excitedly, but as I saw the look on Ted's face I tailed off weakly. "…here any more."

"What will we do then Annie? What will we do when we go home? These few days have been so good."

"You'll be able to sleep in a proper bed." I tried to joke but it wasn't the right moment.

Ted gently took the diary out of my grasp and put it on the desk. Slowly and deliberately he took my hands, holding them tightly, not letting me get remove them from his grasp.

"Annie. We've got to stay together. Do you think you would ever want to marry me?"

"But…" I started, but not being able to think of anything sensible, said nothing more.

Ted seemed to be encouraged that I hadn't looked completely horrified at his proposal and continued. "I've loved these days, being here

294

together. But I've hated every night, you have been so close and I couldn't touch you."

"Oh shit."

He was quiet then spoke gently "Is it that such an awful thought?"

There was so much history between us, I had loved this man for many years in a very different way from the way he was now asking me to feel. We had avoided facing this for the past week. It could be avoided no longer.

"You love me?"

"I'm very much afraid I do."

"Properly?"

"Whatever that means. I want to touch you, to kiss you, to make love to you."

Part of me wanted to say no. But I looked at him. I *really* looked at him. He was an attractive man. He was kind, generous, loving, thoughtful, generous, honest, reliable, steadfast.

What was there not to love?

"Annie! Say something!"

"Shall we just try one kiss? See how that goes?"

He leant towards me, awkwardly, and I let him put his arms around me. I hadn't realised how much taller he was than me. His neck bent as he lent his face down towards mine. I had only a short sight of the hair behind his ear as his lips met mine.

It was a long time since I had kissed anyone properly.

Gentleness became urgency, his hand placed protectively on the back of my neck began to press more forcefully. I was more than aware of every inch of his body as it pressed against mine. Very gently, very deliberately he pulled away from me.

"That went well didn't it?" He asked knowing the answer.

I think I smiled.

"Annie you know that we will have to live with what we do now for the rest of our lives."

I leant up and kissed him. More than I had wanted anything, ever, I wanted this man to make love to me.

"Are you sure?"

I kissed him again.

"Are you absolutely certain?"

Finally he kissed me back.

I'd made love with a few men but never like this. It was comfortable, emotional, satisfying, and completely right. He was gentle, urgent, encouraging, patient, demanding, traditional and adventurous. Nothing had ever felt so right in all my life. Afterwards we lay on the bed, wrapped up in each other, our bodies lying perfectly against the other. I breathed in when he breathed out, and out when he breathed in.

I could just see his face. He was smiling as he traced his finger along my arm.

"Can you face it?" He asked as he turned me over and folded me in his arms.

"What?"

"The world?"

"What?"

"I don't know about you, Annie darling, but that, for me, was a statement of intent."

"What?" I knew I was sounding idiotic.

"I want us to be together. Not furtive, not hiding, not surreptitious, not frightened of what people will say. I want to go back to England hand in hand saying that we are going to live together, that we are going to *be* together. That we are a couple, that you might, one day, actually want to be my wife."

He realised then he had gone too far.

"I can't…I don't …. Please…." Was all I could say as I pushed him away.

"One thing at a time then. Will you come back to live with me but properly live with me, not separate rooms at opposite ends of the landing?"

"I will never get married again." I was sitting up, my knees drawn up to my chest, my arms around my legs. "At least not for a while."

"I'm sorry, I got carried away."

I couldn't bear the pain in his voice.

"But I rather like the idea of trying living together." I felt suddenly shy. "Will people understand?"

"Who's 'people'?"

"The children, Charles, Linda."

"They will be happy for you, for us. They are very fond of you, you know. Linda has done a fabulous job, she has never tried to take over your position as their mother, she has always made them send you cards and letters at Christmas and birthdays and when Bill did something particularly brilliant with his arrows. They care about you far more than you could imagine. In those few weeks after your accident and especially that day after the hurricane they realised they quite liked you as well."

Chapter Thirty-Nine

An hour later we were being driven through the gates of the Thakersey compound. We were shown into what must have been a main drawing room. I looked around me, expecting to recognise many of the items I had looked for over the years.

"You won't find them, my dear Susannah Donaldson." An old man sat in a deep winged armchair, similar to the ones in Max's study. "You won't find any of Max's inventory here."

"Vijay?"

"Indeed and how do you do Mr Mottram?"

Ted and I sat on the sofa opposite him and I was able to see Vijay properly for the first time.

"We are greatly in your debt if you have, as you say, found proof that will persuade young Ramesh of the error of his ways. When I was a young man I would have believed what my elders told me but Ramesh is a different generation. It has hurt me greatly that he refused to accept my word. He has been seduced by the more freethinking ways of the west. Will you show me what you have found?"

I knelt next to Vijay and showed him pages from Maureen's diaries. He showed no emotion as he read the words that showed how much she had loved him.

"You understand why I couldn't go back?" He asked rhetorically at one point. "If I had gone back we would have been unhappy together. It was better she remembered me as I had been."

I picked out the relevant volumes and showed him the pages marked with scraps of yellow paper. He read slowly, nodding occasionally and whispering 'yes, yes, that was so.'

"There was no theft, no fraud, this lady's family helped me. They did not steal from me. Everything you have done has been wrong."

Vijay was standing, talking angrily. I hadn't noticed Ramesh and Sandeep entering the room.

"Will you now believe your uncle that we were not wronged by this family? Will you now stop all your stupidity?"

Ramesh snatched the diary from his uncle's hand and appeared to read the pages before turning to Sandeep and arguing in their own language. They spoke loudly and quickly with a great deal of animated gesticulation before Ramesh handed the diary back to his cousin. There was further urgent conversation between them which Ted and I could not hope to interpret let alone understand until Ramesh turned, somewhat reluctantly, towards me.

He gave a petulant apology before leaving the room.

"I must apologise for my nephew." As Vijay spoke I was struck again by his similarity to Max. "I can assure you he will be dealt with. He will not be in a position to return to your country, he will not be able to harass or threaten any of your family again. Maximilian is not the only man who can arrange such things. But I am in your debt."

I muttered something to the effect that simply not to have to worry about our family would be reward enough.

"Nonsense! Firstly I want you to accept a gift."

We were intrigued as a servant handed Ted a box which he opened to reveal pictures which he carefully removed to show me. I recognised them all. There were three by Gustav Klimt, two were Pablo Picasso and the final one was of a young man in shirtsleeves with a blue tie his hands held awkwardly in the air.

Vijay gave us no time to react. "You are to enjoy the contents for the rest of your lives which I trust you will spend happily together. You will never sell them because you will never be able to establish their provenance, but in many years time perhaps people will have forgotten and your children will display them for all to see."

"They're beautiful." I'm sure it was an inadequate response to a gift worth many millions of pounds but worth nothing. I understood his reasons and accepted them with, I hope, appropriate grace.

Vijay waved his hands dismissively and continued "You will please accept the use of my personal plane to return you to the UK. It may, perhaps, make it easier to carry these into your country. " He smiled mischievously as he indicated the pictures, then grinning broadly he added "Also you may like to spend some time in private to adjust to your new futures."

I had spent years hating and fearing Vijay Thakersey. I had been so wrong about him, as I had been so wrong about so many things.

"But these are practical things." Vijay stood up and held out his hand towards me. He spoke formally, as if the words were immensely difficult and painful to him.

"Most importantly I offer you my sincere apologies for the pain you have suffered at the hands of my family."

Three days later we were being driven up the lane to Greensand Hill. It was almost exactly two weeks since we had left for Maureen's cottage. Ted and I sat in the back of the limousine holding hands, ready to face the family.

"Josie will be so smug she's wanted us to get together for years."

"But what will the boys think?"

"I'm sure they'll be pleased too but does it really matter? We know it's absolutely right don't we?" There was just a hint of uncertainty in Ted's voice

I squeezed his hand and smiled.

"I've had so many false starts in my life, I've made so many mistakes."

"And what would those be?"

"I married Joe."

"But without Joe there would have been no Josie to bring us together. No Al Jack and Bill and, whatever you thought of them when they are younger you have to admit they are wonderful people now."

"I spent all those years wanting Carl."

"Perfectly understandable. He was your knight in shining armour. Every girl has to have one of those so that they can know a real man when they see one."

"And there was Jonathan."

"Well perhaps I'll admit you one really, really bad mistake!"

I was suddenly serious.

"And I believed Maureen. I'm so sorry I …"

Ted leant over and kissed me.

"If you hadn't believed her, just for that short time, you wouldn't have run away and if you hadn't run away I might never have had the courage to find you."

"I love you."

They were words that people used every day without thinking.

They seemed totally inadequate to define the mixture of fear, regret, hope and anticipation I felt, along with the absolute certainty that I would never need to run away again.

Finale

On the afternoon of November 29th 1998 our extended family gathered for the reading of Max's will. Annie had chosen the date because it would have been her mother's birthday and a date that resonated through our story.

I had been busy in the hour I had had on my own before the family arrived. I had arranged my papers, rehearsed what I had to say, and wrapped bundles of the three books together.

There were going to be 22 of us in the room, representing four generations, though, of course, things weren't quite that straightforward.

Max had been the last of the first generation. His contemporaries, David and Edie, had died years before.

Alicia had died even before her parents. Her husband, Arnold, and his second wife Kathleen, Kathleen's sister Maureen they were all gone so the only representative of the second generation was Monika Heller, the woman who had been Max's housekeeper for so many years.

The main group in the room that day would be the third generation, Alicia's children Charles and Susannah, Arnold's son Carl, Linda and her brothers.

And Holly. Sometime wife to both Charles and Carl now married to Linda's brother but also the daughter of Monika's brother. Perhaps Holly was the odd one out.

No generation was simple in this family but the relationships of the third generation of this family were particularly complicated. Susannah and Carl had had a chequered relationship but were still good friends, working together on and off through the years. Charles had married Holly only to be divorced with much ill will. Holly and Carl had then had a short lived marriage during which Carl had an affair with Susannah. When Holly had divorced him she had returned to the man she should probably have been with since she was 17, Linda's brother Crispin. Charles and Linda had lived together for more than 20 years sometimes as friends, but more recently as more than that. They had married a year before Max had died.

The family trouped into the room that had been sacrosanct, Max's study. What would he would thought of the gathering? So many people he would not have wanted in his most private of rooms.

Carl Witherby was just as tall and distinguished as his father had been in his fifties. Annie talked to him. I was not worried about her. I watched them standing together, with easy friendship and knew she would be able to call on him when she needed support as she would before too long. I was getting old and there would be a time soon when Annie would need a friend. We have had 11 wonderful years together for which I will be eternally grateful but it was good to know she would have a friend when she needed one.

Seeing Charles and Carl together in the same room it was impossible not to recognise that they were brothers.

I knew Charles wouldn't speak to his sister. When he realised what had happened between us he had been appalled and said he would have nothing to do with us. Perhaps Maureen had talked to him. Perhaps she had told him what she had tried to tell Susannah.

Perhaps Charles had believed her.

Standing apart were the fourth and fifth generations. Josie, nearing middle age at 35; stood with 11 year old Andy. Her brothers, Al and Jack, stood with their partners next to Bill with his pregnant wife.

Alicia would have been so proud of her dynasty.

Max was unknown to many of them, indeed this was the first time many of them had met each other. I wondered what they would make of the afternoon's proceedings.

I had a very strict timetable to keep to that afternoon, there were formalities to get through and I wanted to avoid the various factions of the family having any time to revive their arguments, so as soon as everyone was in the room I called them to order and began to read Max's first confession.

"I begin with a quotation Exodus Chapter 34 Verse 7

Keeping mercy for thousands, forgiving iniquity and transgression and sin - and that will by no means clear the guilty - visiting the iniquity of the fathers upon the children, and upon the children's children, unto the third and to the fourth generation. "

I can see you all now, pondering that quotation.

Well Charles, Carl, Susannah you are the second generation. Arnold and Alicia, Maureen and Kathleen, they were the first to suffer from the actions of their parents. Susannah, your children are the third generation. I know you and Carl have given them all the love they could possibly need to end the sequence. If God wills it the pain will end now."

I felt it important to put Max's words that I had just read into context So I stopped reading for a moment.

"You must remember that Max wrote this in the autumn of 1976. I do not know why he never changed it. Some of what he says you may find mystifying in the light of what has happened since."

I took a drink of water and began reading once more.

For you all I would say 'Do not judge them too harshly for things they could not know'. Much of this is not your responsibility. Do not blame yourselves.

I could hear the murmur as most of the people in the room became impatient, Charles, Susannah and Carl were the only ones who had any idea what Max was saying.

The first and most important bequest for you all is this book of Ted's. Read it carefully, learn from it. Learn to forgive your elders their mistakes for they make them either unwittingly or through weakness.

I watched as all the people in the room turned towards the table by the door and looked at the parcels I had carefully wrapped in identical paper. Max had not, of course, known of the other books.

I continued reading from Max's prepared documents.

My second bequest is an explanation..."

I was hesitant, knowing that there was no truth in what I was reading.

Monika, I have loved you as a father might for all your life. Your real name is Rebecca Rebmann. You are my dear niece – but I could never tell you for all the memories I knew it would bring up to mention it. As we grew older together I knew your knowing our relationship could not make us any fonder of each other. So I let it be.

Holly stared at Monika realising she gave no reaction.

"You knew." I saw her mouth the words across the room in disbelief, so much of her life had been affected by Max's unwillingness to admit any relationship with Monika. Holly glared at Charles, and, pausing only to exchange obviously angry and bitter words with Monika, walked past me. She hesitated slightly, as if wondering whether it was the right thing to do, before picking up a parcel from the table and walking out of the door.

I followed her. "Holly, you mustn't go. Please don't leave. There is more to tell."

"But Ted, It's so confusing. I looked at Charles and it all came flooding back, all of it. I just couldn't face Monika. She knew. All that time she knew and she let us go through all that pain. She never said a word."

"Do you know why? She said nothing because nothing was said to her."

"We went through hell to keep her safe and she knew all the time."

"No she didn't."

"She didn't care enough about us to try to save us from all that pain. If she had she would have told us she knew."

"But she didn't know Holly, she didn't know."

"But you just read all about it.

"I read the first part. There is more. There is so much more. You must come back to hear it all."

Charles seemed surprised when Holly came back into the room with me. He was standing next to Carl. I wondered what Holly's two ex-husbands would have said to each other.

I walked through the family to stand beside Susannah and waited until silence reigned again in the room.

"I have now fulfilled what Max wanted me to do. I have read the confession Max wanted me to read. But now Susannah must read what Max never wanted spoken in his lifetime. Now is the time."

"I will tell you about Max." Susannah had their undivided attention.

She told them of Max's student days, how he felt disadvantaged, how he was resentful of the men he studied with who had money and families behind them. I closed my eyes as I listened to her reading the words she had carefully composed. How like Alicia's her voice was, the nuances of meaning expressed with subtlety and grace; so like her mother's but so different. There was more strength, more confidence and more maturity than I ever heard in Alicia.

Perhaps it was because Susannah was happy and her mother never had been.

I knew what Susannah had decided to say and so I watched Charles and Monika carefully.

They both thought they knew the truth and were obviously wondering why Susannah was going over this old ground again. 'Why was she talking about Holly's father again', their looks seemed to say, 'we know all this about August and Mattieu and how Monika's brothers abandoned their parents and sister'. They began to be interested when the words Susannah was reading began to stray from their expectations.

They had not expected to hear of Max having a daughter.

I watched Monika as she listened. She realised before the others where Susannah's tale was heading.

Max was her father.

He had never admitted it, had never acknowledged her throughout the 50 years since they had met in Audierne.

Susannah picked up a paper from the desk and read.

On the papers I forged I didn't give her the name she had had when she lived with my sister. Rebecca Rebmann was dead. Monika Heller was born. I gave my dear girl her mother's name.

As the years passed I had to explain things more than I would wish. She asked questions, others asked questions, others thought they knew so I told her something of her past. I resisted telling her all because of the pain it would cause. But again I am disingenuous. I didn't want her to remember because of all the things I had to hide.

Monika Heller, you are the daughter I didn't want, the daughter I denied all my life and the daughter I have loved and wanted to protect for the past 50 years.

All eyes turned to Monika who sat passive and unmoving, but not unmoved.

"Why are you so cruel? Why do you say these things in front of everyone? Do you think so little of me that you use my humiliation as spectacle? Could you not have opened and read these papers to me privately?"

She was so dignified in her distress.

Susannah spoke directly to Monika with compassion but also with authority. "Max cared about you but he hated himself. You might think he wanted to humiliate you but he didn't, he wanted to humiliate himself. He did not want to be remembered with an affection he felt he didn't deserve, he was giving us all a reason to hate him. There is a postscript."

She looked down at the paper in front of her. "Max wrote '*All my life has been a lie. Do not remember me with fondness or affection I do not deserve it.*' I believe he really meant that."

I met Susannah's gaze. We both knew Max would get his wish when I had dealt with the final tasks of the afternoon, the disposal of his assets. Some of the family had been less than interested in the details of Monika's background, many had hardly heard of her let alone known her as a person but they were all interested when I started to read the will. They all had expectations.

I had known Max draw up two wills. In his first, dated 1941, Major Maximilian Fischer left all his property to his wife Elizabeth and daughter Veronica, apart from a substantial bequest to his niece, Rebecca Rebmann. The names had meant nothing to me then.

As I read the second will, dated 1976, I watched the delighted looks on the faces of the family. There were substantial gifts to all the people in the room.

"I have to stop here. I only have read this," I waved the paper in the air like a Victorian preacher "because I am required to. Unfortunately it is all nonsense." I watched the faces change from delight and, in one or two cases outright greed, to enquiry, doubt and worry. "I think at this stage I should hand over to Susannah again."

Heads in the room turned, as one, towards Susannah who slowly walked round to stand next to me. I gripped her hand in encouragement. She looked round the room as if gauging before she began how much what she had to say was going to shock.

"Max enjoyed the finer things in life. He had a good eye and opportunity. He accumulated wealth and influence, but it never made him happy because he had acquired it illegally."

She paused for the murmurs to subside.

"Before and during the war he and others," she hesitated, catching my eye. I smiled in encouragement and she continued. "Before and during the war he and others collected certain things that did not belong to them and to which they had no right. Eventually the façade Max had built around himself began to unravel, his secrets were being exposed to people who also had power and influence. They began to chip away not only at his wealth but at his confidence in himself. Most of what he had kept was stolen from him. The rest he gave to good causes and, as he had less and less he was given his knighthood. It was an empty gesture, given too late by the establishment that had broken him. This house," she waved her arm around the room in an expansive gesture "belongs to the bank, as do all his other properties. They will be sold to repay his debts. There are no investments, no paintings." She paused as she looked at Carl who was staring at her bemused by what she knew and had never told him. "There are no diaries, no books, no papers." She looked away, focussing on no one. "He has nothing. There is no property, no money, no assets. The will of 1976 has no validity whatsoever. None of you will get anything simply because Max has nothing to leave." Susannah stood, flushed, conscious of the effect her words were having.

I watched the faces around me as they realised that they would get nothing. There was a shocked silence, then the first quiet whispers of disappointment, followed by the louder swell of outrage. I caught Annie's eyes and she smiled, this was exactly what she had expected.

"May I say something?" Monika stood up leaning slightly on Charles at first and then, standing free, she turned to the family. No one heard her and I had to ask for quiet.

"I think we all owe it to Monika to listen to what she has to say." And gradually the room quietened and even the youngest turned towards her.

"Why is a legacy only measured in property and money? Why are you all so angry and disappointed. You must know that we have all had the most wonderful legacies from Sir Max."

She spoke quietly and firmly, with the authority of the only person who had really known Max.

"Charles, where would you be without the gifts that Max had given you? Not only did he open his home to us to give you the gift of security he gave you the gift of time. With the money he gave you were able to live well and do the things you loved doing, he allowed to you to spend your early years watching and writing about your birds. Where would you be if you had had to earn your own living? How could you have done the things you have done without Max behind you?"

We had all turned to look at Charles who looked defensive.

"And you Carl. Where would you have been without Max? You may think you have achieved everything on your own, you may think you have been independent and made your own way in the world. But I must disillusion you, you also received a large sum of money on your 21st birthday. But it wasn't his money that was important, it was the gift of achievement. Did you never wonder how you got those first invitations to work on radio and television. There were, no doubt, many young men equally talented who could have been approached but no, you were given special treatment, you were singled out because of contacts Max made on your behalf."

I saw Susannah catching Carl's eye but he could not meet her gaze and quickly turned away.

"And Susannah. Max gave you the gift of freedom. Freedom from responsibility, freedom to make mistakes and to take time to recover from them. He took responsibility for your children, he provided for them, he helped you find a purpose in life. He knew you, not Carl, were the one most interested and most able to do what he wanted you to do.

"Such gifts. Time, security, achievement and freedom, are they not far more important than anything else Sir Max could have left to you?"

No one answered. It would have been too difficult.

"And the rest of you. Why would any of you deserve anything? You neither knew nor cared for Sir Max. But even so he has left you another great legacy, that of independence. You will have to make your own way in the world, you will have to work for what you achieve. What good did all his wealth do him? None. He would have been better off without it. It stopped him living the life he should have led. It made him afraid to acknowledge his past, it made him ashamed of himself and who he was."

Annie turned to me and I saw she was crying, a tear trickling down one cheek as it always did when she was moved. She turned to the room full of her family; her half brothers, her children, the people who were, or had been, important to them all.

"Please fill your glasses, we need to make a toast."

Carl and Charles, helped by Crispin, opened several bottles of champagne while Linda, Holly and Josie handed the glasses around. As Carl passed me a bottle and two glasses Annie gave him a quick hug before turning back to the room.

"To Max" she said "Thank you for everything." We all sipped at our glasses.

Perhaps I wasn't the only one to remember how many times we had drunk champagne in this house over the years. Charles walked to the front of the room.

"I must add a toast."

He held his glass out. I could see him trying not to catch Susannah's eye.

"It is undoubtedly a time for reconciliation. Many things have happened in this family that we cannot hope to understand until we have read these books. Perhaps we have been too quick to judge. Perhaps what Max has said is true '*Do not judge us too harshly for things we could not know*'. Not only have I judged too harshly I should not have judged at all. That is not my right." He looked at his sister and smiled. "Susannah, I am so sorry I have never tried to understand."

My Annie raised her glass towards him, accepting the apology for so many years of distance between them. 'No one ever said life was fair' she spoke silently to him

Charles' voice changed as he raised his glass.

"My toast is to Monika." He turned towards her. "We owe you so much. Please forgive us for not realising how great that debt has been." He spoke with affection and we all repeated 'To Monika' as we took another sip from our glasses.

"And the last toast will be mine." I said believing it was time to bring proceedings to an end.

"We are all one extended family, we have had our good times and our bad, as families must. There have been misunderstandings and misjudgements which is why you will all read these books, mine, Charles's and Susannah's, because they will, I know, make you realise the importance of the subject of this final toast."

I paused, looking round at this disparate group of people. I felt the presence of the ones who were now dead but who had also stood in this house drinking champagne; David and Edith, Maureen and, most importantly, Alicia.

I held out my hand to Annie who took hold of it and squeezed it.

We raised our glasses and spoke as one.

"To family."

The Last Dance

INIQUITIES TRILOGY 1

Winner: David St John Thomas Prize for Fiction 2007

"Ted's Book"

'I couldn't put it down"
"Cracking good read"

Children begin by loving their parents; after a time they judge them; rarely, if ever, do they forgive them.
Oscar Wilde

Softback: ISBN 1-905237-731   Hardback: ISBN 1-905237-936

Walking Alone

INIQUITIES TRILOGY 2

"Charles's Book'

'Brilliant!"
"Powerful page turner"

All that is necesssary for the triumph of evil is that good men do nothing.
Edmund Burke

Softback: ISBN: 1-905886-517   Hardback: ISBN 1-905886-524